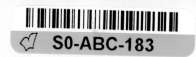

Letters of MARCEL PROUST

Letters of

MARCEL PROUST

Translated, Edited, and Annotated by MINA CURTISS

Introduction by ADAM GOPNIK

HELEN MARX BOOKS ~ BOOKS AND CO., *New York*

First published as *Letters of Marcel Proust*, translated and edited, with notes by Mina Curtiss. Random House, New York, 1949.

ISBN 1-885586-45-0 LCCN 2005933878

Produced by Wilsted & Taylor Publishing Services
Design and composition by Janet Wood
Printed by Transcontinental Printing Inc.

Printed in Canada

To Celeste Albaret,

whom Marcel Proust addressed in 1921 as "ma fidèle amie de huit années, mais en réalité si unie à ma pensée que je dirai plus vrai en l'appelant mon amie de toujours, ne pouvant plus imaginer que je ne l'ai pas toujours connue," this translation is dedicated in tribute to her devotion to her master's memory, a devotion as loyal, as selfless, during the quarter of a century since his death, as was her service to him in the last decade of his lifetime.

Contents

Translator's Preface

The letters in this volume have been chosen, primarily, to provide readers of *Remembrance of Things Past* with clues to the development of the personality and the creative process out of which the novel grew. I have, therefore, attempted, whenever space allowed, to include letters that would disclose Proust as a man who, if always the artist, is, as often as not, a separate person from the Narrator, the Marcel, of the novel. Omissions or cuts in the letters have been made largely to avoid repetition, except when it seemed meaningful. In choosing between letters containing similar subject matter, I have favored those not included in the *Correspondance générale*, since many of them are not easily available even in France. The letters here presented were selected from the following volumes: *Correspondance générale*, edited by Robert Proust, Paul Brach, and Suzy Mante-Proust, Paris, 1930–1936, 6 volumes; *Aux enfers avec Marcel Proust* by Antoine Bibesco, Geneva, 1948; *Au bal avec Marcel Proust* by Marthe Bibesco, Paris, 1929; *Lettres et conversations* by Robert de Billy, Paris, 1930; *Robert de Montesquiou et Mar-*

cel Proust by E. de Clermont-Tonnerre, Paris, 1925; *Du côté de Marcel Proust* by Benjamin Crémieux, Paris, 1929; *Autour de soixante lettres de Marcel Proust*, edited by Lucien Daudet, Paris, 1929; *Lettres à Madame C[atusse]*, edited by Lucien Daudet, Paris, 1946; *Lettres à Maurice Duplay, La Revue nouvelle*, XLVIII, 1929; *Hommage à Marcel Proust*, Paris, 1927; *Lettres à André Gide, Nouvelle revue française*, XXXI, 1928; *A un ami*, edited by Georges de Lauris, Paris, 1948; *Lettres à une amie*, edited by Marie Nordlinger, Manchester, 1942; *Lettres à la NRF*, Paris, 1932; *Comment parût "Du côté de chez Swann,"* edited by L. Pierre-Quint, Paris, 1926; *Comment débuta Marcel Proust*, edited by Louis de Robert, Paris, 1925.

Since the selection of these letters has been based almost entirely on their documentary value, it is only fair to point out to readers unfamiliar with Proust's correspondence in the original French that none of his letters are literary in the sense of "fine writing" or even of conscious artistry. Even if certain critics have seen his novel as a "letter to the world," he himself differentiated drastically between social or friendly communication and the creation of a work of art. Because of his illness—he always wrote in bed, never using a pad or desk, somehow managing to juggle his paper on his knees—his letters were usually a substitute for companionship or afterthoughts to conversations and discussions. The problem of translating them, therefore, is so different from that involved in rendering a work of art into another language that I have not felt shadowed by the brilliant and imaginative work of Scott Moncrieff. I have chosen to be guided by Proust's own attitude as a translator, even though his ignorance of the English language rendered his problem especially difficult.

For Proust, as one of his friends remarked, "would have been hard put to it even to order a lamb chop in a restaurant in English." His translations of Ruskin's *The Bible of Amiens* and *Sesame and Lilies* were accomplished in part by what his friend, Reynaldo Hahn, described as "supernatural divination," but far more by a conscientious, painstaking saturation in his subject, as well as through the aid of generous and devoted friends, both French and English.

This latter aid I, too, have received from Jeanne Saleil of the French Department of Smith College, André du Bouchet of the Department of History and Literature of Harvard University, from Virgil Thomson, as well as from Marie Nordlinger (Mrs. Riefstahl) of Manchester, England, one of Proust's own assistants in his work as translator, who was generous enough to revise my translation of her letters from Proust.

I have not attempted to express Proust's French in the king's English or in the native American tongue. In each of the first few drafts of the translation I changed the convention, feeling around for a style that I hoped the writer—who never wished his letters to be published—might not have found too graceless. And the convention that I finally adopted, or that adopted me, was the use of a kind of English that it seemed to me Proust might have written, had he been bilingual. So, not having tried to make the letters sound as though they had been written by a man to whom English was second nature, I have left in the original

French words or phrases in which the writer's feeling and intention seemed more felicitously expressed in his own language. Although I am aware of the inadequacies of my efforts, I can honestly say, as did Proust of his Ruskin translations, "though I could wish them more alive, at least they are as faithful as love and piety can make them."

If there is a certain deviation from traditional method in the footnotes, it is because, during six months in Paris, I was fortunate enough to spend many hours with Proust's closest friends, to discuss questions raised in the published letters to them as well as many other related subjects. Proust's friends were also most generous in showing me unpublished material, as was the distinguished collector, M. Jacques Guérin. I have chosen, therefore, to share with the reader as much relevant information secured from these sources or from untranslated and little-known memoirs as space permits, rather than to supply the vital statistics of well-known persons, available in any biographical dictionary.

Due to limitations of space, I have been unable to give as many cross references (there are hundreds) between Proust's letters and his novel as I should have liked. The references given refer to The Modern Library Edition of *Remembrance of Things Past*.

Every effort has been made in the translation to adhere to the published text. But an examination of the original copies of many of the letters necessitates my pointing out to the reader that their owners have felt free to delete not only names but, frequently without any indication, whole sentences and paragraphs, thereby definitely distorting Proust's meaning.

I am indebted to Proust's niece and sole heir, Mme Suzy Mante-Proust, whose devoted and knowledgeable guardianship of her uncle's memory is well known. It is due to her generosity that three previously unpublished letters, 32, 36, and 51, from Proust to his mother, appear for the first time in this book.

Through the kindness of M. Daniel Halévy it has been possible to include in letters 111 and 176 portions heretofore omitted in published versions.

For the dating of the letters, a most complex problem, since Proust himself never dated them, I have adopted a lay rather than an academic solution. I have not differentiated between dates determined by postmark and those determined by other methods. Dr. Philip Kolb of the French Department of the University of Illinois, whose book, *La Correspondance de Marcel Proust: chronologie et commentaire*, will soon appear, has most generously and helpfully supplied, with few exceptions, all dates enclosed in brackets; dates not so enclosed are taken from the original French editions.

As a final word I should like to express my gratitude here for the unfailing interest, cheerfulness, and devotion of my secretary, Nellie Miller Sickman.

Mina Curtiss

PARIS, MAY 25, 1948

ASHFIELD, MASSACHUSETTS, SEPTEMBER 2, 1948

Introduction

We read a writer's letters either because we love the sound of his voice, and want to hear it again—rather, overhear it, at moments when the writer, officially, at least, didn't expect to be heard by anyone but the guy he is writing to. ("Officially," only because every good writer secretly expects everything he writes to be read by everybody forever.) Or we read a writer's letters because, loving his voice, we sense in it something willed, and want to find out how he made it. Henry James's letters are of the first kind: if you like the sound of his voice, there is no better place to get it, pure and high, than in his correspondence; the flow is purer when it is not impeded by the necessity of plot. Good instances of the second kind of letter writer are Scott Fitzgerald, sticking to his last amid the Hollywood glitter and gutter, and, in a very different way, Chekhov, "expelling the serf" from himself. Fitzgerald's letters lack the serene sparkle and humor of his stories, while Chekhov is more irritable and argumentative than we might expect, but in both cases the letters tell moving stories of dignity saved and talent kept whole in resistant circumstances—of how a voice was *won*. Fitzgerald's letters are all the more touching for sounding so little like his books: among the drunken apologias and the sheer desperation and the weirdly stern paternal lectures to his baffled daughter, one senses a man at the impossible work of keeping his gift, and his self-esteem, intact when everything else is smashed.

Given the fluency, the genius, the assurance of Marcel Proust, and the safe well of money that kept him from having to hustle or beg for his work, one would expect his letters to be of the first kind—extended footnotes to "In Search of Lost Time," exquisite studies of high life, lyric missives, erotic billets-doux, all written in that tender, probing, circuitous but never meandering voice that by now generations of readers have come to love. But the startling thing about Proust's letters is that they are not particularly "Proustian." They involve very little scene painting, very few self-consciously exquisite moments, very little of what our grandfathers called "purple patches." They do paint a picture of a young man on the make, in one of the most enviable times ever to be alive; and, with the Dreyfus case stirring and the Great War approaching, they also paint a picture of how that time darkened. More movingly than perhaps any other body of literary letters, though, they show a great novelist coming into his maturity. They document the story of a young man finding himself as an artist when everyone thought he had found himself already as a dilettante: Proust had to prove to the world not that it didn't know the score about him but that the score it knew was wrong.

His letters impress us, then, not as stray leaves from the larger Proustian tree but as something less "lyrical" yet more impressive, as the seeds from which the tree grew. That the Proust of the first half of these collected letters—the hyperbolic and sometimes toadying snob, with confused, vaguely aesthetic Ruskinian ideals that seem already out of date as he offers them—became the Proust of the second half of the book, a literary artist absolutely assured in his purpose and almost coldly detached in his search for truths about the mind and human desire, is one of the little miracles of literary history. For Proust, the normal principle of chrysalis was reversed: the social butterfly became a literary caterpillar, crawling his way millimeter by millimeter across an entire world. The cocoon where the transformation happened was woven of his own words.

The Proust of these letters is easy to like but, at first, hard to respect. There are barriers not so much to our enjoyment—the language of obsequiousness is so elaborate and even campy that it's fun to read—as to our admiration, created by Proust's social aspirations, his famous "snobbery." Proust's snobbery, which shows itself in the elaborate language of flunkeydom that he often employs, is, in its way, not entirely unlikable and is in every way peculiarly French. Unlike the snobbery of other writers—of Waugh or James, say—Proust's is worldly, not nostalgic. He is drawn to the way rich people live, not to fantasies about their collective past; his is a snobbery based not on a mysticism of breeding but on a regard for what would now be called a "life style." Given that the rich people he admired were, on the whole, rich people with good taste and wonderful clothes, living in one of the most beautiful of times, in the most beautiful part of the most beautiful of cities, it is hard to be too rough on him. Though Parisian society people of his period could be ignorant, and, as he captured in his big book, criminally indifferent, they weren't dull, and they certainly weren't squalid. You would have to be a bit of an idiot yourself not to want to impress the Comtesse de Noailles or Laure Heyman. (What puzzles us in Waugh is not that he is a snob but that his snobbery is sent into raptures by such dowdy objects, philistine people in moldy country houses.)

And then a great deal of what seems like wildly rococo toadying has to be read as self-conscious flattery, with an ironic edge known to both speaker and hearer—an overcharge of flattery so deliberate that it is a kind of formal dance, set in a civilization where even now it is normal to offer a stranger one's most distinguished possible salutations when ordering linoleum. When Proust writes to the Comtesse de Noailles, "How moved I am when I catch sight of the disciplined tumult of your handwriting, those magnificent spirals of a rhythmic and infinite sea from the bosom of which, sparkling like Aphrodite, your thought emerges as divine and beautiful," we feel, in our small Anglo-Saxon way, for the writer. But of course he was kidding, a little, and she knew that he was, in that way of half kidding and real kidding that only initiates quite understand. Similarly, when he writes to Robert de Montesquiou that he "discovered long ago that you stood far above the type of exquisite decadent with whose features (never as perfect as yours, but common enough in these times), you are depicted," and "I think that never before has this supreme refinement been combined with such energy, and this creative force, typical of the past, with this almost seventeenth century intellectuality," we know that he is both expressing a semi-sincere emotion—he really did have a high opinion of the older man's work—and is also setting him up, with the necessary ruthlessness of a con man. Intimacy is a necessity for the picture he knows already that he will someday want to draw—and the hostility, or at least the strategy, implicit in the naked flattery was, of course, plain enough for Montesquiou to sense. (Countless society favorites have justified their role by that Novel I'm Writing. Proust really wrote it.)

What is still more impressive, though, is the steel in Proust, already there amid the chrysanthemums. His letter to Montesquiou explaining his Jewish origins, after the great man had made an anti-Semitic remark in his presence, is a model of a firm but polite rejoinder, neither oversold nor underwritten. And, on the great issue of his day, the Dreyfus case, the aesthete Proust was courageous and right. Courage and charm are supposed to be opposites, but in Proust they are the same. And the courage rises from a base of sadness, and a sense of having failed. He says flatly, on his father's death, that he "knew that he had been the disappointment of his life." How hard he worked to turn this perception around.

Yet it was work that he was capable of doing; one of the

most striking things in these letters is how much physical energy, despite his asthma and other sufferings, Proust had to draw on when he needed it. Salinger's Buddy Glass says somewhere that no good writer gets a completely failed body issued to him, and Proust is an instance of this truth, against the odds. (There is an anecdote in an obscure English literary memoir of Proust walking twenty miles from Dieppe to arrange a dinner party. He may have appreciated violets, but he wasn't one.)

The hard core gave him a tough mind. Proust wins us throughout these letters not by his delicacy, exquisiteness, or sensitivity but by his robust intelligence and ever-increasing self-knowledge. The real climax of this unplanned autobiography, which is what all letter collections are, occurs as his great book begins to be published, and, one by one, the people around him recognize that this fragile mama's boy of the Faubourg, who wrote such amusing letters and such pretty essays—you know, all about cathedrals and so on—was a great writer, with x-ray vision for their gifts and pretenses, at once brutal, in his way, and limitlessly generous.

He knew how good the book was, and he knew, what's more, that it was better than it had any reason to be, given that it was his book. In all of literature, there is no greater surprise to anyone—including the author—than "Swann's Way." "All this is merely the stem of the book," he writes to his friend Charles Blum, about the famous evocation of memory invoked by taste which begins—but only begins!—the book. "What it supports is real, passionate, very different from what you know of me, and I think infinitely less thin, not deserving the epithet 'delicate' or 'sensitive' but living and true."

Proust was right. What he wrote was different from what anyone knew of him, or even what he entirely knew of himself, and as we turn these pages we share his satisfaction as his contemporaries, often unwillingly, are forced to recognize the genius in the boy-of-the-world they had previously agreed to patronize. One would, after all, have expected from Proust a novel of showy sensibility, with scenes of society life, full of tittle-tattle and settled scores —not unlike what Capote's Proustian novel, "Answered Prayers," was when it appeared. Proust's book is so different: a study of the numinous glow of childhood balanced against the perfect evocation of an unhappy love affair. It is the tenderness of emotion, the gentleness of the pleasures evoked, the achieved simplicity, not the "sophistication," that knocks us out. The heroes and heroines of his work, as he reminds us several times in these letters, are, from the beginning, not the social top but the Jewish middle class and other outsiders: his mother and his grandmother—and, for all his weakness, Swann, who comes from outside the Guermantes way, and ends with a certain heroism, from fidelity to his own illusion, and to his daughter.

The most famous of the delayed recognitions is, of course, that of André Gide, who, having rejected "Swann's Way" for the *Nouvelle Revue Française*, here writes to Proust in a tone that is insulting even as he offers him praise: he rejected what he now recognizes as a great book, he explains, more or less because Proust wrote it. "I thought of you, I shall confess it, as a snob, a man of the world," he says. Proust's reply, preserved here, is a small masterpiece of wounded feelings rising to appropriate dignity: a brave, annoyed defense of his "social" role, ending in an undeservedly graceful compliment to Gide. One feels that he has defended all his behavior more than adequately; Gide is revealed as the real snob, and Proust the realist of snobbery.

Another pleasure these letters provide—and not the smallest, for another author—is seeing Proust engaged in the exasperating business of *being* an author: corresponding with his publisher about editions, sales, failure to respond to success, changing publishers, proofs. Proust speaks for, and sounds just like, all of us, as he tries to protect and project his work. But, of all the pleasures here, Proust's vindication, his defense and explication of his own masterpiece, is perhaps the greatest. Already, upon the novel's publication, the two myths that still bedevil Proustians—the false images of Proust as an aesthete, an exquisist of sensation, and of Proust as a metaphysician, a philosopher of time, dramatizing Bergson and anticipating Einstein—were circulating. Proust rejects them both, clearly and definitively. (He also rejects, with even greater exasperation, the idea that the book is a gossipy, roman-à-clef dramatization of his own life.) Proust separates himself, neatly, from Bergson, and from any overelaborate theory that the book is meant to explicate. His insight, he explains to us, is simple: the past can be recaptured through the mindful acts of imagination and memory. Unlike Bergson, he is never metaphysical or even vaguely obscure. He has simply discovered a way of *being back there*. The brilliance of his book, as he recognized, was that, having become an insider, he recaptured the childlike admiration of the outsider. "I have always been careful in speaking of the Guermantes," he writes to Lucien Daudet, "not to regard them as a man of the world or at least as one who was in society, but from the point of view of *whatever there may be of poetry* in snobbery. I have not spoken of them in the glib style of a man of the world, but in the dazzled tones of someone from whom it is all very remote."

That dazzled and remote tone, hard-won not by abstract philosophy but by particularized writing, is what wins us still. Proust was not a social novelist—a writer who, like Anthony Powell, tries to anatomize a particular historical moment or class. He is less like Powell than like Piaget, a watchful student of the mind. He was a psychological novelist, not in the narrow sense of dissecting motive but in the large sense *of analyzing mind*. He explains in these letters that he would prefer to be called an "introspective" novelist—meaning, as he makes clear, that his writing is done not in the journalistic manner, from the outside in, but in the poetic manner, from the inside out. But, if his object is his own mind, his subject is everyone else's. He looks everywhere, with exactly the dazzled detachment of a scientist, for law, for generalization, for permanent and universal truths about the way people's desires trick them into other desires, always with an eye for the self-deceptions and a limitless sympathy for the self-deceived. His psychology is almost purely "cognitive," in a prescient way: he does not think that heart and mind—or soul and thought, or poetry and reason—are at war in life. He does not accept any of the easy dualities he inherited. He thinks that one part of the mind maps and polishes and creates and wants and idealizes—and another part, equally strong, sees, accepts, judges, and then renews. The constant counterpoint between these two activities creates human consciousness, and neither one is more important; Swann invents Odette; Odette cannibalizes Swann; and his love for Odette produces Gilberte, who becomes idealized in another way. It is a cycle that cannot be broken, but only registered and remade in art. No writer surveys the disillusion of life so well while also honoring its illusions.

He was writing, too, of a time not merely gone by but irretrievably lost. "The war," he writes in a late letter, "has vindicated, consecrated and immortalized the *avant-guerre*." To the normal pain of lost time had come the added pain of a cataclysm. A letter to Comte de Maugny speaks plaintively of how "there has been one death after another." The world that Proust described and analyzed was based, like our own until so recently, on a bottomless supply of money and optimism; it seemed to have committed suicide en masse, even as he was writing what he thought would be only his own elegy. A hundred years later, we can see traces of continuity between our time and his, and, more prosaically, between his Paris and ours, but at the time it felt as if the sky had fallen. Proust is surprisingly alert to the details of the war going on around him as he struggles to finish his great book—he keeps up with the military situation in *Figaro*, deplores the cheap anti-German sentiment among otherwise respectable literary men—but he is writing the epic of a Troy that has burned, and he knows it.

And yet, for all of that, for all the suffering, dying, and sheer loss, which he sees unblinkingly, the keynote of these letters is not sadness but an immense hope, as real as, if more peculiar than, any religious believer's. Proust says, almost as artlessly as this artful man could, that the secret of his book was his discovery that the past was available through memory, that the world was not gone if one struggled to re-create it, that the past can be recaptured, and that he had done it. Proust had a simple shining idea, which he turned into a complex, chiaroscuroed book. The overwhelming emotion of his life, the sense that all that he had loved would just vanish, turned out not to be fatal—the world and our experience of it, however particular and painful, could be restored if we struggled to re-create it from the particular sensations upward, rather than from generalizing memory down. As Alain de Botton has reminded us, this is not a counsel of despair or an artifact of a time that could afford it but a permanent truth about minds and desires and memory. All our experience is made, not found, and our nostalgia is just the demotic form of immortality. This is not merely comforting but true, and challenging in its way—a challenge not just to live, as James wanted us to, but to live mindfully. Proust's letters remind us that among all the other things he was—loving son and elaborate social animal, a metropolitan man of courtesy and malice—the most significant was the one that his metropolitan correspondents might not have imagined him capable of becoming. Marcel Proust was a reasonable man who wrote a rational masterpiece.

Adam Gopnik

PART ONE

Youth and the Years in Society, 1885–1899

Marcel Proust was born July 10, 1871, in the house of his mother's uncle, at 96, rue La Fontaine, Auteuil. His parents had been married September 3, 1870, the day the news of the fall of Sedan reached Paris, the day before the abdication of Napoleon III. The siege of Paris by the Prussians soon exposed Parisians to the terrors and anxieties of continuous bombardment as well as to acute shortages of food and fuel. Horse meat and dog meat became luxuries, and if the armistice in January of 1871 brought a brief respite, the turmoil and violence were soon renewed in the civil war that resulted in the setting up of the Commune in March.

By April, almost everyone who could get away had left Paris. But Proust's parents remained, and Dr. Proust walked each day from 9, boulevard Malesherbes across the Seine to the Hôpital de la Charité to care for the wounded. In the spring of 1871, a stray bullet from the rifle of a Communard nearly struck Dr. Proust, and the shock of this experience caused Mme Proust to be moved to her uncle's house at Auteuil. But she found no quiet in that western suburb of Paris, for even there buildings had been gutted and streets laid waste.

Frequently, during the last years of his life, Proust expressed the opinion that the anxiety and the deprivations his mother had suffered during her pregnancy might well have been a cause of his chronic ill health. So frail at birth that his life had been feared for, Marcel had an early childhood that was, nevertheless, healthy. But when he was nine years old, while on a walk in the Bois de Boulogne, he experienced his first attack of asthma, an attack so violent that he almost choked to death; and from that time on he lived in constant apprehension of repeated attacks. Mme Proust tended her son with a devotion as passionate as his for her, which at the age of fourteen he recorded in a friend's autograph book where he replied to the question "What is your conception of the greatest possible misery?" by writing, "To be separated from Mother."

In spite of his illness, however, Proust attended the Lycée Condorcet irregularly from the time he was eleven. Perhaps the best picture of him as a schoolboy is given by one of his classmates, M. Daniel Halévy, who is mentioned frequently in the letters of this period. ". . . he figured among us as a sort of archangel, disturbed and disturbing . . . with his great oriental eyes, his big white collar, his flying cravat. There was something about him we found unpleasant . . . his kindnesses, his tender attentions, his caresses . . . we often labeled as mannerisms, poses, and we took occasion to tell him so to his face. . . ." When asked nearly sixty years after their schooldays whether he had not been unduly severe with Proust, M. Halévy replied, "Severe isn't the word. Rough. We were rough with him. *Ce pauvre malheureux!*" And in reply to the question of whether any of Proust's schoolmates had had a premonition of his genius, M. Halévy admitted that, whereas his literary talent had been recognized, no one credited him with the willpower ever to achieve a masterpiece.

The following is Proust's earliest published letter and was written during the summer holiday.

1: TO HIS GRANDMOTHER WEIL

SALIES DE BÉARN
HÔTEL DE LA PAIX
[1885 OR 1886]

Ma chère Grandmère,
Please don't be cross with me about this letter. Besides, since my scolding the other day, I am afraid of being punished again. But Madame Catusse has promised me a little song if I start to do a portrait of her for you, a big song if I finish it, and for the whole thing all the songs I want. This means nothing to you, does it? But if yesterday you had heard a certain delightfully pure and marvelously dramatic voice, you, who know all the emotions singing kindles in me, would understand why, while I am being urged to join my comrades playing croquet, I am sitting at the desk of our hostess, Mlle Biraben, to describe to you Madame Catusse.

I am very much embarrassed. Madame Catusse is bound

to see this portrait and, although I shall do it—I swear by Artemis, the white goddess, and by Pluto with the burning eyes—as though she would never see it, I feel a certain reluctance about telling her that I find her charming. Nevertheless, that is the sad reality. Madame Catusse must be between 22 and 25 years old. A ravishing head, two gentle, bright eyes, a delicate white skin, a head worthy of being dreamed about by a painter in love with perfect beauty, framed in beautiful black hair. (Oh, the unbearable task of defying Musset and of saying—particularly when one means it—Madame, you are pretty, extremely pretty. But the divine Melodies of Massenet and Gounod will still my fears.) Her figure is small, attractively formed. But nothing equals the head, which one never tires of watching. I confess that the first day I found her only pretty, but each day her charming expression has seduced me further, and I have arrived at a mute admiration of it. But no more, I shall appear an imbecile to Madame Catusse, and I shall keep the celebration of her physical charms for a letter she will not see.

Madame Catusse's conversation has come to console my multiple sorrows and the boredom that Salies exhales for anyone who hasn't enough "double-size muscles," as Tartarin says, to go searching in the freshness of the neighboring countryside the seed of poetry necessary to existence, and of which, alas, the terrace full of chatter and tobacco smoke, where we spend our days, is destitute. I bless the immortal gods who caused to come here one woman so intelligent, so well informed, who teaches so much and spreads such a pervading charm, "*mens pulcher* [sic] *in corpore pulchro*." But I curse the genii, hostile to the peace of human beings, who have forced me to talk this twaddle in front of someone I love so much, who is so good and so charming to me. It is torture. I should have told you how delightful my stay here has been, how sad I shall be at her departure; I should have tried to paint her features eloquently and to make you feel her inner beauty; I should have tried to show you her grace and to tell you of my friendship for her. But never now! The role I have played is already stupid enough.

I send you a kiss, furious until the time her "melodious accents enchant my ears, put my sorrows to sleep."

Good-bye, Grandmother, how are you?

Marcel

Robert Dreyfus (1873–1937), two years Proust's junior, was his schoolmate both at the Lycée Condorcet and at the University of Paris. Dreyfus became an historian and journalist, the author of several books on Thiers and other figures of the Third Republic, as well as *Souvenirs sur Marcel Proust* and *De Monsieur Thiers à Marcel Proust*. He was for many years on the staff of the newspaper *Figaro*.

2: TO ROBERT DREYFUS

AUGUST, 1888

TUESDAY

Mon cher ami,

The gentleman in question is a little man, thin, dry and formal. Extremely intelligent and well informed. A wonderfully nimble and acute mind. Penetrating to the point of subtlety, almost. A very *distinguished*, very rich, very lively course. Severe, righteous wit. Much more intelligent and, above all, more intellectual than artistic. Nevertheless, he admires Leconte de Lisle. But finds him rather "bizarre"! I can see him now, all movement, all fire—his "lively" little eyes—his manner of a vivisecting psychologist—"This taste for the foreign, the exotic!"

But, on the whole, a very firm and supple intellectual discipline, a notable course of lectures, full of stuff and ideas, the most trustworthy and intelligently cultivated guide for this yearlong journey from Homer to Chénier, with a stopover at Petronius, a little too "lofty" and "serious," too much classroom, too much review, but that can't do you any harm, can it, and he is, without a shadow of a doubt, *by far the best* professor of rhetoric, now that our poor Gaucher is dead. I talked to him about you a year ago, without knowing that you would be taking his course. I shall do it again in the same words. I wouldn't dare repeat them to you because I find it almost immodest and "physically" disagreeable to say it point-blank, but I can assure you he will be ready to admire.

Cucheval is not like him, polite, cold, severe but coarse, vehement, and profuse. A grim old schoolmaster type, worn, rough—but, on the whole, I assure you, very agreeable. This crude, even "direct," Brunetière is not lacking in flavor. It is rather amusing to let oneself be guided by two such different minds. Even though he should ride you, it would do you no harm. Don't tell yourself he is a fool because he cracks idiotic jokes or because he is a barbarian utterly insensitive to exquisite combinations of syllables or cadences. In every other way he is *excellent* and is a pleasant change from the fools who speak in rounded periods. He couldn't do it; he doesn't know how. It's a pure delight. He is the ideally good professor and not at all boring.

M. Dupré is an infinitely more amiable, nice man. He is a very affectionate and delicate soul whose charm I have been able to appreciate in spite of his gruff manner. But he is a bore. True, he knows Dierx and Leconte de Lisle (their works). But what use is there in listening to talk about modern writers from a man who has too many reservations about them? It will bore you and even make you stamp your feet and grind your teeth. You will have endless discussion, for he is a good soul and not at all stiff. But what of it? He will come out of it slightly modernized. And you?

To sum up, Dauphiné is a lecture course, Cucheval a class, Dupré often a conversation. But the lectures are very *extraordinary*, the class is very good, and the conversation boring.

Will you be nice—as you often are—and let me tell you a few more little things that would ease my mind? Here they are. Please don't make fun of me because I am not pretentious enough to compare myself to you. I think much too highly of you for that, and M. Jalliffier can tell you that these are not mere words. But we have something in common with a few others which is that we know a little about the literature of today and we like it, that we have our own way of understanding art and we judge the interpretations of writers or artists according to rather special standards. So I beg of you—for your own sake—don't do what I did, don't go in for evangelizing the professors. I was able to get away with it, thanks to Gaucher's infinitely liberal and charming mind. I wrote themes that didn't read at all like regular themes. As a result, at the end of two months a dozen idiots were writing in a decadent style; Cucheval regarded me as a poisonous influence; I upset the whole class, and many even regarded me as a *poseur*. Fortunately, at the end of two months it was all over, but only a month ago Cucheval would say: "He will be passed because he only did it for fun, but fifteen others will fail because of him." They will want to cure you. Your schoolmates will take you for a madman or a fool. For several months I read all my French themes in class. I was hooted at and applauded. Without Gaucher I would have been torn to bits.

Now, since you are willing to write to me, here is the subject that, to tell you the truth, will interest me most. First, what you are doing. Then tell me in detail about the "sympathetic" personality who hides himself inadequately under the initials D—— H——. Intellectually, I think I know him, and M. Jalliffier, who chatted with me about him for more than an hour, confirmed my opinion of him. But, really what does he want? Why, having been on the whole very nice to me, does he drop me *entirely*, making me very much aware of it, and then, a month later, come up and say hello, after he had stopped speaking to me? And his cousin Bizet? Why, when he tells me he feels friendly toward me, does he drop me even more pointedly?

What is it they want? To get rid of me, to worry me, mystify me, or what?

I thought they were so very nice!

Naturally, I am telling you all this confidentially as a friend. Don't say anything about it. But as their friend, you must know why.

And as my friend, you owe it to me to tell me, because when a person doesn't know where he stands, he risks being either too cold or too clinging.

The horror of being too clinging has always been a nightmare to me. I think in this instance I was. You will tell me, won't you? It would be very nice of you.

Please believe in my sincere friendship.

Marcel Proust

96, RUE LA FONTAINE, AUTEUIL

P.S. Desjardins' articles are very interesting. What he is trying to accomplish seems to me the most beautiful thing that anyone can do. But (particularly because of recent events) his achievement—at least up to the present time—seems to me very inconclusive and hasty.

Forgive my writing, my style, my spelling. I don't dare reread when I have written at full speed. I know very well one shouldn't write at full speed. But I have so much to say. It surges like the tide.

3: TO ROBERT DREYFUS

SEPTEMBER 7, 1888

(Joyant's monogram—I am staying with him at l'Isle-Adam, but write to me at Auteuil where I am returning this evening.)

Cher ami,

Are you trying to tell me politely that Halévy thinks I am raving mad? I must say I didn't understand you very clearly.

I don't believe that a type is a character. I *do* believe that what we think we read in a person's character is only a result of some association of ideas. I shall explain myself, admitting at the same time that my theory may be false since it is entirely personal.

So I am supposing that in life or in a piece of literature you see a gentleman who weeps at the misfortune of another. Since whenever you have seen someone feeling pity it was a sensitive, gentle, and good person, you deduce that this gentleman is sensitive, gentle, and good. For in our minds we build up a character from just the few lines that we see which presuppose certain others. But this construction is very hypothetical. *Quare* if Alceste flees the society of men, Coquelin claims it is because of ridiculous bad temper, Worms because of a noble scorn for base passions. *Item* in life. So Halévy cuts me in a way that appears deliberate; then, after a month, comes to say hello to me. Well, among the different gentlemen of whom I am made up, the romantic gentleman, whose opinion I pay little attention to, says to me, "It was to tease you, to amuse himself and to test you; then he regretted it, not wishing to give you up entirely." And this gentleman presents Halévy, in relation to me, as a whimsical friend, eager to know me.

But the suspicious gentleman, whom I prefer, declares that it is much simpler than that; that Halévy finds me insufferable; that my eagerness seemed to him—sage that he is—at first ridiculous, and very soon tiresome; that he wanted me to feel this; that I was too clinging, and he wished to be rid of me. And finally when he saw that I would no longer embarrass him by my presence, he spoke to me. This gentleman doesn't know whether the gesture was caused by pity or indifference or palliation, but he does know that it has no importance whatsoever, it worries him very little, and then only as a psychological problem.

But there is the question of the letter: is it *x*—is it *y*? That's the whole point. If it is *x* (a combination of the elements of friendship), the misunderstanding has only the importance of a whim, a test or an irritation, and everything depends on the reconciliation.

If it is *y*—antipathy—the reconciliation is nothing, the misunderstanding is everything.

The explanation of my theory has taken up my whole letter, and Joyant is calling me. This letter must wait for another time. But you can verify my psychological research on this question. For you know perfectly well whether Halévy has said to you (and I wouldn't hold it against him): this Proust, what a dreadful bore!

Or, this Proust is rather nice.

It is true that there is a third solution, the most probable: that he hasn't talked about me at all.

I am only a neutral object.

Clear up this little problem for me. I will tell you anything you want to know in reply.

Three apologies: 1st, For not having answered sooner; but my mother went away, and my brother. Then my departure for Joyant's.

2nd, So badly written and hurried from every point of view: Joyant is waiting for me.

3rd, For having bored you with all this. . . . It interests me!

Bien à toi,
Marcel Proust

4: TO ROBERT DREYFUS

SEPTEMBER 10, 1888

Cher ami,

The weather is so beautiful today that I would like to indulge myself in the fantasies of a great nobleman. I would like to conjure up wonderful spectacles. For me that would mean having company or seeing the crowd, escaping from myself, being peaceful or passionate or extravagant or bawdy, according to my mood or even my physical desires; entertaining myself not only with the spectacle of the stupidity of the many, but also with the originality, or simply the character of the few. I should like to tell X — or Y— that I am decadent. But being unable to avail myself of this royal pleasure today, I shall compensate by taking a drive to the Acacias. There, to my mind, the flower of Parisian aesthetics is to be found in full bloom. It would give me great pleasure to study it, if I were a journalist, which it would very much amuse me to be, since I wanted to start a newspaper at school. It would blossom forth on the softest, whitest shoulders in fanciful folds of the most exquisite materials. In this same way a great courtesan, the *modeling* of whose neck—the sloping curve of the nape—has precisely the charming roundness of those amphora in which the patient Etruscans expressed their idea and consoling dream of grace; and the corner of her lip is the same as in those primitive virgins of Luini (Bernardino) or of Botticelli, which I prefer very much to Raphael's—bang! where am I?—wait a minute till I reread this—oh, yes, the kind of courtesan, I was saying, who conceals in the cleverly draped folds of her purple dress more charm than that of many "salons"; above all, it is more modern and very sincere. I mean that they express naturally, with no sense of imitation (as one does unconsciously in painting or in poetry), with no desire either to embody an idea or to shock, what seems to them the height of prettiness, of elegance, in the rarest, most precious materials, in fabrics of a more enchanting pink than the sky at six o'clock, in supple folds as deep as still water. I am afraid I sound rather like Georges Ohnet in all this. But what consoles me about it is that Georges Ohnet and I do not like the same aspects; and that in itself, reality is always changing and of little significance.

Another act would be to criticize our friends. Since I would be putting on a show, being somebody other than myself, I could slander them with no sense of guilt. Myself, too. I would even gladly do my own portrait, a little corner of my portrait: "Do you know X——, my dear, I mean M. P——? I must admit that I don't like him very much, with his perpetual wild enthusiasms, his distracted manner, his great loves, and his adjectives. What strikes me most is that he must be either crazy or a fraud. Take your choice. . . ." If it's a portrait, it's not very flattering and would flatter me less than the portrait I do of you, draped—according to you—in your scorn of the common herd and giving to the public the picture of an imaginary, very ironic Dreyfus.

It goes without saying that if you show this letter to one D—— H——, it is with the express preliminary warning that he mentions it to no one, particularly not to his brother. I suppose that D—— H——, if he sees this portrait, will say of me as before: "It's too honest to be sincere." He would be right.

For I am convinced (it is one of the few things of which I am convinced) that there are certain things which would be loathsome to say about oneself unless it were as a transcendent practical joke. Even then, it is bad taste. Therefore, perhaps, I would really prefer not to have you show this to H——.

A toi,
Marcel P.

5: TO ROBERT DREYFUS

SEPTEMBER 25, 1888
ISLE-ADAM

Mon cher Dreyfus,

A sojourn at Chantilly,

A sojourn at l'Isle-Adam,

A Platonic passion for a celebrated courtesan [Closmenil], which ended in an exchange of letters and photographs,

A not at all complicated affair, which terminated dully in a predictable ending and which gave birth to an absorbing liaison which threatens to last at least a year, to the greater profit of the music halls and similar places where one takes this type of person—all this has kept me from starting all over again my answer to your last letter, an answer which I lost and which I shan't rewrite, but will give you orally; for it is too ticklish since it includes in particular the fact that the "loathsome" and the "transcendent practical joke" in my last letter applied to my portrait of myself, which was beastly, and not to yours of yourself, which was charming, and not in the least "loathsome." There has been a misunderstanding, and I was very sorry that you were cross about it. You may be sure that I have always talked to you with *the most scrupulous frankness*, that if I had to reproach you for anything, I should *by no means* disguise it, and that if my actions and words sometimes contradict each other (I shan't explain myself, but in this I am bound by a decorum which is almost a duty, as Labiche would say), you must believe my words. My words are true. I give you my word of honor and take you affectionately by the hand. I miss your letters. They give me great pleasure. Write to me right away. . . .

Here's to the beginning of term, *mon cher ami*; I wish you a very brilliant rhetoric course, sincere friends, and beautiful mistresses.

Marcel Proust

Dr. Adrien Proust, father of Marcel, was born in Illiers, near Chartres, in 1834. His ancestors had for centuries been respectable Catholic citizens of that little village, where his father owned and ran a prosperous "general store." Dr. Proust went to Paris at an early age to study medicine, and, by 1866, during the great cholera epidemic, he was Chief of Clinic at the Hôpital de la Charité. He was subsequently sent by the French government to conferences in Russia, Persia, and many European countries as technical adviser on sanitation. Inspector-General of Sanitary Services, Professor of Hygiene on the Faculty of Medicine, Chevalier of the Legion of Honor, and a member of the Academy of Medicine, he was credited with much of the progress made in forming the International Sanitary Code. For Dr. Proust was one of the few scientists aware of the necessity for a practice of the techniques of diplomacy in medicine and an understanding of the rules of sanitation in diplomacy.

His relationship with his son was affectionate but lacking in understanding or sympathy. He once asked a woman friend of Marcel's: "Why is he invited to so many places? . . . Is he really so fascinating?" Apart from the basic difference in their natures, Dr. Proust, a conservative, conventional successful bourgeois, could not overcome his paternal and professional exasperation at his inability either to diagnose or to cure his son's illness.

6: TO HIS FATHER

THIS TUESDAY, SEPTEMBER 23
[1889]
I have started fencing again

Mon cher petit Papa,

If I haven't yet started my correspondence with you it's because most of my leave was spent in bed (Mother has undoubtedly written you about it), and I had so much to do yesterday (first day back) that I couldn't even write to Mother. I hope you liked Maupassant. He wouldn't know me because I saw him only twice because of his illness and his journey, but he would have an idea of who I am. I am not feeling at all badly (except for my stomach) and haven't even that general melancholy of which this year of absence, if not the cause, is at the very least the pretext—and consequently the justification.

But I have extreme difficulty in concentrating, in reading, in learning by heart, in remembering.

Having very little time, I am sending you today only this brief evidence of a "thought of you," which is constant and tender. Until tomorrow, *mon cher petit Papa*, remember me to the dear poet, your neighbor and lay my regards at the feet of [his wife] Madame Cazalis. . . . Can you imagine how scandalized the Derbaunes were when some chambermaids of Cabourg, catching sight of the soldier boy—the traditional soldier boy—sent me hugs and kisses. It is the chambermaids of Orléans—forsaken by me—who are taking revenge. And I am punished, if M. Cazalis will permit me to quote a line from one of his most beautiful poems,

Pour avoir dédaigné les fleurs de leurs seins nus.

Je t'embrasse infiniment.
Your son,
Marcel Proust

"*Madame Emile Straus,*" wrote Proust in the copy of *Swann's Way* he was to inscribe to her some thirty years after their first meeting, "the only thing of beauty I loved even in the days of this book's beginnings, for whom my admiration has changed as little as her own beauty, perpetually renewed, as it is, by her charm." His lifelong friend, almost the only one with whom he never quarreled, Geneviève Straus was born in 1850, the daughter of Fromental Halévy, composer of *La Juive,* professor at the *Conservatoire* and permanent secretary of *l'Académie des Beaux Arts.* In 1869 she became the wife of one of her father's pupils, Georges Bizet. This marriage, framed by both public and personal catastrophe—the Franco-Prussian War, the Siege of Paris, the Commune, as well as the indifference of the public to Bizet's music for *l'Arlésienne* and *Carmen*—lasted only six years. Yet on the day of Bizet's death, his widow said to another student of her father's, her former music teacher, Charles Gounod, "There is not an hour, not a minute of the six years of happiness which my married life brought me that I would not gladly live over again."

For the first eight years of her widowhood, Geneviève

Bizet, with her small son Jacques, lived in complete retirement with her uncle, Léon Halévy, and his son, Ludovic. In 1883, however, after the success of *Carmen* had established Bizet's fame both on the continent and in France, his widow permitted herself to be drawn out of her seclusion, to grace certain salons, among them the Princesse Mathilde's. Almost immediately her beauty, her wit, her charm became the talk of Paris. She was surrounded by admirers, among them Guy de Maupassant, and, after a long and persistent courtship, she finally married Emile Straus, a rich and successful lawyer, a connection of the Rothschilds. Her friends and relatives were astonished at her selection of a husband embodying all the solid virtues, but with none of the qualities so characteristic of the Bohemian world in which she had lived.

However, her marriage into the world of wealth and power did not cut off Madame Straus from her old friends. In her salon artists and *gens du monde* found themselves equally at home. Unique among the salons of her day, Mme Straus's was neither the stronghold of one writer, as was Mme de Caillavet's for Anatole France, nor a literary stock exchange, a lobby to the Academy. Among her close friends and admirers were the painters Forain and Degas, the playwrights Hervieu, Porto-Riche, Henry Bernstein, and Robert de Flers, the novelist and critic Abel Hermant, the distinguished and fascinating doctor Professor Pozzi, Louis Ganderax, editor of the *Revue de Paris,* Gaston Calmette of the *Figaro,* and Joseph Reinach, the politician. It was here, too, that *Le Banquet,* a little review, was founded by Proust, Jacques Bizet, Daniel Halévy, and others.

But of them all, Marcel Proust alone rendered her immortal by incorporating her wit and her charm into his portrait of the Duchesse de Guermantes. Introduced into her salon by his schoolmate Jacques Bizet, Proust had known Madame Straus four or five years at the time the following letters were written.

7: TO MADAME STRAUS

[PROBABLY 1890 OR 1891]

Ma chère petite Madame Straus,

You mustn't think that I love you any less because I no longer send you flowers. But Mlle Lemaire can tell you that I go walking every morning with Laure Hayman, and often take her to lunch—and that is so expensive I haven't a *sou* left for flowers—and except for ten *sous* worth of wild poppies to Madame Lemaire I don't think I have sent any since. You were in bed then, beautiful as an angel who looks ill, which is to say beautiful enough to drive mortals mad. And not having dared really kiss you for fear of giving you a headache, I now do it in make believe, most tenderly.

Votre petit
Marcel

8: TO MADAME STRAUS

[SUMMER, 1892]

When you receive this bouquet, I shall be in the midst of taking my examinations at my School of Political Science. I am writing you this because I hope it will bring me good luck and because I shall undoubtedly be kept there too late to come and see you. I have already spent all this week at it and I thought I would finish tomorrow morning. But one professor is endangering my divine Saturday, that day of real happiness, by giving the examination in the afternoon instead of in the morning. Up to now I have passed them all, and I hope I shall do so tomorrow so I can show you that you are quite wrong in thinking me lazy or anxious to be a man of the world. I am a very painstaking worker. I know perfectly well that it is highly unsuitable for me to praise myself in this way. But who else can I count on doing it for me? M. Straus? Perhaps it isn't too wrong for me to boast of the virtues of industry and application, because you value them and because they imply great difficulty in understanding and getting to the bottom of things. I find Jacques very nice now, and I hope that you cast no more severe judgment than that on

Your respectful, affectionate, and sincere

Marcel Proust

9: TO MADAME STRAUS

[1892]

The Truth about Madame Straus

At first I believed you loved only beautiful things and that you understood them very well—and then I saw that you didn't give a hang about them; then I thought you liked people, and now I see that you don't give a hang about them either. I believe you love only a certain kind of life which brings out your intelligence less than your wit, your wit less than your tact, your tact less than your clothes. A person who more than anything loves this kind of life—and who, nevertheless, casts a spell! And it is just because you are enchanting that you must not rejoice and decide that I love you less. To prove the opposite (because you know that what one does proves more than what one says, you, who occasionally say something and never do anything), I could send you prettier flowers and that would annoy you, Madame, since you do not deign to countenance the sentiments which give me the sad rapture of being

The most respectful servant
Of your Sovereign Indifference
Marcel Proust

10: TO MADAME STRAUS

THURSDAY, AFTER LEAVING YOU [1892]

Madame,

I love mysterious women, since you are one, and I have frequently said so in *Le Banquet* where I often wished you might recognize yourself. But I can no longer altogether love you, and I shall tell you why, even though there is no point in it; but you know we spend our time doing pointless and even very harmful things, particularly when we are in love, even though less in love than formerly. You think that to make one's self too available is to allow one's charm to evaporate, and I believe that is true. But I am going to tell you what happens with you. Usually one sees you among twenty people, or rather across twenty people, for it is inevitably the young man who is farthest away from you. But I suppose after a long enough time one manages at least once to see you alone. You have only five minutes and even during those five minutes you are thinking of something else. But even that doesn't matter. If one talks to you about books, you find it pedantic; if one talks to you about people, you find it indiscreet (if one tells stories) and inquisitive (if one asks questions); if one talks about you, you find it ridiculous. So a hundred times one is on the point of finding you much less enchanting, when all of a sudden you grant a little favor, which seems to imply a slight preference, and again one falls under your spell. But you are not sufficiently imbued with this truth (I doubt whether you are imbued with any truth), which *must be conceded* to Platonic love. A person who is not at all sentimental becomes strangely so when reduced to Platonic love. Since I wish to follow your charming rules against bad manners, I shall not be specific. But think about it, I beg of you. Be a little indulgent to a most ardent Platonic love, which binds to you—deign to believe and permit it—

Your respectfully devoted
Marcel Proust

Laure Hayman was born in South America in 1851 and died in Paris some eighty years later. She was of Creole birth, and her beauty and charm attracted to her salon not only the men who had been important in the Second Empire, but young aristocrats and aspiring writers of the nineties, as well. Among her lovers were the Duc d'Orléans, the King of Greece, and the pretender to the Serbian Throne. Paul Bourget made her the heroine of his story, "Gladys Harvey," in which he described her as having "something of the 18th century courtesan . . . not too much of the ferociously calculating prostitute of our positivist and brutal age." In certain minor details Madame Hayman unquestionably served Proust as one of the models for Odette de Crécy, but there was no similarity in character nor did Laure Hayman ever marry. She was the *grande amie* of Proust's great-uncle and was also very closely attached to Dr. Adrien Proust.

II: TO LAURE HAYMAN

THIS WEDNESDAY MORNING
[SUMMER 1892]

Chère amie, chères délices,

Here are fifteen chrysanthemums, twelve for your twelve when they are faded, three to round out your twelve; I hope the stems will be extremely long as I requested. And that these flowers—proud and sad, like you, proud of being beautiful, and sad that everything is so stupid—will please you. Thank you again (and if I had not had examinations Saturday, I should have come to tell you so) for your kind thought of me. It would have amused me so to go to this eighteenth century fête, to see these young men, who you say are clever and charming, united in their love of you. How well I understand them! It is only natural that a woman who is desirable and nothing more, the mere object of lust, should exasperate her lovers, set them one against the other. But when, like a work of art, a woman reveals the utmost refinement of charm, the most subtle grace, the most divine beauty, the most voluptuous intelligence, a common admiration for her is bound to unite, to establish a brotherhood. Coreligionists are made in Laure Hayman's name. And since she is a very special divinity, since her charm is not accessible to everyone, since one must have very subtle tastes in order to understand it, like an initiation of the mind and the senses, it is only right that the faithful should love each other, that among the initiates there should be understanding. So your whatnot of Saxe figures (an altar) seems to me one of the most charming things to be seen anywhere, and bound to be the rarest in existence since the days of Cleopatra and Aspasia. Therefore, I propose to call the present century the century of Laure Hayman and the ruling dynasty the Saxon line. —Forgive all this nonsense and allow me, when my examination is over, to bring you my tender respects.

Marcel Proust

P.S.—On thinking it over, I should be rather embarrassed at becoming part of your collection of Saxe figures. If it is all right with you, I should rather see the one I most want to meet while he is calling on you. In that way if any of them find me tiresome, they will at least not find me indiscreet. And I shall not have to fear the vengeance of dukes or counts for having disturbed the collection.

12: TO LAURE HAYMAN

[1892 OR 1893]

Belle, douce, et dure amie,

Yesterday you made me listen to some brutal truths. They are very precious to me because they are friendly and come from you. But you will admit that if they are merely the fruit of friendship, they are its bitter fruit. —I want at least to exonerate myself from one reproach to which I am particularly sensitive since it is literary. I mean "*comme qui dirait.*" Anatole France, with whom I happen to be at the moment, assures me, and permits me to tell you, that this locution is irreproachable and in no way vulgar. I need hardly tell you that I sacrifice it to you with all my heart and that I should far rather make a slip with you than be on the right side even with the whole Academy. —And France would, too. Indeed, it would be delightful to make a slip with you. *Felix culpa*, as the Church Fathers say.

I throw myself at your feet to receive your absolution, and kiss you tenderly and madly.

Marcel Proust

P.S. If you haven't as yet received my gift of Dresden, it is because so far I haven't found a piece worthy of you. I shall try to get it to you tomorrow.

Robert Jules Daniel de Billy was born in 1869. Now retired, he was for most of his life a member of the French diplomatic corps, having served, among other posts, as his country's ambassador to Japan. He and Proust first met when they were both in military service at Orléans in 1889, and their friendship was an enduring one. In his book, *Marcel Proust: Lettres et Conversations,* M. de Billy, who was brought up in the stern French Protestant tradition, writes, "I owe largely to Marcel my having known the joy of thinking other than by fixed principle."

13: TO ROBERT DE BILLY

[SEPTEMBER 23, 1892]

I am very sad, *mon petit* Robert, and I so wish that you were near me so that we could talk about Aubert together. Do you know as soon as I was alone in Paris—after my parents had left for Auteuil—I took to liking him so very much that his return to Paris was one of the pleasures I most counted on? He was sure of coming back and said so auspiciously, "*No matter what happens*, I shall come back next year." Now those words wring your heart. I think he still expected a great deal from life, still found it full of promise, which makes it even more heartbreaking. And besides all that, his charming melancholy, his defiant and almost apprehensive uncertainty about everything he was going to do, now seem to me like presentiments. Each time we think of him, we can only find reasons for loving him more, which both intensifies and allays our sorrow. I have a photograph of him with some English poetry translated on the back which I don't remember but which was, I think, rather sad. And some letters, the last two of which I was reproaching myself *day before yesterday* for not having answered. Please write me what his illness was, whether he knew its seriousness, what family he leaves, and whether they are like him; tell me all the little details of your trip with him, what he said to you, a thousand things that would not have interested me before, but which now are precious because they are the last things I shall know about him.

I embrace you, my dear friend.

Marcel.

14: TO ROBERT DE BILLY

[JUST AFTER JANUARY 19, 1893]

Mon cher petit Robert,

You wouldn't believe how much I miss you. My frivolity which often binds me to the present, to the immediate moment, has not spoiled my friendship for you. And I think about you all the more desperately since I can't see you, since your charm no longer flavors my daily existence, your gaiety or your wisdom no longer solaces me in my troubles, your advice no longer directs me in the paths of the true and the good.

I was very much touched by a gift that came to me through Boissonnas. It was a souvenir that Edgar Aubert had intended to have sent me. Alas, he will not return; he is gone for an even longer time than you. The days I relive with such poignancy and clarity give me the exact illusion, almost the hallucination, of those return journeys with him when he was so charming, so witty, so good, always modifying any slightly sharp or ironic remark he had just made by a sympathetic look or clasp of the hand. I remember that lunch with him in the tennis *allée* at the Tuileries, his English at the Finalys'.

You complain that I don't tell you anything. I don't dare to because I am going out much too much for you still to respect me if I told you about it. Please be kind enough to send me the list of the four examinations that I have to pass and of the books I should read. I lost it! Please don't forget, *mon petit*. Tell me if I am mistaken but wasn't Edgar a friend of Madame X— and of Madame Z—, two ladies whom I meet fairly often and to whom I could perhaps talk about him. Was it Madame X— or Madame W— whom Y— asked what she thought about making love and who answered brusquely, "I often do it, but I never talk about it!"

The V's (I can talk about this because it isn't social)

played charades the other day with the R's at a Madame U's. It was wonderful and sidesplitting. R— was an old bourgeois in a bathtub hidden by a sheet, but with his feet sticking out so the chiropodist could fix his corns. It was sublime, M. V— was first an old Jew, then a member of the Institute, then president of the Geographical Society, whose members he invited to Madame V—'s Wednesdays where "a thorough knowledge of cards couldn't but be useful to them." This M. V— is very bawdy. He told me that he took advantage of his position on the platform to look down from above at his sister-in-law's and the other ladies' décolletage, and he added, "One could see their busts like the inside of a trunk. Some of them packed only six pairs of socks, others twelve, others none at all. My sister-in-law was obviously equipped for a long journey. . . ."

. . . I dined the other day with one of your colleagues, M. de Florian. Ah, dear Robert, what artistry in his greeting, his handshake, his step, his calm, his silence, his conversation, his politeness, and, that highest form of politeness, his wit. He is the most accomplished diplomat I have ever seen, and his wife appears to be an uncommon person.

Write me, love me, and give me the list I asked you for.

Votre petit ami de toujours,
Marcel Proust

P.S. I went to see your parents lately, who are in perfect health, including your grandmother.

15: TO ROBERT DE BILLY

HÔTEL DES ROCHES-NOIRES, TROUVILLE

[1–15 SEPTEMBER, 1893]

But write me before the end of the month!

After that I shan't be here.

Mon cher petit Robert,

You complain about my silence and don't tell me where to write you. But I think you have gone back to Berlin. I had a very pleasant trip, and, after having spent three weeks at St. Moritz and one at Lake Geneva, here I am at Trouville with mother, at the Hôtel des Roches-Noires. My impressions of it you will read in the *Revue blanche*—not the attached one, which was promised a long time ago and appeared late, nor even in the next one where there will be a very melancholy short story of mine—but later. People? I don't want to talk about them so that my stern Robert won't tease me about my worldliness. I only want to ask you a musical question about a lady—who is neither a duchess nor a princess, but simply a Protestant who, as such, you may perhaps have met—and whom I came to know slightly down there because we had friends in common, Mme X——. I very much admired her talent for the piano, which seemed to me in the grand manner, and I must say that some sensitive and competent music critics—the Princesse Brancovan, a friend of Paderewski and herself a great musician, Mlle d'Harcourt, besides Madame Henri Baignères, whose sound judgment you know and who does not err on the side of charity—all agreed with me. Here,

Madame Z—— said that "she obviously has a vigorous technique, plays in a clean and well-scrubbed" (which is very witty, but to my mind should not be applied to a person I think is a great musician), "but utterly inartistic and odious manner." Even if you have never heard her play, you must know what to think of her gifts, since her talent probably graces the *soirées* where Y—— plays the *roué* and W—— the gallant, where those nuisances MM. R—— and S—— fuss under Madame U——'s rod, and where T——, when he forgets he is a "marquis," looks for a young girl to purify his morals. I am not asking your opinion in order to make up my own mind. The impression she made on me was far too great to be obliterated by what someone else says—but I should decidedly admit that I have no taste—quite the opposite, in fact.

I am very much upset because Father insists that I make up my mind about my career. I am more and more tempted by the *Cour des Comptes*. If I don't want to make a career in the Foreign Service, my career in the Foreign Office in Paris would be just as boring as the *Cour des Comptes*.

Perhaps it would be more difficult for me to prepare for the *Cour des Comptes*, but wouldn't that be counterbalanced by a period that would absorb all the attention I could give to it? The rest of the time I should go walking.

Ah, my friend, more than ever your advice about this would be precious, and I suffer from your absence. Let a good letter cancel it by the all-powerful miracle of communication between two minds. Isn't the bench too discredited? What is there left, after deciding that I am to be neither a lawyer, nor a doctor, nor a priest, nor . . .

Always yours, Robert,
Marcel Proust

16: TO ROBERT DE BILLY

[CIRCA NOVEMBER 1, 1893]

Mon cher Robert,

. . . . I am publishing this year a collection of little pieces, most of which you already know. I immediately thought of dedicating this little book to the memory of two people I knew only a short time but whom I loved, do love with all my heart—Edgar Aubert and Willie Heath—the latter I think you didn't know, but only a month ago he died of dysentery; and after a life of great moral fortitude, he died with an heroic resignation which, except that he died in the Catholic faith to which he had been converted when he was twelve years old (he was born a Protestant), would have been identical with what you told me about Edgar's end. But the mediocrity of the book, the great license of certain portions, the futility of a public tribute, which is always inferior to the unexpressed memory, had deterred me from dedicating it to them except in the wellspring of my heart. But something has happened to make me change my plans. Madame Madeleine Lemaire will illustrate this little book. So it will circulate all over, among the libraries of many writers, artists, and important people who otherwise would not have known of it and who will treasure it for the illustrations alone. It would be a satisfaction to me to have all these élite, who would have appreciated Edgar and Heath had they known them, who would have loved and admired them, become aware of what they have lost, at least through my humble testimonial in a short preface. Heath's family seemed to be pleased with the idea. Never having had any correspondence with Edgar's family, I am asking you to be my representative to them. Happy as I should be if my idea pleased them, I should, of course, withdraw my suggestion if they preferred it—understanding in advance the feeling that would dictate their response. Let them suggest my course of action, which would seem good to me only insofar as by following—or abstaining from it—I could contribute slightly to whatever comfort a knowledge of our inconsolable admiration for him could bring to his people.

When you let me know about their decision, my dear Robert, I shall ask you to tell me in what terms you will permit me to recall Edgar's affection for you.

In the meantime, *mon cher ami*, I send you my sincerest, most affectionate, and most devoted friendship.

Marcel Proust

Comte Robert de Montesquiou-Fezensac (1855–1921), "who was Proust's guide through the inferno or paradise of aristocratic society," was descended from the earliest kings of France, from Blaise de Montluc, the gallant soldier and memorialist under François *premier;* from d'Artagnan, the musketeer, and from a great-grandmother who was chosen as the French governess to accompany Napoleon's unhappy son to Vienna. A living embodiment of French history, his pride of race was second only to his literary ambition. The author of seven volumes of verse, the originality of which Rémy de Gourmont described as "excessively tattooed," of a considerable amount of art criticism, and three volumes of memoirs, he was a friend or intimate acquaintance of Edmond de Goncourt, the Alphonse Daudets, Leconte de Lisle, Mallarmé, Whistler, Verlaine, Oscar Wilde, Pierre Louÿs, Ida Rubinstein, Sarah Bernhardt, and many other artists and writers to whom he introduced his young disciple, Marcel Proust. In the world of society he was famed for his taste and the elaborate fêtes which he set against the fantastic décor of the series of elaborate "pavilions" and apartments he inhabited.

An extraordinarily vain man—he was photographed

over two hundred times and painted by Whistler, Gandara, Boldini, and others—he was equally magnetic and charming when he chose to be. "Incapable of pleasing . . . too different from other people," addicted to "the aristocratic pleasure of offending," he described himself in the words of Stendhal and Baudelaire.

His attitude towards his fascinated young disciple ranged from affectionate appreciation to vindictive envy. On occasion he labeled Proust "a vulgar little creature, uncivil in his bourgeois, plebeian politeness." But if the future self-styled "poet of snobbery" returned insults with excessive flattery, it was not because Proust was himself a snob, as has been claimed, but because, as his friend M. de Billy has written, he had decided early that Montesquiou was "indispensable to the success of his researches [into the Guermantes Way] and, knowing his need for admiration, he flattered his mania like an alienist treating a case of delusions of grandeur." On Proust's clinical approach rests Montesquiou's chief claim to fame. For although he was supposed to have been the model for Des Esseintes in Huysman's *A rebours,* it is primarily as a key to the Baron de Charlus that he is remembered today.

In the letter that follows, Proust is thanking Montesquiou for a copy of *Les Chauves-Souris,* a volume which had been recently published and of which Leconte de Lisle said, "a very subtle and very delicate art [is] in these poems," and Anatole France, they are "fine and great, skillful and sensitive, ingenuous and ingenious, colorful and *nuancé,* new and filled with tradition, charming . . ."

17: TO ROBERT DE MONTESQUIOU

THIS MONDAY EVENING
[APRIL 24, 1893]

Monsieur,

Infinite thanks for your gift. But the inscription is too modest if, thus detached from the piece it summarized, it pretends to describe you. I find that you are equally the sovereign of eternal things. Here is what I mean:

I discovered long ago that you stood far above the type of exquisite decadent with whose features (never as perfect as yours, but common enough in these times), you are depicted. In this period devoid of thought and will, indeed without genius, you excel through your double power of thought and action. And I think that never before has this supreme refinement been combined with such energy, and this creative force, typical of the past, with this almost seventeenth-century intellectuality, so little has there been of it since. (I believe, besides—and not just for the sake of playing with a paradox—that it could be shown how you and Baudelaire derive from the seventeenth century the taste for maxims, the lost habit of thinking in verse.) Did Corneille write a more beautiful line than this one:

Elle y voit mieux en elle,
au déclin des clartés,

a more Cornelian one than this:

Ceux que la pudeur fière a voués au cil sec.

And I believe that this is what has preserved in you this unalloyed generosity which is now so rare—as well as having permitted the most subtle of artists to write poems so powerfully thought out as to insure for themselves an enduring place even in a very slender anthology of French philosophic poetry; which has made the sovereign of the transitory, sovereign of the eternal, as well; and which, finally, prevents our foreseeing the future course of your work, since wherever there is a spontaneous outburst, a fountainhead, a true spiritual life, there is freedom. All this to the great good fortune of your respectful and grateful

Marcel Proust

18: TO ROBERT DE MONTESQUIOU

[MAY 31, 1894]

Cher Monsieur,

I knew there had been a message from you when I came in at 11 o'clock, but I had already been at the *Gaulois*. But what a disappointment this morning! All day long I had made notes for the descriptions of the dresses, all revised and corrected by the most fashionable ladies. What tardy, unforeseen, mysterious, and inept hand corrected that article? I have every reason for finding it inept, first because it suppresses my name, which, with great dignity, came last on the list of guests, also that of M. d'Yturri. Up to now you will say (at least where my name is concerned) that the list remains unchanged as far as the "celebrities" go (for M. d'Yturri is, of course, very well known), but by some equally brash but less harmonious metempsychosis than the one which attributed to Delafosse a kiss from your muse, Sarah Bernhardt's charming remarks on Madame Greffülhe have disappeared. —None of this is very important in comparison to such a fête, but the day after, the account of the refreshments should be given by Potel, the account of the woodwork by the carpenter, and of his notes by Marcel Proust, who sends you a thousand compliments and unexpressed thanks, appropriate only to a fête that was unique in the full sense of the word.

M. P.

Prince Borghese, Mesdames de Broissia, Howland, Talbot and others were omitted. True, M. Detelbach was reinstated. But a number of the descriptions of the dresses disappeared, Madame Potocka's, Madame de Brantes' etc., etc., etc. Instead of an exact description of Sarah Bernhardt's dress—vague banalities; Mlle Bartet's periwinkles became cornflowers.

I confess, however, that all the remaining descriptions (except Sarah Bernhardt, Bartet, Madame Greffülhe) are mine, in spite of one or two changes which make them less intelligible. If I seem to indulge my author's vanity in this, it is really love rather than vanity, for the authors are Madame de Pourtalès, Madame d'Hervey, Madame A.-J. de La Rochefoucauld, Madame de Brissac, Mlle Lemaire, Madame de Fitz-James.

A thousand affectionate greetings to that sublime organizer of the whole thing, M. d'Yturri.

19: TO ROBERT DE MONTESQUIOU

THIS SUNDAY
[AUGUST 12, 1894]

Cher Monsieur,

. . . I was deeply touched to see our great poet, Verlaine, turn critic to talk about you in words unembittered by rivalry with an equal—appropriate and charming words, which carry great weight, falling, as they do, from such heights. I returned to Versailles with M. France, the only person whose company I could have enjoyed in that city where I had seen you and whence you had gone. I need hardly tell you that you were continually evoked with an affectionate veneration, and we were indeed thankful for the memory of you, which so graciously and nobly accompanied or rather conducted us on this walk, which it enlivened and adorned. . . .

Marcel Proust

20: TO ROBERT DE MONTESQUIOU

THIS TUESDAY MORNING
TROUVILLE
[SEPTEMBER OR OCTOBER, 1894]

Cher Monsieur,

An accident—in which my brother was injured—has complicated my life the last few days and has prevented my asking you two favors which have to do with me. One of them is also of interest to Madame Lemaire, who would be grateful for your consent. Here is the favor. Would you authorize me to quote in the preface of my book one or two very ingenious and very beautiful lines which you wrote in the copy of *Chef des odeurs suaves* you gave to Madame Lemaire? Here is the other request. I think I shall dedicate the principal stories or poems in my book to the masters whom I admire or the friends whom I love. In the first category, at least, would you accept one of the dedications? You were very kind indeed to write me such a charming letter from the Engadine. But "it leaves me with a memory both bitter and sweet like an autumn day when the sun shines but the wind is in the north." (*Le Lys rouge*) Perhaps it would be better if I used the felicitous adjective, with its sure and melancholy depths, which you have incorporated into the French language in applying it to Madame Desbordes—"bittersweet." For it is some time since any word of friendship has opened or closed your letters, of whose intellectual and aesthetic value I am aware, at the same time that I suffer from their austerity of feeling. Before I went to spend a month at Reveillon, during which time not a single day passed without talk of you, I happened to see your friend, M. d'Yturri, one afternoon, and I fell again under the spell of his lively wit. What a sensitive, civilized man and what a wild cat, how suave and how vibrant!—I hope that Saint-Moritz has done you much good and that I can see you very soon.

Please accept, *mon cher* Monsieur, my faithful admiration and my respectful devotion.

Marcel Proust

21: TO ROBERT DE MONTESQUIOU

THIS SUNDAY EVENING [PROBABLY 1894 OR 1895]

I was very much annoyed, *cher maître*, that the tardiness of several guests so delayed our leaving the table on Thursday evening that it was too late for me to go to Versailles. In addition, having received no answer to the letter to M. France, which I had attached to my letter to Madame Arman, I inquired about her. She is sailing off the coast of Holland. I don't know whether M. France is in Paris. No one answers the door when I go to call on him. I don't know whether he, or even she, received my letter. If there is no word to the contrary from you, I shall wait to write to M. France again until his return and your own, since I am told that you are leaving for Dieppe. I shall doubtless go to Dieppe, too, and I should be very happy if you would permit me to see you there. For that matter, is there any journey, any place, any circumstance, indeed, in which one does not need your help, as one always needs a penetrating and profound intelligence in order to grasp their full meaning, to sense their full charm. And that is just what I am doing. In lieu of your presence, which, by its lightning glance, the stormy galvanism of the voice, the precision of the silhouette, excites one even more violently to thought, I take every opportunity to consult your writings or your words, whose flame I carefully cherish in my memory and which it illuminates. I hope that M. d'Yturri will be at Dieppe, too, and please remember me to him affectionately,

Your devoted disciple and friend,

Marcel Proust

22: TO ROBERT DE MONTESQUIOU

[NO DATE]

Cher Monsieur,

. . . . In order to simplify a style, which is often unnecessarily complicated, I intend to write several articles for newspapers or reviews. And with an idea in mind that will not surprise you since I have so often expressed to you my sentiments, I should like the first one to be a study of you. In it I shall show, if "Your Grace" will come to my aid, how much you differ from the banal decadent of our time; your willpower and the wealth of your intellectual gifts, wherein you derive from the seventeenth century; in short, what I have already taken the liberty of telling you. I think that insofar as one can hope, through success and public opinion, for the temporal realization of a great spiritual force, this should be your preoccupation or, rather, that of your admirers. I should say it, *first* because I think it is the truth, *in the next place* (or perhaps *first* in sentiment) because I believe that in the present state of public opinion, it is the *only thing* that can be useful to you. The incomplete Montesquiou, as the majority picture him, is enough to enchant sensitive people. Whereas I think, on the contrary, there are a good many intellectuals still to be rallied. I should not undertake this, having no authority and on my part only love, but of what importance is the voice that says, "Read," if, as soon as he has read, the reader is in love with the book, which is a good and charming road to understanding. In case this project should please you, do you think the title (which would seem paradoxical with the legendary Montesquiou, but which the article would soon prove consistent with the real one), "On the Simplicity of M. de Montesquiou," would be good?

Would it please or displease you if I tell (without, of course, mentioning that it was to me you expressed them) your ideas on *success*, how a man of talent ought at the same time to make money with his books (I should tie this in with the pràise of your *willpower*)? Besides, if one day you tell me that I may come to Versailles to ask for advice by word of mouth, I can easily come, and with what pleasure!

Please accept, Monsieur, my most faithful respects.

Marcel Proust

23: TO LAURE HAYMAN

[MAY 11, 1896]

Madame,

My poor old uncle, Louis Weil, died yesterday at five o'clock in the afternoon without pain, unconscious, without having been ill (of an inflammation of the chest, which came on only that morning). Because I know that you were fond of him, I didn't want you to learn it through the newspapers or through an announcement, if any are sent, which I don't know about yet. I did not write you that he was ill because, to tell you the truth, he wasn't, but now I think perhaps you may be a little sad, and it is nicer, isn't it, to tell you this way.

With a kiss, your
Marcel Proust

24: TO LAURE HAYMAN

TUESDAY MORNING

[MAY 12, 1896]

Madame,

I have just this minute received your little note. Thank you for what you say about my uncle. In his religion there is no service. We shall meet at half-past three at his house, 102, boulevard Haussmann, and go from there to Père Lachaise (but I am afraid this would be an effort for you and there will be few women present). But what a fantastic idea to think that you would shock anyone there. Your presence could only be moving. For surely you are a person whom one can't know without admiring and loving, and whom my uncle especially loved very much.

Thank you in advance for doing whatever seems fitting to you, and permit me to embrace you.

Marcel Proust

25: TO LAURE HAYMAN

[MID-MAY] 1896

Madame,

Had I not been "sick as a dog" all this time with attacks of asthma and choking, I should have come to see you, and that is why I delayed telling you how charmed, moved, and overcome I was by your very touching, lovely, gallant thought of the other day. When the messenger on his bicycle, bearing your wreath, caught up with the funeral procession from which flowers were omitted (it was my uncle's wish), when I learned it came from you, I burst into sobs, not so much in sorrow as in admiration. I was so hoping that you would be at the cemetery so that I might fall into your arms there. It was impossible to put the wreath on the hearse then. But after we arrived at the cemetery when mother was told about it she wanted to have my uncle buried with that one wreath, since you were the only person who didn't know about not sending flowers; and that was done. It can, indeed, be said of you as it was about that woman in the seventeenth century, "kindness and generosity were no small part of her elegance." All of this deserves to be talked about at greater length, and one day we shall, shan't we?

With my respectful admiration, your

Marcel Proust

Pierre Lavallée (1872–1947) was an old family friend of the Prousts and a classmate of Marcel's at the Lycée Condorcet. From 1909 to 1937 he was director of the library and the museum of l'Ecole des Beaux Arts. The following fragment is taken from an inscription by Proust in a copy of *Les Plaisirs et les Jours.*

26: TO PIERRE LAVALLÉE

[PROBABLY] 1896

Mon cher Pierre,

. . . .

A copy of a book you read, particularly if it is a copy of my book, cannot resemble others. What meaning hidden to others, what depths—relative—known to you alone, are divulged, if it is you who are the reader. I say, "my book," as though I were never to write another. You know very well that isn't true. If I can finish the one I have started and start on others, don't, I beg of you, be sparing of the inspiration your affection is to me, of the reward of your understanding. Make fruitful and love my defects, which to you represent the best of myself. Our virtues are less a part of us, and there is no need for so free an affection, so intimate a resemblance in order to appreciate them.

Your grateful friend,
Marcel Proust

27: TO LAURE HAYMAN

[CIRCA NEW YEAR'S DAY] 1897

Chère amie, it will be, since you wish no more of "Madame," and you are quite right; compared to the years, you never grow any older, so the only respect I can now pay is that due your mind, your noble character, and your beauty. —If then, *ma chère amie*, I have delayed in sending you this vase, which, with the flowers, is meant to bring you my New Year's wishes, it is because I wanted to find among my uncle's personal possessions some small souvenir that might remind you of him a little. This pin, which could be worn in a hat after having, no doubt, been a scarf pin, doesn't seem too ugly to me, and can, I hope, be a reminder of your friendship without too much offending your taste. Please accept it with the warm affection of one who waits only for a sign from you to come and see you, as is only fitting.

Your
Marcel Proust

28: TO ROBERT DE MONTESQUIOU

THIS TUESDAY MORNING
[PROBABLY 1898]

Cher Monsieur,

I did not answer the question you asked me yesterday about the Jews. The reason why is very simple; while I am Catholic like my father and my brother, my mother is, on the contrary, Jewish. You understand that that is a strong enough reason for my abstaining from that kind of discussion. I thought it was more respectful to write you this rather than to reply orally in front of another person. But I am very glad of this opportunity which permits my informing you of a fact I might otherwise never have thought of stating. Because since our ideas do differ, or rather since I have no choice of opinion on this subject as I might under other circumstances have had, you could involuntarily have hurt me in a discussion. Naturally I am not talking about any conversation that might take place between us two and in which I should always be most interested in your social and political ideas, if you expound them to me, even though reasons of the highest rectitude prevent my agreeing with them.

Your
Marcel Proust

29: TO MADAME STRAUS

[CIRCA SEPTEMBER, 1898]

Ma chère petite Madame Straus,

M. [Anatole] France, at the request of M. Labori, would like to have certain prominent people sign a petition for Picquart, as M. Labori thinks that this might make an impression on the judges. To do this, new names are needed. And I promised M. France to appeal to you for M. d'Haussonville's, to whom you might say, moreover, that you are speaking for France. The petition would be purposely worded in such moderate terms that it would in no way involve the signatories in the Dreyfus Affair itself. And M. d'Haussonville, who has such a kind heart, such loftiness of mind, will perhaps not refuse you. And M. France thinks, as does everyone else, that his name, which is from every point of view beyond comparison, would have enormous importance for the future, not of the Affair but of Picquart, which he feels is much darker. I speak of his future because he himself is calm in a way that wrings, from the usually detached France, words of compassion. But since M. d'Haussonville would be too good to be true, if you don't succeed with him, or even if you don't want to try, could you fall back on Dufeuille, on Ganderax, on any distinguished person you know, or Pozzi, in fact, anything you can do without too much trouble. But this trouble would be a pleasure to you, "because you are beautiful and he is unhappy." But there is rather a hurry about it. I should have been glad to write to

M. d'Haussonville myself, but, since I hardly know him, I am afraid of being ridiculous and, what is more important, ineffectual. I haven't seen you again since the so Balzacian Affair (Bertulus, the police magistrate, in *Splendeur et misère des courtisanes*. Christian Esterhazy, the country nephew in *Illusions perdues*, Paty de Clam, the Rastignac who makes appointments with Vautrin in distant suburbs) has become Shakespearean with its accumulation of sudden *dénouements*. But let us not launch forth on this subject, which we will discuss at Trouville, where I hope Mother will be sent to get well, which she almost is.

Your respectful
Marcel

Don't mention this petition for Picquart, except to possible signatories, so as not to let too much be known about it.

Marie Nordlinger, now Mrs. Riefstahl, was born in 1876. She came from her home in Manchester, England, to Paris in 1896 to study painting and sculpture. A cousin and close friend of Proust's lifelong friend, the musician Reynaldo Hahn, she first met Proust at Hahn's mother's home in December, 1896, where they spent many evenings together, listening to Hahn play and sing, discussing pictures and books. Often they went together to museums and always to Mme Lemaire's famous "Tuesdays" in May. A devout disciple of Ruskin's, Miss Nordlinger was a godsend to Proust in his efforts at translating Ruskin, whom he had read with difficulty in the English editions. Miss Nordlinger not only initiated him into the English texts but supplied him with endless information and assistance. The only woman younger than himself, highly intellectual, and of his own social background with whom he ever seems to have carried on a friendship, Proust saw Miss Nordlinger for the last time in 1908.

30: TO MARIE NORDLINGER

[PROBABLY JANUARY 1899]

Mademoiselle,

Your Christmas card made me very happy. If we were nothing more than creatures of the mind, we would not believe in anniversaries, in birthdays, in relics, in tombs. But since we are also composed of a small amount of matter, we like to believe that it, too, is a part of reality and has (we like to think that what we have room for in our hearts is round-and-about-us externally, too, a little), as the soul the body, its own material symbol. And then, as Christmas gradually loses for us its validity as an anniversary, it takes on a more and more intense reality, in which the light of its candles, its snow, that melancholy obstacle to some longed-for visitor, the odor of its mandarins steeping in the warmth of the rooms, the gaiety of its cold and its fires, the perfumes of the tea and the mimosa, come back to us coated in the delicious honey of our own personality, which we had unconsciously deposited there during the years, when, caught in the spell of our own egotistical designs, we were not aware of Christmas; and now, all of a sudden, it makes our heart beat faster.

There are some of my excuses for having been so pleased with your Christmas message, not counting the ones by which I can excuse the silence you may have misunderstood and which was caused by an illness of my own, followed by a dreadful operation on my mother, just at the time you so graciously wrote to me. She stayed in the hospital for three months. Now she is feeling very well and is entirely cured.

I hope, although I envy you your English life, that you will soon return to Paris. I shall be very happy to meet again your rare and unusual mind, and that graciousness of yours, as fresh as a branch of hawthorn. Please remember me most kindly to your sister, to whom I have not dared to permit myself to write directly since we have never corresponded, and accept for both of you my respectful greetings.

Marcel Proust

Madame Adrien Proust (1849–1905) was born Jeanne Weil, the daughter of a wealthy Jewish family. She was a woman of unusual sensitiveness and culture, with a delightful sense of humor. From his earliest youth she believed in the genius of her sensitive, sickly son. Her devotion to him was obsessive, and from his infancy, when he seemed too feeble to live, she devoted herself to interposing her powerful love between him and every vicissitude of life. Her capacity for self-effacement is always mentioned by Proust's friends. One of them, who spent much time with her and Marcel, sightseeing in Venice, when asked whether she could remember any comments of Mme Proust about the architecture, etc., replied that she could remember only her great courtesy, friendliness, and consideration for her son's friends. When Proust started his Ruskin translations, his mother, because of a knowledge of the English language, which her son almost entirely lacked, was of great assistance to him.

As reward for the countless hours she spent sitting outside the door of her son's room during his attacks of asthma, an ordeal which caused her to be spoken of as "*pauvre Jeanne*" by the members of her large family, Mme Proust has been rendered immortal in the characters of the grandmother and the mother of the narrator in *Remembrance of Things Past*.

31: TO HIS MOTHER

HÔTEL SPLENDIDE, EVIAN-LES-BAINS
THURSDAY, HALF-PAST ONE
[PROBABLY SEPTEMBER 10, 1899]

Ma chère Maman,
Half an hour after I left you (and me already consoled), we saw the shameful verdict posted at the Casino to the great joy of the Casino Staff. Then we went to dine at Villa Bessaraba. As I entered Constantin's châlet to smoke before dinner, I heard someone sobbing. It was the little Noailles (the poetess) passing through, sobbing with all her might, and wailing in a broken voice, "How could they have done that? How did they dare come and tell him? And what will foreigners and the whole world think? How could they?" She wept so violently that it was touching, and we were reconciled. The Prince de Polignac, who "*tutoies*" Galliffet, says that he is incapable of being dishonest in money matters.

. . . Don't be too sad about the verdict. It is sad for the

army, for France, for the judges who have had the cruelty to ask Dreyfus, exhausted as he is, once more to make the effort of being brave again. But this physical torture, this appeal to moral strength in a man who really is already shattered, will be the only one he will have to undergo and that is already over. Henceforth, things can only go well for him, morally in the estimation of the world, physically in the freedom that I suppose has been granted him by now. As for the verdict itself, it will be legally quashed. Morally it has been done. The Princesse Brancovan, and everyone, for that matter, has been charming to me. Madame de Polignac was indiscreet enough that afternoon at Coppet to tell Madame d'Haussonville that I was at Evian, whereupon that lady inquired as to my whereabouts, wanted more details, and told her that she was a very close friend of mine (?). I fear an invitation to lunch . . . all the more since she said to Madame de Polignac about the Affair, "I can very well understand how foreigners like you think as you do." M. de Noailles telegraphed the verdict to his sisters Mesdames de Virieu and Henri de Montesquiou, adding, "As incomprehensible as it is sad." Certainly "extenuating circumstances" for a traitor is odd. But it is not incomprehensible. It is the obvious and vile admission on the part of the judges of their own doubts.

In the hotel and in the countryside absolute calm reigns. I lunched at twelve-thirty (having dined from nine-fifteen to ten-fifteen because the Brancovans stayed to talk over the Affair). I went to bed at the usual time. Advise Robert to be calm. Let him bear in mind that any incitement to trouble will cause extreme embarrassment to the Government, which would be obliged to strike out at his friends. It is better that Millerand should not have to have Jaurès arrested and that those ministers—short-sighted, to be sure, but whom, at least, one is glad to have in power on the morrow of the verdict—be voted time to pass measures for compensation.

Mille tendres baisers au père, au frère, et à toi mille tendres braisers.

Marcel

32: TO HIS MOTHER

HÔTEL SPLENDIDE, EVIAN-LES-BAINS,
MONDAY, HALF-PAST ONE

Ma chère petite Maman,

. . . .

Your answer to my implied question, "Did you sleep well?" was worthy of General Roget: "As soon as we were settled, dinner, then a little chocolate, then a little Balzac—a nap [*somme*] (this I misread *en somme* [in short]), a series of interrupted snatches in the novel, until I really slept." At last, I thought I would find out, but no! Instead of telling me from what time to what time, you say, "A cool night, we left the train well rested." It is terribly like, "Colonel Henry was told to refer it to me. I saw him several days later on official business. The archivist, Gribelin, could inform you on this point. M. de Breuil has shown you Dreyfus dining at the home of suspicious characters with foreign agents. On my soul and on my conscience, I swear, and it is indisputable, that Dreyfus could have handed over documents to them." Alas, one mustn't laugh about it because we see the result.

While I was calling on the C.'s, I asked whether there was any news. Mme C. said, "Yes, the poor man will be cashiered. I swear I find it very cruel, and he should have been spared that." "All the more," added M. Cottin, "since in matters of this kind there can always be doubt. —Even, probably," he added naïvely, "in the minds of the judges."

After this orchestral flourish, I sang my aria and came "to defend the innocent, unjustly accused." They did not compromise themselves, but it is clear that they are anti. However they know so little about the Affair that Mme C. thought that the extenuating circumstances were granted "because in '94 he had been condemned on the evidence of the forged Henry [documents] and that since then it has been admitted that *he* didn't do it."

. . . The "question" at the Brancovans is to find out the names of the two [dissenting judges]. They speak for Beauvais and Brogniard. —Meyer says in the *Gaulois* that nothing is left for France to do but to rediscover her God (which one?). I must say, however, that the *Gaulois* did demand acquittal as a favor to the minority. I am feeling perfectly well.

Mille tendres baisers,

Marcel

33: TO HIS MOTHER

HÔTEL SPLENDIDE, EVIAN-LES-BAINS,
TUESDAY, TWO O'CLOCK
[PROBABLY SEPTEMBER 15, 1899]

Ma chère petite Maman,

. . . I now know that if the Prince de Chimay isn't staying at the villa it is chiefly because of the Affair; he doesn't agree with the rest of the family, although he is very moderate, and they would make life impossible for him. It is also because of hunting, but I don't think he will find any game as worthy as his wife. M. de Polignac told me that he (Polignac) had waged a Boulangist campaign with Barrès and Paul Adam to try and get himself elected deputy. He gave speeches in public meetings and makes very sly fun of himself for the insincerity of the attitude he took. "A working-man having asked me if I was a Socialist, I answered, 'Come now, how could you have doubted it for a moment.' "

Talk to Robert about the League of the Rights of Man and tell me his reply (that of Abel). It is very urgent. . . . Please do see that our letters don't cross in a vacuum but that they reply to each other. Yours give me infinite pleasure. Make them shorter so as not to tire yourself. There isn't a moment I don't thank you mentally for thinking of me as you do and making life as easy for me as it would be sweet, if only I were entirely well. Today I almost am. Kiss Papa and Robert for me. Give my regards to Eugénie, and to the Gustaves, tell them that I have not deceived them about the Affair, that if Dreyfus were a traitor, such hostile judges as he had would not have reconsidered the conviction of '94 by taking so many years off his term of imprisonment and making it milder and less confining—and that two of them would not have wanted his rehabilitation. M. de Polignac told me that the *Petit Bleu* in Brussels came out bordered in black. Chevilly writes me that in a château near Lyons where he was staying they wanted to drink champagne and have fireworks to celebrate the conviction, but someone observed that it was too mild to permit anyone to glory in it. . . . At M. C——'s I saw the *Petite République*, which carried an excellent headline, something like "Cowardly arrest. Why extenuating circumstances." . . . Turn back to page 2 of my letter; one line apart you will see Polignac written three times and with two different P's (dedicated to the graphologists and to Bertillon, a newspaper would say). And yet my letter is not a forged document. Apropos of Bertillon, in the slip-of-paper game at the Brancovan's, one of the questions had to do with circumstantial details about Bertillon (I wasn't there, but Constantin told me about it). Madame de Noailles answered, "*Je ne sais pas, je n'ai jamais koutché* [*couché*] *avec lui.*"

Mille tendres baisers,

Marcel

34: TO HIS MOTHER

HÔTEL SPLENDIDE, EVIAN-LES-BAINS,
WEDNESDAY, ONE O'CLOCK

Ma chère petite Maman,

. . . .

Yesterday I overheard a scene, which I wanted to tell you about on my letter-card, but there wasn't room. General Robillot met the Comte d'Eu at the baths. Greetings, etc. The General, a little deaf, himself, shouted in order to make himself heard, and, from the very first word, he quite naturally, since he was screaming, assumed the tone of command. So that for miles around one could hear, "Has Monseigneur seen how atrociously the Swiss newspapers have treated us in this frightful Affair? What has Monseigneur heard about?"—"I hear very little because I have trouble with my ears."—"General Mercier was admirable; he is to be congratulated."—"But it seemed to me he came out of it very well," replied "the Prince," as Madame P—— would say.

Have Father try to find out through Pozzi whether Dreyfus is really dying, what is wrong with him, whether he (Pozzi) is still convinced of his innocence, and the names of the two officers who voted for his acquittal. . . .

Mille tendres baisers,
Marcel

35: TO HIS MOTHER

THURSDAY, HALF-PAST ONE

[EVIAN, PROBABLY SEPTEMBER 24, 1899]

Ma chère petite Maman,

. . . .

The "Eu" appear to be nice simple people, although I make a point of keeping on my hat and standing aloof in a "not-on-speaking-terms-since-Rennes" attitude. Having found myself in front of a door with the old man, and one of us having to go through first, I drew aside. And he passed me, taking off his hat with a deep bow, not at all condescending or d'Haussonville, but just the bow of a very polite, good old man, the kind I have not yet had from any of the persons from whom I draw aside in the same way, "simple bourgeois," who pass by as stiff as kings. And speaking of kings, Comte d'Eu, instead of walking, glides over the floor as though he were on skates. But I dare not conclude *à la Cuvier* that this is merely good manners, not knowing whether this gliding motion is due to his gout or to memories of the Court. Do not show this letter to my angel of a brother, who is an angel but also a judge, a severe judge who might see in my remarks about Comte d'Eu a snobbishness or a frivolity very remote from my real feelings, rather than my need of telling you what we would love to talk about, and the kind of remarks that amuse us.

M. Joubert, having made the mistake of accepting the office of Inspector from his friend, Fontanes, Regent of the University, managed to ruin his very frail health. He had to stay in bed the better part of each day. "But his friends, deprived of his visits, were unwilling to give up the charms of his conversation, and his bed was regularly surrounded by the cleverest wits and the most charming women. M. de Chateaubriand and the Duchesses de Duras and de Lévis were most punctilious about coming to enjoy his conversation." I hope we are close enough in spirit for you not to think I mean to infer that one should stay in bed, etc., etc. I am copying this with a smile, *cum grano salis*, because of the analogy, except for the part about the duchesses. . . .

Mille tendres baisers,
Marcel

36: TO HIS MOTHER

EVIAN
FRIDAY, THREE O'CLOCK

Ma chère petite Maman,

I am only sending you a line because I had to pay a long call on the C—'s. Monsieur C—, not having seen me for several days (because I had been going up hill and down dale a good deal), came to look for me. He announced to me with a smile the approaching arrival at Evian of General Mercier, because he knows that I cherish no affection for him. But naturally I shall not in any way show my antipathy, since I don't know him. Besides, I don't know whether it is true that he is coming. . . .

I went to see Ch. whose father said to me, "There must

be lots of Jews at the Splendide." Since he is an old man, besotted by the *Libre Parole*, I thought I should be doing a good turn to his family who loathe him by not starting an argument, and I answered, "I have no idea who is at the hotel because everybody there lives to himself." Nevertheless he urged me to go in preference next year to Thonon where the society "is more French, more cosmopolitan." You can understand that as Ch. is sick over the arrest, has become a substitute for Gohier and Gérault Richard, and mentions Reinach every minute, his father does not greatly appreciate this state of mind. And I swear that when I see the brutal fool he has for a father, I admire his courage in admitting his beliefs. . . .

Mille tendres baisers,
Marcel

37: TO MARIE NORDLINGER

TUESDAY, DECEMBER 5, 1899

Mademoiselle,

How annoying that you are not in Paris, and how annoying, too, that when you were here we knew each other so slightly and that I profited so little thereby! For letters like those you honored me by writing the other day excite something other than gratitude; I mean a real sympathy. And sympathy means that people must see each other; the communicating of ideas is not enough. Sympathy is not as philosophical as you are when you say, "I don't know whether I have any living friends." Like friends, books are not enough to sustain it. Forgive my appearing to contradict you. It is you yourself who makes me feel this more exacting and less easily satisfied sympathy, which, stirred by the beauty of your language and your exquisite attentions, does not stop there but goes on to your own self.

I have not been very happy since I had the honor of seeing you. My health, which was already bad enough, has grown worse. And unfortunately, my imagination, which was giving me some slight pleasure, even if it gave none to others (for you are an exception in your taste for what I was writing, as you are in everything), seems to me to have suffered the consequences of my exhaustion.

I have been working for a long time on a long-winded work, but without finishing anything. And there are moments when I wonder whether I am not like Dorothea Brook's husband in *Middlemarch*, amassing ruins.

For the last two weeks I have been busy with a little work apropos of Ruskin and certain cathedrals—absolutely different from what I generally do. If I manage to have it published in a review, as I hope to succeed in doing, I shall send it to you as soon as it appears. If I had published anything else, I would have sent it to you, but until now I have encumbered only my desk.

I don't know whether I have succeeded in telling you how much your letter pleased me. It is not very easy for me, since I hardly dare face your compliments, finding it so ridiculous on my part to have the air of admitting that what you say about my book is more than a kindness on your part, to believe that it tallies with the reality, which would mean that I have a genuine talent. But seeing how much pleasure you have given me, perhaps when you have nothing else to do, you will sometimes take up your pen to send me news of yourself. If ever you should wish some information about French reading, or a French artist, it would be very nice of you to turn to me; and although I am a very poor correspondent because of my ill health—which, however, is a little better, at the moment, but a better that is still wretched—it would amuse me very much to be able to write to you, and it would flatter my vanity to be consulted!

Please remember me to your sister, and believe me, Mademoiselle, to be your respectfully admiring and grateful——

Marcel Proust

PART TWO

Work, Sorrow, and Solitude, 1899–1909

During the ten years 1899–1909, Proust labored at his translations of Ruskin, at his pieces for the *Figaro*, and at the long work, which he appears to have begun as early as 1895. During these years, Proust withdrew more and more from society, particularly after the death of his father in 1903 and his mother in 1905.

The *Prince Bibesco*, born in 1878, diplomat and author, was attached to the Rumanian ministry in Paris at the time he first met Marcel Proust. He was later counselor of the Rumanian Legations in London and Petrograd, and Minister in Washington, 1920–1926, and in Madrid, 1927–1931. Among the many plays he has written are *Jealousy*, *Married Life*, and *The Heir.* Proust wrote of him in 1902: ". . . one person alone understands me, Antoine Bibesco! . . . He is so intelligently kind to me, so intelligent and so kind." In 1922, shortly before his death, Proust spoke of him as "one of the first lovers of *Swann.*"

38: TO ANTOINE BIBESCO

[PROBABLY 1899 OR 1900]

Forgive me chiefly for all the advice, which I really have no right to give you; what I gave you tonight will be the last. Forgive me and tell me whether you don't think it fair that it should reflect my subjective propensities, the jealousy of a masculine Andromeda, always chained to his rock, who suffers at seeing Antoine Bibesco go everywhere without being able to follow him, so that my advice against going out into the social world is nothing but an unconscious, didactic, and pejorative form of the sublime. "The poor flower said to the celestial butterfly: —Don't fly away! I stay. You go! —I envy you, you and Nonelef [Comte Bertrand de Salignac-Fénelon], I envy each of you seeing the other, while my only change is turning over in bed; and yet, how many places I create in my mind and in my heart during this specious rest.

39: TO MARIE NORDLINGER

[TOWARDS THE END OF] JANUARY, 1900

Mademoiselle,

On learning of Ruskin's death, I cannot keep from thinking of you so poignantly that I *must* write to you. Not that it needed this to make me think of you. Having been ill for several days, unable to write easily and unwilling to dictate a letter to you, all my most friendly and grateful thoughts of you, of your letter, of the book [*Queen of the Air*, by John

Ruskin] you sent with its even more precious annotations, are lodged in the very forefront of my being, not in that secluded part of oneself that one visits only rarely, but in that intimacy of the heart where we meet each other several times a day. But when I learned of Ruskin's death, I wanted to express to you before anyone else, my sadness, a healthy sadness, however, and indeed full of consolations, for I know how little death matters when I see how powerfully this dead man lives on, how much I admire him, listen to him, try to understand him, to follow him more than I do many of the living.

I should have liked, a month ago, to ask your advice about some of his works. But a fear of boring you—which is very foolish of me, because I know that you like that sort of thing and one is bored only by the things one doesn't like—stopped me, and I asked it of an English friend. Often since then I have wanted to turn to you again for a word, for a meaning. But, ever since, it has been not only the same fear, but an illness (I caught another stupid grippe, not at all serious, but which aggravated the rest) has prevented my writing to you and has forced me to address myself to the circle of neighbors who can be questioned by word of mouth. But you, you do not have these excuses for not having asked me for any hints (I am vain indeed to believe I could have given them to you) about French authors or any valuable thoughts on life. Would you believe that when you sent me the little book by Ruskin, filled with your gracious notes, placed in each page like pressed flowers, one of which we might well have picked together, since you had delicately extracted it from my book [*Les Plaisirs et les Jours*], I had just been writing some lines about something of Ruskin's, which I have forgotten (which I shall send you when they appear), and which meant something like this: "So it gives us the same kind of pleasure that those people do who send us something they have long made use of themselves with no thought of later giving it away; and it is those presents that are most precious to sensitive minds." And, a moment later, I received your book, bearing the marks of your personal use, so delicate a gift, and so opportune, a book by Ruskin. Oh, pre-established harmonies!

Did Reynaldo tell you that that wicked Ruskin forbade the translation of his works into French, so that my poor translations will remain unpublished? But in some studies I am making of him I shall quote long excerpts.

Most respectfully, your grateful
Marcel Proust

40: TO MARIE NORDLINGER

MARCH, 1900

. . . .

Your verses are charming and evoke in my memory the delightful spring bouquet you once brought me from an excursion of yours, which my hay fever prevented my emulating. But you are a poet and need not go into the fields to bring back flowers. Don't complain about not having learned. *There is nothing to know*. Even what is called technical competence is not properly speaking knowledge, because it does not exist outside of the mysterious association of our memory and the skill acquired by our own inventiveness when it comes in contact with words. Knowledge, in the sense of a thing that is all done outside ourselves and that can be learned as in the sciences, counts for nothing in art. On the contrary, it is when the scientific connections between words have disappeared from our minds and have taken on a life in which the chemical elements are forgotten in a new individuality, that the technique, the skill that recognizes their antipathies, humors their wishes, knows their beauty, conveys their forms, assorts their affinities, can begin. And this exists only when a creature is a soul and no longer so much carbon, so much phosphorus, etc. Victor Hugo, whose *Shakespeare* I am afraid I do not like, says,

> *Car le mot, qu'on le sache, est un être vivant.*
> [For the word, be it known, is a living thing.]

You know it. So you love words, you don't harm them, you play with them, you confide your secrets to them, you teach them to paint, you teach them to sing. And your *horror of yellow* is a *symphony in yellow*, which is wholly exquisite; God himself seems to have wanted to give a sample of everything He possesses in yellow, from the flower in the field to the gleam of the firmament. One could not set this down in painting, yet you have painted it in writing.

This *Poetry of Architecture* of Ruskin's, which you speak of, is there anything in it about cathedrals? Which ones? And the other works you speak of, do they mention anything, even incidentally, about certain cathedrals?

Do you know of any memoir of Ruskin's on flamboyant architecture on the banks of the Somme? In a future letter I shall tell you about Julien Edouard whom I saw a month ago. But he shows only Saint-Ouen and not the cathedral. What did he say to you about Ruskin? He claims that Ruskin said to him that Saint-Ouen was the most beautiful Gothic monument in the world, but in *Seven Lamps* Ruskin says that it is a hideous monument!

Your respectful friend,
Marcel Proust

41: TO ANTOINE BIBESCO

FRIDAY
[PROBABLY 1900 OR 1901]

Cher ami,

Thank you for your nice note, which I hardly dare hope was the expression of some desire on your part to write me, but which, even if it was only an effort to satisfy one you supposed I had, came, for that very reason, from a friend. Just now, in Pascal and La Bruyère with whom I am solacing myself this evening, I have several times found the word "friend," meaning rather "one of two" and "champion."

La Bruyère says, "A man of position should like . . . clever people, he should cultivate them. . . . He will not have to repay (It is not I who am saying this) with too many favors but with too many endearments . . . the lessons and the services that, without even knowing it, he will derive from them. What rumors will they not dispel (at least read what I am writing, Bibesco, because if you don't, it is not worth the trouble of killing myself to copy this wonderful passage), what lying tales will they not convert into fable and to fiction (it is too long, I am skipping the finest part), disseminating, at every opportunity, facts and details that are advantageous, and directing laughter and derision against those who circulated prejudicial statements, etc., etc. . . ."

And Pascal, more briefly and more forcibly (and whom I am astonished to find so well informed about the goings-on at Mme de Saint Victor's), "A friend is an advantage even to great nobles, so that he may speak well of them and stand by them in their absence, even (even is witty, there) if in order to acquire one they must make every effort. But they must choose carefully, because if they go to great pains for fools, it will be of no use to them, etc. . . . even if they [the fools] speak well of them. And they will not even speak well of them if they turn out to be weaklings. Because they have no authority (sublime), and thus they will slander *par compagnie*."

I should like (it is no longer Pascal speaking, and it is, alas, superfluous to tell you so) to have the wit to be of service to you with other people, but you are not utilitarian, and I am not useful. You were hateful yesterday evening, dear Téléphas, and depressed me. But you had previously found the way to my heart. I shall say to you, as people do when one has come to see them for the first time, "Now that you know the way, I hope you will come again." This conclusion of a sentimental *tour de propriétaire* is crude enough to give the Parisian public the illusion of considerable psychological insight. Perhaps you could insert it into *La Lutte*, if you need a cue; the way the skin of an inferior creature was grafted onto Demarsy's divine countenance—or as the Venetians, when they were building their basilica, introduced into their own work fragments brought back from countries they had loved.

Cher ami, enough of letters (I am speaking of my own letters, which are letters, you never send me anything but messages that could be telephoned). All this is paying much too much attention to friendship, which has no reality. Renan says to avoid intimate friendships. Emerson says one must change one's friends progressively. True, men just as great have said the opposite. But I am rather weary of insincerity and friendship, which are almost the same thing. And, old *coquette* of intellectual friendship that I am, I recall what M. Darlu, my philosophy professor, said to me: "Another new friend! What number did you give him when he entered the doors of your heart."

Au revoir, cher ami,
Très yours,
(Since this absurd Franco-English formula pleases you.)
M. Proust

42: TO ANTOINE BIBESCO

[CIRCA 1901 OR 1902]

Mon cher Antoine,

I thought for the moment that it might perhaps be useful for you to correct your faults. But your faults are strangely like your virtues, and they make you what you are, so I shall not correct you. Try to stay the way you are, perpetually regenerating your acts and your words through creative thinking, reserving no place for convention, because what one takes to be simple worldly ridicule or simple malice is the death of the spirit. But continue to live as you do, sincerely, irreverently, spontaneously, and I say this to you not in the religious sense but in the sense of literary immortality. "This do and thou shalt live. This if thou do not, thou shalt die. Die (whatever "die" means) totally and irrevocably."

A toi.
Marcel

43: TO ANTOINE BIBESCO

[CIRCA 1901 OR 1902]

Mon cher Antoine,

I have just read your play [*Mon héritier*]. It moved and disturbed me. Work, work, work, it is your duty. You were very nice this evening, but nevertheless you are the purchaser of my soul, and I should rather be able to repay all your kindnesses, and to recover it and find it the way it would have been if I hadn't sold it, with its secrets undivulged, its reserve undefiled, its tombs and its altars inviolate. At times there appears before me the countenance, defunct and full of reproaches for what might have been and is not; that is to say the better being I should have been if I had not, in order to teach you, and counting no costs, sold what no one ought to be able to buy, and which, indeed, the devil alone does buy; but alas, it *may not be mended and patched, and pardonned* [sic], *and worked up again as good as new.*

About the question of the Ruskin translation—I should rather have made my revision earlier. The revision consists of this: Wherever I am in doubt, I'll put a "?" in the margin. We will leaf through the book, and each time I see a "?" which I have not asked of Humières, I shall ask you (or Nordlinger).

Ton,
Marcel Proust

44: TO ANTOINE BIBESCO

[CIRCA 1901 OR 1902]

Cher Antoine,

Yes, 136 bd. St.-Germain is indeed my brother's address. I was just about to tell him of your great kindness, and he will be, as I have been, very much touched by it.

I dined at your cousin Noailles' and broke her most beautiful Tanagra. I dined at Vallière with the Aimerys. The Lucinges—but it occurs to me that the *Herald* and the *Gaulois* will have described this fête for you, apropos of which I submit the following resemblance: isn't little Lasteyrie, not the one who plays tricks, but the one nicknamed Lolotte, exactly like Léon Blum (I mean only physically)?

I dined in the Bois, another Guiche dinner, with your friend, Tristan Bernard. But this was a very small dinner, while at Vallière there were thirty people. I gathered together (but previously) Bertrand's friends (not all) and Bertrand at my house the night before he left, and this ended in a supper, also at home. You know Albu is not the only one of my friends who is getting married. Guiche is also engaged, and he, too, seemed quite happy (but less so). However, Albu comes to see me even oftener than before, if that's possible, and is delightful. But I know very well in spite of what he says that it can't stay the same afterwards. . . . Yet I am too fond of him to consider his marriage from my point of view alone.

Since you are interested in medical matters, and you also like to think that I am a little mad, I will tell you that I have consulted a doctor who, along with Faisans, is considered the best, a Dr. Merklen, who told me that my asthma has become a nervous habit and that the only way of curing it is to go to an antiasthmatic establishment in Germany (I doubt whether I shall go) where they would make me "lose the habit" of my asthma like the demorphinization of morphine addicts.

I should be delighted to see your brother when he passes through, but is it really necessary to wait until then to disclose what is going on? You know how discreet I am and you could easily write to me. Well, decide for yourself and see. I should like to have your brother tell me what is most interesting at Poitiers or at Nevers.

I am giving you a purely frivolous account of my life since your departure, but you know, don't you, that "*This is the apparent Life*," and that "*The real life is underneath all this*."

But now I must leave you. What else is there to say? I reproached Barrès (without mentioning you, as coming from me, because it was my own feeling from the first moment) about the end of his article. I said to him that "the Comtesse de Noailles" had never been for Dreyfus, that it was unlucky enough just to be innocent, but to be innocent when convicted was indeed unfortunate. He simply laughed and said, "What is the meaning of this sudden explosion of Dreyfusism?" There was a M. Vaschide there, who gave forth some absurd medical theories (*Tombeau*), but who was charming, nevertheless, a Parsifal difficult to engage for the Opera because he has too much accent, talks too quickly, and is so eager to amplify his special field that he keeps saying all the time, "*C'est nelveux.*" What a blow, *mon vieux*, that broken Tanagra.

Au revoir, my dear Antoine, *mille amitiés* for Emmanuel and for you.

Marcel Proust

45: TO ANTOINE BIBESCO

[CIRCA DECEMBER, 1902]

Mon petit Antoine,

Although I had been thinking of your grief all the time and picturing it to myself cruelly, when I received your poor letter, when I saw your little handwriting entirely changed, almost unrecognizable, with its dwindled letters, shriveled like eyes shrunken into slits from weeping, it was a fresh blow to me, as though for the first time I was experiencing the clear sensation of your distress. [The Princesse Alexandre Bibesco, Prince Antoine's mother, had died recently.] I remember when Mother lost her parents, which was such anguish for her that I still wonder how she could go on living, I tried in vain to see her every day and every hour; once when I had gone to Fontainebleau and telephoned her from there, suddenly her poor shattered voice came to me through the telephone, stricken for all time, a voice quite other than the one I had always known, all cracked and broken; and in the wounded, bleeding fragments that came to me through the receiver I had for the first time the dreadful sensation of all the things inside her that were forever shattered.

. . . .

Everyone speaks of you with deep and mournful sympathy. Several of your friends whom I have known for a short time, like Mme le Bargy and Mme Tristan Bernard, were very touching when they spoke to me of you, but I want to tell you what touched me the most. I went to Gallé's to have something arranged in a vase. I was told that the workmen couldn't work because M. Gallé's father had died that very day. I said to the employee that it must be a great sorrow to M. Gallé. "Monsieur Gallé doesn't know it." "How is that?" "He is at the moment in such a state of despondency, and his health has been affected to such a point, that no one dares give him the news, which might prove fatal to him." "Is this despondency caused by his father's illness?" "No, he didn't know that his father was ill, but a month ago Monsieur Gallé lost the person he most admired in the world, the Princesse Bibesco, and since that day he has been so prostrated that he has had to be isolated, forbidden any work, and, Monsieur, we all understand it, she was such a good woman, etc. . . ."

And this employee didn't suspect that I knew you, and I have heard the same thing said a hundred times.

. . . .

I have dined several times at your cousins' who are very nice, but you are the only person I should really love to see at this time, and I embrace you as I love you, with all my heart.

Marcel Proust

The Comte (now Marquis) *de Lauris* was one of the group of young noblemen, including the Duc d'Albuféra, Prince Léon Radziwill, Comte Bertrand de Salignac-Fénelon, the Duc de Guiche, Prince Antoine Bibesco, and Comte Gabriel de La Rochefoucauld, whom Proust met at the turn of the century. M. de Lauris is the author of novels, short stories, a life of Benjamin Constant, and, in 1948, of his memoirs, which also include the introductory essay to *A un ami*, a collection of the letters Proust wrote him. A number of the most attractive qualities in the character of Saint-Loup Proust borrowed from M. de Lauris and other members of this group of friends. Explaining the following letter, M. de Lauris writes, "The echoes of the Dreyfus Affair still continued. . . . One evening I defended Combes' anticlerical laws, but I think I was arguing not with Marcel but with some other speaker."

46: TO GEORGES DE LAURIS

[JULY 29, 1903]

After Albu left I started thinking again about your blessed laws, and, in a strange state of depression and stupidity—perhaps inseparable from the side I have set myself to defend—I am noting down my humble little reflections, merely simple common sense, reflections far beneath the level of Yves Guyot, or, I admit, the high plane on which our discussions have so far been conducted. So tear up this letter at once; I should blush too much if someone else should happen to read it. Up to this point I have been thinking only of the virtues and dangers of Christianity and of its right to existence and freedom; but now I am trying to get down into the very nature of your laws and what they can mean to you. I have no idea whatsoever what you want. Is it to create *one* France? (As your ideas about granting a subsidy to Saint-Cyr, and your other ideas, which are too specialized for me to be able to discuss, would lead one to believe.) I don't think that you want all Frenchmen to be alike, a dream not likely to come true—luckily, because it is stupid, but no doubt you do wish all Frenchmen to be friends or at least to be able to be, outside of the private and personal reasons they may have for hating each other; and thus that no prior hostility could pervert the ends of justice, should the case come up, as it did a few years ago. And you think that the private schools teach their pupils to detest Freemasons and Jews (this evening it was, in fact, education particularly that seemed to arouse your anger to the point of making you question my good faith concerning Cochin, etc.), and it is true that for the past few years Jews have no longer been received socially by those who come out of these schools, which in itself makes no difference to us, but which is an omen of that dangerous state of mind that fostered the Affair.

But I can tell you that at Illiers, the small community where two days ago my father presided at the awarding of the school prizes, the curé is no longer invited to the distribution of the prizes since the passage of the Ferry laws. The pupils are trained to consider the people who associate with him as socially undesirable, and in their way, quite as much as the other, they are working to split France in two. And when I remember this little village so subject to the miserly earth, itself the foster-mother of miserliness, where the only upward thrust towards the sky, often dappled with clouds, and often, too, a heavenly blue, transfigured each evening at the setting of the sun—there on the plain of La Beauce where the only upward thrust towards heaven is still the lovely church steeple; when I remember the curé who taught me Latin and the names of the flowers in his garden; when above all, I know the mentality of my father's brother-in-law—town magistrate down there and anticlerical—who, since the decrees, no longer takes off his hat to the curé and who reads *L'Intransigeant*, but has, since the Affair, added to it *La Libre Parole*; when I think of all this, it doesn't seem to me right that the old curé should no longer be invited to the distribution of the prizes, as representative of something in the village more difficult to define than the social function symbolized by the pharmacist, the retired tobacco-inspector, and the optician, but something which is, nevertheless, not unworthy of respect, were it only for the perception of the meaning of the spiritualized beauty of the church spire—pointing upward into the sunset where it loses itself so lovingly in the rose-colored clouds; and which, all the same, at first sight, to a stranger alighting in the village, looks somehow better, nobler, more dignified, with more meaning behind it, and, with, what we all need, more love than the other buildings, however sanctioned they may be under the latest laws. In any case, the gulf dividing your France in two is widened by each new stage of anticlerical politics, and that is very natural. Only, at this point, you can answer me by saying that if you have a tumor and live with it, in order to remove it I have to make you very ill, indeed; I shall give you a fever; you will have to recuperate; but, afterwards, you will be in good health. Such, indeed, was my reasoning during the Affair.

If, therefore, I thought that once the religious teaching orders were destroyed, the ferment of hatred among the French people would be destroyed as well, I should consider it a very good thing to do; but I think exactly the opposite. In the first place, it is only too clear that everything we find detestable about clericalism—first of all, anti-Semitism or, for that matter, clericalism itself—is wholly distinct from Catholic dogma and Catholic faith. Alphonse Humbert, Cavaignac, radical anti-Semites, seem to me a breed that must not be allowed to multiply. And the priests, not necessarily the Dreyfusards, but the tolerant ones, seem to me tolerable only insofar as they themselves are tolerant. Today the great supporters of Catholicism are not believers (and be it said to the shame of Catholicism, which accepts their support, although we should remember that we have accepted Gohier, and heaven knows how many others, some really bad and anti-Semitic at heart), and the clericals don't give a hang because they know that a country curé, a monk, a bishop, or a pope can support the Government, but that an editor of *La Libre Parole* cannot, so they pardon them completely for not going to church, for insulting almost all the clergy and, first and foremost, the Pope. With the religious schools gone and Catholicism extinct in France (if it could be extinguished, but not through legislation; ideas and beliefs die out but only when whatever they held of truth and usefulness to society is corrupted or diminished), the clerical unbelievers—all the more violently anti-Semitic, anti-Dreyfusard, anti-liberal—would be just as numerous and a hundred times worse than before.

The influence of the teachers (the professors in the schools), supposing they are bad, does not mold the opinions of young people (except for those who go on into higher education and whose fervor as partisans of a Boutroux or even of a Lavisse, depends on whether they went to Stanislas or Condorcet), the trouble is with the press; if instead of restricting the freedom of teaching we could restrict the freedom of the press, we might perhaps lessen a little the ferments of discord and hatred, but an "intellectual protectionism" (the existing laws are a Mélinist form of it a hundred times more obnoxious than Méline himself) would have many disadvantages, too. In all of this, we are talking only about other people, about those who hate us. But what about ourselves—have we the right to hate, too? A unified France would not mean a union of all Frenchmen, but the domination, etc. I am too exhausted to go on with it. I shall take an example in which there is no hatred, but, on the contrary, only a little gentle malice on your and Bertrand's part. When Bertrand snickers over nuns being forced to travel, when you are annoyed at seeing a clerical reading *La Libre Parole*, your state of mind, although it is not on edge, is, nevertheless, not perceptibly different from that of a very nice officer who, himself reading *La Libre Parole*, is annoyed at seeing a Jew on the train reading *L'Aurore*. Believe me, for those who will never have open minds, the Schoolmaster is *L'Echo*, *L'Eclair*, *Le Journal*, or the world they represent, which, in turn, supplies and formulates their conversation and ideas—if, among such people, you can call them that. For those whose minds are in the process of being enlightened, the Schoolmaster is the professor at the Sorbonne or the abbé with "modern ideas," and so, whether a man is born Fénelon, Radziwill, Lauris, Gabriel de La Rochefoucauld, Guiche, or simply Marcel Proust, the ideas are the same (as are even those of the more advanced Orders).

You may be sure that the act of requiring a degree for military service has done more for the cause of a progressive liberal Republic than all the expulsion of the monks. The others who haven't "studied," do not go beyond the political ideas of their society, that is, of their newspapers. Besides, none of this even skims the surface of the question. And it is less simple than you believe. Thus, we all speak very lightly of the Jesuits—even I, and Albu, too. But if we were better informed, we would know things about the Jesuits that would give us pause, notably the fact that Auguste Comte—whom General André admires, but probably knows only slightly—had such admiration for the Order of Jesuits and believed so strongly that nothing good could be done in France except through them, that he got in touch with the head of the Order about combining into a single organization the Positivist School and the Order of the Jesuits. However, since the head of the Order was suspicious, the negotiations miscarried. We are always told that absolute monarchies could not tolerate the Jesuits; but does that imply a very serious defect in the Jesuits? Nevertheless, I believe that in the long run I should be against them, but let the anticlericals at least draw a few more distinctions and at least visit the great social structures they want to demolish before they wield the axe. I don't like the Jesuit mind, but there is, nevertheless, a Jesuit philosophy, a Jesuit art, a Jesuit pedagogy. Will there be an anticlerical art? All this is much less simple than it appears.

What is the future of Catholicism in France and in the world? I mean for how long and in what form will its influence continue to be felt? It is a question which no one can even ask because the Church grows in the very process of change and, since the eighteenth century, when it seemed to be the refuge of the Ignoramuses, it has assumed an influence even over those who were supposed to combat and deny it, which the preceding century could never have foreseen. Even from the point of view of anti-Christianity, the strides they have made (in the Catholic sense) from Voltaire to Renan are tremendous. Renan is, indeed, still an anti-Christian, but one who has been Christianized; *Graecia capta* or, rather, *Christianismus captus ferum victorem cepit*. The century of Carlyle, of Ruskin, of Tolstoy, even if it was the century of Hugo, of Renan (and I am not even saying if it were never to be the century of Lamartine or of Chateaubriand), is not an antireligious century. Baudelaire himself was in touch with the Church if only through sacrilege, but in any case, this question has nothing to do with Christian schools. *First*, because the Christian spirit isn't killed through closing Christian schools; and, also, if it were to die, it would die even under a theocracy. And, *second*, the Christian spirit and even Catholic dogma have nothing to do with the party mind we want to destroy (and which we imitate). It is all too much and so, farewell.

Always yours,
Marcel Proust

As for Denys Cochin (I am not speaking of Aynard, who is an admirable man, a great spirit), he must, I suppose, be fairly well tainted with conservatism, reaction, and clericalism. But his speeches enchant me because he speaks so well and voices opinions I like, and is all the more liberal, now that, for the moment, all he cares about—naturally—is freedom (just as we used to talk about nothing but justice and love when all we were asking for was an act of justice and love). I shouldn't go so far as to offer him a portfolio, but, although I am very advanced, a ministry supported by him would no more alarm me, than, in 1898, M. de Witt, a royalist, was alarmed by a ministry supported by the collectivists, because then the most urgent concern was to reform the injustice of the General Staff. Today it is to reform the injustices of the Government, if we do not want a powerful party to rise up against us with that potential strength such parties have when their ranks are swelled by the force of justice (for example, Dreyfusard socialism). At this time, the socialists, by being anticlerical, are making the same mistake that the clericals made by being anti-Dreyfusard in '97. They are paying for it today; we shall pay tomorrow.

47: TO HIS MOTHER

MONDAY NIGHT, AFTER DINNER, 9 O'CLOCK, DINING ROOM
45, RUE DE COURCELLES
[PROBABLY AUGUST 24, 1903]

Ma chère petite Maman,

. . . .

My numerous dinners in restaurants have made my stomach as good as new. Yet I eat a great deal more there. But much more slowly. Besides, eating out is my own personal

Evian, my change of scene, my summer holiday for me who never has any. Also, people think I look very well. My asthma having apparently subsided, I think that if my worries would abate . . . but, alas! —On this subject you say that there are people who have just as many and who, in addition, have to work to support their families. I know it. However, the same worries, even much greater worries, even infinitely greater worries, do not necessarily mean the same suffering. For there are two sides to all of this: the material aspect of the fact, which causes the suffering; and the capacity of the person—according to his nature—to suffer from it. But, of course, I am convinced that many people suffer as much, and even more, and work at the same time. But then we learn that they have had some illness or other and that they have been forced to abandon all work—and too late! And I have preferred to do it too soon. And I have been right. For there is work and work. Literary work makes perpetual demands on the emotions that are linked with suffering (*quand per tant d'autres noeuds tu tiens à la douleur*). It is like the pain one feels when one moves an injured part of the body that should be held still. What I need, on the contrary, is frivolity and distraction. But this is August. And besides, in spite of everything, I am better, at least at this moment. Today I even feel happy! . . . I kiss you with all my heart.

Marcel

48: TO MARIE NORDLINGER

SUNDAY [PROBABLY SEPTEMBER, 1903]

Ma chère amie,

Please don't think that I have forgotten either the blooming rose of Manchester or the withered heather of Varengeville. But I have taken across France, from Roman vestibules to Gothic apses, an intense curiosity and a more and more ailing body. And of the monuments I visited, only the hospital at Beaune was suited to the acute state of my illness. I have no doubt that in an emergency I should have been admitted. Viollet-le-Duc said that it was so beautiful it made him want to fall ill at Beaune. It is easy to see that he didn't know how it feels. Since you are in Paris, as I am (Reynaldo told me that you were here, and that is how I know where to write you), perhaps, if I recover, we might see each other one of these days. And please, in the meantime, accept for the present with my warmest gratitude, scented with amethyst and gold and the even dearer memory with which it is perfumed, my respectful friendly greetings.

Marcel Proust

49: TO GEORGES DE LAURIS

SEPTEMBER, 1903

Mon cher Georges,

Thank you with all my heart for the nice things you say to me. I shall answer them better by word of mouth. But why do you go back to "the beginnings of our friendship?" Do the succeeding ones seem to you less good? There were other things I didn't understand. However you were probably prompted to say all that out of pure kindness of heart and to please me, without remembering anything about it yourself. Since you ask me for news of my health, here it is: after I left you, the restorative company of Albu did not succeed in lessening my fever, and I left in an indescribable state. I didn't even think of sleeping on the train. I saw the sun rise, which hadn't happened to me for a long time, and it was beautiful, a most charming reversal, I thought, of a sunset. In the morning I was taken with a mad desire to ravish the little sleeping cities (be sure that you read little sleeping *villes* and not little sleeping *filles*), those that lay to the west in a dying vestige of moonlight, those that lay to the east in the midst of the rising sun, but I controlled myself. I stayed on the train. Arrived at Avallon around eleven o'clock, visited Avallon, took a carriage, and after three hours arrived at Vézelay, but by that time I was in a fantastic state. Vézelay is prodigious, enclosed in a sort of Switzerland of its own on a mountain that dominates the others, visible for miles around in a most thrilling harmony of landscape. The Church is immense and looks as much like a Turkish bath as like Notre Dame; it is built in alternating black and white stones, a delightful Christian mosque. If I weren't so tired (I have been sending post cards and this is the first letter I have written), I would tell you what one feels on entering it, a curious and beautiful experience. But that will be for the next time, because I am exhausted. In the evening I went back to Avallon and was taken with such a fever that I couldn't even undress. I walked up and down all night. At five o'clock in the morning I found out that there was a train at six. I took it. I caught sight of a splendid little *moyen âge* city called Semur and arrived at Dijon at six o'clock, where I saw some beautiful things, along with those great tombs of the Dukes of Burgundy, of which the casts give no idea because the originals are in polychrome. And at eleven at night I arrived in Evian. But this frantic and sleepless journey, in spite of illness, this "journey towards death," had changed me so much that I no longer recognized myself in the mirror; people in the railroad stations asked me whether there was anything they could do for me, and I understood the gentle wisdom of your advice (by which mother is still very much touched) not to leave home like this. Since then I have spent all my time trying to get well. . . . You seem to be overwhelmed with attentions and I am happy about it. For the first time, in your letter, you again alluded to Madame X. I never mentioned her to you again as I didn't know the state of your heart. You seem, from the happy and calm tone of your letter, to be undergoing the charms of convalescence or the uncertainties of a resuscitation. May it be blessed by all the forces of life and happiness that have already given you so much and which your friends so fervently wish for you.

Marcel Proust

Comtesse Anna-Elisabeth Brancovan de Noailles (1876–1933), whose poetry, included today in every anthology of French verse, and which, according to François Mauriac, expressed "the spiritual torment of a whole emerging generation," was as much a personal as a literary influence. By her dramatic appearance, her stylized mannerisms, her brilliant conversation as well as by her writing she enchanted the intellectual élite of her day.

Proust said of her: "Madame de Noailles is a man of genius—not only that—but the best and most perfect creature imaginable, as well."

Of Proust, Mme de Noailles wrote, "He is the only person who ever made me change a line, suppress a stanza; I am not saying that he was right in effecting my sacrifice . . . but to take a stand against Marcel, against the seer, the sorcerer—I couldn't!"

50: TO THE COMTESSE DE NOAILLES

MONDAY [EARLY OCTOBER, 1903]

Madame,

You are infinitely nice. I should be enchanted to dine Wednesday. But I have to go out Thursday (and can't do anything about it; it's something I have postponed four times already because I was always ill). And I can't go out two days in succession, because each time after I go out I am sick for several days. Occasionally this life, in which every pleasure is paid for without its even having been enjoyed, fills me with that sort of "sad repugnance, of poor and desperate feeling" that poor, dear, sublime Sabine felt at seeing the furniture in her salon moved and her servant sweeping. I should like at least to be in retreat, industrious and productive in some great monastery where, all in white, you would be the splendid abbess (although my clericalism is momentarily attenuated because I have just reread the history of the freeing of the communes and because I see all that these poor bourgeois and peasant enthusiasts had to suffer at the hands of all those pigs). This struck me all the more because the most grievous story, and the one that produces the greatest "civic" shudder, as you would say, is the one of that poor commune of Vézelay to which I went a month ago—at the cost of how many attacks of asthma—to admire without bitterness and conscientiously the marvelous abbey church, never suspecting the cruelty of the abbott, Pons de Monboissier. But I shall forget all that because of my love of churches, to which I always return "as the wasp flies to the open lily," and then, too, because those bourgeois were even more ferocious, if that is possible. Besides I don't know a word of history. And I have just read *Vieux papiers, Vieilles maisons*, and *Batz de Lenôtre*. And, nevertheless, it is shocking that Clemenceau makes capital out of the Terror and, nevertheless, does not permit the isolating of the Bloc.

Madame, you are not my confessor, and I don't know why I don't spare you a single one of my absurd ideas, and I am trying to blot out this audacious effusion with the most passionate respect.

Marcel Proust

51: TO HIS MOTHER

[OCTOBER 3–11, 1903]

Ma chère petite Maman,

I have come in so exhausted by an *incessant* cough that I tried it discreetly outside your door to see whether you were asleep. But there was no response to "that voice of the heart," which, Lamartine says, "alone reaches the heart."

A solemn reconciliation this evening at the Noailles' between myself and Barrès, with whom I did not mince matters, either political or moral. But he took it very well and was very nice. And in succession, for his behavior towards Rouvier, Picquart, Labori, he gave me excuses, none of which, however, was valid.

I was obliged to keep a closed carriage waiting from

half-past six to quarter-past one, and, by the desperate financial straits into which this has flung me, I can appreciate the improvement your own finances must have undergone since you no longer pay for my summer months at Roche (a sentence which you will be taking quite the wrong way if you find it not very nice. But I don't always find "the way to your heart"). Thank you infinitely for the fruit, the *Secret de Polichinelle*, and the *Mercure*. —Will you leave me a line telling me whether Tuesday, the 13th, is a good date for the dinner, at which I am wondering whether I could have just the Noailles, the Chimays, with a literary couple—I am hesitating between the Barrès and Pierrebourg-Hervieu. I should think Calmette might enjoy it.

Marcel

I am trembling for fear the sentence about my keeping the carriage for seven hours and about Roche will annoy you. In which case I should be greatly distressed. I only said it so that you would have some idea. . . . I feel ill, meaning that I am coughing miserably, but there it is. In case any day next week is convenient to you for the dinner, will you have this [attached] letter taken to Radziwill (there will be an answer if he is there). If he is not in Paris, have them ask whether he has a telephone at Ermenonville and the number (and whether he is at Ermenonville). If, on the other hand, the different days next week are not equally convenient to you, or are not convenient at all, keep the letter and don't send it.

Dr. Adrien Proust died November 26, 1903. A few days before his death, he remarked, "I have been happy all my life," and in the eulogy delivered at his grave he was described as, "Epicurean enough to enjoy things without taking tragically the little miseries of life, Skeptic enough to be indulgent towards those who stray from what we consider the paths of virtue, Stoic enough to face death without flinching."

The translation of *The Bible of Amiens*, published in 1904, bore the following dedication: To the memory of my father, stricken in the midst of his work the 24th of November, 1903, died the 26th of November, this translation is affectionately dedicated.

M. P.

52: TO THE COMTESSE DE NOAILLES

THURSDAY [EARLY DECEMBER, 1903]

Madame,

You are too kind. In ages of faith, how natural it was to love the Holy Virgin—for she let the cripples touch the hem of her gown, and the lepers, the blind and all the sad of heart. But you are kinder still, and every new proof of the infinite generosity of your heart gives me a clearer understanding of the unshakable foundation of your genius, rooted, as it is, in eternity. And if it annoys you a little to be an improvement on the Holy Virgin, I shall say that you are like the Carthaginian goddess who inspired lascivious ideas in many and longing for holiness in a few.

Madame, you must not pity me, although I am most unhappy. I have not even the courage to picture honestly what life can now mean to poor Mother when I realize that she will never again see the only person she lived for (I can't even say "loved," because since the death of her parents any other affection was so much less in comparison). She gave him every moment of her life to a degree hardly credible to those who did not actually see it. Now, each moment, empty of its impelling purpose and its sweet savor comes in some different form, like innumerable bad fairies, ingenious at torture, to typify the unhappiness that will never leave her. However, no one would ever guess it. Mother has such energy (the kind of energy that doesn't look like energy, and in no way suggests the exercise of self-control) that there is no apparent difference between her a week ago and today. But I, who know the depths, the intensity, and the duration of this drama, cannot help being afraid. You, who saw Father only two or three times, have no way of knowing how kind and simple he was. I tried—if not exactly to satisfy him, for I am well aware that I was always the disappointment of his life—at least to show him my affection. At the same time, there were days when I revolted against some of his remarks which seemed to me too sure, too positive, and the other Sunday, I remember, in a political discussion I said some things I shouldn't have. I can't tell you how unhappy I am about it now. It seems as though I had been harsh with someone who even then was no longer able to defend himself. I'd give anything if only I had been all affection and gentleness that evening. But I almost always was. Father's nature was so much nobler than mine. I am always complaining. Father's only thought when he was ill was to keep us from knowing about it. However, these are things I can't yet bear to think about. They cause me so much grief. Life has started again. If only I had an aim, an ambition of any kind, it would help me to bear it. But that isn't the case. My own vague happiness was only the reflection of Father's and Mother's, which I always saw around me, not without remorse, which is even sharper now because I was its only shadow. Now the little incidents in life which made up my happiness are filled with pain. However, it is life starting again, and not just a blunt and brief despair, which could only be temporary. So I shall soon be able to see you again, and I promise no longer selfishly to talk to you about things I can't even explain, because I never spoke of them. I can almost say that I never thought of them. They were my life. But I didn't realize it.

Tell the Princesse de Chimay that I have been wanting to write to her one of these days before I must start answering letters, which will be unbelievably tiring. But when Mother suddenly heard that I had given up the Ruskin, she took it into her head that Father cared about nothing else, that he had waited from day to day for its publication. So I had to countermand my orders, and I am about to start all over again on the proof sheets, etc. So tell the Princesse de Chimay that I shall have to go several days without writing her, but not a moment without indulging in the only balm I know, her unbelievably kind words, the kindest anyone has written me. Please accept, Madame, my very respectful affection.

Your grateful admirer,
Marcel Proust

53: TO LAURE HAYMAN

[PROBABLY DECEMBER, 1903]

Chère amie,

When this thing, which you could not have borne to see, happened—Father, who was so well when he left in the morning only to be brought home on a stretcher—you were one of the first persons I thought of, as soon as I could think of anyone besides Father and Mother. Father loved you so much. And I knew from my brother that you sent wonderful flowers. I thank you with all my heart for having always been so sweet to Father and for having been even more so since, and I am sure you will cherish his memory. He always mentioned you when he wanted to cite an example, not only of elegance, youth, and beauty, but also of intelligence, of taste, goodness, tact, of sensitiveness, and warmth. You know that you had become a subject of conversation in the family. In the past, before I was sick and also before we were involved in our quarrel, each time Father saw you and learned some little thing from you about me, he took such elaborate, obvious precautions to prevent my knowing who had said it. "Someone saw you . . ." "It appears that . . ." And I always guessed at once that you had been to see him that day. For several years it was no longer possible, but he spoke of you no less frequently. And whenever he wished to crown an enthusiastic eulogy he was delivering to me of the charms of heart, mind, and beauty of some woman, he would add at the end, "To a lesser degree, she almost reminded me of Laure." My ill health, for which I am unceasingly grateful in this case, resulted in my spending much more time with him in the past few years, since I never went out anymore. During this time, when we spent so much time together, I had to repress—and there are even moments when I seem retrospectively to use the word "suppress"—the traits of mind or character which wouldn't have pleased him. So that I believe he was reasonably satisfied with me, and it was an intimacy that wasn't interrupted for a single day and the sweetness of which I savor, now that even in the least important things I find life so bitter and hateful. Other people have some ambition to console them. I have none; I lived only this family life and now it is destroyed forever. I thank you with all my heart, Madame, my dear friend, my dear Laure, for having guessed this and for having been thoughtful enough to write me such compassionate and kind lines, you who are so kind to all unhappy people. I kiss you very sadly.

Your respectful,
Marcel Proust

54: TO MARIE NORDLINGER

[JANUARY, 1904]
I am very ill.

Thanks for your nonaromatic balsam. All the more balm, indeed, for me, since it is odorless. Seeds, a *spirituel* present (in the humoristic sense of the word, "*spirituel*," which it loses because of your cursed English infiltration) for someone who loves flowers and fears their perfume. Seeds, flowers for the imagination, as Bing's dwarfed trees are trees for the imagination: the one, the future of flowers, the other, the past of trees—all in a small present. In the Whistler itself, I do not wish to write; the copy is rare, and it would be criminal to mark it in any way. Besides, it is really the book of too great a man to bear a name as unimportant as mine. Or I should be the Cockney who inscribes his name on the Cathedral of Amiens (see *The Bible*, IV).

Ruskin and Whistler were mistaken about each other because their *systems* were opposed. But there is one truth, and they both saw it. Even in the action against Ruskin, Whistler said, "*You say I painted this picture in a few hours. But actually I painted it with the experience of my whole life.*" But at that very moment Ruskin was writing to Rossetti, "*I prefer the things you do quickly, immediately, your rough sketches, to what you work over. What you work at you spend, say, six months in doing; but what you sketch at one swoop is the expression of years of dreams, of love, and of experience.*" On this level the two stars strike the same point with a ray perhaps hostile, but identical. There is astronomical coincidence.

Thanks to Reynaldo (everything I have ever done is *thanks to Reynaldo*), I met Whistler one evening, and he told me that Ruskin was absolutely no judge of pictures. It is possible; but in any case, even while he was rambling on about other peoples' pictures, out of his misjudgments he painted and drew marvelous pictures, which must be loved for what they are. And to explain and acclimatize them to France, in the form of conscientious and impassioned copies, we shall attempt together.

Yours affectionately,
Marcel Proust

55: TO MARIE NORDLINGER

FEBRUARY 7, 1904

Chère amie,

. . . . I worked like a nigger on *Sesame* and have done over the whole beginning, and the entire first notebook, *nec varietur*. There is only one thing with which I am still dissatisfied: that is *careless writing*. I have replaced "*entretien fortuit*" with "*dans le négligé de la causerie*." It is not as good, but at least it is not pretentious, which would be the worst kind of mistranslation. I have written the commentary for several passages of this first notebook, a commentary destined to be used either as preface or as notes. As soon as I am in a condition to receive you, I shall write, for I am all on fire for *Sesame*—and for you.

Your
Marcel Proust

56: TO MARIE NORDLINGER

[CIRCA FEBRUARY 14, 1904]

Chère amie,

To your reply (if you need to reply) will you add another piece of information. Ruskin says, "*Eisenach* (*name of it iron-ach*) (I found *ach*, it is "water"; that means nothing at all, so much the worse), *significant of Thuringian armories*." "Significant" means "reminiscent of," doesn't it? But "armories" is in no dictionary. Is it "armorial bearings" or "arms"? (The sense seems to me rather to be "armorial bearings.") This old man is beginning to bore me.

Your respectful friend,
Marcel Proust

57: TO MARIE NORDLINGER

[MID-APRIL OR MAY, 1904]

Chère amie,

Thank you for the wonderful hidden flowers, which enabled me to "make a Spring of my own," as Madame de Sévigné said—a harmless, fluvial spring. Thanks to you my electric darkroom has had its Far Eastern spring.

Thank you too, for the beautiful translation, which I shall go over carefully and, with your permission, change, although hesitantly, with affectionate respect. But nevertheless change. You speak French not only better than a French woman but like one. You write French not only better than a French woman, but like one. But when you translate English, all the original characteristics reassert themselves; the words revert to type, to their associations, their meaning, their native rules. And whatever charm there may be in this English disguise of French words, or rather in this phantom English cast of mind and countenance breaking through its French garb and mask, all this life will have to be cooled off, gallicized, removed farther from the original, and the originality obliterated.

No, I shall certainly not go out to seek the *coup de grâce* from Manet and Fantin when Clouet and Fouquet have already half killed me.

Your friend,
Marcel

What is *la perle du Rosaire de Venise?*

P.S. (Monday) As my letter was forgotten, I am adding a short postscript. I am afraid you will be angry about *Sesame*, for I have upset everything; however, I could put back your words if you prefer. But I don't think the text you have translated is the same edition as the one from which I am working, for there is continual variation. Or else you have several times skipped words. It would be better for me to revise what you have done by myself and afterwards we will discuss all of it together. The other day I was sleeping; I heard the bell ring. In the first drowsiness of wakening, I didn't ask right away who had rung. When I did ask and discovered it was you, it was too late; you had already gone. However, even if you had still been there, I wouldn't have been in any state to see you. I still have not gone out again, but I shall risk it soon (only in the evening, not in the day-time any more!).

Mille respects, mille affections,
Marcel Proust

58: TO MARIE NORDLINGER

FRIDAY, MAY 27, 1904

Chère amie,

. . . . Mother would like, however painful she might find the comparison between the exact and gentle picture of my father that she bears in mind and a necessarily rather inaccurate work of art—Mother would like, for those who will succeed us and who might wonder how my father looked, to have a bust in the cemetery that would give them the simplest and most exact answer. And she intends asking some gifted and docile young sculptor to be good enough to try, using photographs, to give in plaster, in bronze, or in marble the form of my father's features, with that maximum of exactness which even then will be remote enough from our memories and which might make them even sadder, but which, for those who did not know him would, nevertheless, give more of an idea of him than just his name carved on the stone. *Would you like to be this sculptor?* I should have liked to talk to you about it, but since I couldn't see you, I wanted at least to write you. Tell me yourself what you think about this project.

Our *Sesame* will appear in the *Arts de la vie* as soon as it is ready; but when will it be? *I am doing it over from top to bottom.* I have not asked how much we will be paid, but I don't think it will be too bad for that review. Can you believe that I found all my notebooks (six notebooks) of *Sesame and Lilies*? By pure chance. Here's what prevented my finding them before. I said to everybody: Look for *green* notebooks. And the first three, those that we had, were indeed green. But the next three were yellow. So seeing notebooks that weren't green, no one even looked into them.

My fatigue and, above all, my scruples about starting everything all over again made me so late that I wish you would try, so that we can gain ground, a rough draft of whatever *verses* there are in *Sesame*. As to the preface, since it is the one for *Sesame and Lilies* and not just for *Kings'*, I think it could, if absolutely necessary, be dispensed with. If we wanted to be conscientious and give it, we would have to choose between the one in your copy and the one in mine. The one in mine is thirty pages, the one in yours six. That might mean giving preference to the one in yours, which is, however, I think less good. . . .

Your friend,
Marcel

59: TO MARIE NORDLINGER

SATURDAY

[SEPTEMBER 17, 1904]

Chère amie,

I don't know what you must think of me and yet [my silence] is not for lack of thinking of you! And not only all the things I have to tell you, but to answer as well. Because I haven't caught up with you, since a letter of yours, written the day after my visit to Auteuil, a very charming letter, although, coming from anyone else but you, it might have appeared to be a little ironic and scornful. For on to the dreadful state of health I was in, tumbled the proud words, "I am overflowing with health, with life, with energy, with the power to be happy, etc."

Chère amie, please don't think that I read this with bitterness! And believe that, on the contrary, I understood the charity of those words, which were like an offer of a moral blood-transfusion. And I also had so much to reply to the rest, although I am so little the person who could respond to it. For I understood the melancholy of your solitude. But I was so much the last person who could break it down, since I don't feel well two hours a week, etc., etc. I have tried for two weeks to husband my forces in order to have those two hours, and I went to Versailles to dine with poor, convalescent Reynaldo, to bid him good-bye, because I hadn't seen him since he left for Germany, and it is always possible that at the first ray of health I shall go away for a few days, which might perhaps stretch out into a longer stay. I didn't find him looking bad, and no trace of his horrible suffering. Is your journey to America (on which subject I may perhaps be permitted to give my opinion, which you might, perhaps, think bizarre; I am very much in favor of it if the idea amuses you and the financial arrangements are favorable; for the offer itself, I find it very flattering, and the sort of thing that any art-loving person would be delighted to do) working out in any definite way? And has your stay in the Venice of the North thrown some light on the matter?

Why don't you want your name to be associated with mine on the cover of *Sesame?* You answered me evasively. Respond, "*dic nobis, Maria quid . . . ?*" (Easter Day Service).

I think our walks in Venice, *St. Mark's Rest* in hand, had very little charm for M. Abel Hermant, for, in an article in *Gil Blas*, incidentally a stupid one, he speaks of English women (according to him I assume your sex and your country for the occasion) who think they must bend over backwards to see the capitals of St. Mark's extolled by Ruskin. Apropos of all this, isn't this touching? A bookseller in the Piazza San Marco writes me that he obtained my address through M. Maurice Barrès and that he wants me to translate *St. Mark's Rest* for him. I think I shall refuse because otherwise I shall die without ever having written anything of *my own*. . . .

Marcel Proust

60: TO MARIE NORDLINGER

SATURDAY

[SEPTEMBER 24, 1904]

Chère amie,

. . . . I don't know when Mother is returning. I write to her every day, but have been careful not to tell her that you were here for fear of making her return. However, if you need to see her, let me know at once, for in that case she would reproach me for not having done so. Otherwise, since she has only been in the country five days and will certainly not go away again once she has returned, I shall say nothing. But naturally if her presence is useful or urgent tell me so.

No, I didn't receive your letter from Liège. And did you receive mine at Hamburg? I rejoice at the thought of seeing you again and wish I could be a little surer of being able to one of these days.

Yours with all my heart,

Marcel

The idea that you find your visit "improper" in Mother's absence seems to me enchanting and has made me laugh a lot. As if it were you who were the young man and I the young girl. Yet I was alone at Auteuil at your house. Only it would be too stupid to come when I am in bed or to make any other useless kind of effort.

Mademoiselle Louisa de Mornand was for many years an actress at the Vaudeville Theatre in Paris, her first role there in *Maman Colibri* having been acquired through Proust's introduction of her to Henri Bataille, the author of the play. She met Proust around 1904 at the Restaurant Larue, where, each night after the theatre, she would join Proust's friends, the group of young noblemen and artists who met there regularly. The mistress of one of Proust's close friends, she remembered, a quarter of a century later, having immediately been struck by Proust's "superiority." *"Une amitié amoureuse"* was established between them in which there was no element of "banal flirtation or of an exclusive liaison, but on Proust's side a strong passion tinged with affection and desire, and on mine an attachment that was more than comradeship and that really touched my heart."

61: TO LOUISA DE MORNAND

THURSDAY [PROBABLY 1904]

Chère amie,

Your souvenir is precious to me, thank you for it. How I should love to walk with you in the streets of Blois, which must be a charming frame for your beauty. It is an old frame, a Renaissance frame. But it is a new frame, too, since I have never seen you in it. And in new places the people we love appear to us somehow new, too. I should find your beautiful eyes reflecting the lightness of a Touraine sky, your exquisite figure, outlined against the background of the old château, more moving than seeing you in just another dress; it would be like seeing you in a whole new costume. And I should like to see the effect of the pretty embroidery of one of the blue or pink dresses you wear so well, against the delicate stone embroideries worn by the old château with a grace which, even if a little ancient, is to my mind, nonetheless becoming. The pen with which I am writing you all this is so bad it will only write wrong-side up. My brain is a little that way, too. So don't be surprised if the result isn't brilliant. Besides, I only know how to tell women I admire and love them when I feel neither one nor the other. And you—you know that I admire you very much and love you very much. So I shall always express it to you very inadequately. Don't think that all this is an indiscreet, pretentious, and awkward way of trying to flirt with you. Not that this is of any importance, because if it were, you would have sent me quickly on my way. I should rather die than make advances to a woman who is adored by a friend whose noble and sensitive heart endears him to me more each day. At least a small amount of friendship and a great deal of admiration may be permitted me. . . . You will decide how you want it. While awaiting the verdict, risking all to win all, and with a boldness that is perhaps a result of the great distance between the rue de Courcelles and the chaussée de Saint-V——, I am going to do something (while mentally asking A——'s permission) that will bring me mad happiness if it is realized other than in just a letter. I embrace you tenderly, my dear Louisa.

Marcel Proust

If, as I hope for his sake and for yours (for the hours that you spend apart seem to me long, indeed, when I think of your sadness as well as his), A—— has returned to you, tell him chiefly please not to call me "Proust" anymore and, incidentally, that I like him very much. I send my respects to your sister, whom I don't know, but who must indeed be charming if she resembles you. If she combines your gentleness and your loyalty (which I appreciate most in you and which, if I am not mistaken, the future alone will fully reveal), she must be an accomplished person. But I suspect that I prefer you, nevertheless!

62: TO MARIE NORDLINGER

FEBRUARY 9, 1905

Chère amie,

The words "I have been so ill, I am still so ill" have been spoken by me so often, meaning an almost habitually painful state of health, although not one that excludes from time to time the possibility of epistolary relationships, that I am rather afraid they come, colorless and with no power of pardon or absolution to your ears, too long inured to them (I certainly do not mean incredulous). But there it is; I had been in terrible pain, almost constantly in bed and without the strength to keep up any relations with my friends except those disembodied ones of friendship and memory. But those, be assured, were not interrupted and the accusations of forgetfulness harbored by me against myself were not justified where you are concerned, for I have thought of you a great deal; and what you tell me rather mysteriously, but very forcibly, about your intense happiness has delighted me. Happiness—that is something I have occasionally ceased to hope for myself, but have never stopped wishing for others. And I bless the Whistlerian magician who has brought you happiness, because I don't think that circumstances alone have given it to you, and I have a feeling that people are involved. . . .

I regret to think that your new friend, since you have been good enough to talk to him about me, must, as a good Whistlerian, be very scornful of an admirer of Ruskin's. But really, I think that if their *theories*, which are the least intimate part of each one of us, were opposed, *at a certain depth* they agreed more often than they themselves believed. . . .

Having had a slight respite these days I have started *Queens' Gardens*, which I have decided to add to *Sesame*. My charming, old, English scholar of whom I have told you will act as my "Mary."

I have received as a New Year's gift the splendid new edition of Ruskin. You will enjoy reading it when you come back. And you will see some magnificent new illustrations.

I have a friend—M. Lucien Daudet—who studied painting with Whistler. If the information he might perhaps (?) furnish your friend could be of interest to him, I should be delighted to ask him. I myself did not know Whistler—except for one evening, when I made him speak a few kind words of Ruskin! And from which occasion I kept his charming grey gloves which I have since lost. But I have heard him much spoken of by Robert de Montesquiou and by Boldini.

Tell your friend that in my deliberately bare room there is only one reproduction of a work of art, an admirable photograph of Whistler's *Carlyle* in a serpentine overcoat like the dress in the portrait of his mother. The more I think of Ruskin's and Whistler's theories, the more I believe they are not irreconcilable. Whistler has occasion to say in *Ten O'Clock* that art is distinct from morality. Yet Ruskin, too, utters a truth on another level, when he says that all great art is morality. But this is too much chatter, so without further ado I send you my respectful and grateful affection.

Marcel Proust

Madame Catusse was a friend of Proust's mother and, from time to time, an interior decorator and dealer in antiques and curios.

❧

63: TO MADAME CATUSSE

SPRING, 1905

Chère Madame,

What to read? Really, I have nothing on Laon. Rather vague memories of the cathedral itself and of Mâle's splendid book on religious art in which there is naturally very little to do with Laon. It is chiefly from the point of view of architecture that Laon is curious, more savory than any other because the green shoot is not yet open. There, better than in subsequent growths, one can see the first flowering of the Gothic and how "the marvelous flower emerges slowly." But how to show this except on the spot, under the vaults of the magic forest! The iconography would lend itself more to epistolary accounts if my recollection of it were more exact. Erudite, wholly impregnated with the scholasticism that was taught there, Laon will offer you with delightfully pedantic insistence the liberal arts in its portal, in the stained glass of its rose window. You will recognize Philosophy with the scale ladder (of learning) leaning against her breast; Astronomy with eyes towards the heavens; Geometry with her compass; Arithmetic counting on her fingers; Dialectic with her wily snake. Architecture is very beautiful. As for Medicine, she is rather banal, not as at Rheims, where she is examining a sick man's urine (pardon me, Madame). On the portal, too, you will like the Erythraean sibyl with a verse by Saint Augustine, and the Foolish and the Wise Virgins. But the great thing about the portal, one of the essential pieces of sculpture, is the life of the Virgin told, in anticipation, with the aid of the Holy Scriptures. I confess I am too tired this evening to describe it to you. But will you refer to my *Bible of Amiens*? I say a word about it there in a note (p. 326). The windows are interesting, particularly those in the choir, because of interpretations, which are still slightly Romanic, the legend of the Midwives coming to examine the virginity of the Virgin undoubtedly figures there for the last time, a most singular fish adorns the Lord's Supper, the good Thief (why?) goes along on the Flight to Egypt. If I remember correctly, the artist did not dare (this is very Romanic) represent Christ resurrected. Only the Holy Women cry at the tomb. Lovely vase of flowers between the Virgin and the Angel of the Annunciation.

Your respectful friend,
Marcel Proust

64: TO ROBERT DE MONTESQUIOU

MONDAY EVENING
[APRIL 24 AND FOLLOWING, 1905]

Cher Monsieur,

Had I not been worse the last two days, I should have thanked you sooner for the trouble you were kind enough to take in sending me that letter from Neuilly without waiting for me to send for it. Since I was unable to get up, it was uncomfortable for me to write. You are, Monsieur, more cruel than the cruelest Catholic theologians, who wish us to regard our illnesses as punishment for our sins. You wish us to consider them as sins in themselves and think that we should not only suffer physically for our ills but feel remorse for them as well. No matter how inevitable and painful they are in themselves, they must in addition be sinful. I confess that there is something else in your letter which I strive not to think about, for it would embitter my rare days of health, add to the worry of others, and would end—with an invalid's egotism—in introducing a nervous resentment into my admiration, my respectful and grateful affection for you. It is the idea that when once every fortnight I can get up, dress, go out around ten o'clock at night for an hour or two, this single innocent relaxation can be considered as a deliberate recovery (which would imply that the illness, too, is deliberate), with an eye to enjoying vain pleasures. I know perfectly well that a number of people, because I was ill on such and such a day and could not do a certain thing, would rather I should not be seen a single day in the year, and, otherwise, say: Come now, you're well enough to do the things that amuse you.—But that *you* should say practically the same thing and not realize that if I could get well for the occasions I most enjoy, it would always be to go where I can see and hear you—that is very painful to me. When shall I meet the person who truly understands my real life, my intimate feelings; who, after having seen me, because of illness, miss some great pleasure, when he catches sight of me an hour later (a thing which, however, doesn't occur in so short an interval!) in the most commonplace gathering, would come up to me and say sincerely: —How fortunate that your attack is over!

Most unfair, and unjust, too, your reproaches in regard to what you call the La Rochefoucauld orangeade. On the last four Thursdays I have wanted to go to rue de l'Université to thank Mme de La Rochefoucauld for having come to see me since I cannot visit her, as I never go out in the daytime and since she receives in the evenings at an hour which is convenient and not tiring for me. But I haven't yet been able to manage it in three years. The idea you seem to have that my choice of outings is guided by snobbishness (which if true would always lead me to the places where you are speaking) astonishes even more than it humiliates me. The shuffling and reshuffling of choice of amusements during an illness, which deprives one of practically everybody, is so natural and honest that it inevitably seems to us that everyone ought to understand something so transparent, that directs our actions towards noble and very disinterested ends or would so direct them, if the body could obey. If you knew all the things for which

I have committed indiscretions and all those which have left me with a profound sense of regret, you would see that worldliness plays little part in them. That doesn't preclude, on the evenings when I do go out, my going to a place on that particular evening where I can find refuge and see some human faces, as long as it is a place that does me no harm. There are such places; at a time when the country in the afternoon was fatal to me, I could always miraculously go to the "Pavillon des Muses" without feeling any ill effects.

Forgive me, *cher* Monsieur, for boring you with tiresome explanations. It will seem singular to you that I even dream of offering them. But all this arises from a state of introspection induced by your letter. You don't know the nervous depression that overwhelms an invalid when he feels himself misjudged by someone of whom he is fond, when he feels that his most innocent periods of rest will be construed against him. It can be the source of serious wrong. I remember when I fought with M. Lorrain, at a period when I was not yet spending the whole day in bed, but only the morning, my sole worry was that the duel might take place before noon. When I was informed that it would take place in the afternoon, the duel itself became a matter of no importance. So, you see, the suffering of neurasthenics is not in proportion to the importance of the cause of their suffering.

Another thing I should find very distressing would be to have you come and see me, since it is very painful and practically impossible for me to receive in the daytime; and it would be such a Tantalus-like good fortune and honor that you should come to sit with me without my being able to enjoy it, the more so because my hay fever is about to begin and I am wondering with dread whether, instead of being able to sit up at nine o'clock in the evening, I shan't have to wait until one in the morning.

Monsieur, forgive my letter, which is so stupid that I feel myself turning into a *catoblépas* as I write. And having thought so much about what that wonderful reading must have been like, I have failed to say a word about it or about you; I have spoken only of myself. But you are always so kind to me that I wanted to tell you that you had hurt me. How I wish I were well and could go and hear you in Brussels. Perhaps after a cure I shall be able to do things like that.

Give my friendliest greetings to Yturri, who seemed well and was so kind the other day, and believe, *cher* Monsieur, in my respectful and grateful affection.

Marcel Proust

And I didn't tell you why I couldn't go to the lecture. If you only knew!

65: TO MADAME STRAUS

FRIDAY [APRIL OR MAY, 1905]

Madame,

. . . . I have worked so hard for the last two months, whenever my attacks permitted, that I have not even been able to have friends come to see me even at home. There will be a very small piece of my work in the *Renaissance latine* of June 15. By then you will have returned, and if it doesn't tire you, I will give it to you. One of the times I went out (it isn't very proper, but we are both ill, after all), coming out of a concert I heard Mme de X— making involuntarily obscene remarks as she does *every* time I hear her speak. She found the songs very badly sung. "My dear, I shall have myself Plançon." (I suppose she meant have him sing for her.) "That will be a real pleasure. Next Thursday at ten o'clock. Notice to amateurs who would like to be present." An eddying of the crowd separated me from her and I couldn't hear any more, but I was flung back towards her again and this is what I heard: "My dear, say what you like, Madeleine likes good cooking. I prefer to give you good music. She gives two thousand francs to her cook, I prefer to give it to my artists. It's the same amount of money. Madeleine likes having it put in her mouth, I prefer having it put in my ear. Each one to his liking, my dear, we are all free, after all, I always think. . . ."

I am worn out by letters from Montesquiou. Every time he gives a reading or a fête, etc., etc., he *refuses* to admit that I am sick, and beforehand there are summonses, threats, visits from d'Yturri, who wakes me up, and, afterwards, there are reproaches for not having gone. I believe it would still be possible to get well if it weren't for "*les autres*." But the exhaustion they cause you, one's helplessness at making them understand the suffering—sometimes lasting a month—that follows the foolhardiness one has committed for the sake of what they imagine to be a great pleasure: all that is death.

I read so much every night that without tiring you, I could send you countless extracts from books. But they are so boring and so serious that I don't know whether it would please you. Tonight I have been reading Mme Desbordes-Valmore's letters, crammed with pretentiousness in the style of Mme D——, etc. Come to think of it, we are wrong in making fun of pretentiousness, of irritating ways. Talented people are like that. She sends Sainte-Beuve notes like this one:

Si vous étiez toujours notre ange
Et sans qu'un tel vol vous dérange
Vous viendriez demain
A votre soeur serrer la main.
Pour la reposer de la terre
On nous l'envoie en Angleterre
On la mettra sur un bateau
Où j'irai la chercher malgré ma peur de l'eau.

The frightening thing in these letters is to see how egotistical love is. As soon as the lover is dead, since nothing more can be expected of him, it's all over (not that that is true of everybody of course). Still she had been madly in love with Latouche. He had been dreadful to her. Nothing had been able to make her forget him. He dies. Sainte-Beuve, who wants to do an article on Latouche, asks Mme Desbordes for some information about this man "who had passed so close to talent" (isn't that typical of Sainte-Beuve?). "I should like to speak of him," he adds benevolently, "with the forbearance one owes a man who did not do all the harm he might have done." I thought that Mme Desbordes, indignant, would at least beg him to do a good article. She lets some time go by and then answers. First, protestations of grief, "I write you, my eyes dimmed with tears, which flow unceasingly," etc., etc. Then she comes to the projected article. "You wish to speak of him with all the forbearance one owes a man who didn't do all the harm he might have done, you say, etc. Oh, that's it, that's really it, he did plenty of harm, but, etc. This man who passed so close to talent. How apt that is! To tell you the truth I am not even sure of that and can give you no information, for *I was afraid to open his last books for fear of finding them too bad*. Everyone told me they were worthless, etc." What a dirty trick! And when you think that she was at his feet, mad with joy because his Christian name (Joseph de Latouche) repeated itself in hers (Josépha). "Thy name! Thou knowest heaven deigned to write it into mine!" (Which made people think that since she was also called Marceline, these letters were addressed to a M. de Marcellus.) Of course, I may be interpreting her letter to Sainte-Beuve incorrectly; one would have to ask someone who knew more about the question. I had always been told she was an angel. I must say I was rather surprised.

Madame, I hope you get well immediately, and I send you my profound and respectful affection.

Marcel Proust

66: TO MADAME STRAUS

SUNDAY, MAY 7, 1905

Madame,

. . . . I found myself in a salon filled with a dreadful group of people, from the midst of whom rose barnyard screeches. It was a very courteous row between Mme G——

and a big woman with yellow hair, a sort of queen of the roost, who, not listening to what Mme G— was saying any more than Mme G— would have listened to her under similar circumstances, kept repeating, "No, no, Madame, how could he have founded *Psst* (they were talking about Forain) when he owes everything to the Straus's, when he owes them his bread and butter, when without them he wouldn't have known how to draw." I think Mme G— agreed with her, but since the other one kept on shrieking without listening, Mme G— seemed to be being contradicted, which was not the case. "No, Madame," she started over again, "I repeat, when a man has behaved so infamously, when without the Straus's he would have had no food, etc. . . ." After these premises, I expected some such conclusion as, "A man who has done that is the lowest man on earth," or something like that. Not at all. "When a man has behaved so infamously, when he owes his living to the Straus's, etc., do you know what he is, Madame? Well, I am not afraid to say it though you may find the expression a little coarse: he is a DUMMY!"

—I thought that after such an exordium the word was rather feeble. But that didn't appear to be the lady's opinion. She seemed so enchanted by the word that she repeated it three or four times in an airy way, "He's a dummy, he's a dummy," then rose and departed. I asked X— the lady's name, he said Mme U— (?), and since he sensed that I didn't seem to admire her, he said with an air of authority intended to hypnotize me, "She is one of Mme Straus's best friends." To me she seemed more like a boring old cocotte than one of your best friends. But I said nothing. Besides she did very obligingly speak to me as she left.

Something else concerning you (as Goncourt said, that alone is always interesting). I think I told you I did not go to Montesquiou's reading, which made him furious and which resulted, under the pretext of contrasting my small handwriting with his, in his comparing himself to Solomon and me to an ant. Since this comparison rather irritated me, I answered that he always tried to give himself the star part (I also said some better things than that), to which he replied, "Where do you get the idea that I take the star part? I do not have to take it: *I have it.*" In the end, to console me for not having heard his reading, he announced that he would come and give one at my house at such-and-such a time, but only a month from now or I don't know when. But on this solemnly announced occasion (which has prevented my sleeping ever since I heard of it, although I told him it was impossible) there is to be an audience of only *three* listeners! At the head of the list: Mme Straus. I wrote him that you were not in Paris and since, of course, you were irreplaceable it would be best to await your return. I don't know what he will answer. I can't tell you, Madame, how enchanted I was by your little card, so charmingly, so cleverly written. Anything coming from you today gives me a hundred times more pleasure than in the past. I am so constantly grateful to you for being convalescent. What a marvelous way of writing you have! While I was doing the thing that will be in the *Renaissance latine* for

June, I kept saying to myself all the time: Ah, if only I could write like Mme Straus! And I said it, I can assure you, with deep feeling, with an intense longing for all that lucidity, for the beautiful balance that makes your sentences so enchanting. But don't, I beg of you, write to me. I love you so much that the pleasure you give me is bound to be lessened by the painful thought that I may have tired you.

Please accept, Madame,
my respectful, my profound friendship.
Marcel Proust

67: TO GEORGES DE LAURIS

[1904 OR 1905]

Cher ami,

I am exhausted after two days not only without sleep but without going to bed, and I can't even make up my mind to lie down. Before the sandman closes my eyes completely, as children say, let me cast a last glance at the curious character I recently ran into and submit to you the outlines (very sketchy) of a portrait that I could draw of him if I weren't so tired.

Although it is possible at first glance to discern in his double heredity of foolishness the combination of a slightly silly Parisian and the heavy stupidity of an Eskimo, at a little distance he appears to be a distinguished young man, patiently cut out of seal skin to be shown at some exhibit of the products of the Urals, and on the whole not at all badly modeled. The eyes—if I may say so—have a sort of superficial depth, a specious luster, a squint that suggests independence, a myopia resembling concentration, all of which bear the same relation to thoughtful eyes as the figured stucco of motley staircases to Byzantine mosaics. But at a little distance, the optical illusion, blatant though it be, doesn't prevent a slight deception, and it would be easy to say about him, as one does about certain animals or the figures in a waxworks museum: only the power of speech is missing.

If the eyes are those of a thinker, the nose proclaims a *muscadin*. This nose stands erect, quarrelsome; rebels, gets out of bounds; it was the nose of a moujik, squat and large; now it wants to be the nose of a patrician. As a nose it has some distinction, some poise easily achieving haughtiness; yet, original and mischievous, this nose holds itself aloof from the rest of the face. (*Here a few lines that would be easier to say aloud.*) Besides, for the last few months or so, aware of its own importance and its existence as an entity, this nose has thought it could afford to treat itself to a large pimple that glows peacefully beside it like a castle on a hill or the purple in an escutcheon. And he has hitched it to the left, a little to one side at the tip *à la Russe*. This young man is articulated, he wags his head and shrugs his shoulders, wears his topcoat swagger and his jacket open. He says: "How-do-you-do, M. So-and-so." . . . "Good-bye, M. So-and-so," and if he isn't forced to talk at the same time, he can assume a manner both clever and forthright. However, the gentleman in seal skin must be kept at a slight distance, because he is like those dolls who, from far away, appear to be smiling, but close up make a face or leak sawdust. *Cher ami*, I have no strength left and can't finish this splendid sketch.

Your,
Marcel

Maurice Duplay, the author of many novels, the best known of which is *Nos médecins,* is the son of the well-known surgeon, Simon Duplay. A classmate of Dr. Adrien Proust's in medical school, Dr. Duplay occupied the chair of Surgery on the Medical Faculty while Dr. Proust was Professor of Hygiene. Although considerably younger than Marcel and Robert Proust, Maurice Duplay was from childhood a family friend.

68: TO MAURICE DUPLAY

[JUNE] 1905

Mon cher Maurice,

I wanted to write you about your book and some articles. Here is why I haven't done it. M. de Montesquiou is coming to read me an excerpt of his new book, and he asked me to invite seven persons whom he designated. I wrote to ask him to add several others, among them you, and it is only this instant that I have had his answer in which he denies my request *en bloc*, saying that it would change the character of the reading, etc., etc. Actually, I am delighted; for if I had invited you, I think that on the day itself I would have begged you not to come. I still don't dare see you in front of that one person. But at a reading! I think it would have been the most scandalous outburst of *fou rire* imaginable! Only I waited for his answer to tell you everything at the same time. His refusal is a great relief to me, and I dread the attack of *fou rire* less because you won't be there. Nevertheless I shall have it.

The book: I find it even more amazing than the first time. A thousand sentences reveal the great writer, the old men lying on their beds like tombs, the gold and amethyst windows, a hundred magnificent things. I am amused by your thesis, which is splendid and probably false, but that doesn't matter at all. Rousseau's, Flaubert's, Balzac's theses, among so many others, are doubtless false. And if absolute monarchy and clericalism are not the only refuge for France, does that make *Le Médecin de campagne* a less fine book, or Barbey d'Aurevilly's novels. . . . Now the question is, have you morally the right to say that? I believe so, *but I don't go as far* as that point of view. My feeling is even more favorable to you on this point. But I am too tired to express it. Curious, in any case, that we two, who are both rather good, should have regarded the regiment, you as a prison, I as a paradise. But what difference does that make? Because the sunset exists, it doesn't prevent the dawn's being beautiful, another moment of truth; a painter can't paint everything at the same time and, good

God, you have already painted enough as it is. In spite of the thesis, Lucien Daudet was going to have the book bought for the Empress Eugénie. At least he said so as he left. —As for the articles, I shouldn't want you to think that I am not helpful because I swear that isn't true. But look here: when I did *La Bible d'Amiens*, I thought my literary friends would take the utmost pains for me. The preface was dedicated to Léon Daudet, who writes for *Le Gaulois*, for *L'Echo*, etc.; I let it be hinted to him that an article would be acceptable to me. *Never a word, not an allusion*, no mention of my name in articles where he mentions everybody in the world. Don't say anything, but I still haven't swallowed it. I turned to Hermant and let him know that it would please me. In each of his articles, I kept seeing the subject evoke this phrase: *La Bible d'Amiens*. Not a word! What's more, he spoke at length of Ruskin in an article in *Gil Blas* and didn't breathe a word either of Marcel Proust or of *La Bible d'Amiens*. What do you say to that? It isn't that I didn't have excellent reviews. But *all* from people whom I didn't know, who fell from the blue, unforeseen, contrary to all expectations. After that what do you want me to say to you? Talk about it to the two I know best, Hermant, Daudet? They won't do anything. And it is more complicated because of the subject. Send your book to Brancovan without asking for a review, saying that you met him with me, and he will be touched. In the meantime I shall have someone tell him that your sending it is amazing, so it will seem very natural; perhaps he will do a review, although he is no longer really a literary critic. I shall tell all the artists I see that it is amazing; I shall try to have them read it; it is the only thing to be done. I will try to have someone speak to *L'Humanité* and to *Essais*. If by chance you have already had any promises in that direction, let me know, because it wouldn't be worth while my tiring myself to write *those letters*. You don't know how much you make me want to see your beautiful countryside, fluvial and laden with grapes.

Ton,
Marcel

69: TO MARIE NORDLINGER

SATURDAY, JUNE 24, 1905

Chère amie,

.... You arrived in Paris like the Messiah, but you left like a demon, and your passage through was like a fleeting dream. What an idea of yours not to have warned me that you were leaving so soon! I would have tried to see you instead of accepting the accomplished fact from an odious "Manchester, Victoria Park, etc." I also regretted very much not having seen and met M. Freer, from every point of view a very natural temptation for me, both out of curiosity and fellow-feeling. My respect and esteem for him have infinitely increased, as you can well imagine, when I tell you that the other day, facing death (and, alas, almost finding it) at my usual bedtime, tired out, I took a cab and went to look at the Whistlers. It's the sort of thing one would not do for a living person. But one does it for a dead man, probably in a misguided passion of conceit, which gives one the illusion that one's eyes perhaps, are among those with which this nomad beauty, on its way to Boston [actually Detroit], would like to have been beheld. But it would have been a hundred times better for me to have gone to Boston. It would have made me less ill. When I saw that all the most beautiful Whistlers belonged to M. Freer, even in my death agony I cried out Ruskin's words on the unknown man who sculptured and painted the delightful archivolt of St. Mark's: "I don't know who this man was; but, just seeing this archivolt in which he has put his joy and delicacy of perception and taste, I can proclaim to the heavens that he was an artist, a happy man, and a holy one." This I would say of M. Freer, excepting the "happy man," since I am not as convinced as Ruskin that taste brings happiness. But it can happen.

You know that at present the artistic élite of France are having a frightful reaction against Whistler. He is regarded as a man of exquisite taste who, because of it, was able to pass himself off as a great painter when he was nothing of the kind. Jacques Blanche, in the *Renaissance latine* (did you read my article in the same number which Beaunier praised so exaggeratedly in the *Figaro*?) has expressed the same opinion with more fairness and some warmth. It is not at all my own. If the man who painted the Venices in turquoise, the Amsterdams in topaz, the Brittanies in opal, if the portraitist of Miss Alexander, the painter of the room with the rose-strewn curtains, and, above all, the sails at night belonging to Messrs. Vanderbilt and Freer (why does one see only the sail and not the boat?) is not a great painter, one can only believe there never was one.

Chère amie, I am already a little tired of writing, and I have not yet said anything about practical matters. I waited for months for your return from America, then weeks, from Manchester, to send you my manuscript, there being much to ask you about *Lilies*. And now I am obliged to send it off. It can no longer appear at this time; it is too late; but I can always have it printed so that, if I am in a sanatorium this winter, it can appear without me, *vox silentiae*. I am sending it to the publisher, but I should like your criticisms, and if you will give them to me, I shall ask for the manuscript back for two days to make corrections. Would it be possible for me to send you to Manchester—Gladville and all the rest—my copy of *Sesame* in which I have made crosses and underlined wherever I was in doubt? I am not swearing that you will resolve my doubts, but, after all, it's possible. This never applies to more than one or two words at a time. Does it seem to you practical? But you mustn't lose my copy, which contains all my wisdom, and which after that, you will return to me.

If you find this complicated, would it annoy you if I turned to someone else for help with *Lilies*? You know that I have anglicizing friends, less effective than you, but who might perhaps tell me a little. If not, I shall send you the book. Tell me what you think. The note against which you protested was not the one in this volume, but the only note I put in the review in which the translation appeared (*Les Arts de la vie*), having held back the other notes for the book.

I do not regret not having been able to listen to you (it had already appeared), because *Les Arts de la vie* is read by all the really intelligent artists in France. Besnard and Carrière and Rodin often contribute to it and read it assiduously, and I should like your name to be very well known there. In the book, I shall be as temperate as you could wish; I shall say that you are completely lacking in talent and even in capacity, if you like, and that I shall encourage you to pursue another course. Is that what you would like? If your so charming Venetian aunt, the passionate and fastidious friend of art, of virtue, and comfort, so full of good will for the writer of this letter, is now living at mysterious Victoria Park, which I can never picture to myself, please give her my very respectful compliments, and believe, *chère amie*, in my sincere affection.

Marcel Proust

70: TO ROBERT DREYFUS

JULY 4, 1905

Cher ami,

. . . .

You are very nice about "La Lecture." It was the article I wanted to send you. Then when it appeared, it disgusted me so much that I no longer dared. I thought that you who know how to say so much in half a line would be exasperated by sentences that run to a hundred. Ah, how I should love to be able to write like Madame Straus! But I must perforce weave these long silken threads as I spin them, and if I shortened my sentences, the result would be little fragments, not whole sentences. So I continue like a silk-worm, and live in the same temperature, too, or rather like an earthworm ("in love with a star," that is to say, in contemplation of the unattainable perfection of Madame Straus's conciseness). Apropos of Madame Straus, the desire to see her again will, I think, force me to change my hours a little. After this reform, should it succeed, I shall write to you to try and at last arrange a meeting.

Affectionately *à toi,*
Marcel Proust

71: TO LOUISA DE MORNAND

FRIDAY [CIRCA JULY, 1905]

Ma chère Louisa,

Thank you with all my heart for your letter. I didn't see you again. But how can I blame anyone but myself. All I can hope is that because of my health I will be forgiven the odd behavior that force of circumstance imposes on me. But far from having to forgive you, all I can do is to beg your pardon. It is only natural when you telephone a lady at ten o'clock to ask her if she can come at midnight that she would hardly be there on the alert waiting for you. I shall have, my little Louisa, more serious defects in friendship with which to reproach you. But I have abandoned this kind of attitude and correspondence with everybody. People are what they are, and resentment on our parts doesn't empower us to change their feelings. I am glad to know you are at Trouville since that gives me the joy of picturing one of the people who pleases me most in the countryside which I love best. This merges two beautiful pictures into one. I don't know exactly where your Villa Saint-Jean is. I suppose it is on the elevation between Trouville and Hennequeville, but I don't know whether it looks out on the sea or the valley. If it looks out on the sea, the view must be through the foliage, which is so lovely, and in the evening you must have wonderful views of Le Havre. Those roads are fragrant with leafy branches, milk and sea salt, a blend more exquisite than any of the more refined "*mélanges*." If you give on the valley, I envy you the moonlight, which opalizes its depths into the semblance of a lake. I remember one night returning from Honfleur by those paths from above. At every step we stumbled into pools of moonlight, and the mist in the valley seemed like a vast pond. I recommend to you a very pretty walk called "les Creuniers" (I don't answer for the spelling). From there you will have a splendid view and a sense of peace, of the infinite into which you, yourself will dissolve. From there all your worries, all your sorrows will appear as small as the ridiculous little fellows you can see on the beach down below. Really one is right up in the sky. For a carriage ride I recommend an even more beautiful one: *Les Allées Marguerite*. But once you have got there, you must open the little fence (unless you do that you will have seen nothing), have the carriage drive in (if the owner isn't in residence), and walk for hours in this enchanted forest with the rhododendrons around you and the sea at your feet. Beaumont, too, is a splendid promenade, but on the other side. The entrance to Honfleur by the old route from Caen, between the great elms, is very beautiful. Also, there are thousands of other walks, which you must already know much better than I who have spent so little time there and so long ago. . . .

My little Louisa, your letters are always exquisite. But the last ones are even more wonderful. For some time a remarkable change has been taking place in you, one in which I think the different kind of life, the precocious maturity of your thoughts, also the theatre, reading—all have played their part. . . . To judge by my little Louisa's delightful letters and her great feeling for life, which I have always known she had, I shall not be surprised if one of these days a book by her is announced and she adds this literary ornament to her crown of art and beauty.

I go from bad to worse. It's three weeks since I have set foot outside my house. My beard is so long it doesn't even make me look dirty anymore. If you go to see the poor little church at Criqueboeuf, nestling under its ivy, speak to it tenderly for me, and also to an old pear tree, broken but unswerving, like an old servant who, with all the strength of her age-gnarled but still robust arms, buttresses a little house in the neighboring village, from whose only window the pretty faces of little girls frequently smile, girls who are perhaps no longer either little or pretty or even girls, for that was a long time ago.

All my tender thoughts,
Marcel

My respects to your mother, if she is with you.

72: TO ANTOINE BIBESCO

[PROBABLY SUMMER, 1905]

. . . . Nothing I am doing is real work, just documentation, translations, etc.

There are passages that are very difficult to understand; Nordlinger has helped me, so have you, and I am infinitely grateful.

It is enough to rouse my thirst for accomplishment without of course gratifying it in any way. From the moment I emerged from that long torpor and for the first time turned my eyes inward towards my thoughts, I have felt the complete void of my life, while hundreds of characters for a novel, thousands of ideas beg me to give them body, like those shades in the *Odyssey* who ask Ulysses to let them drink a drop of blood to bring them back to life and whom the hero disperses with his sword. I have awakened the sleeping bee and I feel far more keenly his cruel sting than his impotent wings. I had fettered my intelligence to my peace of mind. In undoing its chains I thought only of freeing a slave. Instead, I have given myself a master whom I lack the physical strength to satisfy and who will kill me if I don't resist him.

A toi,
Marcel

73: TO MARIE NORDLINGER

SUMMER, 1905

Chère amie,

. . . . My notes were madly illegible, and I see that there are several that you read wrong, or rather right, since you read them as they appeared to the eye, which in no way resembled what my absurd hand had meant to write.

I understand nothing about this prolonging of your exile, if one can so term a sojourn in one's mother country. As for me, my imprisonment, my isolation (which has nothing splendid about it, like that of the land of the Marys') go from bad to worse, without my even having, like the Pope, with whom I hold the record for voluntary imprisonment, the gardens of the Vatican to stroll in, which, however, would doubtless be very bad for me.

This evening, came an unexpected visitor whom I received in spite of my fatigue—since for once my breathing was not too bad; it was Reynaldo, back from an astonishing lot of beaches where he lived the life of a vaudeville-writer rather than a musician, if I believe in his accounts of how, thinking that he was going to M. X.'s by the front door, he found himself entering M. Z.'s by the service stairs, which didn't matter, for he knew M. Z., too, etc. He is back, very much taken with the *Iliad*, which, by a coincidence which is not at all odd, I was reading at the same time. I say "not at all odd," because it was the reading of Lemaitre's *Contes* and the desire to reply to it which made me take up this wonderful old book again, while Reynaldo was prompted to read it by the view of the beaches which he *felt* were Homeric. He confessed to me his sadness over knowing that this *Iliad* was an anonymous and collective work, and not the work of the "old Homer." I consoled him when I informed him that this idea of a collective work was no longer credited in any way by scholars and that, besides, it never had been by people with good sense. He was still in doubt; but I gave him a *Revue de Paris* where an excellent article by M. Bréal formally proved to him that Homer existed like Massenet, that the *Iliad* was composed like *Sesame and Lilies*, and even written and not recited. All this seemed to revive him. But while fetching this liberating review, not two steps away, I caught a cold which for weeks has been annihilating me, the result is that my eyes are too bad for me to write you about what affects literary history and even just plain history to a lesser degree than the authorship of the *Iliad*, the opinion of Bréal and the opinion of Reynaldo. What particularly struck Reynaldo in the *Iliad* was the politeness of the heroes. Since they spend their time calling each other, "You dog," and bashing in each other's heads, I do not agree with him. But it is true that even when they insult each other, they say, "Know, O magnanimous Hector, that I shall kill you like the dog that you are. . . . Vile soul, a match for the bitches of Hell, irreproachable Helen!"

Chère amie, I wanted to blow all the way to Gladville a little of the air of Courcelles and Alfred de Vigny. But really I am too exhausted for this kind of undertaking and too lacking in "breath" this evening.

Thank you again and always yours,

Marcel Proust

74: TO LOUISA DE MORNAND

[1904 or 1905]

Ma chère Louisa,

What a beautiful, what a delightful letter you wrote me. How dearly I shall cherish it. If you knew how I reread it, how I admire it, how it touches me. Withdrawn for a moment from the restlessness, the surge, the froth of Paris, you have looked into the depths of your heart and there you have begun to see, to discern pictures of the past. It is to that I owe your letter, and it is that which moves me so much. I am nothing to you except that I was identified with some sweet and sad moments in your life. I am like the man who held the horse or was next to the carriage in some great historic event. His name isn't even known. But in all the "views" of the event, he inevitably appears because chance or Destiny placed him there. In the same way our memory often shows us "views" or historic events in our own lives, not always easy to discern, a little like the ones we try to distinguish through the tip of a penholder made of sea shells, a souvenir of a seaside resort. But in these views where our memory brings back happy or tragic days, which still control our destiny, we begin to see inevitably the subordinate character, the supernumerary who happened to be there, the Marcel Proust whose memory is tinged for us by the color of the picture as a whole. This supernumerary asks for nothing more and rejoices silently in these windfalls of friendship, which, according to the Gospel, cannot be taken from him. As for the matter that preoccupies me, my little Louisa, and that hinges less on this question: "Could I see Louisa one of these days?" than on this other one: "Could I soon after the holidays see Louisa regularly and often?"—it is not at all isolated in my mind. It is only an aspect, more particularly preoccupying to me, it is true, of that other question, which it is time, finally, to resolve: "Shall I continue until my death to lead a life, which even seriously sick people don't lead, deprived of everything, of the light of day, of fresh air, of all work, of all pleasure, in a word, of life itself? Or am I going to find a way to change?" I can no longer put off the answer, for it is not only my youth, it is my life that is going by. . . . And from this point of view, I should be inclined not to postpone the solution, which would enable me to see you often and for a long time, even by running the risk of seeing you now, in the state I am in, when, as a man, it would annoy me to have you see me disguised in a long unkempt beard. But shall I have the courage not to say good-bye to you? It would be more sensible to write you an immediate *au revoir* in the hope of frequent and regular future meetings. But, as always, I shall probably do the least sensible thing.

Yours affectionately,
Marcel

75: TO MADAME STRAUS

[BEFORE SEPTEMBER 26, 1905]

Madame,

A day or two after receiving your letter (your first letter)—the one of all those I ever received from you that gave me the most exquisite joy—moved to tears that you should think enough of me to talk to [Doctor] Widmer about me, that you should tell me that I could visit you in Trouville, etc., two days after that letter, full of the optimism, which it poured into me, I left for Evian and Mother. I was happy! *Two hours* after our arrival, Mother was seized with vomiting and dizziness, and fell gravely ill. I had to bring her back to Paris. But the journey back finished her, and she is now in a terrible state. Nothing else could have kept me from thanking you for your letter and the charming postscript that you added several days later. But I am so unhappy that I am hardly able to write. Mother, who loves us so much, does not understand how cruel it is of her not to want to take care of herself. As a result, she left for Evian with an uremic condition, which no one knew about, and which we discovered only after we returned to Paris, because even at Evian it was impossible to get her to have an analysis made. Alone with her at Evian, at the height of her attacks of vertigo, I was distressed to see her go down to the lounge even in the morning, no matter what I could say, when she needed two people for support to keep her from falling. How weak her condition continues to be you can imagine just from the fact that she has taken nothing to eat in two weeks, has to be helped out of bed, to be washed and dressed every day, which is hateful to her. And it is impossible to make her take any medicine or nourishment. I need hardly tell you of my distress, and if I had the strength to write you more, you would see that it is even greater than you can imagine and that nothing more hideous could have happened. Still, there is a slight improvement since yesterday, very little, but the doctor (to the extent that Mother consents to see him) assures us that if Mother succeeds in overcoming this crisis, she will regain her former health. But I find it hard to believe. And I am sure she is convinced of the opposite and that mentally she suffers horribly. I had always hoped she would die before I did so that she should not have the grief of losing me. But I don't know whether the anxiety she must feel at the thought of having perhaps to leave us, to abandon me, so little equipped to cope with life, alone; that she may perhaps live handicapped, frail: whether all that doesn't torture her even more. Of all the sad things I ever imagined when I tried to anticipate future sorrows, I had never feared this. Forgive me, Madame, for giving you all these details, but you are so kindhearted it seemed to me more affectionate to write in this way. If one of these days there is, as I think there may be, the slightest improvement, I shall write you. But I beg of you don't write me, I know that you will be full of pity for me, and it would be useless and would only grieve me to have you tire yourself by writing to me.

Most respectfully yours,

Marcel Proust

76: TO ROBERT DE MONTESQUIOU

[BEFORE SEPTEMBER 26, 1905]

Cher Monsieur,

I cannot tell you how moved I am by your kindness, nor the depth of my gratitude. I beg of you not to send for any more news, thereby inconveniencing someone who doubtless has to come from Neuilly. Whatever hope the little day-to-day improvement gives us (and I can't tell you how this word "hope" thrills me; it seems to restore the possibility of my continuing to live), from the depths where we were, the ascent returning will nevertheless be so gradual that each day's progress, if God is willing for it to continue, will be imperceptible. Since you are kind enough to be concerned about my anxiety, I shall write you if there is any decisive improvement to deliver us from our torment. But don't take the trouble to send [for news]. I can't tell you what I have suffered. You don't know Mother. Her extraordinary modesty hides from almost everyone her extraordinary distinction. And in front of people she admires—and you she admires infinitely—this excessive modesty becomes a complete disguise, with the result that, except for a few friends, I am almost the only one who knows how incomparable she is. As for the uninterrupted sacrifice that her life has been, it is the most moving thing in the world. She knows I am so incapable of living without her; so vulnerable in every way of life, that if, as I fear and dread, she has the feeling that perhaps she is going to leave me forever, she must have known cruel and anxious moments, which are a most horrible torture for me to picture. I wish we could tell her of our hopes and our reassurance and share them with her. Perhaps she wouldn't believe us. In any case, her absolute calm prevents our knowing what she thinks and how much she suffers. Permit me to thank you again with all my heart for your exquisite kindness, for which I am infinitely grateful.

Your respectful admirer and friend,
Marcel Proust

77: TO THE COMTESSE DE NOAILLES

[27 SEPTEMBER, 1905]

Thank you, Madame. My poor mother admired no one as much as you; she was infinitely grateful to you for your kindness to me. She died at fifty-six, looking no more than thirty, since her illness made her so thin, especially now when death restores to her the youth of those days before all her sorrows had come to her; she hadn't a white hair. She takes my life with her, as Father took hers with him. She wanted to stay alive after him for us, but she couldn't. Since when she married Father, she did not change from the Jewish religion, because in it she saw a refinement of respect for her parents, there will be no church service, only at the house at high noon tomorrow, Thursday, and at the cemetery; but don't tire yourself, don't come, or, in any case, only to the house. But if you do, come at noon; since there won't be any prayers at the house we shall leave right away. Today I still have her, dead, still receiving my caresses. After that I shall never have her again.

Your respectful friend,
Marcel Proust

I wanted to catch the person you sent, but she had gone, because I had left word that I was not to be disturbed for anyone.

78: TO LOUISA DE MORNAND

[END OF SEPTEMBER OR EARLY OCTOBER, 1905]

Ma petite Louisa,

Having been in bed for several days, I can't write well, but I want to scrawl these few illegible words, the first I have written, the only ones I shall write for some time, to tell you that never in my life shall I forget that you wanted to pay homage to Mother's memory by sending that huge wreath of wonderful flowers. I shall always be infinitely grateful to you. . . . You can imagine my sorrow, you who have seen me, always all ears and heart, on watch at Mother's door, where I used any pretext to return and kiss her again and again, where now I have seen her lying dead, but happy even so to have been able to kiss her again. Now the room is empty, and my heart and life itself. I was embarrassed by the extravagance of your royal gift of magnificent flowers, but I can't stop thinking of it with infinite gratitude, which I beg of you to find in this most affectionate and heartfelt expression.

Marcel Proust

79: TO ROBERT DE MONTESQUIOU

[END OF SEPTEMBER OR EARLY OCTOBER, 1905]

Cher Monsieur,

I don't know how I could ever thank you for so many kindnesses. When I am not less unhappy (for that I shall never be, but less acutely sick than now), as soon as I can talk and get out of bed, I shall come to see you. Your compassion for my distress is a new and magnificent interpretation of "for the petal of the lily is opening outwards" in sympathy. And it is in these particular moments that more than anyone else you are "more splendid than Solomon in all his glory." For "the greatest of these is charity." My life, from this time on, has lost its only purpose, its only sweetness, its only love, its only consolation. I have lost her whose incessant vigilance brought me in peace, in gentleness, the only honey of my life, which at intervals I still savor with horror in the silence with which she was able to surround my sleep all day and which still, inert, in the habit that she formed in the servants, survives her zeal, now ended. I have been overwhelmed by so much sorrow; I have lost her, I have seen her suffer, I can even believe that she knew she was leaving me and couldn't make suggestions to me, which it may have been distressing to her to pass over in silence; I have the feeling that because of my poor health I was the sorrow and the burden of her life. The very excess of my need for seeing her again prevents my visualizing anything when I think of her, except in the last two days two particularly painful visions of her illness. I can no longer sleep, and if by chance I do fall asleep, sleep itself, less frugal of sorrow than the awakened intelligence, crushes me with excruciating thoughts, which at least when I am awake, my reason tries to temper and to contradict when they become unbearable. One thing has been spared me. I didn't have the anguish of dying before she did and of knowing the horror my death would have been for her. But leaving me forever, knowing how incapable I am of contending with life, must have been a great torment for her, too. She must have understood the wisdom of parents who, before dying, kill their little children. As the nurse who took care of her said—to Mother I was always four years old. Forgive me, *cher* Monsieur; Hesiod has said: unhappy people are wordy and complacent in talking of their troubles. But there is among all sorrows a kind of fraternity. "That way, the poor man is the brother of Jesus Christ." I shall never forget your gentleness, your kindness, your magnanimous compassion.

Your profoundly grateful
Marcel Proust

80: TO MADAME STRAUS

NOVEMBER 9, 1905

You will understand, Madame, that if I haven't written you it is because my accumulated and constant thoughts of you would overflow twenty letters, a hundred letters, into which I should like to put all my affection, all my gratitude, all my sorrow, which I lack the strength to do; I am exhausted. If I don't write it is chiefly because my first visit must be to you, and each day I hope to be able to go out again the next day, and then I can't. Going out, even as sick as I am, would mean nothing but *coming back*, when my first word was always, "Is Madame here?" And before there was time for an answer, I would catch sight of Mother, who didn't dare come near me for fear of making me talk if I were too depressed, and who was waiting anxiously to see whether I had come back without too bad an attack.

Alas, it was this worry added to her sorrows that now consumes me with remorse and prevents my finding a second of comfort in the memory of our tender times together, which I can't even call incessant, for in that memory alone do I breathe and think; it alone surrounds me. When the anxiety that is intermingled becomes too strong and drives me mad, I try to control it, to lessen it. But in the last few days I have again been sleeping a little. But then in sleep the intelligence is no longer there to dispel, even for a moment, a too agonizing memory, to drug it with sorrow, to blend it with gentleness; then I am defenseless against the most dreadful sensations. However at times it seems as though I were accustomed to this unhappiness, that I shall regain my taste for life; then I reproach myself and at that very moment a new sorrow casts me down. For one does not have just one grief; regret takes on a new shape at every instant, suggested by some impression identical with one out of the past; it is a new misery, an unknown woe, as excruciating as the first time it occurred.

I think perpetually of your health; I should so like to know whether your stay in Switzerland merely repaired the damage done at Salsomaggiore or improved a little on the condition you were in when you left for Salsomaggiore; what I should like to know is whether you are better than when you came back from your first visit to Territet. I am afraid that these cold spells, these fogs, and, most of all, these incessant changes in weather are very bad for your health. I wanted so much to talk to you about Dubois. Perhaps he could do something for you. But he is very arbitrary, very little the doctor. I have not written to Jacques or to M. Straus, but I think they understand. I am grief-stricken, indeed (for I am like Mother, who, even after the misfortune that destroyed her, continued to have sympathy for every kind of event in life—even happy ones—and even more for sorrows), over the death of that poor Robert Fould. His parents must be in a state of despair that it hurts me to picture.

Your respectful friend,
Marcel Proust

Forgive me if I don't write you from time to time; I shall have hundreds of letters to write. And, sick as I am, it isn't easy!

81: TO MADAME STRAUS

[CIRCA DECEMBER 1905]

Madame,

How can I ever thank you for what you have done. I can't tell you how infinitely grateful I am. I *think* that I shall let him come. But the reason for my doubt and for what I told you is this (which I am telling you in confidence): I was supposed today to go into Déjerine's nursing home (for three months), and I wanted, in a supreme effort, wishing particularly to do what Mother would have liked, since I have no other aim here below, to ask M. Sollier whether he wouldn't much more simply, without isolation, without making me stay with him, doing nothing but changing my hours, my meals, etc., make me a little more capable of leading a normal life. But I know very well at bottom that all his talent would not do what a radical cure would, and I cannot do that for Déjerine at Sollier's. Don't tell this to Sollier, it is unnecessary. If I decide to wait (but the room in rue Blomet is waiting for me, and I was waiting to give it up until I found out whether Sollier would look after me at home without isolation), there will be no need of my talking about that (Déjerine) to Sollier; I have too good reasons, unhappy as I am, to fear isolation and being away from home. I have told you all this so that you will be *convinced* that I would not have permitted myself to ask you abruptly this way, on the very day itself (I am not so ill mannered) if it had only been a case of nerves. There was this serious reason. So if I decide in any case to give up Déjerine, or to have him wait further, I don't have to telephone to Sollier, do I, and I shall expect him at half-past six tomorrow.

Thank you with all my heart, and I wanted to tell you all this to show you that my feeling for you would have recoiled against such abrupt behavior without a major reason.

Most respectfully yours,
Marcel Proust

If by chance you know in general whether Sollier intends treating me at home without isolation, or if you know the contrary, it would be helpful if you would tell me. If you don't know, don't take the trouble to write.

82: TO LOUISA DE MORNAND

[CIRCA DECEMBER 6, 1905]

Ma petite Louisa,

Your letter comes to me in a nursing home, which I have just entered, and where I shall not be able to write. Out of affection for you I am making an absolute exception by writing you this little note. I should liked to have seen you (alas, it is physically impossible) to tell you (although I don't know exactly what, and it is purely an impression) that you must take yourself in hand a little; you know I have always given you good advice at times that I believed important. In a month and a half I shall be out of here, perhaps sooner. Have courage enough between now and then to be the way I advise you to be. I think it is very useful at this time. Knowing no more about it than I do, I can't tell you anything more. You know that I should approve of your giving in to temptation if it involved a real decision, but since this is not the case (at least, I don't know whether it is, not having seen you), I sense symptoms that you should check. Don't make a mess of one relationship that is happy until you have another. And there will always be time enough to talk about it again in a month and a half. Try to make as good use of it for your happiness as I shall for my health.

Always my tender admiration, affection and devotion,

Yours affectionately,
Marcel

83: TO THE COMTESSE DE NOAILLES

[1905 OR 1906]

How moved I always am when I catch sight of the disciplined tumult of your handwriting, those magnificent spirals of an infinite and rhythmic sea from the bosom of which, sparkling like Aphrodite, your thought emerges as divine and as beautiful. But when, by some excess of kindness or refinement of graciousness like your letter this morning, it overwhelms me by rousing in me a sense of gratitude I feel I could never prove to you, then this joy is touched with sorrow, mingling "the foam of pleasure with tears of anguish." When Father, who was as active as I am lazy, and who got up in the morning, brought up the mail, he would say to me, knowing my joy, "A letter from Mme de Noailles," and Mother would scold him and say, "But don't take away his pleasure by telling him ahead of time." And I assure you that it was a very touching little comedy (not for you, perhaps, but for me, particularly now), the air of sovereign indifference that mother assumed when she brought up a letter from you, with the air of saying: these are nothing but insignificant papers—so that my joy might be complete. —No, I shall come, but have you heard that I am sick, a rheumatism in my back, which hurts only when I make certain motions, but atrociously then, and gives me a fever. I don't think I can go out before two or three days at the earliest, and my first expeditions will be rather cautious and not perhaps a visit like going to your house. Since I never have rheumatism, I don't want to start.

I think that Constantin will not delay his return, and since he has behaved not at all nicely to me, I shall write him some harsh things so as not to see him until afterwards, either here or at your house, because in conversation one sometimes, if one gets angry, says more than one intends. True, I already feel better about it. One shouldn't get angry at people about things having to do with a review. And, besides, I am in no way angry at him. But his conduct towards me on three successive occasions in one month has been so extravagant that, since it is my habit when someone is nice to me to dissolve in thanks, in affection, and tears, it is in the same way necessary, when someone is too much the opposite, also to say so, if only so as not to deprive the nice, kind people of the whole value of the gratitude I show them (unnecessary to tell you that you are not among the nice people to whom I show gratitude! You are the sublime goddess who will be no less blessed the day that she turns her favors away from me). So don't be angry at me if you find that I have written Constantin a rather severe letter. You may be certain that loving him and esteeming him highly, I was *obliged* to do it to get the affair over, and that this was necessitated, besides, because I wrote him an almost insanely nice one three weeks ago, the second day before I discovered the folly of his conduct! As for Antoine [the Prince Bibesco], my difficulties with him are serious because they are sentimental troubles. But those will not be terminated or sanctioned through letters. "Only silence is great." The

Renaissance latine (I am speaking of the *Renaissance latine* as far as its administration goes, not as the sanctuary, forever rendered illustrious through the perpetual adoration of *La Nouvelle espérance* and *L'Exhortation*) is not worth the effort of *silence*.

Your respectful friend, your adoring admirer,
Marcel Proust

84: TO MADAME CATUSSE

1906

Chère Madame,

. . . .

I regret so much that I am not able to go out, that I am afraid of the dust. I should so love to wander with you, guided by that Beatrice of archaism, through what Balzac would call "the infernal circles of curio collectors," about which I haven't *the shadow of a notion*, and wouldn't want to have too much because it is bad for a writer (which, I no longer am, however); but I should love to go *bibelot* hunting with you, and even without you, to teach myself to collect. At the moment I dream of someday buying, on the one hand, a Venetian primitive, on the other, a Tuscan, Sienese, or Roman primitive, if I could discover an inexpensive one. I do not call primitive those painters, who are not the least bit in the world primitive, but labelled so by people in society—Botticelli, Mantegna, etc., whom I nevertheless adore. More modestly, I think of much more ancient painters, Vivarini, for example, one of those works, if one owned it, would be the motif of endless reveries; or of some Sienese or Roman painter, one of those to whom Ruskin imperturbably attributes the works of Taddeo Gaddi or Simone Memmi in the Spanish Chapel, when all that is definitely known about them is that they are by neither one nor the other. If I were rich, I should not try to buy masterpieces that I should leave to museums, but those pictures that retain the odor of a city or the dampness of a church, and that, like their curios, hold their illusion as much by association with an idea, as in themselves.

Your respectful friend,
Marcel Proust

85: TO MADAME STRAUS

SUNDAY
[PROBABLY MAY, 1906]

Chère Madame Straus,

The thought of you keeps me such delightful company each day that to receive a letter from a person who never leaves my mind seems to me at the same time entirely natural and almost miraculous. I experienced this when I went to Venice; when my dream became my "address," my *villégiature*, it seemed to me unbelievable—and so simple! Most of all it seemed to me charming. This charm, at once easy and mysterious, your letter gave me. Yet isn't it a little your own charm, peculiar to you? Wouldn't the device, "Mystery and Simplicity," express it rather well. And the mystery increasing with the simplicity. Often I read

(I don't dare say, "sometimes I write") things that it seems to me you would like. I put them aside. And that makes quantities of books which I have to bring you and objects, too. And other things besides. In the end I shall get around to it! Only in order to get up for an hour, something other people do every day, I need at least a month of preliminary exercises; to do more special things I need such a long time! If I can only not die until I have fulfilled the chief desires of my mind and heart! For I have no others! Not any longer. I am very sad at your being ill. I hope Grasse has done you no harm! What is so frequently disgusting about our attempts to be reasonable is that unreasonable inertia makes almost all the infallible calamities avoidable. For weak constitutions, every attempt to get well is such a hazardous undertaking that one is like the people who feel obliged to work and to launch out into business to earn money and who end by losing it in every venture and finding that what is still least expensive is simply to spend their money. I hadn't been up since I went to see you, but this evening I did get up at eleven o'clock and went to the *Figaro*. They were congratulating themselves on the outcome of the elections, which disturbed me acutely, given the people who were there, and the fact that those who formerly thought as we do were the worst. However it is probably not very important and only a few of the returns were known. I hoped very much that Reinach was elected. He is the best deputy in the Chamber, yet that is no reason for his election. How much I shall have to say to you about people, about books! For me there is something missing when I read the paper if we don't all three discuss it together. Which is to say that there is always something missing! And that irony of Cabourg, now that I can no longer get there, renders even more cruel, perhaps, the useless and precious fact of our having been neighbors. You know (I have told you often enough!) that I am finishing a long work. I think it reasonable, as long as it isn't finished, not to risk being unable to finish it. But once the last page is finished, I shall select the folly closest to my heart and carry it out. And that will probably be to try to see you constantly *jusqu'à la rupture de la corde*. And since that last page, at my invalid's pace, can be put off for several months, perhaps even longer, I shall go hither and yon to see you a little late and trying not to get too tired. I do everything Yvel recommends in the *Figaro* and nothing succeeds. Rubber stocks, oil stocks, and the rest always wait until the day after I buy them for the bottom to drop out of the market!

Adieu, Madame. Your respectful and grateful friend.

Marcel Proust

86: TO MADAME CATUSSE

MAY, 1906

Chère Madame,

. . . . It is very ironical about poor Ruskin who did not, in fact, write his masterpiece on Florence. I think that if one used only these "Mornings" as guides to Florence, one would see nothing there is to see and would wear oneself out climbing to the top of a ladder at seven o'clock in the morning to distinguish some entirely repainted Giottos not worth the trouble. No matter, if I ever go to Florence it will be "to place my footsteps in his." Venice is too much a graveyard of happiness for me to feel strong enough yet to go back there. I want to very much, but when I think about it as a distinct project, too many pangs are aroused and stand in the way of its immediate realization. If after you have come back, I am a little better, for right now the hours I keep are deplorable, and if you are kind enough to come and see me once more, I will show you a copy of *Mornings in Florence*, an admirably illustrated edition, which I have just received and in which I should so enjoy seeing you re-experience your impressions and having you tell them to me. I haven't seen Lucien Daudet since I saw you, not being in a condition to receive anyone. So I don't know how he took "the blow" of the elections, which I myself take very badly. . . .

Your respectful friend,
Marcel Proust

87: TO MADAME STRAUS

[CIRCA MAY, 1906]

Madame,

If my response to Ruskin was "of the same quality" (which your friendship makes you believe, but which I can't), your response to me is of an infinitely rare quality, so delightful and so simple. What you say about the wit, the gaiety of people who are sad, is exquisite, profound. You are a marvelous person, and your talent goes hand in glove with your kindness. It makes it more precious. But it also gives it a supreme distinction, a moral charm and refinement. Madame (this has nothing to do with my thanks, which I should have sent anyway, even if I had nothing to ask you), do you know what Doctor Sollier charges for his visits. I owe him for two that he paid me, one the day I entered the sanitarium, the other the day after my return. They were not included in my bill. And when I objected to Mme Sollier, she answered that it had nothing to do with her, that I could send what I liked. But since I have asked several times, I shouldn't want you to ask Sollier. That would worry me. Just if you know how much he charges for his visits in general, I should like you to tell me. He himself is exquisite, but I am convinced that he pays no attention to the bills for the sanitarium, because Mme Sollier's is terrific. (Which, naturally, I did not tell him!) He came to see me the other day, but I was asleep. He did, however, leave me an extremely witty note. Since then he has written to give me the names of the superintendents, for which I asked him. Unfortunately it was impossible for me to read them. I have been told some very amusing stories, but so improper that it is impossible for me to write them. This one, on the other hand, is very proper, but perhaps you know it; it comes from Degas, reported by Forain (not to me!), and is about Gustave Moreau: "He taught us that the Gods wore watch chains." I don't, however, find it at all wonderful, and I find that it smacks rather too much of Forain to come from Degas.

Reynaldo was touched to an extraordinary degree that you took the trouble to come to Mme Lemaire's to that gathering where one was not supposed to know why one had come, and above all at your appearing enraptured at being given a score of Mozart, which he had been wondering how in the world to get rid of! Which, however, he would certainly not do. He repeated some delightful things you said about me, and I am even more grateful to you for not having said them to me.

Your respectful and grateful admirer,
Marcel Proust

88: TO MADAME STRAUS

JUNE, 1906

Madame,

. . . .

Although I think that Dreyfus is idiotic and indiscreet to persist in a rehabilitation that the whole world (the Dreyfusard world, the other will never be converted) has sanctioned, I, who had somewhat forgotten all this, find it rather moving to read about again and to think that this could have happened a few years ago in France and not among the Apaches. The contrast that exists on the one hand between the culture, the intellectual distinction, and even the glitter of the uniforms of these people and their moral infamy on the other, is frightening. But I think that only two or three of them were infamous and the rest were sincere.

Your respectful friend,
Marcel Proust

89: TO ROBERT DREYFUS

[CIRCA JUNE 10, 1906]

Mon cher Robert,

How I should like not only to have you believe what you tell me (for I am sure you do), but to believe it myself! I cannot. It would make me happy, because since Mother's death that word no longer has any meaning for me (and it did have before. People pitied me mistakenly, thinking that I led a very sad life when actually it was very sweet). But at least the torture I feel at having caused her so much worry over my health would be blended with the feeling of having done something good, which would have pleased her. Besides, she knew this preface, for I need hardly tell you all this was done before her death, and it was about to appear when suddenly she left me.

Your letter is enchanting, and I promise you I am not saying this to reciprocate. If each of us thought as well of himself as we do of each other, how much more useful and pleasant it would be—for even the most formal praise from people whose unquestioned competence we recognize and respect, cannot take the place of this direct knowledge, this sort of awareness of one's own talent, which certain of our friends have the luck to possess to such a high degree, along with the talent itself. What you say about my preface delights me and, indeed, there are ideas in it which seem to me quite deeply fathomed, although in general I feel that I write much less well than at the time of *Les Plaisirs et les Jours*. As for the notes, they are pure chit-chat and I would much rather work seriously. But a minimum of physical well-being is necessary not only for working but even for taking in impressions of the outside world. And when the discomfort does stop for a short time, and impressions do come through, then one enjoys them like the pleasures of a convalescent, without the strength, which is incessantly at work repairing the ravages of illness, being shifted and made available for the incarnation of what one has felt. . . .

Tout à toi,
Marcel

I am very happy over what you tell me about Beaunier's liking my book. He has been so incredibly nice to me that I am disturbed at not knowing how to thank him. If you ever think of anything I could do to give him pleasure, it would make me very happy. If by chance you sometimes see Daniel Halévy, tell him that recently in the *Chronique des arts*, apropos of a translation of *Stones of Venice*, I made an allusion to his article on Venice in *La Revue de Paris*.

90: TO ROBERT DREYFUS

[CIRCA JUNE 20, 1906]

Mon cher Robert,

. . . . I can't tell you how happy and unhappy I was about Beaunier's article on *Sesame*. Knowing Calmette's charming intentions in regard to me—and I have never been able to understand why, with such admirable forethought, considering he sees me only once every two years and knowing me so little, he has been so kind to me—I had asked him if he did have me mentioned, not to ask Beaunier to do it. He paid no attention to me and it was Beaunier who did the "paragraph." I was disturbed by it, but I had no further fears. For how could I surmise that this was merely a beginning and that Calmette also wished to have an article about me. So much fuss about a translation. I am afraid that Beaunier will take a dislike to me, and I like him so much that it would cause me great distress. I shall never again have a line of mine published (which is, alas, probable from every point of view) without first asking him for a written pledge that he won't discuss it. Besides it is frightening and shows how little interest there is in literature as a whole to see how incapable our most intelligent contemporaries, to say nothing of the others, are of *reading* even so much as a newspaper. You know that I see nobody, but during the last few days I have been able to receive one or two of my most faithful friends. Not one of them (they are all subscribers to the *Figaro*) had read the article by Beaunier!

Reynaldo, whose eager and inquisitive mind you know, came to see me the day after the article was published and said: "Did you read the *Figaro* yesterday?" I modestly answered, "Yes." —"So you read Varennes' article?" After he had talked to me about Varennes' article and when I saw that he wasn't going to talk about anything else, I said: "How did you like Beaunier's article?" "I didn't see it!"

Albuféra (whose whole family subscribe to the *Figaro* and who takes it himself) wrote to tell me how strange it was, since I knew Calmette, that the *Figaro* hadn't mentioned *Sesame*. And when I said that on the contrary they had talked about it too much, he said: "*You must be mistaken*, because my wife reads the *Figaro* every morning from one end to the other and there was absolutely nothing about you in it."

Finally, I mentioned it in a letter to Lucien Daudet, who replied: "I saw neither the paragraph nor the article you mentioned (he reads the *Figaro* every morning), could you send them to me?" —I may read very little, but I don't read like that. I assure you (I *swear* to you) that the reason this strikes me so forcibly isn't because it has to do with me; on the contrary, just because it does concern me I shall cut short my examples here and omit the most striking one of all. . . .

The thing that made me happy about Beaunier's article (while always giving the word *heureux* its sad connotation, with its counterpart of heartsick anguish that I mentioned the other day: but one really must resort to simple words ever to get to the end of a sentence) and about last year's article, too, after this preface appeared in the *Revue*, was that it seemed to have been done in collaboration with the friends I most valued. Last year I received a remarkable letter from a woman whose genius I think you acknowledge to be as great as I do, Madame de Noailles, who said exquisite things about this preface and: "We read yesterday in Beaunier, etc." The next day Beaunier's article arrived and I still seemed to breathe in "the perfumed memory" of the flowery praise of the day before. In the same way, this year, you write to me: "I read yesterday in Beaunier, etc." And the next day and the day after that, a whole efflorescence of praise from Beaunier, which made your exquisite and graceful lines serve no less as harbinger. But what people say about it is not what I like best about my preface. Enough talk about me, however. I want you to know that this letter was chiefly to talk about you, of my grateful friendship for you.

I picture you to myself in the Bois recently, at a tea where there was a woman who admires you and who is, indeed, so beautiful. Naturally I couldn't go, but I am touched to think that people still think of me. It tires me to write, so this letter will have to do for a long time.

Tout à toi,
Marcel Proust

91: TO ROBERT DREYFUS

END OF JUNE, 1906

Cher Robert,

. . . . Yesterday, while writing to you, I thought of X—— (I really don't know why!). And when it came to addressing the letter, I automatically wrote on the envelope: Monsieur X——. Fortunately I noticed it in time! Think of all that might have happened, and how out of the generalizations induced by his rancor, all the works of Ruskin, not to mention the *Entente cordiale*, would have been condemned in all the conversations in which, having run into Barthou or Briand, he gives them advice, particularly emphasizing that if in their own interest, of course, they want, at small cost, to make a name for themselves in history, they should take him as minister, as anything at all! I think as you do about him, perhaps a little more kindly. I admire his marvelous intelligence, a property of his profession (his own special profession!), which has long since attained perfection, segments of true greatness, including the impenetrable crust of naïveté, which has preserved in him a spontaneous and delightful freshness of spirit. But in spite of all that, one can never listen to him without smiling. When there are a number of people, this serves as a pretense to signs of intelligence. In talking to him about almost anyone, one could say what Caumartin said when, without M. de Clermont-Tonnerre's having the slightest suspicion of it, he ironically received him into the Academy, where his inordinate pride made him a laughingstock: "When you are with the King, no one can help noticing the delighted expression on his face. As long as you are there, he has a kind of gaiety, etc." M. de Clermont-Tonnerre swallowed the whole story with a simper and only the meanness of the Archbishop of Paris several years later (all this is a little vague in my memory) disabused him and let him know that he had been made a fool of.

I know a quite different example, close to us, of an even more excessive pride, which induces laughter, but it is done deliberately. Or, at least, perhaps just as Baron comes by his comic voice naturally and, having become aware of it, puts it to specific use, so M. de Montesquiou (it is he) makes a work of art of his own absurdity and has stylized it marvelously. Ah, X— is not one to stylize his: he isn't even aware of it! I don't know under what convention, perhaps the one observed in the theatre, he doesn't hear the laughs around him, or so indistinctly that like Harpagon in Plautus when he hears the laughter in the audience (coming from people who were unreal to him) asks: "What are all those people laughing about?" But personally he doesn't make me laugh because I understand so well everything he says, and I find him so sympathetic. But his being considered a priceless joke is understandable. I remember in the beginning I didn't know Montesquiou knew that he was ridiculous at his first "reading" when everyone expected him to be dressed in pink or green, and he appeared as severely dressed as a notary's clerk and said to me: "I wanted to arouse this feeling: to have them expect the ridiculous, and to be disappointed." It is a kind of disappointment which X— rarely provides. For all that, he is charming, exquisite, and admirable.

Tout à toi,
Marcel Proust

92: TO THE COMTESSE DE NOAILLES

[CIRCA MID-JULY, 1906]

Madame,

Post-scriptum to my letter to tell you that I think Barrès was very courageous and noble the other day at the Chamber. Tell him so and that I shan't write him because I should immediately have to add that Dreyfus is innocent just the same, and that in spite of my great pity for General Mercier, he is a first-rate scoundrel; and so many distinctions would be wearing both to write and to read. Nevertheless, when I think that I organized the first list for *L'Aurore* to ask for a revision of the trial and that so many politicians who were then passionate anti-Dreyfusards are hounding to death this old man of sixty-six who had the courage to appear, surrounded by a hostile pack, with nothing to say, knowing that he would have no evidence to give except that the procedure (of the Court of Cassation!) had been *irregular, illegal,* and *behind closed doors.* It would be unbelievably humorous but for the fact that the paper says: the very pale General Mercier, the even paler General Mercier. It is horrible to read, for even in the most evil man there is always a poor innocent brute with a heart, a liver, and arteries in which there is no malice, which suffer pain. And the most splendid hour of triumph is spoiled because there is always someone who suffers.

Your respectful friend,
Marcel Proust

93: TO MADAME STRAUS

[AFTER JULY 13, 1906]

Madame,

It was too kind of you to write me such exquisite letters, and I thank you for them with all my heart. What you say about the Dreyfus affair is naturally the most humorous, the most profound, and the best-written thing that could be said on the subject. You have the infallibility of your wit and grace. It is curious to think that life—so unlike fiction—for once resembles it. Alas, in the last ten years, we have all had many a sorrow, many a disappointment, many a torment in our lives. And not for one of us will the hour strike that will change our sorrows into exaltation, our disappointments into fulfillment, and our torment into exquisite triumphs. I shall become more and more ill, more and more I shall miss the ones I have lost, and all that I dreamed of in my life will be farther and farther beyond my reach. But for Dreyfus and for Picquart it is not so. For them life has been "providential" after the fashion of fairy tales and serial thrillers. That is because our suffering was founded on fact—on truths—physiological truths, human and emotional truths. For them, suffering was founded on error. Fortunate, indeed, are those who are victims of error—judicial or otherwise! They are the only human beings for whom there are redress and restitution. I don't know who the stage manager is in the final scenes of this restitution. But he is incomparable and even moving. And it is impossible to read this morning's latest scene: "In the courtyard of the Military College with five hundred participants," without having tears in one's eyes. When I think of the trouble I had sending a copy of *Les Plaisirs et les Jours* to Picquart at Mont-Valérien, where he was imprisoned, it almost takes away my desire to send him *Sesame et les lys* now because it is too easy. . . .

A man who should be profoundly happy and who deserves it, the most enviable man I know for the good he has desired and achieved, is Reinach. I regret that his triumph in the newspapers and the Chamber of Deputies is so modest. He did a great deal more than Zola. . . .

Your respectful and grateful friend,
Marcel Proust

94: TO MADAME STRAUS

VERSAILLES,
[JUST BEFORE AUGUST 23, 1906]

Madame,

. . . . Here at the Reservoirs I have a huge, wonderful apartment (which is now much more expensive than Trouville!), but it is terribly sad, dark, chilled, and filled with pictures, tapestries, and mirrors. It is the historic type of room, one of these places where the guide tells you that here Charles IX died, and you glance about furtively as you hurry to get back to the light and warmth and the reassuring present. But when you not only can't get out again but must accept the inevitability of having to sleep there—it is enough to kill you. I don't know how the room could have been oriented so that the sun never penetrates at any hour of the day. I asked whether the chimneys smoked and was told no, which is true, Jesuitically speaking. For indeed, the chimney in which you light a fire doesn't smoke, but when a fire is burning it sets all the other fireplaces in the house to smoking so violently that the whole apartment is nothing but a cloud of smoke.

Please forgive my writing you such boring details, but I must avoid getting tired, for I have a violent fever.

Your respectful friend,
Marcel Proust

95: TO MADAME STRAUS

VERSAILLES
OCTOBER 10, 1906

Madame,

You are probably at a loss to account for my silence, and, alas, I can't yet break it. Having had to decide to leave rue de Courcelles, for the last month I have been having apartments viewed for me, and my reluctance, my anxiety, my tentative leases and the subsequent cancellation just as the lease is to be signed have deprived me of so much sleep that I barely have strength enough to write you. In the end, I couldn't make up my mind to go and live in a house that Mother had not known, so for this year, as a transition, I have sublet an apartment in our house in the boulevard Haussmann, where I often went to dinner with Mother, where together we saw my old uncle die in the room that I shall occupy. Of course, I shall be spared nothing! Frightful dust, trees under and against my window, the noise of the boulevard between the *Printemps* and *Saint-Augustin*! If I can't stay, I shall leave. And the apartment is too expensive for me to stay there always. But this year, since it was sublet to a tenant who is paying for it without using it, I have gotten it for comparatively little. How much I shall have to tell you, what affection to lavish on you, and even jokes to amuse you! But I am too tired, and want only to say that I have never loved you so much.

Marcel Proust

For two and a half months since I came to Versailles I have succeeded (*Unberufen*) [sic] in not seeing Mme X——! A little reading and that's all! Your card (your postcards) from Bayeux were intoxicating. Ah, there is a house I should like to live in. And Jacques's cards from Brittany! I haven't had the energy to thank him.

Comte Bertrand de Salignac-Fénelon (1878–1914), a descendant of the writer, Fénelon, a member of the French diplomatic service, was one of the many models for the character of Robert de Saint-Loup.

96: TO BERTRAND DE SALIGNAC-FÉNELON

[END OF NOVEMBER, BEGINNING OF DECEMBER, 1906]

For a long time, my dear Bertrand, I have wanted to thank you for your charming card from Göttingen, which gave me great pleasure. And I shall have a lot to say to you about it—the charm with which you can talk about cities like that, like Veere, like Delft, is so unusual that I found myself thinking this: if I had more talent, more life, more time, if I were a better friend, I would, with these really exquisite postcards as starting point, and with what I myself have been able to gather in relation to their author, do what Sainte-Beuve did for the striking people of his period who, without him, would have been forgotten because they wrote only the kind of letters, spoke only the kind of distinguished words that need to be combined and interpreted, since they are nowhere recorded. But it unfortunately seems probable, whether because of excessive work, or laziness, or contempt, that you will not write any imaginative work, any books of your own. The only resource you have left is a portraitist, a conversationalist with a good memory who will be able with talent, painstakingly, affectionately, attentively, to catch the physiognomy which would otherwise risk being unknown. Since my pen was too early broken by sorrow, find another, a golden pen.

I am expressing all this very badly, my old friend, in the bustle of moving and perhaps (although I shall stay another month at Versailles) a lawsuit against some people from whom I sublet the apartment in Paris and who haven't had the repairs finished in time; however I wanted you to know that I think of you very often. You know that the desire to travel and the impossibility are always with me. So each letter that comes from a place I should love to see gives me a sense of the poetry of an imaginary voyage. But when the letter is from you, the impression is intensified, and because of my having experienced my chief travel impressions with you, a letter of yours sends me not only on an imaginary voyage as do other letters, but on a voyage in memory, too. I hope that you are happy, as they say, and I send you my friendliest remembrances.

Marcel

97: TO MARIE NORDLINGER

DECEMBER 8, 1906

Chère, chère, chère, chère Mary
First:
Did Reynaldo tell you, as I told him, that I had sent a letter, then *Sesame* to the strange place and address where *Detroit* is the name of the city, isn't it, *Avenue*, of the province, and *Lake Ontario* of the country? But never any answer, and I can well see that nothing arrived, since you ask me, "And *Sesame*?" Here it is, enclosed in reply.

Chère amie, how near you are to my heart, and how little your absence has separated you from me! I think of you constantly with such tenderness and indestructible regret for the past. In my ravaged life, in my demolished heart, the place you hold is sweet. *Chère amie*, permit me in a few words to talk to you about something trivial. If you have not yet received any author's fee for *Sesame*, it is because the review in which it first appeared, the *Arts de la vie*, has gone bankrupt and paid nothing, and the publisher of the book, the *Mercure*, will not settle with me until it is more nearly sold out. If you wish me to send you an advance from here, nothing could be easier; you know that, alas, I no longer have to account to anyone for the use I make of my money.

You are in Manchester, I see. I, for the last four months, at Versailles. Can I say Versailles? Since I took to my bed on my arrival and have not left it (unable to go even once either to the Château or to the Trianon, or anywhere, and I don't wake up until nightfall), am I at Versailles rather than elsewhere? I know nothing about it. I should be in Paris, but I have had apartment troubles, the beginning of a lawsuit, and since October I have rented an apartment that I can't get into. . . .

Are you working? I no longer am. I have closed forever the era of translations that Mother favored. And as for translations of myself, I no longer have the courage. Did you see some beautiful things in America? What strange folly to have sent back the little textbook! If I went out in the daytime, I should love to see this Egyptian and Assyrian art, which appears to me to be very beautiful. Does M. Bing sell Egyptian and Assyrian things, and Gothic?

How are your people? How is your aunt, to whom I beg you to remember me, and who remains in my mind as one of the most curious *stones of Venice*. Nothing could soften her, nothing could budge her inflexible principles. But how she delighted me, and how much she seemed to love you! And she represents for me the *Mornings in Venice* that I never saw . . . the "early riser" who ignores the "slug-a-bed."

I have not, *chère amie*, ceased thinking of you always, a great deal, constantly, and I shall never stop. I kiss your hands in infinite friendship.

Marcel Proust

98: TO MADAME CATUSSE

[VERSAILLES]
[PROBABLY LATE OCTOBER OR EARLY NOVEMBER, 1906]

Chère Madame,

I have been so ill these last few days that not until this morning could I look at my letters and read yours. Then I fell asleep. I slept until this evening, I got up around eleven o'clock at night, I am writing to you, my letter will go out tomorrow at dawn, but in the meantime what must you think of me! You will think me ungrateful! You will say to yourself, he was in a hurry to write when he needed me; now that I have done him a service, he doesn't take the trouble to thank me. Madame, the idea that you might be thinking this up to the time you receive this letter grieves me. I am so grateful for your kindness! Everything you said seemed—through the haze of vanishing *malaise*—perfect. I wasn't as attached to the red paper as you thought. It was that Empire paper especially which seemed beautiful to me even though red. But it couldn't go there. And I have no objection to red; on the contrary. I am glad to know that the *boiserie* can be used; I thought the hall would be too small, and it will give me great pleasure to find it there again, for Mother always took so much pleasure in it, loving her hall as she did. And even apart from this satisfaction, it will please me in every way, because it was charming.

Alas, what you tell me about the apartment in the boulevard Haussmann I know only too well! It is at least fifteen years since I have seen it, but I remember it as the ugliest thing I ever saw, the triumph of the bourgeois bad taste of a period still too near to be inoffensive! It isn't even old-fashioned in the charming sense of the word. Old-fashioned! It is too ugly ever to be. But I have explained to you the strength of the tender and sad attraction, which drew me back there, in spite of my even greater horror of the district, of the dust, of the Gare Saint-Lazare, and so many other things. The friends who, with such exquisite devotion, looked around for me, since I couldn't look myself, and who knew my instructions, my taste, and my recommendations—no trees, no noise, no dust, a high part of the city, etc., have not yet recovered from seeing me choose the "beautiful apartment" of a less rich and much later Nucingen. But I told you the reason: perhaps I have told no one else. If I can make up my mind to leave it, it will at least have been the transition between the place where Mother rests, which is not the cemetery but the apartment in the rue de Courcelles, and an apartment which she had never seen, completely strange. And besides, all this is mixed up with other things, too long to explain by letter. What you say about how beautiful a golden autumn at Versailles should be pains me! For can you believe that except for the very first days when I saw the last rays of the sun from my bed I have never waked up until nightfall, and I know nothing of the charms of the season or the hour. I have spent four months at Versailles as if I had spent them in a telephone booth without having seen any of the surroundings. And in the past I was always going from Paris to Versailles, because I love so much those incomparable places, which our sorrows have rebuilt into something more beautiful than they ever were in their first splendor and which have so increased in beauty from the time of Louis XIV to Barrès! I haven't your letter at hand, but it seems to me that you say that the little salon could not be made into a room *all* tapestried. That is what I should have liked, to remind me of the hall at the rue de Courcelles or the "tapestried study" at the boulevard Malesherbes. But that can be done in the dining room. . . . Madame, I should like to stay with you even longer to thank you for the trouble you have taken for me, but really I can't go on; I thank you with all my heart and beg you to accept my respectful gratitude.

Marcel Proust

As for pictures, I don't want to see much of any of them except the small and oldish shepherdess with the monstrous, well-bred air of a Spanish infanta, the portrait of Mother, and my portrait by Blanche. However, the exact copies of the Snyders will do very well in the dining room. I know that the Govaert Flinck ("Tobias and the Angel") is a valuable picture and is, in fact, the very good, if a little too somber, painting of one of Rembrandt's best pupils. But I intend to leave it for Robert (and for that matter, everything he wants) as well as the very beautiful portrait of Father by Lecomte de Noüy, which Jacques admired, but I think Robert would be very much pleased to have it. I shall send him also, if he is willing to store them (or I can hang them in the shadow), "Esther and Haman," "Roman History," and the "Metsu." Still, if he doesn't take them right away, I shan't hang them in the shadow so my sister-in-law will not turn up her nose at them. But for my part, any picture that one has not *desired*, bought with suffering and love, is atrocious in an apartment. William Moriss [sic] said, "Have nothing in your apartment except things you have found beautiful or which you have judged as beautiful." A chest, a table, even if they are ugly, even if they are useless, still evoke an idea of utility. But a picture that isn't satisfying is a horror. And I can say that of all those that will be there, good or bad. . . .

99: TO MADAME CATUSSE

VERSAILLES

[BETWEEN SEPTEMBER AND NOVEMBER, 1906]

Chère Madame,

. . . .

How true was Vogüé's article on the separation when he said that it was only a word, that Church and State would by no means be separated for that, and that it was not viable, that the law would have to be improved, made over, that there should have been an understanding with Rome, etc. I had been thinking it was all false. How true it was! Prophetic! What power there is even in a mediocre Pope, since all Briand's admirable intelligence, his sublime "good will" have just come to grief there, even though upheld by the forces of wealth. All the same, what a difference between today and former times. Formerly never a Philip-Augustus, never a Louis XIV, never a Napoleon would have accepted a quarter of what Briand puts up with from the Pope. Formerly, too, the clergy would never have had this elevation of spirit or at least this disinterestedness, which, in obedience to the Pope, makes them renounce all their property. Power amounts to very little, however, because since the Pope no longer has either army or land, he is more powerful (even in France, and there he is least so) than he ever was in the days of his material power. I hope, nevertheless, that this crisis will come to an end. And I hope that Briand's law, which is so fine, so wise, so truly and abundantly just—so desirable even for the Church—can become the statute of the Catholic Church. . . .

Marcel Proust

100: TO LAURE HAYMAN

[PROBABLY 1906 OR 1907]

Chère amie,

I was so touched when Coco told me of your exquisite thought. As my brother said so nicely when I told him about it, "How comforting it would be to have a bust of Father made by a member of the family." I doubt whether it will be possible to have it placed in the cemetery. I haven't talked to my brother about that (you know I am in such a state of health that I can hardly ever receive even him, and when by chance I am well enough, it is usually only for a few minutes). In any case, I can talk to him about it, but as Mother made all the arrangements as they now are, we cling to the superstition of not changing what she arranged, though we know, as in this case, that she would have been happy to replace an effigy too little like him for a statue created directly out of the living memory of a long friendship. But, in any case, even if this isn't possible, and I don't think it is, if you pursue the project of making this bust, there are other places where it could be placed, in your house or in ours. And if the latter, after we are gone, either in the Luxembourg or the Faculty or Academy of Medicine, where Father's statue would be perpetuated affectionately, and faithfully kept.

. . . .

In spite of everything I have so often been told about your remarkable talent, the sight of the bust would never give me as much pleasure as the knowledge that you still think of my poor father and that you still remember him. I still recall how distressed he was when the letters you wrote him at the time you were so upset never, for some unknown reason, reached him. Although he was already preoccupied with the fear of soon having to leave us forever, the thought of it often came back to him and he was so afraid that you might not believe him—he who had never lied.

Allow me to offer you, Madame, the expression of my admiration, my friendship, and my regard.

Your respectful friend,
Marcel Proust

101: TO ROBERT DE BILLY

[FIRST QUARTER, 1907]

Mon petit Robert,

Who could possibly have told your friend that I was translating *Praeterita* and the parts of Ruskin's correspondence and journal that the publishers added to it? I didn't think I had talked about it. In any case, it is barely started, and I would gladly give way to your friend as I have already done for M. de X. and his *Selections*. The only thing I take into consideration in matters of this sort is: "What is most advantageous for Ruskin? Who is able to make him better known, etc.?" But in my present state of health it is so improbable that I could bring such a long work to a successful conclusion that it would be preferable to have your friend do it. But is he a poet? *Praeterita* is written in colors that are "thought"; what evocative powers one must have to translate them! Has he a bit of magic in his pen point? Will he do notes? They are indispensable. If he is afraid of not knowing enough, he could do what the translators of *Mornings in Florence* did, have the notes put in by someone else (they were even done by ten others, which is a good many). In that case, if he wished to entrust me with the proofs of the translation when it is finished, I would gladly annotate it, if they give me plenty of space, several months, and complete freedom of opinion.

Mon petit Robert, since *The Bible of Amiens* says that present-day Protestantism conceives of the Cross as a raft destined to carry intact our movable values all the way to Paradise, don't be scandalized that I go from Ruskin to the Pins des Landes, and let me know, please, where one can buy them and whether they are worth more at the moment than the Harpener or the Gelsenkirchen about which you talked to me.

Affectionately yours,
Marcel

102: TO ROBERT DREYFUS

FEBRUARY 3, 1907

Mon cher Robert,

How nice you are, what real friendship I feel for you and how secure and solid this friendship is (so few are), since it is really rationally and indestructibly based on pride amply gratified. But I am slandering myself, for I assure you that my feeling of friendship is not because you appreciate my writings. If only I could hold myself in more esteem! Alas, it is impossible, and I am wondering if you are not telling a charitable lie to an invalid when you say my article is good. In any case (and unfortunately this does not explain its deadliness, for it hasn't even the charm of improvisation; it is both laborious and hurried, icy and rhetorical), to explain to you the repetition of words, the slips (particularly of the type-setter), Calmette asked me for this article Wednesday morning in a letter which, because of an attack, I didn't read until Wednesday evening at ten o'clock. At three o'clock I got up, started it immediately, and wrote until eight in the morning in only one draft on the sheets that went to the *Figaro*. Since it wasn't finished and my hand (unaccustomed to writing) hurt, cramp in the fourth finger, I went to bed, leaving word that I should be awakened during the day to finish it. But since some frightful construction going on overhead woke me up at half-past eight, I felt so miserable that I gave up finishing the article and sent it off unfinished without having reread it, to appear as it was. At eleven o'clock at night they brought me the proofs, which had to be returned at midnight; I intended to start correcting them. But then I had an idea for a really rather good ending. As there wasn't time to do everything, I preferred to give up correcting the proof, and underneath I wrote the ending.

At midnight the proof sheets were taken back to the *Figaro* (I neither go out nor get up—once a week I get up, but don't dress), and I let them know that they could cut what they liked, but that not one word of the ending must be changed. They published all of it, however—almost all—but they suppressed the ending, not a word of which was there. And I don't dare give the reason which I am not supposed to know, but here it is: Cardane [managing editor of the *Figaro*] found that my ending was immoral and constituted an encomium of parricide. I assure you this is so. . . .

All yours with most affectionate thanks,
Marcel

I don't know what you hear Beaunier and the people at the *Figaro* say about Calmette. I don't myself know how

I shall find him on closer contact. But for considerateness (which, to this extent, is really kindness and charm), I know of no one comparable. I can give you an idea when I tell you that this newspaper editor wrote me three times in three days for no other reason than to give me pleasure and in this tone: "Your article is admirable; it moved me more than I can say, it will be an ornament to the paper; there will not be a reader who won't reread it and thank you for it with a feeling of the utmost enchantment, etc., etc., etc." When, like me, you have not slept for more than a fortnight and when you are *half crazy*, I assure you that letters like that—even if at the same time he is saying, "What a bore this article is" —do you good, and you bless an editor so different from Arthur Meyer.

103: TO MADAME STRAUS

FRIDAY, JUNE 21, 1907

Madame,

Forgive me for bothering you again but have you perhaps an idea now of how you will feel Monday, the first; do you think you could come for dinner or not until after dinner. I feel that it is hateful of me to pester you. But what can I do? Six people sent the same kind of answer you did! So if I am left uncertain until the last day, or if I count on the people who don't come, I am threatened with being left tête-à-tête with Mme d'Haussonville, without her husband, and Mme de Clermont-Tonnerre, both of whom are definitely coming, but which would make me very uncomfortable for them, since I know them very slightly—or if to guard against this I invite more people now, and at the last moment the six others come, I am threatened with more ladies than I know how to seat or, at least, whom I should seat badly. And if you would say that on the first of July at seven o'clock you will come to dinner, I should be frantic with joy, but I should seat you badly if the six others came and I invited still others now.

I invited Mme de L——, whom I have not seen for years, but with whom I should like you to be friends because I am sure that something very fortunate could come of it for the Princesse de X——, who is in the process of *killing* her daughter. But she was, unfortunately, not free. My other guests are all people you know. But when I invited Dufeuille, I told him the truth, that I was afraid that you would only come in the evening. He, too, wrote me a letter saying that he wouldn't know up to the last moment whether he would be free. But I had to stop there and not tell him that I would keep his place because I needed men and didn't want, if he came at the last minute, not to know where to put him. I already have Fauré, who is not young, Calmette, for whom I am giving the dinner, Béraud, who is very susceptible, M. de Clermont-Tonnerre, who is younger, but descended from Charlemagne—and some strangers. Since it kills me to write, I do all this on the telephone, which kills me just as much although I don't do the telephoning myself—I mean that it is done while I am asleep—so that a second person is asked when the first has already accepted. I have been at pains, in case you find you are too tired to come to dinner, to have something in the evening that will amuse you and not necessitate your talking. And that is why I am having Fauré. You will be played things you like; I think Fauré will play (alas, Reynaldo will be in London), and since we shall only be about twenty, I can still have the pleasure of your being there, of your eyes during the music.

La musique parfois me prend comme la mer
Vers ma sombre étoile
Je mets à la voile.

But naturally I could enjoy you even more if you came to dinner. I intend inviting Robert Dreyfus for the evening, but I have begged him not to talk about it because since I don't even know whether I shall invite my sister-in-law, I don't want anyone but the guests to know about it. I shall send someone to every paper to be sure that it isn't mentioned. Because of that and also because it would make me too tired to have my apartment put in order (it is still in the state it was when I moved in and has not been arranged) and to have people smoking there, etc., I think I shall try to find at the Ritz, or preferably Madrid or Armenonville, a room that is shut off, where one can be at home: I think I should be less likely to choke that way.

I thought of inviting M. Reinach, whom I have not seen for a long time. But since M. de Clermont-Tonnerre—which I didn't believe, but which appears to be true—is very anti-Dreyfusard and very violent, and since M. Reinach is so completely the incarnation of Dreyfusism, I thought that it was better at such a small dinner to avoid the encounter the first time I was having M. de Clermont-Tonnerre, who has invited me so often while M. Reinach never has. If however it would be pleasant for you, I think it would be possible to ask him.

I still have three miserable hideous little Japanese trees for you. Having seen them announced at a sale, I sent my pseudo-secretary to buy them. What a disappointment when I saw them! However, they will get to be nice, and they are so old and so little. It is like when one looks at Mont Blanc on the horizon through an opera glass and says to one's self it is 4810 meters high. I wanted to have all this explained to you when I send them by the so-called secretary, who will bring them to you one of these days, because writing tires me so and I so love to write to you. Mme de Chevigné, according to formula, said to be sure to keep her place for her at all events! But since then she has refused. Nevertheless I am sorry. She is so very nice. Mme Lemaire doesn't know whether she will be back from London, Mme de Brantes whether or not she will have lost a cousin, Mme d'Eyragues whether she will be on the banks of the Loire, M. Dufeuille whether his friends from the Basse Normandie will have returned (word for word). My dear little Madame Straus, don't forget the date, July first; if you decide only at the last moment to come, don't blame me for seating you badly, and if bad luck has it that you don't come for dinner, don't fail to come as soon as possible afterwards to hear Fauré and see me. I shall have you informed of the place.

Your respectful friend who would like to write at greater length if he weren't so tired.

Marcel Proust

I forgot that Mme de Noailles is in London and will probably not be back until the second, Mme de Chimay is in Holland and doesn't know yet whether she will be back before the third!

Unnecessary to remind you that my invitation, either for dinner or the evening, is meant to express the *strongest desire* to have M. Straus come.

104: TO MADAME STRAUS

END OF JUNE, 1907

Madame,

. . . . After you telephoned me the other day, it never occurred to me that even if you couldn't come for dinner you wouldn't come in the evening. I thought it was decided. You had told me that you were going to the theatre. I am ashamed of talking to you this way. It makes me think of the people who say to me, "But you must be well since you are giving a dinner party," and who don't know that it is on the one day in two consecutive months that I have spent in bed without getting up even for an hour. But if that is an evening when you can go to the theatre, would listening to Fauré tire you as much? I don't think so, although I should not like to appear as unintelligent as the people who decide what does and what doesn't tire us, and who find that what gives them pleasure couldn't tire us. God knows I would forgo all the pleasures in the world rather than have you tired for a moment! But if it wouldn't tire you! Gabriel de La Rochefoucauld (about whom I talk to you excessively, considering that I never see him) knew the scheme of my dinner because I had asked him to invite his mother. He came the other day to bring me his mother's reply, get news of me, but above all else, knowing it was what I wished most deeply, he asked me abruptly when he came in, "Is Mme Straus coming to dinner?" "No." "*Oh, my poor friend!*" I shall always be grateful to him for that remark.

Mme Straus, don't come, don't tire yourself, don't go to bed later on my account, be assured that I can subordinate my pleasure to yours, all of which is a way of expressing my friendship for you. It is just my luck that M. Straus, too, will be tired and unable to come, even in the evening. *Entre nous*, I know very well that he doesn't like all those people and that it is perhaps rather good for that reason that he shouldn't come. You know what it is all about; I planned a dinner solely out of compliment to Calmette, who is very nice to take my long articles, which are so little to the public taste. And paying a compliment consists in inviting him with fashionable people. But the greatest compliment I could pay him was you. When I spoke your name, he let out an exclamation of joy, saying that he liked you so much and hadn't seen you for such a long time. I went to the *Figaro* about that article on Mme de Noailles which has caused me so much trouble. It is a place you can go at midnight. And not knowing how to thank him, I said I should like to have him to dinner someday. I thought that would be the end of it, for how could I have imagined that I should be giving a dinner until years off, before my death (less remote perhaps)? Very amiably he took out his engagement book and looked for his free dates. That is how it was set so far ahead. He certainly never suspected the difficulties in which he was involving me. For only unimportant things are troublesome—and love. But I am no longer in love. If you see him, don't tell him that I thought it pleasanter for him to be invited with the aristocracy. Because that would seem to imply that I was flattering him, which would make him angry; he would quarrel with me when he can be so useful to me and so agreeable. These are the things one feels obliged to do to be pleasant, like having lots of courses, etc., which nobody really likes. In any case, if M. Straus doesn't like them very much, he mustn't complain, because I learned all this at your house!

Madame, I say good-bye because I can't go on; I shan't plague you anymore, I shan't ask you again to come, I shall only have you informed by telephone of the place when I know it. You know that all this is relevant only in case you are feeling well that day—*and only in that case.*

Your respectful friend,
Marcel Proust

105: TO MADAME STRAUS

END OF JUNE, 1907

Madame,

. . . If you have a minute it would be so nice of you to tell me how I should seat respectively the non-nobles (the nobles I sacrifice), Fauré, Béraud, Calmette, and Dufeuille. . . . And while I am about it, dare I ask you if you would make a *menu de grand dîner*, tell me what I ought to order (only things you like and which still wouldn't harm you too much if you should come). Do you know about wines? Please accept, Madame, my respectful compliments.

Marcel Proust

106: TO MADAME T.-J. GUÉRITTE

102, BOULEVARD HAUSSMANN

JULY 27, 1907

Madame,

I was seriously ill (and still am), and I had to go away to try (ineffectually) to recover. So I have only in the last few days found the delightful letter you did me the honor of writing; I have read it, reread it, I am relishing at length this tardy and profound joy. I am really very proud that such a fastidious admirer of Ruskin's should, with such warm approval, have sanctioned an effort, the value—and even the legitimacy—of which I have often doubted. "Let the dead bury the dead," those harsh and singular words from the Scriptures, the imperious and splendid significance of which can be understood only by sensitive spirits, can be applied to translations, to apologues, to latria. I felt your reproach for not having published Ruskin's preface. But I explained in a note that I was unable to give the third lecture. It was not my fault but the publisher's. And then the preface to *Sesame and Lilies*? Which preface? Ruskin did not write just one, as you know. Which to choose? It was difficult. As for mine, it is in fact less literally Ruskinian than the one to *The Bible of Amiens*, but I think that in itself it is worth something, and the other little more than nothing at all. In a volume of *Mélanges*, if I ever again find the strength to assemble the already existing pieces, I shall certainly include the preface of *Sesame*, and if I give one or two excerpts from the one to the *Bible*, that will be all. As for Ruskin, I have stopped translating him; people are starting to do it on all sides, not always in the way that seems to me the most respectful and the most sensible, but then this fire is spreading and that is enough. I regret very much that you did not pursue your project of translating his work. To be interpreted by a woman of an intelligence as rare and sensitive as yours would without doubt have been a great pleasure to him. But is it as easy to have translations of Ruskin published as their recent multiplicity seems to indicate? For my part, I had all the trouble in the world getting mine accepted by the *Mercure*, and they would not have taken a third.

Excuse me, Madame, for interrupting here an interview I should like to have prolonged, but I am so very weak; excuse the disparity of these different-sized sheets of paper; I am staying in bed and my box of letter paper is not at hand; and accept my grateful and respectful compliments.

Marcel Proust

Prince Emmanuel Bibesco

(1874–1917), the elder brother of Antoine, was a man of rare culture, gentleness, and charm. His deep and scholarly love of the arts—particularly architecture—prompted him to visit most of the churches and cathedrals of France, pilgrimages on which Proust frequently accompanied him. His exhaustive collection of architectural photographs was endlessly stimulating and useful to Proust. A "great mystic of friendship," he was among the very few whom Proust excepted when he deplored "the indifference of friends."

107: TO EMMANUEL BIBESCO

GRAND-HÔTEL—CABOURG

[CIRCA AUGUST 15, 1907]

Cher ami, thank you with all my heart for your charming card. I was so pleased that you liked my little article; it was indeed good of you to tell me so.

I have been at Cabourg for a week (Grand-Hôtel), from

where I go across Normandy to see churches. If you have any scenery or any monuments to recommend to me, you would make me very happy. But hurry, because I shall soon be leaving this part of the country for Brittany. It is true that there, also, you could tell me of some places that seemed to you really stirring. You would be astonished to see me on the roads every day. But it won't last. . . . I hope Antoine is well, calm, industrious, happy, everything that I am not! I have never been so upset, so sterile, so unhappy. But he, he who has such a future ahead of him, it is absolutely essential that he feel well, be happy, work. I think I could do him a great deal of good, because I know what is good without having the strength to do it, and, besides, for me that no longer has any importance. *Cher ami*, I love you very much, both of you, and I send you the best of my thoughts. Victor Hugo expressed it much better—my thought, the best of my possessions.

Marcel Proust

108: TO MADAME STRAUS

102, BOULEVARD HAUSSMANN
MONDAY [OCTOBER, 1907]

Madame,

I left Cabourg the same day that you left Trouville, but not at the same time! Just before arriving at Evreux (where I spent four or five days), we went down into a small valley where the mist was visible in the distance and one could imagine the coolness. And ever since that moment up to today (and until I don't know when in the future), I haven't stopped choking and having incessant attacks. And that is why, although you were in my thoughts practically all day long, I haven't written; I haven't had the courage to take up my pen. Naturally, it wasn't the little valley that brought on my attacks. But from that moment I did nothing but make for Paris, and even at Evreux I was very ill. There I saw by daylight a bishop's palace with a not very beautiful interior; and at nightfall a church of Saint-Taurin, which I found very pretty (Romanesque and Gothic, if I am not mistaken, now that you are familiar with the different styles), with some rather curious baptismal fonts and beautiful stained-glass windows. Then a cathedral, which you have doubtless seen, combining all periods, with beautiful windows, which found a way of being luminous even near dusk, which was, when I saw them, in grey weather under a cloudy sky. And from all the dreariness of a day, which even at dawn had resembled the night to which it would give way, they were able to steal jewels of light, sparkling purple sapphires gleaming with fire; it is incredible.

I went to Conches right near Evreux, to see a church, which still has all its sixteenth-century windows; many of them are by a pupil of Dürer. It is like a pretty little German Bible with Renaissance illustrations in color. Each window has its inscription written above in Gothic characters. But the windows of that period do not interest me very much, they are too much *pictures* on glass.

. . . .

While I was at Evreux I went one evening to see M. and Mme de Clermont-Tonnerre at Glisolles (right near Evreux), a very attractive place. They were supposed to show me some very beautiful things in the neighborhood, but I was so disgusted with Evreux I left the next morning and went on none of these excursions, not even a visit to Claude Monet's garden at Giverny, near the lovely bend where the river is fortunate enough to see you, through the mist, in your salon. If I can find it in a nice edition, I want very much to give M. Straus a delightful work which was loaned to me and which I had, as a matter of fact, read before, but which is very pleasant to read and look at again, the *Dictionary of Architecture* by Viollet-le-Duc. It is unfortunate that Viollet-le-Duc has spoiled France by restoring with scientific accuracy, but without any feeling, so many churches, whose ruins would be more moving than their archeological patching up with new stones, which say nothing to us, and mouldings identical with the original, but of which they have kept nothing. Nevertheless, he did have a genius for architecture, and that book is admirable. . . .

Your respectful and infinitely grateful friend,
Marcel Proust

109: TO ROBERT DE BILLY

SHORTLY AFTER NOVEMBER 8, 1907

Mon petit Robert,

Although I have been wanting to write you for the last century, I am so worn out that you will have to let me send you just a note. Thank you a thousand times for having been willing to recommend my protégé to your father-in-law. . . .

I was told something—very scandalous or, rather, very insinuating—about two ladies who are, I am sure, members of your inner circle. Did you know about it? It may, of course, be entirely untrue.

What do you think about all this homosexuality trial? I think they have hit rather at random, although about some of them it is very true, notably the Prince, but there are some very comic things about it. Will you remember me to M. Paléologue?

Your affectionate and devoted
Marcel

110: TO MADAME STRAUS

DECEMBER 28, 1907

Madame,

It is more than good of you to want me to write. It is a welcome change from the people who take infinite pains to avoid talking to me about my articles, while pretending not to do it purposely, for fear of hurting my feelings by admitting that they find the articles absurd, and who attach such stupid importance to their words and to *sincerity* that they are unwilling to pay me a courtesy compliment. I am astonished, besides, to see what even very intelligent people admire and sanction. For example, a speech of Bourget's in which puns worthy of L—— are quoted and in which there is a credo of faith in anti-Semitism, which it would have been more delicate for him to have kept to himself if it is sincere, since he has had the misfortune for an anti-Semite of having been launched by a Jew, endowed by a Jewess, and married to a convert. I have seen people of taste find D——'s speech charming. I myself have never read anything so silly and so really "academic." For in order to find it humorous, scandalous, devilish to "dare" say, "flunk an exam" ["*pousser une colle*"], etc., at the Academy, one must be terribly academic and have a mind imbued with the same prejudices one sanctions by the very act of thinking it extremely daring and clever to challenge them. He and Bourget looked like two bigoted old maids delighted to have dared to use a slightly off-color word in front of their curé. Basically this whole spirit derives from the same idiocy that makes cretins like R—— write, "I don't give a hang, as Bossuet said." It's disheartening. And the whole discourse, as to style, was counterfeit! What is less like Honfleur than his Honfleur to those of us who have seen the real thing? Poor Porto-Riche deserved far more to have been elected, he, who at least did *Le Passé*.

The truth of the matter is that people believe love of literature, of painting, of music has become very widespread in the social world, but actually there isn't a single additional person who can tell good style from bad, and D——'s speech from a really well-written essay. Madame, forgive this half sheet because I have no more paper, forgive this stupid letter, forgive everything; I hope to see you soon, very soon.

Your respectful friend,
Marcel Proust

111: TO MADAME STRAUS

FRIDAY

[CIRCA JANUARY, 1908]

Madame,

Infinite thanks for your enchanting, funny, nice letter. And at almost the same time I have been reading the article by Ganderax. How I should love to have known you that way (to be able to call you "my friend since the days of Bas-Prunay"), to know all these things, have been capable of writing about them. In which case it seems to me that I should have written them—a little differently. By that I am not saying anything against M. Ganderax, who has great gifts, a man cast in a mold that is really no longer very usual, which will be seen less and less, and which I, for my part, prefer to those of today. But why does he who writes so well have to write like this? Why when one says, "1871," add, "the most abominable year of all"? Why is Paris immediately qualified as "the great city," Delaunay as the "master painter"? Why must emotion inevitably be "discreet" and candor "smiling" and mourning "cruel" and a thousand more beautiful examples that I don't remember. One wouldn't think of it if Ganderax himself, when he corrects others, didn't think that he was being of service to the French language. For the glory, no. Nor as defense either.

The only people who defend the French language (like the army during the Dreyfus Affair) are those who "attack" it. This idea that there is a French language that exists outside of the writers who use it and that must be protected, is fantastic. Each writer is bound to create his own language as each violinist must create his own "tone." And between the tone of some mediocre violinist and Thibaud's tone (for the same note) there is an infinitely small difference that embodies a whole world! I don't mean that I like original writers who write badly. I prefer—and it is, perhaps a weakness—those who write well. But they start to write well only on condition that they are original, that they themselves create their own language. Correctness, perfection of style do exist, but not this side of originality, but through and beyond it. Correctness this side of "discreet emotion," "smiling candor," "the most abominable year of all," simply does not exist. Certainly, Madame Straus, the only way to defend the language is to attack it! Because its unity is created only by the neutralizing of opposites, by an apparent immobility which hides perpetual, vertiginous activity. For one "holds one's own" and cuts a fine figure in comparison with the writers of the past only inasmuch as one has tried to write quite differently. And when one wants to defend the French language, one actually writes quite the opposite of classical French. For example: the revolutionaries, Rousseau, Hugo, Flaubert, Maeterlinck "hold their own" beside Bossuet. The neoclassicists of the eighteenth and early nineteenth century, and the "smiling candor" and the "discreet emotion" of all epochs clash with the masters. Alas, Racine's most beautiful lines—

Je t'aimais inconstant, qu'eussé-je fait fidèle!
Pourquoi l'assassiner? Qu'a-t-il fait? A quel titre?
Qui te l'a dit?

would never have been accepted—not even in a review nowadays.

Marginal note for the "Defense and elucidation of the French language." "I understand your thought; you mean that since I loved you when you were unfaithful, what might that love have been if you had been faithful. But it is badly expressed. It could just as well mean that it was you who would have been faithful. Having been appointed to defend and elucidate the French language, I cannot allow this to pass." I am not making fun of your friend, Madame, I assure you. I know how intelligent and how well informed he is. It is a question of "doctrine." This man who is so skeptical has grammatical certainties.

Alas, Madame Straus, there are no certainties even in grammar. And isn't it more fortunate that way? For thus a grammatical form can be beautiful, indeed can only be beautiful if it bears the imprint of our choice, our taste, our uncertainty, our desire, our weakness. Yes, this intelligent man has known your whole life. He has already made a little headway into that life; he turns and looks back, the diversity of the planes should multiply the beauty of the lighting for him. But grammatical dogma keeps him in chains. Discreet emotion, smiling candor. And then this so gay Carmen, is she really you? Isn't there in you, too, a part of Perdita, a part of Imogene? In spite of everything, it was a beautiful testimonial to one life in relation to other lives, sad and beautiful, in their radiance of glory. I read it with a great deal of enjoyment. And I found the description of your portrait delightful. Recently he gave a marvelous little talk to some children in a school. It was much better. Madame, what grim folly to set myself to writing to you about grammar and literature! And I am so ill! In the name of heaven *not a word* of all this to M. Ganderax. In the name of heaven—in which neither one of us believes, alas.

Respectfully yours,
Marcel Proust

112: TO GEORGES DE LAURIS

1908

Mon cher Georges,

Thank you with all my heart for your delightful letter, which brought to my isolation and my sadness a feeling of friendship. I didn't, Georges, mean to send you "disturbing" books, but only the sort of pornography that mortifies the senses. There are two secret Verlaines, filthy and stupid. But I have only two other "improper" books (and not very improper, either), which, if you don't know them, might help you to spend half an hour. Seven letters from Mérimée to Stendhal and from H. B. to Mérimée, which I shall ask you to return for an hour in a few days and then you can keep them. But they are nothing wonderful.

Georges, if your innocence is finally beginning to weigh heavily upon you, I can quite understand that you would not want to have *cocottes* come to your house, but people claim that . . . As for me, I love only (at the moment I love nothing, as you can imagine) *jeunes filles*, as though life weren't sufficiently complicated as it is. You will say marriage was invented for that, but then she is no longer a *jeune fille*; one only has a *jeune fille* once. I understand Bluebeard; he was a man who loved *jeunes filles*. Speaking of people who like to complicate things, there are the Rothschilds, who besides everything else they ask of a future daughter-in-law require her to be a Jewess. . . . I remember on a train hearing some people say, "You see, rich as they are, the Rothschilds can't find any Catholics to marry them." Dear Georges, how do you want me to work since I don't sleep, don't eat, don't breathe and this letter represents a labor of Hercules.

Adieu, cher Georges, à bientôt,
Ton
Marcel

113: TO MADAME STRAUS

FEBRUARY 3, 1908

Madame,

It is so charming of you to defend yourself for having been ironical over that article about which I am now afraid I was not ironical enough. *Talent* is a great deal. I meant to say that the article isn't as stupid as people in society say it is.

But society people are so imbued with their own stupidity that they can never believe that talent exists in one of their own set. They only appreciate writers who are not in society. But at the same time (again a result of their stupidity), the only writers they appreciate are those who express their own mentality—that is the mentality of people in society. They find Mme de Noailles's books dull and Bourget's sublime. As for A——, although he may have done several articles in which he shows a really gracious wish to express things that we like, the merit of the one I mentioned lies only in its good intentions and its aura of virtue. But still there is this about him, too; he is a journalist and a man of the world who does not make virtue consist in anti-Semitism. And the whole thing adds up finally to a character more sympathetic than his physical appearance, which, I admit, is more worthy of Sem's pencil than of our apologies. I realize that in saying *our* I am being presumptuous indeed! . . .

Your grateful and respectful friend,
Marcel Proust

114: TO ROBERT DREYFUS

MAY 16, 1908

Mon cher Robert,

. . . .

Meanwhile my project is taking form. It is more likely to be a long short story, so there will be time to consult you again. But just for the same reason (namely, that art is too much above life, as it is judged through our conscious minds and described in our conversation, to be satisfied with any counterfeit of life) that I think the importance of art and its superconscious reality prevents certain anecdotal novels, however pleasant they may be, from wholly deserving the rank you seem to give them—so this same reason does not allow me to make the realization of a dream of art depend on material just as anecdotal and too directly drawn from life not to be part and parcel of its casualness and unreality. Besides, put in such terms, the whole thing seems, if not false, at least banal enough to deserve some stinging slap in the face from a resentful existence (like Oscar Wilde's saying that the death of Lucien de Rubempré in Balzac was the greatest sorrow he had had, and discovering a little later, through his trial, that there are more real sorrows). But you know that this banal aestheticism could not be my aesthetic philosophy. And if fatigue, the fear of being a bore, and chiefly this *pencil* prevent my making myself clear, credit me, if not with its truth, with its seriousness.

Marcel

115: TO MADAME STRAUS

[JUNE] 1908

Madame,

I was stupefied and disgusted to read that S— has presented himself for admission to the Academy. Although I am afraid of running afoul of the timid and time-serving spirit of the *Figaro*, I intend to write (which, alas, does not mean acceptance and publication) an article about him. I shall substitute perfidy for insult so as to have more chance of being printed!

Only, I should like to have certain information and wish you would ask Reinach for it when you see him. Naturally I shall not compromise him nor mention my sources.

1st. Is it true that S——'s works are not by him but by R——?

2nd. Has S—— any scientific standing whatsoever? Are there any members of the Academy of Inscriptions who have more than he has? Which ones (all of them, I suppose, but I want some names to quote)?

3rd. Is it true that he was only elected through some sort of fraud and no longer would be today? That, to be specific, he behaved badly to Maspéro?

—*Finally*, I wish that if you see Hervieu or any other member of the Academy, you would ask him whether there is any *possibility whatsoever* of S——'s ever being a member of the Academy or whether he will never get more than two votes. Forgive me for bothering you, but you understand my feelings. Reinach can write me the information without any fears; I shall return his letter so that he won't worry, and I shall compromise only myself.

Your respectful friend,
Marcel Proust

116: TO MADAME STRAUS

MONDAY EVENING
[JUNE, 1908]

Madame,

Naturally I shall not talk about the Affair. But perhaps it would be wise, so that he can't claim that there is political vengeance, to say that I am enchanted at Barrès's election to the Academy; that I should also be at Léon Daudet's; that if I find S——'s election absurd it is not because of his opinions but his stupidity; that a ducal party in the Academy is legitimate (I don't think so, but perhaps it is better to put it this way), but a snob party is excessive; that if being a duke is enough to make one an Academician, seeking out the company of dukes is not sufficient; that it would be all right if S—— were nothing more than a snob and had been elected for that reason, but he has written books, and there is something offensive in the thought that he could be elected because of those books. Finally, I shall say all this better, less seriously, less charitably, drawing attention to his feet, without any pretense of good taste and barely any of good faith. . . . But, seriously and exclusive of all political reasons, if they want to find someone in the related sciences (as though there weren't enough writers), it is *shameful* of them not to elect: either scholars who are the brilliant and undisputed glory of these related sciences; a Boutroux, a Bergson, a Maspéro, a Bréal, an Alfred Croiset, and so many others. *Or* even better, a rare and little known talent in one of those very sciences whose name the Academy might launch rather than consecrate: an Emile Mâle, an Abbé Vignot, an Abbé Huvelin, a Darlu, a Brunschvicg, and so many others. And then, quite simply, Porto-Riche, Régnier, Boylesve, Hermant, Francis Jammes, Maeterlinck, etc. And if *snobisme* is to dictate the choice, let it be a great nobleman who has never written a line; it is understood that he is elected only because he *is* a great nobleman. Or even an aristocrat of distinction and intellect, Galliffet, or your friend, the Prince d'Arenberg, or why not Montesquiou? But S— seems to me a national disgrace, the triumph of everything vile and senseless, of knowledge without intelligence and even, which is unprecedented, without seriousness; this type of idiotic knowledge, the solemnity of which is its only excuse for being, is, in him, utterly frivolous. Also it is servility become arrogant, the ugly venom of a striking reptile; a life supposedly dedicated to science (and actually a science that admits of no more understanding and which produces no more "elevation" than the science of bridge) which is crowned by devotion to ideas which Louis XIV found superannuated and Vauban barbarous, and all this without the excuse of loyalty to principles, which he never had, to friends when he was sixty and who are not his friends, for they can only despise his shameful obsequiousness in their presence; and with the added insult of all the denials and all the surrenders. I shan't say all of this; but it will be the secret motive power, the priming charge of fire and anger that could make me decide to do an article, me, who can't even write a letter without its giving me a headache. But then, there is the fun of portraying this prehistoric buffalo, mustachioed like a patriot, intimidated and blushing before all the ladies, converts of the X— and Z— families. Madame, how I must bore you; how grateful I am to you! Will you give my deepest thanks to M. Reinach?

Your respectful friend,
Marcel Proust

117: TO MADAME STRAUS

[JUNE, 1908]

Chère Madame Straus,

This "poor man's" writing paper, as the Baroness James [Rothschild] used to say, will tell you only that as I entered the Murats', before even catching sight of the masters of the house, I saw seated with them to receive the guests, wearing the falsely bashful look of a man who for sixty years has pretended a horror of society, S— This gave me the pleasure of passing in front of him twenty times to greet other people without saying how-do-you-do to him. Someone said to me: "Don't you know M. S—?" I answered very loudly: "I shall say how-do-you-do to him when he says how-do-you-do to Madame Straus, who doesn't care whether or not he speaks to her, but I do care." I "spoke" my article to practically all the guests, so that he must by now know my intentions. Mme de Chevigné was sublime, which restored all my affection for her. Besides being nice about a young girl whom I love, she assured me that she said to S—— about the Academy: "You will pay for all your cowardly acts." There are good people. *Adieu,* Madame, it is so late that it seems almost indiscreet to write you. The bashful buffalo smiled inanely each time I passed him, thinking that I was coming to greet him, and his enormous hooves left fossil footprints on the carpet.

Your respectful friend,
Marcel Proust

118: TO GEORGES DE LAURIS

[CIRCA OCTOBER—NOVEMBER 1908]

Mon petit Georges,

. . . . Today the exposition at the Autumn Salon, which I wanted to see more than any other, closed, El Greco and Monticelli, the two painters I am most "in love" with, and I couldn't go there. Before your accident when I didn't expect to come back to Paris (which was most helpful to me and useful to you), I said to myself that no matter where I was, even if it were Venice, I would come back for forty-eight hours to see this exhibition, which may not be sublime, but which would have been so fruitful for me because it happened to be held just at the moment in time that coincided with my desire to see it. And it wasn't even possible for me to find a wheel chair in which I could have been taken there and in which I would quite shamelessly have gone. I think I shall get better. I think I shall go to see you.

Georges, when you can, *work*. Ruskin somewhere made a *sublime* statement that the two great commandments of God (the second is almost entirely his own, but that doesn't matter) were: "*Work while you still have light*" and "*Be merciful while you still have mercy*"; we should bear these in mind every day. Léon Blum, I assure you, has never said anything as good. After the first commandment taken from Saint John, comes this sentence: "For the night comes when one can work no more." (I am quoting incorrectly.) Georges, I am already halfway into that night, in spite of certain temporary signs which don't mean anything. But you, you have the light, you will have it for long years to come, *work*. Then, if life brings bitterness, there is consolation, for the true life is elsewhere, not in life itself, nor afterwards, but outside, if an expression that takes its origin in space has any meaning in the world that is free of it. And as for compassion—you have had something even better: a love so sweet that the death of your poor mother doesn't for the time being seem so horrible when I think of all the hope she left, of how exactly you are fulfilling her prayer. As for your life with your father, you know what I think about that and how it delights me to think about it. With me you are very kind if I refer to my sense of gratitude, less affectionate than kind, although you think the opposite, and your kindness has limitations which have to do with the lack of security in your character. *Adieu*, dear Georges, forgive this evangelical sermon, but accidents like yours, which I keep picturing to myself, should be a warning. Work, since God has left you the light to work by. No, dear Georges, it is useless to search in Léon Blum, or even, in spite of what our friends will swear to, in Claude

Anet; you will find nothing as good there. Which doesn't prevent Ruskin's work from frequently being stupid, eccentric, maddening, false, and irritating; but it is always significant and always great. He was, you know, much admired by George Eliot, who, in spite of what Léon Blum may think, is worth all the Marguerittes and, perhaps, who knows, even the Rosnys. She spoke of "these great works which allow us to reconcile our inward despair with the delightful sense of a life outside ourselves." Dear Georges, it is a great effort to write, but it is pleasant to remind someone of fine ideas, which he already knows, understands, and from which he can draw sustenance, and in whose opinion the literature of our great and near-great acquaintances is of purely relative value.

Yours with all my heart, even now, at one in the morning, in spite of endless coughing and a fever, with three windows open in an effort to combat the steam heat.

Your
Marcel

119: TO THE COMTESSE DE NOAILLES

THURSDAY [1908 OR 1909]

Madame,

Will you permit me without preamble to ask your advice? I should like, although I am very ill, to write an essay on Sainte-Beuve. The subject has taken shape in my mind in two different ways, and I must choose between them. But I lack both determination and clarity of mind. The first way would be as a classical essay, an essay in the manner of Taine, only a thousand times less good (except for the content, which I think is new). The second starts with an account of the morning, of waking up. Mother comes to my bedside to see me, I tell her I have an idea for a study of Sainte-Beuve; I submit it to her and develop it for her. Could you tell me which way you think best? I shall have so many apologies to make to you, which I am too exhausted to do, but the reason for my mad impertinence also makes it forgivable; because you are our greatest writer, it is outrageous to bother you with these trifles, but it is also why your advice is irreplaceable.

Please deign, Madame, to accept my deepest and most respectful admiration.

Marcel Proust

I can't telephone, otherwise I should not have bothered you with a letter.

PART THREE

Swann's Way and the War, 1909–1918

The long book that was undoubtedly an outgrowth of the writings mentioned ten years earlier in a letter to Marie Nordlinger seemed, in the years just preceding the World War, to be approaching completion. Proust's expressed attitude towards his work took on greater seriousness, and he began to write on critical matters with greater freedom, as though his book—for which he soon sought a publisher—gave him the necessary *cachet*.

But if he had begun to feel that the book of which he was proud was almost ready for publication, and if his letters display a quiet confidence in it and in himself, there were few to support that confidence. Long regarded in his family both as *malade* and *écrivain imaginaire*, he remained the *écrivain imaginaire* in the eyes of the literary and social worlds. And when, after numerous rebuffs from publishers, *Swann's Way* was at last published at the author's expense in 1913, it was as little noticed, save for a few reviews, as that first sensitive indication of his gifts, published almost twenty years earlier, *Les Plaisirs et les Jours*. Soon, however, *Swann* began to acquire admirers, devoted if few.

In August, 1914, the war came. Friends were scattered, and friends were killed. Proust withdrew more and more into himself and his work, but looked out upon the world of Gothas and Americans "from far away" with an absorbed interest, living in the war, he once wrote, as men in the past lived in God.

Princesse Marthe Bibesco,
Romanian-born author of many novels and plays written in French, is a cousin of the Prince Bibesco.

120: TO PRINCESSE MARTHE BIBESCO

102, BOULEVARD HAUSSMANN
MONDAY, MARCH 29 [1909]

Princesse,

. . . .

Mme de Noailles has, in my opinion, obliterated all possibility for at least fifty years of anyone else's addressing cities in direct discourse, etc. . . . Everything done in this style, in this pattern, no matter how sincere, how true to life, how anterior to her it may be, will appear to be an imitation of her; her radiance will outshine all our lights unless, unless we go deeply and endlessly down into ourselves, to the heart of our heart or rather the brain of our heart, to find a different and entirely individual expression. I very pretentiously say "our" because I myself had to burn almost all of a volume on Brittany written before I had ever read anything of hers where:

Quimperlé! . . .
Pont-Aven! . . .

seemed to come from the *Shadow of Days* or *The Domination*. My sacrifice was necessary but bloody. It will perhaps not be definitive. Literary sacrifices rarely are. From this point of view I regret the choice for the *Figaro* supplement where the reader could justifiably be misled, where I myself didn't immediately find the originality which later enchanted me in the book. But the admirable thought that you quote and that closes the book, rather ties it to certain passages of Ruskin, which you certainly do not know, and which in themselves detract nothing from such a different kind of originality.

Please deign to accept, Princesse, all my respects.

Marcel Proust

121: TO GEORGES DE LAURIS

[APRIL OR MAY 1909]

Mon cher Georges,

. . . . I am glad that you have read some Bergson and liked him. It is as though we had been together on a great height. I don't know *L'Evolution créatrice* (and because of the great value I attach to your opinion I shall read it immediately). But I have read enough of Bergson, the parabola of his thought is already sufficiently discernible after only a single generation, so that whatever "creative evolution" may have followed, I can, when you mention Bergson, know what you mean. Besides, I think that I have told you of my great admiration for him and even, which is less interesting—although it gives him a moral quality—of the great kindness he has always shown me: in fact it was he who reviewed the *Bible d'Amiens* at the Institute. I see that Pius X has forbidden the priests to attend his courses or to read his books. That's how I discovered that they do read them, and it pleased me because I was under the impression that they read only *La Libre Parole* (which is not, however, forbidden them by Pius X). I remember that when I entered Sollier's sanatorium, one of the first things he said to me concerned Bergson, whom he had been obliged to read because he felt that their province was the same: "What a confused and narrow mind!" he said. I felt a da Vincian smile of intellectual pride pass over my face. Which did not add to the success of my psychotherapeutic treatment. *Adieu*, Georges, writing you is tiring me. I did nothing while you were away. I intend starting work . . . in an hour. But that is a practical expression, which doubtless means never. The *Mercure de France* and Fasquelle have refused to publish my *pastiches*. You mustn't say so because I have offered them to Calmann-Lévy, who will also, without doubt, refuse. . . . I read the name of the young heroine (of your novel), agreeably quoted by Hurst in an article on Mademoiselle Dorziat.

Affectionately yours,
Marcel

122: TO GEORGES DE LAURIS

[MAY 23, 1909]

Mon petit Georges,

. . . .

Do you know whether *Guermantes*, which must have been the name of some people, was even then in the Pâris family or rather, to use a more suitable expression, whether the name of the Count or Marquis de Guermantes was the title of a relative of Pâris's, and whether it is entirely extinct and available to an author? Do you know any other pretty names of châteaux and of people? What was your property called?

Affectionately yours,
Marcel

123: TO GEORGES DE LAURIS

1909

Mon petit Georges,

I know I owe your divine letter to your blind friendship for me, but that gives it all the more value. Since I am more affectionate than conceited, it is pleasanter to see that you love me than to believe that I have talent. From the point of view of discretion you can very well say that I had you read the beginning of my book, and if anyone can find that an exclusive privilege (about which I in no way flatter myself), I am only too happy to state and to underline my predilection for you. What I ask is that you should not repeat the subject nor the title nor, in fact, anything that might be informative (not that it would interest anyone), but more than that I wish to be neither hurried nor harassed nor conjectured nor anticipated nor copied nor explained nor criticized nor embarrassed. There will be time enough when my thought has worked itself out to let others make fools of themselves. According to the directions I am leaving, you will be given with the two notebooks (second and third), two pages of the first to replace those similarly paginated with a passage which will seem worldly to a worldly reader but where you will see a meritorious attempt to express some ideas which do not express themselves of their own accord. As for the notebooks I am sending you, in spite of some words crossed out in ink at random when I discovered some monstrosities, they are much more the copyist's work than mine. And I count on your intuitive and affectionate collaboration.

Your grateful
Marcel

Don't think that I like George Sand. It is not a piece of criticism. That's how it was at that time; the rest of the book will rectify it.

124: TO MADAME STRAUS

CABOURG

[END OF AUGUST, 1909]

Madame,

Your delightful card causes me, along with tremendous pleasure, a little pain, because for several days I have been going to write to you, because my letter turns out to have changed into a reply, because you no longer are aware of the initiative of my desire and the flight of my heart, which goes twenty times a day to *Les Mûriers* and tires me out more in my restless and vagabond immobility than would a journey which would at least fill my eyes with the picture my memory is endlessly painting. I did, in fact, leave Paris, feeling very ill, and I have stayed so here. I do, however, get up for a little while around half-past nine at night, but I have bad, damp rooms, which I can't settle into very easily. I go from the hotel to the casino, which is about two minutes away, and that seems so to tire me that I wonder how I could go to Trouville. But I shall go. I prefer that to seeing you at Cabourg, where the surprise of your arrival, the fear that you may catch cold, the excitement of the music and the crowd, the shock of seeing you without the preparatory pilgrimage during which I gradually become worthy of you during my meditations on the way, practically prevent my realizing that you are here. I think only of the drafts that must bother you, of the chocolate for which M. Straus has gone off secretly to pay, and only when your automobile has gone, when I am left alone, when I say to myself, "That was Mme Straus!" do I become painfully aware of the happiness I have not felt. And I try to identify all the affectionate thoughts, the beauty and admiration that your name means to me with the vanishing image that I have looked at for an hour without seeing. I shouldn't want you to take too seriously those often stated threats which may this time become more effective, but I think you will see me fairly frequently in Paris this year. But before that, you will read me, more than you will like, for I have just begun—and finished—all of a long book. Unfortunately, my leaving for Cabourg interrupted my work, and I am only now about to go back to it. Perhaps a part of it will appear serially in the *Figaro*, but only a part because it is too improper and too long to be given in its entirety. But I should so like to finish, to come to the end.

I am very glad, not being able to see either you or Helleu, that you are seeing him. I know that it makes him very happy and I should think that you would like him. Even physically he is charming, and Montesquiou was right when he said that few descendants of those who were guillotined have as much "breeding" as the descendant of the executioner. And it is very true. I wish you could see his establishment in Paris. We think we are *blasé* about pretty houses because everything is alike and it bores us. But it is the same way with novels; we are tired of them until the day an original book appears that restores our freshness of impressionability and our desire to read. I am sure you would like this arrangement in exquisite taste and that it would please him greatly to show it to you. For he has the very simple nature of the true artist, and if very few people can make him happy, of those very few, all do. You know La Bruyère's remark, "If one is with the people one loves, whether one talks to them or is silent doesn't matter if one is only with them." (I am not quoting very accurately.) This is unfortunately not one of my pleasures, and I am never with the people I love. In Paris I at least have the consolation of not being with the ones I don't love, either, and I haven't it at Cabourg. . . .

Adieu, Madame, I shall come to see you soon and I never tire of seeing you. Please accept for you and M. Straus my respectful expression of deep and grateful affection.

Marcel Proust

P.S. Since I have written this letter I have been obliged to stay in bed the whole time, having caught a slight fever; this may perhaps enable me to change my hours and to come to Trouville soon.

125: TO MADAME STRAUS

VERSAILLES, OCTOBER 27? [1909]

Madame,

I am very sad over your not being well, very sad that our "treatments" separate us without bringing any improvement. I keep saying to myself that if I had to climb stairs, I should be even worse, and that if you were seeing people in Paris, instead of being in Switzerland, you would be even more tired. The medical profession is lucky that it is impossible for us to know what would happen if, other things being equal, we had followed another course of hygiene. But things aren't equal, and how can one distinguish between the part time plays, the thousand unknown causes, the capriciousness of the illness itself. We have—or, rather, I have—for some time past fallen into a bad habit where you are concerned. As soon as I am near you, I am paralyzed by an unfamiliar timidity, I sense a sort of spell between us, and I behave in such a stupid way that it exasperates me all the more because away from you it is not so continuous. The feeling that you regard me as a gossip, the necessity for always supplying you with news and scandal perhaps has something to do with it. I am, for the time being, very poorly stocked because since I saw you I have hardly left the house, and at home I see no one. Only Reynaldo tells me from time to time what goes on in "society," where I never go. But the fact of having known various individuals at your house in the past enables me to be more interested in his stories. I know that Mme de F— your friend (who was mine!) met M. de G— the other day, and he reproached her for never inviting him to her house. She replied, "Not at all, I shall invite you— But, no, come to think of it, I couldn't. You remind me too much of my poor Robert!" An indisputably authentic remark reported by three people who were present. Her rival made several pleasant remarks. But really to repeat other peoples' remarks to you—except involuntary ones—is too stupid. Even on the merest postcard yours are so much better. . . . I am always seeing announcements in the papers of exhibitions that tempt me. But I keep saying to myself that I shall wait to go and see pictures again until we can go together. And besides I haven't seen any since they say I went to Durand-Ruel with you to see Claude Monet's wonderful water lilies. I think the last evening I went to your house was the one when Helleu expected me. Fancy my having been indiscreet enough to tell him that a picture of Versailles, a sketch, was the best thing he had done. A few days later it arrived! I am so embarrassed by his kindness that I don't know what to do, and I should like to find something nice that would please him with which to thank him. Everyone is so nice to me that it makes me unhappy that I myself don't know how to give pleasure. *Adieu*, Madame, I hope that you will be coming back soon and that I may go and see you.

Your respectful admirer who loves you,
Marcel Proust

I wrote an extremely affectionate letter to Jacques recently. But he never answered.

126: TO GEORGES DE LAURIS

BETWEEN NOVEMBER 21 AND 25, 1909

Mon petit Georges,

. . . . You will perhaps learn some news from me very soon, or rather I shall ask your advice. To share my ghastly life with a delightful girl, even if she isn't frightened of it—would that be a crime?

. . . .

Georges, I shall set to work, for I read the beginning (two hundred pages) to Reynaldo and his attitude encouraged me deeply. Any evening you wish I will read it to you. I feel that it is my duty from now on to subordinate everything to trying to finish this. And afterwards I shall have only one aim: trying to see you a great deal.

Affectionately yours,
Marcel

Could you lend me Mâle for twenty-four hours? Which of your books have I besides *Port-Royal*, which I shall send back because I shan't use it for several months?

127: TO ROBERT DE BILLY

[CIRCA DECEMBER, 1909]

Cher Robert,

. . . . I have just been reading something very beautiful which unfortunately slightly resembles what I am doing (only it is a thousand times better): *The Well-Beloved* by Thomas Hardy. It doesn't even lack that slight touch of the grotesque which is an essential part of all great works. When you are talking to Lister, ask him if he knows Thomas Hardy and Barrie, what kind of men they are, men of the world, ladies' men, etc. It is curious that in all the different *genres*, from George Eliot to Hardy, from Stevenson to Emerson, there is no literature which has as much hold on me as English and American literature. Germany, Italy, very often France, leave me indifferent. But two pages of *Mill on the Floss* reduce me to tears. I know that Ruskin loathed that novel, but I reconcile all these hostile gods in the Pantheon of my admiration.

Adieu, dear Robert, I should love to know that you are well, that neither Mme de Billy whom I picture again almost every day so rosy and so sweet in the boat that took her to Lion-sur-Mer, any longer has a temperature, nor your daughters whom I don't know. *Adieu*, dear Robert, I love you very tenderly, very deeply.

Your,
Marcel Proust

128: TO MADAME GASTON DE CAILLAVET

[PROBABLY 1910]

Madame,

Strange to love opposite physical types! For here I am, in love with your daughter. How naughty of her to be so gracious, for her smile, which has made me fall in love with her, colors her whole personality. Had she frowned, I should be completely at peace. I am trying to think of the flower with petals just like her cheeks when she smiles. I should indeed like to see her smile again. True, if I saw her again she might thumb her nose at me, a symbol, rather, of her parents' attitude towards me and notably of her father's, to whom I have written so affectionately. If ever Calmette finds the time to publish an article of mine which he has had for a long time and which is the memory of a childhood love of mine (not my love for you; that was *before*), you will see embodied in it some of the emotion I felt when I wondered whether you would be at the tennis party. But what is the use of remembering things when you have taken the absurd and malicious attitude of pretending you never noticed them in the first place! How prettily your daughter smiles! How pretty she is! She pleases me infinitely.

Your respectful,
Marcel Proust

129: TO MADAME STRAUS

MAY OR JUNE, 1911

Chère Madame Straus,

. . . .

I am very unhappy about not seeing you and two or three other people. But, apart from that, people complain to me about things which aren't really very sad, the cruelest of which they seem to think is the fact that I have to get along without seeing *them*. But nothing could be more delightful. All the more so since the ones I caught sight of *the* evening I went out to see *Saint Sebastian* seemed to me much worse. The nicest ones go in for intelligence and, alas, in society people—I don't know how they manage it—intelligence seems only to multiply stupidity to an unprecedented degree of power and magnificence. The only possible ones are those who have had the wit to remain stupid. . . .

Adieu, Madame. I hope to see you soon.

Your respectful friend,
Marcel Proust

130: TO MADAME STRAUS

MAY OR JUNE, 1911

Chère Madame Straus,

Life goes by and only makes more cruel this complete separation from you. I am always expecting my book to end and it is not yet finished. I can't tell you how much I constantly try to console myself for being deprived of you by thinking of the happier days when I could see you. Sometimes I evoke one day, sometimes another, I am surrounded by them. I am sending you two little engravings, one of which requires no explanation; I am afraid that it isn't very suitable, but since the frame is nice you could hang it in a dressing room at Trouville. As for the other: the first time M. Straus came to see me at boulevard Malesherbes, at the time when he thought I was having a bad influence on Jacques (or at least he had just stopped thinking so), I received him in our hideously medical little salon, which retrospectively I find more touching than many beautiful rooms, and in which the bronzes, the palms, the plush, and the mahogany played their respective roles. M. Straus wanted to say something agreeable, he looked around, and at that moment he encountered the "Château Florentin"; when he finally caught sight of a little drawing of Henri Monnier's that Caran d'Ache had given Father, who was his doctor, he said several times that it was nice. Ever since then I have looked at this mediocre little drawing with pleasure because of the epoch it brought to mind. And I should like henceforth to have it in your house in an obscure corner, in an upstairs corridor. I think with such melancholy and such enchantment of that happier time when I received my first letter from you, and, in order to be able to reexperience a little of the emotion, I have asked Leuchars to send me paper like yours. But what he sent me a month ago, a sample of which I am sending you in this letter so that you can know that the friend who never sees you thinks of you endlessly, is so different from your mauve-lined paper scented with *peau d'Espagne*, that up until now I have hesitated to order any. There were the pink cards from the *Trois Quartiers*, too. But that was later. I am not writing to you at greater length because in addition to my other worries military worries have come along. A medical major came to see me the other day at nine in the morning, and a second visit is imminent.

If I could know of some little object that would please you, I should be so happy to send you a little souvenir and it would be so nice of you to tell me what. Won't you, please? It would at last give me something pleasant to do, something with which I could associate a thought of you.

Please accept, Madame, and share with M. Straus, my respectful affection.

Marcel Proust

131: TO MADAME CATUSSE

[CABOURG, PROBABLY OCTOBER OR NOVEMBER, 1911]

Chère Madame,

. . . . To my increasingly failing strength, which always makes me put off until next day what I couldn't do the day before, is added the hope of soon finishing the novel I have started and which has already for a very long time made me postpone until its conclusion the carrying out of precious plans, which I have promised myself as celebration once it is finished. But the work stretches out ahead of me and my strength diminishes. . . . I went this year again to Cabourg and was better there than in Paris. But even this better is growing worse, at Cabourg. The first year there I could take long automobile rides, the second I could go down to the beach, the third go downstairs in the hotel every day, but the fourth, this year, I could go down to the beach only once in two and a half months and only every two or three evenings around eleven downstairs in the hotel (and to the casino which is in the hotel). What stories I shall have to tell you. And it will be amusing to talk to you about art, literature, philosophy, politics, even financial affairs! I shall tell you about my "Kracks," the stupid stocks they made me buy and which have dropped to nothing! All of this fortunately to a sufficiently negligible degree not to affect my life. I doubly regret no longer seeing Bénac, for I would have asked his advice. And, besides, the sight of him is now so rich for me in that daily diminishing treasure of days gone by. They are, chiefly, what I should love to talk to you about, you whom I loved in days that were happy and in heart-rending days; you whom I first told on the telephone from Evian of Mother's condition and who saw her at the station carried to the train, and by whom, the day you came to Evian, she wanted and still did not want to be photographed, wishing to leave me a last picture but fearing that it would be too sad; you whom I saw first on my return from Evian. I wanted to write only a line. But with you I never can! I have so much to say, I talk to you, I imagine I am seeing you, I can't bear to leave you! But I shan't write again because I must concentrate all my energies (if I dare say so) on my book. I still get up once or twice a month, and on that day I generally go out to the *Concert Mayol* to hear that singer who has the double advantage of not singing until eleven o'clock and of having a great deal of talent! . . .

Please, Madame, accept my respectful and fraternal affection.

Marcel Proust

Jean-Louis Vaudoyer, born in 1883, is a novelist, essayist, and critic, formerly curator of the Carnavalet Museum, now director of the Charpentier Gallery.

132: TO JEAN-LOUIS VAUDOYER

[CIRCA THE 21ST OF] MARCH, 1912

Cher Monsieur et ami,

Your letter gave me great pleasure. I shouldn't have dared send you the *Figaro*, but there is no one whom I should rather have had read my article. When I saw that an unknown hand had added that disgraceful title, "On the Threshold of Spring," as well as an absurd sentence, I thought right away of several artists, among them you, and of the opinion they would have of me if that copy of the paper happened to catch their eye. But then I thought it showed great conceit on my part, because people do not pay that much attention to what they read, and it showed a lack of faith, too. Surely, a mind as active as yours at in-

terpreting laws knows from the start what my literary possibilities and impossibilities are and could no more give credence to "On the Threshold of Spring" than to a flying bull. There are also natural laws for the mind, as well, and they are governed by determinism. You speak of some verses you are sending me; I await them impatiently, but shall perhaps delay thanking you for them, for I am very ill. Although I have already told you of my condition with a precision and directness that offended you and embarrassed me myself, I am forced to tell you again lest you think it is indifference on my part that makes me ask you not to come and see me. I haven't received my brother for a year, my doctor for two years. My attacks come and go without forewarning. I take inhalations every day. The only rest I take is frequently put off until four or five o'-clock in the morning. How can I receive anyone? Certainly there are some less bad days. I make use of them by getting up and going out, but I don't know in advance. I can only be patient and hope. After the book of which I have told you has appeared, I shall risk a great deal to see you. Between now and then I should not want to be too imprudent. And what precious advice you could have given me, practical advice, too. My book will be between eight and nine hundred pages long. You would have decided whether there should be two volumes, two titles, hundreds of things! I saw that you had a novel in the *Revue de Paris*. More than anything else I envy you your talent, your immeasurable and diverse richness in which all your diverse (alas, I have used diverse twice) gifts are united by

the originality of a quality of intelligence. But I envy you, too, being able, young as you are, to have both a platform and a framework. Just realize (and I beg of you to believe that this is no entreaty to recommend me to someone! I hope for nothing—except to read you and, if I am better, to see you)—although I had connections with Ganderax, the editor of the *Revue de Paris*, even before he became editor, some poems and a story of mine and an essay on Ruskin (commissioned) lay for years around the office of this gentleman who, torn between his personal friendship for me and his horror at my writings, ended by rejecting them out of "conscientious duty." The essay on Ruskin should have appeared because, in the interval, Ruskin having grown old and died, the manuscript, however wretched it may have been as literature, turned out to be admirable in its news value. Some other critic declined to do one. The editor-friend, caught in the dilemma of letting his review appear without an obituary of this great man, or of publishing what was later my preface to the *Bible d'Amiens*, still preferred the former disaster. And the reason for his rejection, which he gave me consistently, sadly, affectionately in all his letters was that "he didn't have enough time to *reorganize*—and *write* them." The writings which were deprived of this collaboration were combined with others to make up *Les Plaisirs et les Jours*; the verses were inserted there, etc. I shall not continue the list of my humiliations, especially since I bore them with an indifference that is basically very contemptible. But I am happy to think that a person like you, who is good enough to be ignored, is lucky enough to be understood and loved, and

to enjoy through that audience the wide publicity that is precious, indeed, because only through it is there the chance of our words being brought to the attention of our forever unknown brothers who would know how to understand (experience) them. For the same reason, since I never go out, I prefer to "intimate" meetings great "brawls," where in the surge of the crowd we sometimes catch sight of a face that we can dream about for a long time afterwards.

I am miserable over your letter in which you speak of the *cards* you sent me from Spain and Italy. I received only *one*. The one I had from Italy was a year ago and from you alone.

Yours very affectionately,
Marcel Proust

I don't know whether it would be entirely fortunate for us to have a real conversation together, for you would discover very quickly that we don't like at all the same things (I mean in literature, which is the only important thing). Nevertheless, I like what you write; well—you should write what you like, too.

133: TO PRINCESSE MARTHE BIBESCO

WEDNESDAY [MAY 1, 1912]

Princesse,

. . . .

Your *Alexandre Asiatique* really came like "the face of the sun." Unfortunately, the book itself has proved to me that our disagreement was more profound and that it had to do with ideas. Not that I haven't great admiration for these jewel-like words in their setting of silence, so boldly, so cleverly reticent that what you say is but a small part of what you have thought, so that if a commentator enlarges on what you have passed over in silence (although you outline it like a circumference the diameter of which one has measured but which one does not trouble to draw out), he would have to write a longer book than yours. And this silence is also a pedestal and indicates to what heights one should climb to read you; it is a usage, too, which permits of a concert between your actual or future thought and the distant images, making these profound sentences flower like a meadow in a tapestry or the chirruping of a bird. But, unless the book meant only to lead no further than where you conclude (and why not?), nothing is so alien to me as to look for happiness in the immediate sensation, or even less so in its concrete realization. A sensation, however disinterested it may be, a perfume, a ray of light, if they are there, are still too much in my power to make me happy. It is when they bring back to my mind some other sensation, when I savor them between the present and the past (and not in the past—impossible to explain this here), that they make me happy. Alexandre is right in saying that to cease hoping is despair itself. But although there is no end to my desires, I never hope. And perhaps, too, the great sobriety of my life in which there are no journeys, no walks, no society, no light, is in itself a contingent factor that adds fuel to my perennial desire. And when one no longer thinks of one's personal pleasure, one even finds a certain amount of it in determining the laws that deprive us of what we thought we could keep, even of the very heart itself. And our own interest in these laws, through which what we would never have believed we could attain is finally brought to us—this interest is able to compensate us for the disappointment of possessing what, as long as it was merely a desire, had seemed to us beautiful. I notice that after having told you that I never think about myself, I talk of nothing but me and the joy I feel in thinking about you. But I also notice that it is an exegesis of yours that I should talk about myself. For are not these last words singularly in accord with Alexandre's: one ends by no longer hoping as desperately for what one has as for what one will never have. Doesn't the death that you extol resemble the life I lead? But the latter will always lack the delightful and really perfect grace of your words when you say the "story of his life ends in a bird's chatter." That is perfection itself, the supreme art, which rejects useless riches, and which, still in the same sense, is a kind of reticence.

Please deign, Princesse, to accept my admiration and my grateful respect.

Marcel Proust

134: TO MADAME GASTON DE CAILLAVET

[JUST BEFORE JUNE 7, 1912]

. . . . Could you by chance give me some little details and explanations about dressmaking for the book I am finishing? (Please don't think that this is the reason I telephoned you the other day; then I was thinking only of how much I wanted to see you.) But I do need lots of details, words that escape me, but which I know in advance you couldn't give me because they are too out of date. You were too young. But perhaps you could do this. Have you seen dresses like those Mme S—— and Mme G—— wore at the Opera one night for an Italian performance of the Monte Carlo? Mme G—— took me to the Opera with Mme S——. And I had the impression of two quite different, quite opposite approaches to dress, to style. I don't think you could have seen them that evening because they were in a stage box, very dark (about two months ago), but you may perhaps have seen them separately at other performances. I shouldn't want either of them to know that this interests me (otherwise I should quite simply have asked Mme G——, whom I have often seen since) because the two women whom I shall drape in their dresses (like two mannequins) bear no relation to them; because there is no key to my novel; because if I talk to them about it and after that my invented women turn out to be poisonous or incestuous, or no matter what, they will be convinced that I meant to say they were. I'd rather not! . . .

Your respectful friend,
Marcel Proust

135: TO MADAME GASTON DE CAILLAVET

[JUST AFTER JUNE 7, 1912]

. . . . I go out once in a while when chance permits, and it is generally to see the hawthorns, or the furbelows of three apple trees in their ball gowns under a grey sky. But when much more rarely I go into the world, not of things, but of people, the ladies' dresses, far less delightful in color than the apple trees, puzzle me just as much. For when I have an impression, I need exact words to interpret it. And I don't know what they are. So I peruse botanical books or books on architecture or fashion magazines. And naturally, what I need is never there! Little P——, of whom I was talking to you the other day, undertook only last year to ask his botany professor about some of these things. I thanked him effusively for his information—which was of no use to me. I have just seen again the two ladies of the *soirée* before which I had wanted to come and see you. But I was no better able to describe them. By the way, you may not know Mme S——'s remark to the other one. The other one, borrowing Mme Récamier's remark, said that she would know she was no longer beautiful when the little chimneysweeps stopped turning to look at her as she passed. And Mme S—— replied, "Oh, don't worry, my dear, as long as you dress that way, people will always turn around and look at you."

I think you know, also, the letter that Montesquiou wrote to Maurice de R——, from whom he had asked the loan of some jewels for a fancy dress ball and who had sent him only a tiny brooch, asking him to be careful of it because it was a family jewel. "I didn't know that you had a family, but I did think that you had jewelry."

I am compensating for months of solitude and sadness by a quarter of an hour of frivolity with you, but I am afraid you may find me excessively frivolous. From time to time my memory and my imagination present me with stereoscopic views of your daughter's smile, and phonograph records of her voice. I label this pastime with the slightly out-of-date title: "The Pleasures of Solitude." My affectionate greetings to Gaston and my fond respects to you.

Marcel Proust

136: TO MADAME STRAUS

OCTOBER, 1912

Madame,

. . . . This letter is attached to a copy of Sainte-Beuve I wanted to have bound with some extracts from other volumes where the name Halévy is mentioned, and to preface it with a little essay by me, but in the light of this perpetual postponement, which, much against my will, my life has become, I want at least to enable you to read Sainte-Beuve's essay, and so I am sending it to you. I don't doubt but that you know Sainte-Beuve well. But in reading aloud to you certain pages of his on Flaubert, on Balzac, on Stendhal, you would have had a more exact focus, a sort of "scale" that these pages need and without which they will seem very cold to you, but with which, if you really know his style well and his customary opinions, they would seem most complimentary. In any case, I think they will interest you. . . .

Please share with M. Straus my respectful compliments.

Marcel Proust

Louis de Robert (1871–1937) was a prolific novelist best known for his *Le Roman d'un malade* (1910), written after ten years of severe illness spent in sanatoria. A friend of Loti and of Zola, a successful journalist during the nineties, he was a passionate Dreyfusard and attended daily the court sessions of Zola's trial. Too ill to attend the trial himself, Proust had listened eagerly each evening at Mme de Caillavet's salon to de Robert's accounts of the proceedings.

137: TO LOUIS DE ROBERT

102, BOULEVARD HAUSSMANN
[BETWEEN 7 AND 15 OCTOBER, 1912]

Cher ami,

. . . . You know, perhaps, that ever since I have been ill, I have been working on a long book, which I call a novel because it isn't as fortuitous as memoirs (it is fortuitous only to the degree that life itself is), and the composition is very severe although difficult to appraise because of its complexity; I don't know how to describe the *genre*. Certain parts take place in the country, some in one kind of society, others in another kind; some have to do with family life and much of it is terribly indecent. Calmette, to whom the book is dedicated, promised me to have Fasquelle publish it, and we didn't speak of the matter again because it was all understood (at least understood by Calmette and me, I don't know whether he had talked to Fasquelle first). Only this is what happened. My novel is so long (although from my point of view very concise) that there will be three volumes of 400 pages each or, better still, two volumes of 700 and 500 each. I was told (not by Calmette, whom I haven't seen again) that it was useless to ask Fasquelle to publish a work in two or three volumes, that he would *force* me to have a different title for each volume and an interval between the publication of each one. This upsets me very much, but I am told that it would be the same with other publishers. Besides, I am ill, very ill, and consequently in a hurry to be published, and Fasquelle has the advantage (as well as many other advantages) of being willing to publish the book immediately (I hope!)—that is, if Calmette really has the influence he said he had. But I now am told that Fasquelle goes over books very critically, that he demands changes, that nothing must be allowed to interfere with the *action*. What advice would you, who have had so much experience with this sort of thing, give me (who have published only an illustrated book with Calmann-Lévy, for whom my present work would be much too indecent, and translations in the *Mercure*)? Do you think that if Calmette took my book to Fasquelle, the latter would publish it with its lyric sequences, without changing them? (I shall resign myself to dividing the work into two parts, but as the approach to the subject is very slow, there would be a great advantage in having the first novel run to 700 or 650 pages, very compact, like the pages in *L'Education*.)

Do you think I would do better to give up the idea of Fasquelle and look for a purely literary publisher (like the *Nouvelle revue française*, which would perhaps be willing to publish me in three volumes; I don't mind paying the expenses of publication, but if one does that, I believe the publishers no longer take any trouble about the book)—do you think, then, that such a publisher would have more luck in making readers accept a book that, really, in no way resembles the classical novel? You who have been ill can understand what it means always to keep saying to yourself that tomorrow you will have finished, and then to spend months without being able to take up a pen, and always to fear there may not be time to finish. Thank God, there are actually 600 or 700 pages that are all ready to be printed. And during that time I could revise the rest. One of these days, if I can get up, I shall go to see Calmette, who fortunately receives late at night when there is some respite from my attacks. But before then, if by chance you are free for a moment, I should like some advice from you. Only don't judge me too much by yourself who have written an admirable book which is not a novel. You were already known. I am known only to a very few writers. To the majority I am *entirely unknown*. When on rare occasions readers write me care of the *Figaro* after I have had an article published, the letters are sent to Marcel Prévost because they think my name is just a misspelling of his.

Most cordially yours,
Marcel Proust

138: TO MADAME STRAUS

[OCTOBER OR NOVEMBER] 1912

Madame,

. . . .

This desire to write about Sainte-Beuve, that is to say, about your family regarded as a Tree of Jesse, of which you are the flower—and also about Sainte-Beuve himself—is an old one, for I can remember that three years ago when I thought my novel was about to appear I warned Beaunier, who was planning to write on Sainte-Beuve, that he would have me trespassing on his domain. But my novel blocks everything, and the collection of articles can't even appear until afterwards, because if I published it now, people would think that the book that my friends have announced as so very good, was merely this collection of articles. Unfortunately, since the novel will be in three volumes and since Fasquelle would certainly not publish them except under three different titles, at six month intervals, it will take a long time and you know I have no assurance that I shall be alive tomorrow. And by the way (please don't think that the point of this digression is to minimize in a casual way the favor I am asking you), if you see Calmette soon, whom I can go to see only with great difficulty, could you give him this message. First, however, you must know that he wanted this novel, which is dedicated to him, to be published by Fasquelle and to be submitted to Fasquelle by him because he was confident he could have it accepted. So that there is nothing to ask of him in this connection. But Calmette has much to do, many things on his mind. If you see him (and if it would be in no way embarrassing to you, otherwise it is quite simple to have someone else remind him), tell him that you have seen me, or that we have corresponded, that I have asked you to remind him of my book, and that I should be very grateful if he could discuss it with Fasquelle as soon as possible, so that the 1st volume (where, alas, your red dress and red slippers will not be; they won't come until the 2nd, for the Duchesse de Guermantes appears only for a moment in the 1st volume) can appear as soon as possible. Otherwise I shall be dead long before the 3rd (no need to tell him that). If in the meantime some complication has arisen about talking to Fasquelle, let him tell me so frankly. I did not particularly care for Fasquelle, and I had other contacts. I prefer him now because of the time lost and because friends of mine and of Fasquelle's who have a somewhat exaggerated idea of me have, I believe, talked to him about me enough so that I don't feel myself among strangers. I can, however, go somewhere else, if Calmette does not care to see him at this time. Above everything, and I can't say this often enough, if for any reason at all you prefer not to say this to Calmette (there is nothing to ask him, just to *remind him not to forget*. It is he who offered)—don't say a word to him, I can so easily have someone else tell him. . . . As for me, my manuscript is ready, recopied, corrected, etc. What you say about a "Conquest of the Past" is just another proof, as you say, that we feel about things in the same way, and I can't give you better proof than that one of the titles I have thought of for my book is *Le Temps perdu* for the 1st volume and *Le Temps retrouvé* for the 3rd. But you are wrong in thinking that it was just a whim. I assure you that physically—and if you had read the recent physiologists you will know age is a physical ill—you have certainly achieved a "conquest of the past" this summer. I didn't want to bore you at Trouville with any remarks about "how well you are looking," because you must have grown tired of them, but you must surely have realized yourself how much better you were. The philosophers have certainly persuaded us that time is a process of reckoning that corresponds to no reality. We know that, but the ancient superstition is so strong that we cannot escape it, and it seems to us that on a given date we are inevitably older, like the government, which finds that because it should be warm the 1st of April, after that central heating is no longer needed. For a long time we have found this ridiculous of the government, but for age we don't find it so. I can say that I have known few people as young as Prince Edmond de Polignac (and, alas, he was carried off accidentally, which can happen at any age), who was eighty years old and who, besides, it seems, from youth up, had had the face of an old man. Alas, I can achieve no conquests of the past in this sense of lasting rejuvenation, since my illness is organic and serious. But you, thank heaven, have this terrible illness which is stupidly called "having nothing wrong," which persecutes nervous people especially in their youth, because with them everything is transposed and not until later in life are they granted health, equilibrium, the prerogatives of youth. Their life is, like certain years, thrown off its orbit. However, you must feel all this yourself from your own intimate experience of your body. I am profoundly convinced that thinking of you, not only because of the joy your graciousness gives me, but because of all the long happiness I foresee for you, is a great reason for consolation in my life, which is so sad, so barren. All this is badly put, the nuances, the essential approach omitted, but I am crushed with fatigue. . . . However, I had so hoped to see you that I had to write. And this is a sort of written promenade, an epistolary aftermath of the promenade we have not taken, a transference of strength, a transformation like that of the electric stove which gives me light when I don't want to use it to heat my milk because I am too ill to drink it. But at least these lines because they were lived and acted may perhaps become powerful enough to convince you, to give you reasons for being happy, full of hope and faith in life. What good would that do me!

Your respectful friend,
Marcel Proust

Above all say nothing to Calmette if it bothers you *the least little bit* and besides it can be *at any time*, provided that *he* hurries, or restores to me my liberty of action, for I don't know that I have much time ahead of me.

139: TO MADAME STRAUS

[CIRCA NOVEMBER 10, 1912]

Madame,

. . . .

The thing I liked best about the idea of Fasquelle as publisher, was that *Les Plaisirs et les Jours* having been my only published book—and in a most deluxe edition, illustrations, etc., I should like this second work, which will certainly be the last (except for collections of articles, of critical essays) to appeal to a larger public, to people who take trains and buy a badly printed book before getting into the coach. . . . I shall not talk about this any longer because you will end by thinking me terribly utilitarian, and there is no point in my having written nothing during twenty years and then making up for it in a month by scheming to be published, behaving like a bounder, and getting drunk on printer's ink. I feel so strongly that a piece of work is a thing which, although born out of ourselves, is still worth more than we are, that I find it natural to take trouble for it, like a father for his child. But I must not allow myself to talk like this to other people about things that, alas, may only interest me. Hervieu said very properly in the *Figaro* the other day that the conditions of the tournament were years of work to be judged in a few hours. And what's more, people listen to plays, but books they do not read. . . . I cannot believe that this book will leave you quite indifferent. I cannot say like Joubert: "Whosoever comes under my shadow grows wiser," but perhaps happier, in a sense that it is a breviary of the joys that can still happen to people who have been denied many of the joys of the human race. I didn't at all try to have it that way. But it is a little, I think. If you are at home tomorrow evening, order the *théâtrophone*. The charming opera, *Gwendoline*, is being given. You probably know it already, and the ideas are not always discriminatingly chosen, as generally happens in Chabrier. But the slightly vulgar but nevertheless bewitching charm of the melodies is compensated by such delicacy, such refinements of orchestration as were new then and have remained new. I don't know whether you are like me, but I adore this sort of thing. *Adieu*, Madame, I don't know how to leave you.

Your respectful friend,
Marcel Proust

140: TO GEORGES DE LAURIS

1912

Mon cher Georges,

. . . .

I have subscribed to the *théâtrophone*, which I use rarely because one hears very badly. However, for the Wagner operas, which I know almost by heart, I make up for the inadequacies of the acoustics. And the other day a charming revelation which even oppresses me a little—*Pelléas*. I hadn't thought of it! Antoine Bibesco has subscribed to

Gide's review for me. There is a story of Gide's in it; it's not bad, but it doesn't bowl one over. *Adieu*, dear Georges, I no longer sleep, I no longer eat, I no longer work; there are many other things I no longer do, but those I have gone without for a long time. Nevertheless, with a little fortitude, my book will be ready in two months, but shall I ever have those two months.

With all my heart,
Your
Marcel

141: TO ANTOINE BIBESCO

[NOVEMBER ? 1912]

Mon cher Antoine,

Here is the only copy of *Swann*. Give it to Gide and to Copeau to read. I am giving you some points about my novel, which you already know, but which might be useful for your readers.

Du côté de chez Swann is the fragment of a novel, which will have as general title *A la recherche du temps perdu*. I should have liked to have published it as a single whole, but it would have been too long. They no longer publish works in several volumes. There are novelists, on the other hand, who envisage a brief plot with few characters. That is not my conception of the novel. There is a plane geometry and a geometry of space. And so for me the novel is not only plane psychology but psychology in space and time. That invisible substance, time, I try to isolate. But in order to do this it was essential that the experience be continuous. I hope that by the end of my book what I have tried to do will be understandable; some unimportant little event will show that time has passed and it will take on that beauty certain pictures have, enhanced by the passage of the years.

Then, like a city which, while the train pursues its winding course, seems to be first on our right, then on our left, the varying aspects the same character will have assumed to such a degree that they will have made him seem like successive and different characters, will project—but only in that one way—the sensation of time passed. Such characters will later reveal themselves as different from what they were in the present, different from what one believes them to be, a circumstance which, indeed, occurs frequently enough in life.

But not only the same characters who reappear under varying aspects, in the course of this work as in certain of Balzac's cycles, but there is one continuous character. From that point of view my book will perhaps be like an attempt at a sequence of novels of the unconscious. They are not Bergsonian novels, for my work is dominated by a distinction which not only doesn't figure in Bergson's philosophy but which is even contradicted by it.

Voluntary memory, which is above all the memory of the intelligence end of the eyes, gives us only the surface of the past without the truth; but when an odor, a taste, rediscovered under entirely different circumstances evoke for us, in spite of ourselves, the past, we sense how different is this past from the one we thought we remembered and which our voluntary memory was painting like a bad painter using false colors. Even in this first volume the character who narrates, who calls himself "I" (and who is not I) will suddenly rediscover forgotten years, gardens, people in the taste of a sip of tea in which he found a piece of a *madeleine*; doubtless he remembers them anyway, but without color and shapes. I have been able to make him tell how as in the little Japanese game of dipping into water compressed bits of paper which, as soon as they are immersed in the bowl, open up, twist around and become flowers and people, so all the flowers of his garden, the good folk of the village, their little houses and the church and all of Combray and its environs—everything that takes on form and solidity has come, city and garden, out of his cup of tea.

I believe that it is involuntary memories practically altogether that the artist should call for the primary subject matter of his work. First, just because they are involuntary, because they take shape of their own accord, inspired by the resemblance to an identical minute, they alone have the stamp of authenticity. Then they bring things back to us in an exact proportion of memory and of forgetting. And finally, as they make us savor the same sensation under wholly different circumstances, they free it from all context, they give us the extratemporal essence. Moreover, Chateaubriand and Baudelaire practised this method. My novel is not a work of ratiocination; its least elements have been supplied by my sensibility; first I perceived them in my own depths without understanding them, and I had as much trouble converting them into something intelligible as if they had been as foreign to the sphere of the intelligence as a motif in music.

Style is in no way an embellishment, as certain people think, it is not even a question of technique; it is, like color with certain painters, a quality of vision, a revelation of a private universe which each one of us sees and which is not seen by others. The pleasure an artist gives us is to make us know an additional universe. How, under these conditions, do certain writers declare that they try not to have a style? I don't understand it. I hope that you will make them understand my explanations.

Ton
Marcel Proust

Gaston Gallimard, born in 1881, is a French publisher, managing editor of the *Nouvelle revue française* during its existence, and now director of the publishing house bearing his name.

142: TO GASTON GALLIMARD

NOVEMBER (?) 1912

Monsieur,

I cannot tell you what pleasure your letter gave me; you used the simplest and most effective words to dispel the slight anxiety I was feeling, and I want to thank you for it sincerely.

You couldn't come yourself to fetch the typescript for you have no idea how heavy it is. I shall have it brought to you tomorrow. It isn't collated with the actual text; however, it will give you an accurate idea. It has been only slightly improved since. Page 633 of this typescript could, if necessary, end the first volume. Actually, it would be a little more because there are pages designated *bis, ter*, etc.

. . . But there are others that have been removed and since a page of print is much longer, I think it would make only about 550 pages. As to the second and third volumes, I can't easily give you the manuscript as I have only my rough draft. However, I could lend it to you if you think it absolutely necessary. For naturally I couldn't have the 1st volume published without being sure that the 2nd (or the 2nd and 3rd, if there is a third) are published. You can see from this that it will be a work interrupted in the midst of publication. Still, if you like, I could tell you in a few words what this second part is all about. But it will be very confidential, for it is a very curious subject and I should prefer not to have it known in advance. As for the intervals between the volumes, my sincere thanks for offering to make them so short (knowing how disagreeable it is for a publisher and realizing with what sensitive feeling and acute understanding you are allowing for my condition). But I don't believe it will be necessary. I believe that the 1st volume (which we will not call 1st volume, but to which a subtitle will be given; for example, general title: *Les Intermittences du coeur*; 1st volume, subtitle: *Le Temps perdu*; second volume, subtitle: *L'Adoration perpetuelle*, or perhaps *A l'ombre des jeunes filles en fleur*; 3rd volume, subtitle: *Le Temps retrouvé*), I believe if the 1st volume appeared in February or March (better February), the second wouldn't have to appear before November to allow for the normal assimilation of such a bulky fragment, and the 3rd in February, 1914. Alas, could all these plans, the charm of which has revived since you have told me that I was mistaken, be carried out?

I don't know. You know my situation and since it is not with the publisher but with my friend's nephew that I deal, I must ask you formally to say nothing about it, even if I outline it to you with the right names. My book was taken by C[almette] to F[asquelle], who accepted it under the most delightful conditions, such as not wanting to read it before promising to publish it, in order to show his regard for me. I am not silly enough to think that it could be any satisfaction to a publisher, whose house does as admirably as F[asquelle] does, to publish a work so different from his usual novels. But there is a delicate question of the utmost importance in relation to him, to C[almette], and to some charming friends who, because I was unable to get out of bed, have shuttled back and forth between the two. Perhaps if I feel better in a few days, a conversation with my friends, if I can go and find them, would resolve the whole thing. But each day that slides by makes everything more uncertain. If I receive my first proofs, there will be nothing more I can do, and in that case I will telegraph you immediately. As for our seeing each other, here's the situation; I think the best thing to do is to wait a little while. If you publish me, even if it is difficult because of your hours and mine, we shall have to see each other. And if you do not publish me, it would be even more agreeable for us to see each other with no underlying professional prejudices. Since I have written you such a long letter and since it tires me to write too often, I should like very much (2nd confidence) to tell you what is shocking in the 2nd volume, so that if it seems to you unpublishable, you would not need to read the first. At the end of the first (3rd section) you will see a M. de Fleurus (or de Guray, I have changed the name several times), who is vaguely reputed to be Mme Swann's lover. But as in life, where reputations are often misleading and it takes a long time to know people, the reader will see in the second volume that the old gentleman is not at all Mme Swann's lover, but a pederast. It is a character I believe to be rather novel, the virile pederast, in love with virility, detesting effeminate young people, actually detesting all young people, the way men who have been made to suffer by women are misogynists. This character is sufficiently scattered throughout parts of the book that are entirely different so that this volume has none of the quality of a special monograph such as *Lucien* by Binet-Valmer, for instance—nothing, indeed, could be more completely opposite. What is more, the pederast is not crude. And you may be sure that in the long run, the metaphysical and intellectual point of view predominates throughout the work. Still one does see this old gentleman taking up with a janitor and keeping a pianist. I prefer to warn you ahead of time of anything that might discourage you.

I think I have told you everything I had to tell you, and this is the last letter with which I shall bore you. I have almost arrived at the point of hoping that you will not like my work and will want none of it, as then I could spare myself both my present anxiety and the regret I should feel if I did receive the proofs from F. tomorrow, now that I have seen the possibility of collaborating with you. I am like those travelers who, unable to make up their minds to give up a tempting journey, try to make themselves late, to miss the train so as to be forced not to go. But, no, I shall be really happy if you like my work because I greatly value your judgment. I have read you in the *Nouvelle revue française*. And if my book is not one of those works you like because "they are as curly as a head of Savoy cabbage," there is nevertheless infinitely more spontaneity in it than the arbitrary juxtaposition of rational analysis and intuitively perceived evidence would lead one to believe in the first place. The third volume, *Le Temps retrouvé*, leaves no doubt in this respect.

I must ask you again to keep secret the name of my other publisher. For absolute discretion is my only chance of arriving at a satisfactory solution without any unpleasantness. I must ask you again, also, to keep the subject of my second part secret, and while asking you to excuse this endless letter and to believe how much pleasure yours gave me, I am yours sincerely,

Marcel Proust

143: TO LOUIS DE ROBERT

[BETWEEN DECEMBER 24 AND 31, 1912]

Cher ami,

I have so much to tell you I hardly know where to begin. And, chiefly, alas, I have favors to ask. The more I swear, because of my friendship for you—and I am so aware of each new proof you give me of yours—not to add to it the burden of worrying you, the more intricate becomes the network of favors I have to beg of you. The more I am caught in the fatality of circumstances, the way that character in Dostoevsky becomes involved in crime.

Here, to begin with, is the most disagreeable part of my letter. I have not even had to decide whether or not I should leave my manuscript with Fasquelle. I had a letter from him (which I must admit, gave me a better, more sympathetic opinion than I would have believed possible of his intelligence, of the painstaking attention he gives to what he does, of the staunchness with which he takes the responsibility for his preferences and antipathies), saying that he didn't think he could undertake the publication of so considerable a volume, one so different from what the public is accustomed to reading (here I may perhaps be confusing my recollection of his letter with a conversation he had, just about the time I received it, with my friend, Hahn, who by a completely fortuitous coincidence found himself dining with him at the house of some friends, where he had invited himself at the last moment and where Fasquelle, too, arrived unexpectedly). Be that as it may, his rejection is clear-cut, definite, and there is nothing more there to reconsider. So I recalled what you told me about Ollendorff. Let us not delude ourselves (if I really dare use the word "us," as though it were something in which you, too, would be interested; but you have so thoroughly proved to me that it is). All publishers could have the same objections as Fasquelle. And Fasquelle's point of view, which is perfectly fair commercially, is not unintelligent

t have as neighbor the writer whom I most ad-
cis Jammes. I don't know him, but . . . but I
nother line. Even these are barely legible. As
u said, paleographers spend three years trying
a few lines of my letters.

even from the literary point of view (you can see that I feel no bitterness whatsoever against him); I think he is wrong, but one can be mistaken in an intelligent way. So, in order to avoid exhausting ordeals with publishers, requests for changes, etc., I wish now only to have the book published at my own expense. Not only will I pay the expenses, but in spite of that I should like to share with the publisher any profits there might be, not out of generosity, but so that he would want to have the book succeed. Do you think Ollendorff would publish the book under these circumstances (perhaps I ought also to pay for the publicity). Will you tell me what you think? And will you ask him? It's a question of two large volumes, each one approximately 650 pages (it might be a little less but I should rather not err in the wrong direction). I should like to have the first volume appear in the spring (without making that a condition *sine qua non*) and the second about ten months afterwards, for instance in February, 1914. If asking him would bother you in the slightest degree, whom would you suggest that I have ask him? I am a good friend of Hermant, whom I believe they publish, with Barrès, with Régnier. It seems to me they all know him, but I should prefer you. I say Ollendorff because you mentioned his name. I have no preference if someone else seems better to you. I hold out for only one thing, that it shall be published at my expense so that I can remain free and have absolute *certainty*. I thought I had it with Fasquelle because of his promise to Calmette. It is curious, however, that, as I understood it from you, he did seem attached to Calmette; he told me so in his letter and what's more he asked Reynaldo several times whether he thought Calmette would be annoyed. And for that matter he talked to Reynaldo so much about my articles in the *Figaro* that I am not sure I shan't suggest his collecting them in a little volume, which would be in no way abnormal or too long.

In his letter he didn't speak of Rostand, but he told Reynaldo he had received a long communication from Maurice Rostand. I don't know how much good that did. In any case, now that the break is definite, I shall be able to write to Maurice Rostand to thank him, for I think it is infinitely kind of him to have done this without knowing me. Besides, he has amazing gifts as a poet and I have always had a sympathy for him rather than the antipathy he imagines. But I think it would be better if you didn't talk to him about me.

. . . .

It is true that I went to the dress rehearsal of *Kismet*, the first occasion of that kind I have gone to in fifteen or even twenty-five years. This is why: Mme Straus wanted to ask me something. But not once was I able to see her because I can't get up before eleven at night and she goes to bed at ten. She let me know that that night she could see me until one in the morning because she was going to this rehearsal. And I arrived there at half-past eleven. What's more, I absentmindedly put on my morning coat instead of evening dress with my white waistcoat. Thereby providing Guitry with the good luck of having a clown in the stage box, an effect which the production certainly seemed to

need, but which we had n
happened a week ago Tue
out of bed, not even for
row I shall get up for a
another two weeks in b
enough idea of my lif
does me no more harm
more, which is why I n
and recognized (which
plain that I am not dea
in a thousand compli
pened, too; because I
went on stage with he
as not to be seen I stay
"holy of holies," hic
a charming face, wh
of the *Orestea*. It tur
even stranger, becau
has, Lemaitre in his
nized me!

But who could h
to anyone but He
people I used to
mask which age ar
longer have enou
you with a shake o
and grateful frier

You mus
mire, Fran
can't write
Montesqui
to decipher

René Blum (1878–1943), a journalist and art collector, brother of Léon Blum, is perhaps best known for his collaboration with Diaghilev in producing the *Ballet Russe* in Paris. He died in a concentration camp in Germany.

144: TO RENÉ BLUM

FEBRUARY, 1913

102, BOULEVARD HAUSSMANN

Be sure to keep this address because letters are always going astray and the post office puts unknown, *alas. Telephone: 29205*

Cher ami,

I telephoned you last night at the *Gil Blas*. But since I am very rarely in a condition to telephone and exceedingly rarely able to go out or to receive, I think it is preferable to tell you by letter of the great favor I want to ask you. It has to do with Grasset, the publisher, who is, I believe, a friend of yours. I hope that M. Grasset will publish at my expense, with me paying for the printing and the publicity, an important work (let's call it a novel, for it is a kind of novel), which I have finished. This novel is in two volumes of about 650 pages each. In order to make a concession to the prevailing custom, I am giving a different title to each volume, and there will be an interval of ten months between the publication of each volume. However, I shall perhaps put at the top of the title-page a general title, as France, for instance, put *Histoire contemporaine: L'Orme du mail*. If for any reason whatsoever it would embarrass you to talk to M. Grasset, tell me so very frankly without any qualms; for I know a lot of people who are, I believe, connected with him. But if you do it, I want to tell you first of all that if I have asked you this without any oratorical precautions, so as to be more frank, I have no less the sense of your doing me a great service. You will easily understand about it; I have been working for a long time on this book, I have put the best of my thought into it; it now requires a tomb that can be achieved before my own is filled, and in helping me realize its success you are doing something very valuable for me, all the more so since the state of my health makes it very difficult for me to do anything about it myself. Secondly, if you can do me this favor, do it the way I ask you to; that is to say, don't, as everyone I know says, say, "But, *cher ami*, Grasset will be enchanted to publish you at his own expense, offering you excellent terms. You have too much talent to pay for being published like an amateur. Besides it is a wretched idea, it will become known, make you ridiculous, and a publisher will take no trouble about a book published under these circumstances." All this (except for the talent which I don't know about) is true. But, *mon cher ami*, I am very sick, I need security and rest. If M. Grasset publishes the book at his own expense, he will read it, make me wait, suggest changes—having a number of small volumes, etc. And be right from the point of view of success. But I am looking rather for the intelligible presentation of my work. What I want is for you to be able to say to me in a week, this *affair* is concluded! Your book will appear on such and such a date. And that is only possible if one pays one's own expenses. So that M. Grasset will put more effort into its success, I should be grateful to him for accepting from me further a certain percentage of the sales. In that way he would not spend a cent, might make a little (for I have no hopes that the book will sell, at least not until the public has gradually become accustomed to it), but I think that the book which is very much better than anything I have ever done will one day do him honor. I must add, so as to mention all the objections in the beginning, that in the first part which I can have submitted to M. Grasset within twenty-four hours if he accepts it, there are some very indecent pages; and in the second part (the one which would appear ten months later) others that are even more so. But the quality of the book is so serious and the approach so literary that this cannot be an obstacle. —Finally, I should like (but this is only of secondary importance) to have this kept for some time between you, M. Grasset, and myself; I mean the request to be published at my own expense. Not out of vanity: I shall announce it very openly when the time comes. But for the time being I fear certain complications. So I have said to certain people (and the letters I shall show you will prove that I was speaking the truth) that a very well-known publisher asked to publish this book at his own expense and with terms that were fine for me. Everyone will think I lied if they picture me asking as a favor to have it published at the author's expense. Or else they will think I am a grotesque type and the "Tristan Bernard character" quality of this letter will be emphasized. I can see Antoine Bibesco telephoning M. Grasset right now that I have lots of talent, that he [Grasset] should pay me, etc. I think it is better to avoid nonessential complications with a publication that is very important to me and very trying for a publisher confronted with a work of this length. Remember that I am so unaccustomed to this sort of thing (I have never published anything except *Les Plaisirs et les Jours*, which Calmann published at his expense, and my Ruskin at the *Mercure* with the same advantageous terms) that I don't know whether in spite of everything I am offering, I am not still asking a *favor* of M. Grasset. If you think so and think that in order to have it granted it would be helpful to have me recommended at the same time by a man of "standing," I am sure that Barrès or Hervieu or Régnier or Calmette would be very glad to do it. The only thing I am afraid of is that they will not approve of its being at the author's expense. Which would result in delays, indecision, uncertainty, and perhaps rejection. And then new wear-and-tear, another publisher, etc., everything I wish to avoid at any cost. Tell M. Grasset everything that you think would make him say a firm and irrevocable yes; don't tell him I have talent, first because it may not be true, then because people should not be too much discouraged at the start. But I am told that he is so intelligent that even that might not discourage him. For several years I have heard wonderful things said about him. I am even sorry to think that I shall have so little to do with him. Because unless my presence is indispensable, it will be Reynaldo who will go to see him for me: for it is so difficult for me to move. Don't tell him the reason for my condition either. Because if afterwards you still go on living for a little while, it is not forgiven you. I remember people who have "hung on" for years. People acted as though they had been putting on an act. Like Gautier, who delayed so long going to Spain that some people said to him, "You have come back"; so if they are unable to admit that I am not dead, they will say that I am "reincarnated." . . . Finally, *cher ami*, one last thing, for it tires me so to start a letter that I want to tell you everything in this one (and I have left out three quarters), will you make a note not to telephone me about this (or at least, if you do telephone, to speak only to me and if my *valet de chambre* answers, not to give him any explanations) and seal your letters with wax (and M. Grasset, too). I should like M. Grasset to say when the book can appear so that I might perhaps send out some excerpts. I should hope "MAY," but I don't know whether I could correct that many proofs quickly enough. At least I want them to start right away. And apropos of this, don't think that my book is a collection of articles. My last two articles in the *Figaro* were extracts from it, but that has nothing to do with it. My other articles in the *Figaro* I shall make into a collection if I can find them again, but later and with another publisher. As for this book, it is, on the contrary, a deliberately formed whole, although the composition is so complex that I am afraid no one will grasp it and that it will appear to be a series of digressions. It is quite the opposite. See if you can do this favor for me; it is tremendous; but only if it is complete, definitive, and assured.

Your wholly devoted
Marcel Proust

145: TO RENÉ BLUM

FEBRUARY 24, 1913
102, BOULEVARD HAUSSMANN

Cher ami,

Thank you with all my heart. It is a great favor that you are doing me. And you, too, must try to find one that I can do for you so that my satisfaction may be complete. Concerning M. Grasset, I do not scorn the "precautions" of which you speak, although I don't know the terms (you will tell me). But above all I should want the *formal* promise of publication (without my being obliged to abridge), the first volume to be published as soon as possible, and a delay of about ten months between the first and the second. It would be very nice of you if you write me to put a *wax seal* on the envelope. As for telephoning, that seems difficult to me; it would, on the contrary, be very easy if you would leave the initiative to me. In that way when I am not too sick, about once a week, I get up for an hour or two. On that day (which, unfortunately, I do not know in advance—and which is imminent, for I have been in bed a long time) it is very easy for me to telephone and to stop by to see you at the *Gil Blas*, if you like. On other days, alas, the same attacks that keep me in bed and prevent my receiving anyone do not make telephoning very easy, either. And I should not want you to talk about this on the telephone to anyone but me. —I have taken the liberty of telling M. Louis de Robert that I asked you this favor. (I told him in a letter, for it is more than fifteen years since I have seen him); he wishes my writing well in a way that touches me deeply. He has replied, but his letter, very nice about both you and me, is so excessively appreciative of my writings that it would be indiscreet to send it to you. I have also told Reynaldo, who arrived from Germany last night, about the favor I had asked you. —I have spoken to no one else. —You might tell M. Grasset, for I believe that he is sensitive to this kind of thing, that since I have published nothing for a long time, for an extremely long time, I think that the friends of my writings will make this book profit by the sympathy they have for my ideas. If it could be any satisfaction to M. Grasset, I could submit it for some Goncourt Prize or other; I say this rather at random. In any case a prize like the "*Vie Heureuse*" would be impossible because of the extreme license and indecency of certain portions.

Thank you again, *cher ami*, your very grateful

Marcel Proust

I don't know whether I have told you that this book is a novel. At least it deviates least from the novel form. There is a Monsieur who narrates and who says "I"; there are a great many characters; in the first volume they are "prepared" in such a way that what they do in the second is exactly the opposite of what one would expect from the first. From the publisher's point of view, unfortunately, this first volume is much less narrative than the second. And from the point of view of composition, it is so complex that it will not be clear until much later when all the "themes" have begun to be combined. You see, there is nothing very engaging about all this. But under the conditions we have discussed, it seems to me that M. Grasset cannot lose anything, and, literarily speaking, I do not think that he will be "*déclassé*" because of it.

146: TO MADAME STRAUS

[END OF FEBRUARY OR EARLY MARCH, 1913]

Madame,

Don't think that I have forgotten you! You have never been more in my thoughts. But I have been very ill; I was supposed to leave for Valmont [Dr. Widmer's sanitarium], and I didn't come to any decision about it. And I have had a lot of other worries, too. One thing, however, pleases me; my hours have improved, and I hope that I can come and see you earlier. Unfortunately they have improved in the following manner; I am awake during the day, but it doesn't make me sleep at night. So I am even more tired.

I am talking too much about myself, but it is about me only in regard to you, relative to the possibilities of our seeing each other. For I miss you very much; and it seems to me that all my troubles might be a little less cruel if I told them to you. And they are sufficiently general, sufficiently human so that they might interest you. But not really; I should rather talk to you about other things. There are some very lovely ones that I wish very much to see, and I have never thought to ask you whether you knew them. I don't even know whether you ever were in Florence. But I don't want to start off that subject this evening; I am too exhausted; I shall come to see you one of these days. Are you a subscriber to the *théâtrophone*? They now have the Touche concerts, and I can be visited in bed by the brook and the birds of the Pastoral Symphony, which poor Beethoven enjoyed no more directly than I do since he was completely deaf. He consoled himself by trying to reproduce the song of the birds he no longer heard. Remote as I am from genius, and without talent, I, too, compose symphonies in my own way, when I portray what I can no longer see!

Your respectful, admiring friend,
Marcel Proust

147: TO LOUIS DE ROBERT

[SUMMER ? 1913]

Cher Louis,

It is very difficult for me to reply to your objections because I can't answer by word of mouth. In conversation, the very inflection of the voice would dispel from your mind the suspicion that there could be anything cutting or arrogant in my remarks. I admire you too much not to believe that you are right in thinking of those "unknown friends" of whom Sully Prudhomme spoke in verses, which are no longer fashionable, but which to my taste remain exquisite. "The true essence of friendship is community of feeling," but without—I swear it—believing that my conception of art is better, I deny myself the ease of theirs; I defer to a universal truth that keeps me from considering people I like any more than those I dislike; the praise of sadists, once my book is published, would distress me as a man; it would in no way modify the conditions under which I search out the truth, and which are not at all determined by any whim of mine. Besides, I know we agree about this, and explanations would tax your strength as a reader and mine as a letter-writer, and we ought to spare ourselves. And yet, among the charming and excessive compliments you pay me, there is one I cannot accept (at least not as praise), except in a special sense. You speak of my gift for the meticulous detail, the imperceptible, etc. How successful I am in what I do, I do not know, but I do know what I want to do; except in the passages that I don't like, I omit every detail, every fact (following an instinct analogous to a carrier pigeon's; I'll explain this to you more clearly someday when I am in less pain), I include only what seems to me to reveal some universal law. But since that sort of detail is never revealed to us through the intellect, since we have in some way to fish for it in the depths of the unconscious, it is, indeed, imperceptible because it is so remote, so difficult to grasp. But it is never just a meticulous detail. Nevertheless, a mountain peak in the clouds, although very small, can be higher than a nearby factory. For example, you could say that the taste of the tea, which I don't at first recognize and in which I later rediscover the gardens of Combray, is imperceptible. But it is not merely a meticulously observed detail, it is (at least such is my ambition) a whole theory of memory and consciousness, although not directly projected in logical terms (in any case, all that will appear again in the third volume).

The sad thing about letters, particularly when they are written by a hand as tired as mine, is that they seem to want to say the opposite of what one thinks. If you don't sufficiently realize my affectionate and humble gratitude for your exquisite kindness you will think that I find you underestimate me while actually I think you overrate me! But of course I'm wrong; you do understand me; we mean the same thing and need fear no misunderstanding.

How happy I should be if you would discover a title for me! But I should like something quite simple, quite grey. The general title, you know, is *In Search of Vanished Time*. For the first book, which will be published in two volumes (if Grasset allows a box for two volumes), would you have any objection to *Charles Swann*? If I do a single volume of 500 pages, I am not in favor of this title because the final portrait of Swann will not be included in it, so my book wouldn't carry out the implications of the title. Would you like, *Before the Day Has Started*? (I shouldn't.) I had to give up *The Heart's Intermissions* (original title), *The Wounded Doves, The Past Suspended, Perpetual Adoration, Seventh Heaven, In the Shadow of Young Girls in Bloom*, titles which, however, will be chapter headings in the third volume. I have told you, haven't I, that *Swann's Way* comes from the two ways of going to Combray? In the country, you know, people say, "Are you going M. Rostand's Way?" But I don't want this book to appear with a title that is offensive to the only friend whom, in spite of my effort to emerge from my "phenomenal me," I have been unable to put out of my mind while writing it. So I shall take another title. I should take *Charles Swann*, if I could explain that these are only the early portraits of Charles Swann.

Yours with all my heart,
Marcel Proust

P.S. Would you like as a title for the first volume, *Gardens in a Cup of Tea*, or *The Age of Names*. For the second, *The Age of Words*. For the third, *The Age of Things*? The one I prefer is *Charles Swann*, if I could make clear that it is not all of Swann; *First Sketches of Charles Swann*.

148: TO LOUIS DE ROBERT

[SUMMER ? 1913]

Cher ami,

I should like, without wearing myself out, to tell you that however much my occupation as an artist precludes my taking into consideration the feelings of one person or another (because, at a time like this, one becomes individual—impossible to explain here; I shall postpone that until later), I do not think, on the other hand, that I need fear, as you seem to think I should, the sympathy of sadists. This is even more striking in my third volume (in part pederast), and a magnified example will make you understand better what I am trying to say. If, without mentioning pederasty at all, I depicted healthy adolescents, tender and fervent friendships, without ever implying that there was anything more there, I should then have all the pederasts on my side because I should be giving them just what they love. First, because I do dissect their vice (I use the word "vice" without any implied reproach), do show their sickness, I am saying exactly the thing that fills them with the greatest repulsion, namely, that this dream of masculine beauty is the result of a neurotic defect. The best evidence is that a pederast adores men but detests pederasts. Further, since my pederasts are elderly men, their situation borders on the ridiculous (at least for the reader, actually it is rather touching), which will exasperate them even more. And so for my sadists it is rather the same thing. The scene I have painted is anything but voluptuous. The commentary which, according to you, gives me the appearance of a defense lawyer (and perhaps you are right, I mean in thinking that I appear to be, for actually I am in no way a special pleader) is exactly, alas, what may perhaps turn away from me not only the sensitive spirits, but also, and chiefly, the sadists. Nothing could be more disagreeable to the people who seek out cruelty than to say to them: "Yours is a perverted sensibility." The idea of the scene was suggested to me by a number of different things, but above all by this: a very well-known man of great distinction was the lover of a prostitute, although he was married and the father of a family. But in order to achieve complete satisfaction, he felt impelled when speaking of his own son to this prostitute to call him "the little monster." At home, however, he was a very good father.

Cher ami, I think of calling my first volume *Spring*. But I continue not to understand why the name of that road at Combray which was called "*le côté de chez Swann*," with its earthy reality, its local color, hasn't as much poetry as these abstract and flowery titles. If you read my first part, you will have seen that around Combray there were two ways of going, the Méséglise—La Vineuse way and Swann's way. And those two ways take on a meaning for my inner life. But since, furthermore, this whole volume takes place on Swann's way, I found that title unpretentious, true, grey, drab, like a furrow from which poetry could spring. . . . To change the subject, Grasset doesn't want the two books sold together; there will have to be one 520-page volume and one 680 pages. I will agree to the 520 only if you see a great advantage in it, because the 680 ends superbly (inasfar as my feeble gifts permit), and the 520 one ends very poorly. At present, I should rather be read. Thank you again for all your kindnesses, your forbearance, and chiefly for your severity.

Your

Marcel Proust

Lucien Daudet (1878–1946) was the younger son of Alphonse Daudet, at whose house Proust was frequently a guest in his youth. A student at Julian's studio during the nineties, Whistler's only French pupil, Daudet abandoned painting and became the author of a number of novels and books of memoirs. An intimate friend of the Empress Eugénie, a member of the group known as the "Farnborough boys," he spent much time with the Empress in England and wrote several books about her. He was for many years a devoted friend of Proust's, but they rarely saw each other after 1913.

149: TO LUCIEN DAUDET

[AUGUST, 1913]

Mon cher petit,

. . . . As to your "lack of self-confidence" in relation to me, I shall take the liberty of ignoring it, for I am sure you know perfectly well how much I admire and love you and there is no need of my stressing it. Indeed, I was on the point of bothering you over and over again while I was writing my book. For there is a special aspect to our relationship—I am the one person who needs precise information, who must have an exact knowledge of the things I am talking about—and you are the only one who has it. And writing you, doubtless, would have spared me the interminable letters I have exchanged with horticulturalists, dressmakers, astronomers, genealogists, pharmacists, etc., which have been of no use to me, but which may perhaps have helped them a little. For I knew just a little more than they did. . . .

Mon cher petit, you know that I am very ill, very worried, very unhappy. So please understand that if my letter is an inadequate reply to much of what you said, it is because writing tires me so. I, who am even less self-confident than you, hardly dare propose sending you, in case it should amuse you to glance through them, the proof sheets of my first volume (for, alas, the book will be divided into three volumes—and ridiculously, too, because no one will be able to tell from the first volume what the whole will be like). God knows if I shall ever be able to publish the other two, which are written, but I am changing them in proof, and I don't know how long it will be before I can get back the proofs of the second and third volumes, which I haven't even given to the publisher yet.

Ton
Marcel

150: TO LUCIEN DAUDET

[AUGUST, 1913]

Mon cher petit,

I don't believe that my admiration is merely the result of my affection for you, but I do believe that what you call your admiration for my book stems from your great kindness to me. And it has never, perhaps, shown itself more strikingly or wonderfully than in your immediate reading of my proofs, and in your letter which followed so promptly that when I saw the handwriting just now and hoped that it might, even this soon, be an "appreciation," as the Comtesse A. would say, I figured that it would have been impossible for the proofs to have gotten to you before your letter was sent.

Mon cher petit, in the second volume you will see a diplomat *Gd Seigneur*, who is so polite that no one who receives one of his letters can ever believe that he has replied so soon, but always thinks that the letters must have crossed, and that special mail collections must exist for him. Really, I felt the same way when you were so miraculously kind. Just as when we are in love but not loved in return (the form in which I habitually know this emotion), we figure out a thousand devices to prove to ourselves that it would have been physically impossible for the woman to write, no matter how much she might have wished to. And, yet, when a person wishes to do something sublimely kind, he can write you by return mail ten pages that condense, extol, magnify, stylize, and fathom five hundred.

Mon cher petit, how can I ever thank you. . . . Here is my answer to some of the points you made. I haven't any proofs at hand, but I am almost sure I never said that a chicken was killed the same day it was eaten (although actually it happens frequently in the country). Françoise cooks a chicken every night, but it is not the one she has killed that day.

About the flowers, I assure you, I have many doubts; for instance, in the first version of the hawthorns (which appeared in *Figaro*) there were wild roses on the same road. But having discovered in Bonnier's *Botany* that roses do not bloom until later, I made a correction and put in the book "not until a few weeks later could one see, etc." As for the verbena and heliotrope, it is true that Bonnier points out that the former blooms from June to October, the latter from June to August! But since Bonnier is dealing with wild flowers, I thought (and the horticulturalist to whom I wrote assured me) that in a garden (and not wild like thornbush or wild rose) they could be made to bloom in May while the hawthorns are still in bloom. If it is impossible, what shall I put instead, would mignonette or jasmine be possible, or what others? And while we're on the subject, what does the "American oak" look like? In any case, you will tell me whether there are mistakes in the new ending, which you will get. I can't tell.

Mon cher petit, you tell me that in the book there are also a certain social significance and repercussions; I accept this double compliment; you will see how true it is when you know the other two volumes. Indeed, the significance of most of what you have read will not be clear until you do; and when I have talked of place-names in this volume, it is not a digression. The last chapter is called: "Place-Names: The Name." The principal chapter of the second volume is called: "Place-Names: The Place." And this instance is nothing, *François le Champi* comes in again at the end of the third volume, etc.

Often, as you know, people say that a great artist "apart from his genius is merely a narrow-minded old fool," but knowing about his genius beforehand we do not picture him to ourselves as being really narrow and ridiculous. So I found it more striking to picture Vinteuil at first as an old fool before giving any hint of his genius, and in the second chapter to speak of his sublime sonata, which Swann hasn't even for an instant thought of attributing to that old fool. Similarly, it is not a mistake if you have read on the second or third page of the first chapter, "Can I be at Tansonville at Mme de St.-Loup's house?" whereas Tansonville belongs to Swann; but in the third volume, Mlle Swann marries Robert de Saint-Loup, whom you will meet in the second volume.

I tell you all this, *mon cher petit*, to give you my most intimate confidence, to divulge to you, ahead of time, all my poor little secrets.

Mon cher petit, as to what you say about doing an article, I need hardly put on a pose with you, a thing which, for that matter I would not do with anyone. If you will and you wish, it would give me deep satisfaction or rather many and varied satisfactions, not the least of which would be the far from disinterested satisfaction of hearing someone like you talk about me so favorably in public. I should be so delighted by it purely from the sentimental point of view that I can tell you frankly that my vanity would also be very much gratified. It is not often indulged. I sent the "Soirée at Madame de St.-Euverte's" and some other excerpts to —— and to ——. M. X. and M. XX. both rejected them, which is not too surprising. But other excerpts sent to —— (intelligent people) were also rejected. As a last resort I sent "St.-Euverte" to the supplement of *Figaro*. Chevassu found it "penetrating," which X. had already found it, but too long, and he sent the whole thing back. As for M. Hébrard, he has all along been asking Reynaldo and others to send him things for *Le Temps*. I sent him an article on the *Colline Inspirée* (I must tell Barrès who doesn't know about it and who has, I am told, written me a long letter which I never received). . . . He didn't accept it and didn't even reply.

But with your "signature" it would be very easy! If you don't change your mind (and you have already written me an enchanting letter. Don't tire yourself if you have something to do right now or if you are traveling), but if, after all, you still want to do it, you could send me this article (if you have no preference about which paper publishes it), and Reynaldo, who is angry that *Le Journal* and *Le Temps* have recently refused my things, would perhaps like to retaliate by making one of them put in your article. Or perhaps my publisher who, it seems, excels at making his authors known and who fought a duel because the Academy gave a prize to a book of Romain Rolland's instead of to the one he had published, and who is very well versed in these matters, might undertake to approach some *Echo de Paris* or other. I know Lafitte (of Cabourg) slightly. I don't know whether he still has the *Excelsior* or whether it is a sufficiently literary paper. If Calmette were willing, the *Figaro* would be the most natural place, since the book is dedicated to him.

In a word, if you have no special preferences I could give *carte blanche* either to Reynaldo, to Grasset, or I could try Calmette (a rather more delicate matter). All this in case it didn't seem to you that *L'Action française* would readily welcome the article, because that, of course, on account of your brother and Maurras, would flatter me the most.

Mon cher petit, I leave you because I am so miserable that I don't even know how I've been able to write you today; I am, at the moment, very sick and weighed down with sorrows, but your letter made such a profound impression on me that it should bring about an immediate recovery of health and happiness. How I should love to be your miraculous cure, *mon petit!* In any case, you have enacted a miracle of exquisite kindness, acted and reenacted it like a masterpiece, and, with all my heart, I thank you.

Ton
Marcel

151: TO LUCIEN DAUDET

[END OF AUGUST, BEGINNING OF SEPTEMBER, 1913]

Mon cher petit,

. . . . Thank you for the names of the flowers, but pansies (which I adore and about which I have often written) are not right for me because they are wide, flat flowers without any perfume: I need something more like verbena. Perhaps, for lack of anything better, I shall decide on hyacinths, which in no way resemble verbenas, but which are at least not wide and flat. But they hardly seem to be bedding flowers. Mimulus is delightful but too Latin and requires explanation (unless there is a common name), but don't trouble to answer me just for all this.

Naturally, if Cocteau is nearby, you could perfectly well tell him that you have my proof sheets, but not to judge me by them. Not only is it impossible to anticipate the whole work from this single volume, which derives its meaning from the others, but the proofs have not even been corrected: they abound in mistakes and, above all, in the second part certain very important little incidents that tighten the knots of jealousy around poor Swann are missing. And even when it is ready to appear, it will be like those pieces which, when played separately at a concert, we fail to recognize as *leit-motive* until later when we are able to place them in the work as a whole (thus the lady in pink was Odette, etc.). . . .

I found the passage about the chicken, and it does imply that it is the same day. But I don't know whether I could fix it because my illness is taking the form of holding me up for months on some one word I am incapable of changing. . . .

Ton
Marcel

152: TO ROBERT DREYFUS

NOVEMBER 29, 1913

Cher Robert,

. . . .

. . . . Z, delightful writer that he is, wrote me an agreeable but unjust letter. He says: "You report everything!" But that isn't so; I report nothing. It is he who is the reporter. Not once does a character of mine close a win-dow, wash his hands, put on an overcoat, or go through the forms of an introduction. If, indeed, there were anything new in this book, that would be it, although not at all deliberately so; it is just that I am too lazy to write about things that bore me. . . .

Marcel Proust

153: TO RENÉ BLUM

DECEMBER, 1913

Cher ami,

Very briefly because I am very ill. First, because I have been worse I have not been able to undertake the condensation of a part of the novel into a short story for you. And it seems rather late for that now. If I can't do it, I shall in any event send you a little excerpt when the book appears; but I am giving some to the other papers, so don't use it unless you like it. On the other hand, Grasset would like any time now to have *Gil Blas* commit what he calls a "literary indiscretion" about me; it seems that this is a specialty of *Gil Blas*, even a practice, if I understand correctly. And it mustn't be delayed. It consists in announcing the book and saying a few words about the author. It embarrasses me very much to ask this of you. —And if it bothers you, don't do it. —*Cher ami*, I have spent my life pestering people so that I should not be talked about (you may perhaps not believe it, but ask Henry Bordeaux, Flamont, Chaumeix, and how many others, chiefly Calmette), and now in deference to my publisher I demand a "literary indiscretion." However, it is true that I attach infinitely more importance to this book into which I have put the best of my thought and even my life than to everything else that I have done up to now, which really amounts to nothing. If you would like to know something of what the book is about, Cocteau, Louis de Robert, Lucien Daudet have read it and can tell you (but under no circumstances ask any of them to do this simple announcement). What I hope most of all, particularly if you say that the book is dedicated to Calmette, is that people will not think that it is a collection of articles! My *Figaro* articles I shall perhaps collect later, but this has nothing to do with that. . . . It is an extremely real book, but supported after a fashion by a peduncle of reminiscences to imitate involuntary memory (which in my opinion, although Bergson does not make this distinction, is the only valid one; intellectual and visual memory give us only inexact facsimiles of the past, which no more resemble it than pictures by bad painters resemble the spring, etc. So that we think life is not beautiful because we don't *remember* it, but once we smell a fragrance out of the past, we are suddenly intoxicated! And in the same way we think we no longer love the dead, but it is because we don't remember them; when suddenly we come across an old glove, we dissolve in tears). So one part of the book is a part of my life, which I had forgotten and which, all of a sudden, I rediscover while eating a bit of *madeleine* which I dip in some tea, a taste which enchants me before I have identified and recognized it as one that I had formerly known every morning; immediately my whole life at that period is revived and, as I say in the book, like the Japanese game in which little pieces of paper dipped in a bowl of water become people, flowers, etc., all the people and gardens of that period of my life arise out of a cup of tea. Another part of the book brings to life the sensations of waking up, when one doesn't know where one is and imagines oneself two years earlier in another country. But all this is merely the stem of the book. What it supports is real, passionate, very different from what you know of me and, I think, infinitely less thin, not deserving the epithet "delicate" or "sensitive," but living and true (I swear to you that that doesn't mean "truth").

Cher ami, if you see any possibility, announce the book, but it is very urgent (I mean in two or three days or even sooner). Naturally I had no idea that I should have to ask you this the other evening when I was at the *Gil Blas*. It was only the day after the next that I saw Grasset. Please don't think that there is any duplicity on my part and that I wanted to "prearrange" this. And if it annoys you, oppose it as energetically as you did Maurras's malevolences or the signing of the Questionnaire the other evening.

But naturally there is no need whatsoever of its being signed. . . .

unfinished

André Gide was one of the founders of the *Nouvelle revue française* in 1908 and, until 1940, a determining influence in its policies.

154: ANDRÉ GIDE TO MARCEL PROUST

[JANUARY 1914]

Mon cher Proust,

For several days I have not put down your book I am supersaturating myself in it with rapture I am reveling in it. Alas, why should it be so painful to me to like it so much? . . .

The rejection of this book will remain the most serious mistake made by the N.R.F.—and (because I bear the shame of being largely responsible) one of the most poignantly remorseful regrets of my life. Without doubt I think that we must see in it an implacable act of fate, for my error is certainly not adequately explained by my saying that the picture of you in my mind was based on a few meetings in "society," twenty years ago. For me you were still the man who frequented the houses of Mmes X. and Z., the man who wrote for the Figaro. *I thought of you, shall I confess it, as* "du côté de chez Verdurin"; *a snob, a man of the world, and a dilet-*

tante—the worst possible thing for our review. And your offer to help us out financially in publishing the book—a gesture which I can understand so well today and which I should have found charming then if I had only interpreted it correctly*—served only, alas, to plunge me deeper into error. The only one of the notebooks of your manuscript I had to go by, I opened absent-mindedly, and as ill-luck would have it, my attention fell immediately into the cup of camomile tea on page 62—then stumbled over the sentence on page 64 (the only one in the book that I don't understand clearly—up to now, for I am not waiting to finish before writing you), where there is talk of a pediment with some vertebrae showing through.*

And now it is not enough for me just to love *the book. I have fallen under its spell and under yours, with a very special kind of affection, admiration, predilection.*

*I can't go on. I feel too much regret, too much pain—*above all *at the thought that perhaps some repercussions of my absurd rejection may have affected you—hurt you—and that I deserve at present to have you judge me as unfairly as I judged you. I shall not forgive myself—and it is only to lighten my own pain a little that I am confessing to you this morning—begging you to be more indulgent towards me than I am toward myself.*

André Gide

155: TO ANDRÉ GIDE

[12 OR 13 JANUARY, 1914]

Mon cher Gide,

I have often found that certain great joys require our first having been deprived of a lesser joy, which we had the right to expect and without the expectation of which we could never have known that other joy, the most splendid of all.

Had there been no rejection, no repeated rejections by the N.R.F., I should never have had your letter. And if the words of a book are not entirely mute, if they are (as I believe them to be) like a spectrum that teaches us the inner nature of those remote worlds, embodied in the lives of other people, it is impossible for you to read my book and not know me well enough to realize that the joy of receiving your letter infinitely surpasses any I should have had at being published by the N.R.F. I can say this all the more because I made no pretense of indifference when I was undergoing the antagonism of the N.R.F. Your friend (I think I can almost say our friend), Monsieur Copeau can tell you that a long time after my final rejection by the magazine when I was wishing him luck with his theatre, I wrote him the following (I can no longer remember the exact words, but this was the thought), "The opposition you will meet from people who cannot understand your effort will be less cruel than what I undergo at the hands of people who ought to understand mine. Remember that in order to feel that my book was placed in the atmosphere which I deemed suited to it, I made small shrift of my pride, refusing to be deterred; although I already had a publisher and a newspaper, I left them in order to beg you for a publisher and a magazine who would have none of me in any form, thereby exemplifying the eternal truth of the Evangelist: 'He desired to enter into his heritage and he was *denied*.'" I can remember quoting this sentence to Copeau and saying that it was easy to condemn the boulevard, but at the same time wrong to force back to the boulevard those who are not made for it, and who write for the newspapers only because the magazines, where they rightly belong, will have none of them.

If I tell you all this, my dear Gide, it is to show you that I am intensely sincere in saying that the feelings I continue to have for you (apart from my profound admiration) are only those of the most deeply felt gratitude. If you regret having caused me pain (and you did it in another way which I should rather tell you by word of mouth, if ever my health permits my doing so), I beg of you to feel no more regret, for you have given me a thousand times more pleasure than pain. If you are good enough to rejoice or to grieve according to the good you have done (and I know about it through your admirable *Notes d'un juré*), be happy. How I should like to be able to give someone I loved as much pleasure as you have given me. May I tell you something I remember, too: just now I was saying that I had wanted to be published by the N.R.F. so that I might feel my book had found its place in the dignified atmosphere which it seemed to deserve. But that was not the only thing. You know how when after all kinds of indecision we finally make up our minds to go on a journey, the pleasure that has determined our going, the haunting vision that has finally triumphed over the inconvenience of leaving home, etc., that pleasure frequently turns out to be a very small one, arbitrarily chosen by our memory from among the souvenirs of the past—like the eating of a bunch of grapes at such and such a time of year in such and such weather. And when we have returned, we find we have not savored the pleasure we went in search of. But if I want to be entirely sincere, I must admit that the particular little pleasure that made me decide all of a sudden, sick as I was, to take the absurd step I did in relation to M. Gallimard, to persevere at it, etc., was, I very well remember, the pleasure of *being read by you*. I said to myself: "If the N.R.F. publishes me, there is every chance that he will read my book." That, I remember, was the refreshing bunch of grapes the desire for which enabled me to rise above the annoyance of unanswered telephone calls and all the rest, at a time when, "*du côté du boulevard*," I received such charming summonses. But, more fortunate than the traveler, I finally attained my pleasure, not the way I thought I should, not when I thought I should, but later and in a different much more splendid way, in the form of that letter from you. In that form, too, I "recaptured" *le temps perdu*. I thank you and leave you only to stay with you, to follow you all this evening through *Les Caves du Vatican*.

Your very devoted and grateful
Marcel Proust

156: ANDRÉ GIDE TO MARCEL PROUST

[JANUARY OR FEBRUARY, 1914]

Mon cher Proust,

I am writing you again, having heard yesterday that your contract with Grasset does not actually bind you to giving him your other two volumes of A la recherche du temps perdu. *Can that really be true?*

The N.R.F. is prepared to undertake all costs of publication and to do the impossible in order to have the first volume take its place in the series of subsequent volumes as soon as the present edition is exhausted. This was the unanimous and enthusiastic decision of the N.R.F. at its meeting yesterday (I came back from Florence to be there). I have been appointed to inform you of this—and I am speaking in the name of eight fervent admirers of your book. Is it too late?—ah, in that case, do send me a line to check my hopes as soon as possible.

Your devoted
André Gide

157: TO MADAME STRAUS

JUNE, 1914

Chère Madame Straus,

.... The characters you are kind enough to wish to see again (although perhaps it is already too much to have devoted 500 pages to them—in ordinary print, a thousand—in the first volume) will reappear and have quite as much space in the third volume; and they will have a little in the second. Only I preferred to give excerpts from the part of the second volume where they do not appear, to make it look more varied. If I had published the whole second volume serially, you would have seen Swann and Odette and Gilberte and Mme Cottard again, while waiting for the third volume for the Verdurins. But as I was giving only fragments, I preferred to contrast the sea with the landscapes of Combray, and Charlus with him you call Swann-Haas. (Although it is not Haas and nowhere are there either keys or portraits.) I will send you the July number of the *Revue* where some excerpts—still very long ones—will appear for the last time, but they have been so much and so awkwardly cut that they are very difficult to read. However, don't be disheartened. I think you will find certain portions about sorrow and about love that you may not dislike too much. There is a separation and also a scene where the same woman is seen by two men, one of whom loves her, the other who doesn't, and which, it seems to me, is not without a certain pathos and "human nature." But I am ashamed of talking about myself this way. Blame this tardy and ridiculous boasting to my inexpressible weariness, and please deign to accept my respectful expressions of grateful admiration.

Marcel Proust

158: TO EMILE STRAUS

JUNE, 1914

Cher Monsieur Straus,

. . . . Agostinelli was an extraordinary being (a fact I had not suspected at Cabourg, where I knew him only as chauffeur, and after years during which I didn't see him again) and gifted with perhaps the greatest intelligence I have ever known! Last year, having lost his position, he came to ask me to employ him as chauffeur, but I couldn't hurt Albaret by taking him. I suggested, without expecting much, that he type my book. That is how I discovered him; how he and his wife became an integral part of my existence. Alas, today I have the sorrow of thinking that if he had not met me and had not earned so much money through me he would not have had the means to learn aviation. Unfortunately all of his family were far from being up to him. We ended by quarreling and, after an incident beyond the limits of ingratitude, I wrote him: "If by any misfortune you ever have an aeroplane accident, make it very clear to your wife that she will find in me neither a protector nor a friend, and that she will never get a cent from me." You can well imagine that in the face of this disaster I have forgotten all that and, besides, she had known so well that I would that I was the person to whom she sent the first desperate telegram. I did everything to keep him from going into aviation, but his wife was convinced that he would earn a million. I shall come to their aid as best I can, but the difficulty is twofold. The terrible financial speculations about which I talked to you and which I intended stopping at the first rise in stocks, I was forced to continue without stopping, the Bourse having declined without closing, so each month I pay nearly thirty or forty thousand francs to brokers, and my capital will not hold out long. In the second place, the Agostinellis are the kind of people who, when they have fifty francs, spend twenty francs for peaches, twenty francs for an automobile, etc., and have nothing left the next day. And "this example is drawn from smaller animals," I mean lower figures, but if I told you about their life, you *would not believe me*. . . .

Marcel Proust

159: TO EMILE STRAUS

JUNE—JULY, 1914

Cher Monsieur Straus,

. . . . It seems that Agostinelli's wife, who always said "my husband" in speaking of him, as he said "my wife," and who signs all her letters, Anna Agostinelli, was not married to him. I knew very well that she was a former mistress of his, that he wanted to get married, and I thought it had been done a long time ago. Since I was mistaken I would seem to have acted in bad faith and to have caused you to act in bad faith towards the Prince of Monaco, since we have tried to move him to pity for a widow who is not one legally. I consider her Agostinelli's widow just the same because (although I don't like her and was on bad terms with her just before the death of the man I supposed to be her husband, but who was only her "man") I have to recognize the fact that she adored him; she has already tried to kill herself several times since his death; as for him, although he was unfaithful to her (which she didn't know because she was insanely jealous and would have killed him), he loved her better than anyone in the world. His love for her in the first place is inexplicable, for she is ugly; nevertheless he lived only for her, and certainly he would have left her everything he had. Only the rest of his family who, I am afraid, are not worth much and who did not like her (which I can well understand) have suddenly, right in the midst of a grief which may be sincere, become terrified at the thought that someone is interested in the wife and that if the body is recovered it would be to her, not to them, that the money he had on him (five or six thousand francs) would revert. This sort of thing, shocking as it is, happens every day at the La Rochefoucaulds' or the Montmorencys' whenever a question of self-interest arises. The same thing has happened in the Agostinelli family. I have been told that they have gone so far as to telegraph the Prince of Monaco that the "widow" was not legitimately married to the deceased. I don't know whether it is true; I don't believe it is. The fact remains that the Prince did send word that he would interest himself in the widow, but nothing ever came of it. I think, though, that it is my duty to have the Prince informed that I was mistaken, that Anna Agostinelli was not legitimately married to Alfred, but that she nevertheless deserves consideration, for I have seldom in my life seen a couple so tenderly united, truly living one for the other.

For the same reason I should like to find out from the Prince if they really did telegraph him or whether I am being "taken in." So as not to bother you any further about all this, I should like to have him informed, since it is very urgent, by someone else who knows the situation. But since I not only feel compunction towards the Prince but towards you, whom I deceived first (without wanting to), I have preferred before taking any steps to ask you whether you would not prefer taking them yourself. To sum up: to apologize to the Prince for the mistake about the legality of the marriage, while telling him that the widow's love and her relations with the deceased were more affectionate than in many a legal union (without asking for anything for her, just restating the facts); to find out whether they did write to the Prince to tell him of the illegality.

I am really distressed to admit that you should have a grievance against me and that in wishing to help people who were never nice to me I should have deceived you and caused you to take steps which were based on an error.

Your respectful, grateful, and disconsolate friend,
Marcel Proust

160: TO EMILE STRAUS

JULY, 1914

Cher Monsieur Straus,

My heartfelt thanks. I should have thanked you right away, but I was taking a little rest after a bad attack. I herewith return to you the documents, while thanking you again most deeply for what you have done. I hope my *gaffe* about the widow, from whom I asked no documents, as Mme Martini would have done, hasn't caused a "coolness" between us. For since then, "*Mon cher Marcel*" has been replaced in your letters by "*Mon cher ami,*" then by nothing at all. But I think it is pure coincidence, and I am not alarmed about it. I regret not being well enough to come to see you. I regret it for many reasons, but most of all because I should have brought you some of poor Agostinelli's letters, and I think you would have been astounded to read from the pen of a chauffeur sentences worthy of the greatest writers. You certainly would have had much difficulty in reconciling with these sentences the only idea you could have formed of him at Trouville (and, moreover, the one I had, too). France, indeed, spent many years near Gobineau without suspecting that he had genius. And he, of course, was a cultivated man of the world. It is true that a given station in life is no more essential than it is sufficient for the birth of talent. It is sad, indeed, that so gifted, so young, so courageous a creature should have ended in this frightful, stupid way, while imploring aid which his teachers did not give him. . . .

Marcel Proust

161: TO LUCIEN DAUDET

[November 17, 1914]

Mon cher petit,

Even if it weren't such a joy—at least as much joy as it is possible to feel at this time—to receive a letter like yours from a person I think of daily with ever increasing affection, what a relief to read these pages where there is neither "*Boche*," nor "their *Kultur*," nor "I could have wept," nor "loved ones," nor any of the rest. However, one suffers so much, thinking of the martyrdom of the soldiers and officers, is so overcome by their sacrifice that all this talk is easily enough borne.

Nevertheless, if the press, notably ——, would only express themselves with more dignity, victory would be even more splendid.

Frédéric Masson, whose veteran's style I have often liked in the past, is today really too much the embodiment of French "culture." If he is sincere in finding *Die Meistersinger* idiotic, forced on us by snobbery, he is more to be pitied than those he proclaims victims of "Wagneritis." If, instead of being at war with Germany, we had fought with Russia, what would have been said of Tolstoy and Dostoevski? But because contemporary German literature is so dull that the only recognizable names or titles are those the reviews of "foreign books" announce to us from time to time, only to be forgotten, they fall back on Wagner, not knowing whom else to attack.

I don't know why I talk to you about this so stupidly because, in being so summary, I am completely falsifying my meaning, which is quite different from what you will think it is. But, *mon cher petit*, you didn't write me before all this happened, not for two months, not since before the war; in spite of which there has not been a *single day* when I haven't spent hours with you. *Mon cher petit*, you wouldn't believe how much new significance my present affection for you, grafted onto the older one, has assumed; but I am sure you won't believe me. Well, you will see. . . .

I shall write to your brother. I was going to do it anyway to tell him of my admiration. The war has, alas, vindicated, consecrated, and immortalized the *Avant-guerre*. Not since Balzac have we ever seen so powerful a discovery by a man of imagination of a social law (in the sense of Newton's (?) discovery of the law of gravitation). . . . I hope that even if his prophecy was not listened to we shall at least know how to "apply" his discovery and put into practice the *Après-guerre*, ourselves. But I don't think that it ought to consist in reducing us to an inferior position (and I think that is also your brother's opinion, although I have not read his articles), in depriving not so much our musicians, but our writers, of the tremendous fruitfulness of listening to *Tristan* and the *Ring*, like Péladan, who no longer wishes us to learn German (a language of which, happily, General Pau and General Joffre are masters).

Mon cher petit, I have also worried about my brother. His hospital at Etain was bombarded while he was operating, the shells exploding on the operating table. He was also cited in the order of the day, not for that, but for the many other courageous things which he never stops doing. Unfortunately, he exposes himself to the greatest danger, and until the war is over I shall never know what the next day's news will bring. . . .

I hope you haven't too many friends among those "dead on the field of honor," but one loves even those one doesn't know, one weeps even for the unknown. And while I am on this subject, *mon cher petit*, I was dumbfounded by something that was told me: meagerly informed as I am about genuine greatness and the fixed brightness of the new stars that have been shining lately, I thought very great respect was due a certain M. Z——, whose work I have never read, but who I had been told was a genius. But the other day certain remarks of his, which were quoted to me, made me sick, and I couldn't believe they were accurately reported. I will copy them for you, word for word, since they have to do with people whom I don't know, whose last names I could not have invented, much less their Christian names: "Oh, yes, this war! Well, at least it will bring about the reconciliation of Célimène and Alceste (the Count and Countess of X—, née —). Oronte told me to tell you that Valère has behaved very well." (Don't these Christian names stand for M. de A— and the young Duke of B—?) "What I really can't stand is to learn of the death of one of the right people (in other words, chic people). Oh, yes, for me to learn that one of the —'s has been killed is a frightful blow!"

Is this sort of thing really possible? I wouldn't have believed even M. Y— or any other such clown capable of speaking, much less of thinking this way, but a writer, a philosopher! I hope all this is not true. I repudiate nothing—and I believe that the "right people" are sometimes righteous. But their death can cause me no more sorrow than the death of others, and because of my other friendships, it has happened that up until now they have caused me much less. But as to the war dead, they are admirable, and in a very different way from what people say. Everything that has been written about poor Psichari, whom I didn't know, but about whom so many people have told me, is so wrong. For that matter, the men of letters who think they are "serving" at this moment by writing, give a very false picture of all this, except for one or two. There are exceptions; did you read "The Three Crosses" by Daniel Halévy in the *Débats*, a paper in which, by the way, there is a daily article called "The Military Situation," by I don't know whom, which is remarkable and clear. Nevertheless, all these important men are as ignorant as children. I don't know whether you read General O's article on the origin of the word *Boche*, which, according to him, goes back to last September when our soldiers, etc. . . . He, too, must have talked only with the "right people," otherwise he would have known that servants, working people, have always said: "He's a filthy *Boche*." I must say that when they use the word, it's often very funny (like the admirable account of Paulhan's mechanic). But it makes my flesh creep when the academicians say, "*Boche*," with false heartiness, trying to appeal to the people, like grownups who prattle when they talk to children.

Mon cher petit, I am paralyzed with fatigue and no longer have enough energy to give you news of Reynaldo. He was at Melun; and having asked to go to the East, was sent to Albi and from there is to leave, alas, for "the trenches." I can't tell you how many proofs of moral courage he has shown since the beginning of the war. I don't mean just about the war, but indirectly, too. Really, Reynaldo is a rock of virtue on which one can build and live. . . .

Marcel

162: TO LUCIEN DAUDET

[DECEMBER 1914 OR EARLY 1915]

Mon cher petit,

. . . . I am very much depressed by the letters I get from Reynaldo; not that they aren't courage itself in any matter that concerns him; but the remark "someone is too good a soul, too sensitive to watch endless suffering and dying around him," which is stupid when not applicable, is true about him, and this sadness has assumed proportions for him which at first I didn't understand and which now make me unhappy.

Mon cher petit, I, who find the newspapers so irritating with their misplaced patriotism, had a real "patriotic" emotion myself the other day. I went to see — whom I thought was going back and at whose house I found several people whom it is unnecessary to enlarge upon because you know them from as far back as Adam and Eve, and your opinion of them, if, indeed, you have any, is unlikely to change. . . . Apart from these people, there was M. Z—, whom you probably know but I don't. This man talked of France with great admiration, told with such power, such grandeur of the visit General A— had permitted him to make to the battlefield of the Marne that I can't tell you how deeply I was moved. And the most pointless thing is that what most made me want to cry was his saying over and over again, "You have routed the Germans, you have overpowered them, etc. . . ." On the one hand I was embarrassed by this *you* because I had done nothing at all; on the other hand, I felt he meant that I was French, which was just the thing that called forth my emotion. Then some unbelievable anecdotes which I can't tell you here. Later I regained possession of myself a little and wondered whether this warm, vivid (and sincere) man hadn't really taken us in a little (in his story). I'll explain the nuance to you by word of mouth. . . .

Ton

Marcel

163: TO LUCIEN DAUDET

[CIRCA MARCH 1915]

Mon cher petit,

. . . . If you see Madame de X— —it would be overdoing it for me to write her just for this—will you deny something she said that makes me miserable. She said, I am told, that when someone talked to me about the war, I answered: "War? I haven't had time yet to think about it. I am, at the moment, studying the Caillaux affair." I have never given much thought to the Caillaux affair, since I don't know the Caillaux's. Moreover, I never told anyone I was studying the Caillaux affair. It's not only inaccurate, it's an absurd invention. As for the other part of the remark, it's even more pointless. I have all the reasons in the world, alas, for not having stopped thinking about the war for one minute since the eve of mobilization when I took my brother to the Gare de l'Est, and, in a rather touching and ridiculous way, I have even followed strategy, on a General Staff map. It is true that *Boche* does not figure in my vocabulary and that things are not as clear to me as they are to certain other persons, but never have I said it did not interest me, for I worry about it all the time. I am sure if Madame de X— said this, it is because someone told her (and I should very much like to know who). She has been told a stupid lie, which can't have for excuse or bait some misunderstood word, since I never said anything of the kind. . . .

Ton
Marcel

164: TO LUCIEN DAUDET

[CIRCA MARCH 1915]

Mon cher petit,

. . . . As for Madame de X's gossip, I've stopped thinking about it. Since in the course of events we find out what we want to know once we have stopped trying, I have learned that the story was invented by —— who thought he was "synthesizing" my hothouse life and was very much surprised to find that I wasn't delighted.

I can't tell you how strongly this shows (granted my affection and admiration for ——) how little I understand him in certain respects. I have always lacked the measure of buffoonery and of metaphysics necessary for the "invention" of these "syntheses." As far as practical jokes go, you are perhaps closer to —— than I am, but, on the other hand, *mon cher petit*, I believe you and I have a trait in common, a trait which is specially peculiar to us and which for some time will give people a lower opinion of us than we deserve. With both of us, you see, when there is communication on the "trip" out of life into literature (life nourishing literature), there is no contrasting communication, no "return ticket" back from literature to life. We do not allow literature to tinge, to warp our social relations or to distort the customary ethics of these relationships. At least it's an idea that I thought up, which would be really clear only if fully developed, if I were less sick and you more patient.

While I was looking through a drawer, I again found the

beautiful letter from Jammes of which I have often told you and which I regretted not having shown you, for it is my great pride. I can't decently say to you: "Such and such a person has said of Swann that, etc.," but you know Jammes; to show you his letter would have been so natural and so flattering. Oh, well!

Au revoir, mon cher petit. I promise to think a great deal of your Dickensian isolation. I embrace you tenderly, *mon cher petit*.

Your
Marcel

P.S. I happened by chance to open a volume of the Goncourt journals (veronal has so affected my memory right now that I realize I had entirely forgotten this volume, *not a word* of which I remember at all). It is fantastically and overwhelmingly horrible to remember nothing. You can't imagine the incredible things I found in the journal on the day of Victor Hugo's funeral! I thought I was reading a *pastiche* done by you or me. . . . And the same thing is true of what he says about the idolizing of his book on Lapland. You, who saw the Princesse Mathilde when you were very little, must describe one of her costumes for me, a spring afternoon, the crinoline-like dress she wore in mauve, perhaps a hat with streamers and violets, just as you must have seen her, in fact.

Jacques-Emile Blanche (1861–1942), the fashionable French portrait-painter, had known Proust since childhood when they were neighbors in Auteuil. His portrait of Proust, with an orchid in the buttonhole, painted in the early nineties, is well known. During the Dreyfus Affair they were alienated, but later became reconciled. Until 1940 Blanche was an Anglophile and spent much time in England, where he painted portraits of Thomas Hardy and Henry James, among others. Proust gained much of his knowledge of James from Blanche, who was the author of a number of volumes of art criticism and of memoirs.

165: TO JACQUES-EMILE BLANCHE

102, BOULEVARD HAUSSMANN
WEDNESDAY [CIRCA JUNE, 1915]
No, I never received the letter.

Cher ami,

.... Since I can't get out of bed (except very occasionally), I could not receive you any place except in my bedroom.

In any case, if we are able to meet, I should like better to see you to chat with and then go over the proofs you speak of when you are not there. I value what you write too highly to be satisfied with knowing it superficially; but I read thoroughly only when I read to myself and alone. Anything read aloud must penetrate through the intervening personality of the reader. Intent on that reader and on conveying to him my impression, I do not have the leisure, the opportunity to let it take shape in the depths of my being; I inhabit my own outer surface, and not until I am alone again do I go back down into the hole where I see some light. It is there that I want to read you. During the "readings" like those France, Montesquiou, and others have sometimes given me, I hardly know what I am listening to, and part of the meaning escapes me. Granted all this, everything shall be as you wish it and will in every way give pleasure to your affectionate and grateful admirer.

Marcel Proust

166: TO LUCIEN DAUDET

[CIRCA JULY, 1915]

Mon cher petit,

. . . .

I have been visited and revisited by some majors I didn't know (I don't even know their names); they did not know that Father was a doctor and that Robert is one, and each time they would say to me, "You are an architect, aren't you?" But I was so sick that there was no doubt about the decision. It is a recommendation that is destined to become more and more cogent up to the time of my death, and I hope with all my heart you will never have it. However, it isn't always effectual because the examinations are frequently so brief and superficial. Reynaldo was witness at the following visit.

"What is wrong with you?"

"I am a cardiac case."

"No, you are strong enough for service in the army." And the sick man dropped dead of a stroke. It is quite possible that the same scene will be enacted with me. But in that case, the cause of death will certainly not be my emotion at having to go. My life in bed for the last twelve years is indeed too sad for me to regret losing it.

In going over the first proofs of *Swann*, which are different from the later ones, I find Françoise saying, "War isn't fair. Only those who want to should be made to go." A naïve sentiment (but not really so much so, since that is the English system) that would have spared us the invasion, for how many Germans want to fight a war?

Affectionately,
Marcel Proust

167: TO LOUISA DE MORNAND

[1915 ?]

Ma chère Louisa,

I can't express to you briefly the great sorrow your letter has caused me. This great sorrow is only too natural; loving you as I do love you, I can't but be cruelly struck by the idea of your suffering. And you know that under those circumstances one thinks all the more of the people one loves, even though we are hurt by the thought, as when one is ill one makes just the movements that cause one pain and that one shouldn't make. If I write you in too scanty a way about my affection and my grief, it is because this morning while I was taking my inhalation, and, because probably even my antiasthmatic powders are less well made during the war, a pinch of the powder caught fire, flared into my eyes, and burned a corner of one eye. I haven't seen a doctor and I don't think it will amount to anything, but it keeps rather hurting me and it took the news of your misfortune to make me risk the fatigue of writing. I am not surprised that L— wrote you a wonderful letter. As I was saying recently to a number of ladies who were more or less brought up with him and who, nevertheless, do not perhaps know him as well as I do, he has the greatest heart that I know and there are no letters I like as much as his. I infinitely admire what you are doing for your poor brother's family. And, just imagine (it seems to me I told this to L—), merely from a photograph that I saw of him I developed a great curiosity about knowing him; I have always been curious about what it is that can make the transformation in the face of a friend or a loved one of the masculine sex into the feminine, and vice versa. Because of this three years ago I very much wanted to see little B—, the brother of a woman who, when she was fifteen years old, was the great love of my youth and for whom I wanted to kill myself. That was many years ago. In spite of that I was curious to see her young brother. Alas, he died almost at the beginning of the war. I could cite you a number of other examples if my eyes weren't really abandoning me, among others, M. de F— (whom, however, I never saw) and who is the son of a woman with whom I played in the Champs-Elysées, although she was considerably older than I. . . .

Your wholly devoted,
Marcel Proust

Sometime I shall tell you how I was so sure it was you I recognized in a restaurant that I had them ask whether it really was Mlle de Mornand. The lady was called, if I remember correctly, Mme Dussaud. Does she look like you?

Comte Clément de Maugny was an old and close friend of Proust's, whose loyalty and warmth towards him was uninterrupted. During the late 90's Proust used frequently to visit him at his family château at Thonon on Lake Geneva.

168: TO CLÉMENT DE MAUGNY

APRIL, 1915

Mon cher Clément,

I write you out of the blue, afraid that my letter may not reach you because your address seems quite incomplete, but, in any case, I am trying; I have thought of you so much since learning of the death of M. de Ludre. I know how much you loved him and to lose him like this, without having seen him again! Young as many die these days, they, alas, are at war! How I should have liked to have been near you, to have tried, by dint of kindness and friendship, to ease the sadness of your good, your so sensitive heart, the sorrow that no one there in the country could have solaced. My heart, my dear Clément, always so devoted to you, forgets its own grief to think of yours. Yet my own grief is very great; you don't know, because of the way our lives have now drifted apart, of a friend whom I lost a year ago, who with my mother and father was the person I loved best in the world. But since then, there has been one death after another. Bertrand de Fénelon, who, when you stopped seeing me, became my Clément and proved himself an incomparable friend, Bertrand de Fénelon, who did not have to join up and who was far more useful where he was, wanted to go, and was killed. Ten years had gone by without my seeing him, but I shall mourn him always. D'Humières's death caused me much sorrow. My brother has just been decorated for acts of heroism, which also show the risks he runs. And so I can say that it is with an aching heart I think of you and of all you must suffer in this life, so glorious but so filled with sorrows.

Your
Marcel

Marie Scheikévitch came to Paris from her native Russia as a child. Her marriage to the son of the painter, Carolus Duran, lasted only briefly, but through her father-in-law she was introduced to the artistic world of Paris and later her salon brought together a wide variety of talented persons. Among her friends were Anatole France, Jules Lemaitre, Paul Valéry, the Comtesse de Noailles, d'Annunzio, Jean Cocteau, as well as many distinguished journalists, politicians, and statesmen. She is the author of *Souvenirs d'un temps disparu.*

169: TO MADAME SCHEIKÉVITCH

[PROBABLY NOVEMBER OR DECEMBER 1915]

Madame, you wish to know what Mme Swann turned into as she grew older. It is rather difficult to sum it up for you. I can tell you that she became more beautiful!

"But another reason for this change lay in the fact that, having reached the turning point of life, Odette had at length discovered or invented a physiognomy of her own, an unalterable character or style of beauty; and on her incoherent features—which, for so long exposed to every hazard, every weakness of the flesh, borrowing for a moment, at the slightest fatigue, from the years to come, a sort of flickering shadow of anility, had furnished her, well or ill, according to how she was feeling, how she was looking, with a countenance disheveled, inconstant, formless, and attractive—had now set this fixed type, as it were an immortal youthfulness."

You will see her social life revive; however (without knowing the reason until the end), you will always find Mme Cottard there, exchanging remarks like the following with Mme Swann:

"But you're looking very sweet today," Odette says to Mme Cottard. "*Redfern fecit?*"

"No, you know I always swear by Rauthnitz. Besides, it's only an old thing I've had done up."

"Not really! It's charming!"

"Guess how much. . . . No, change the first figure."

"Oh, it's very bad of you to give the signal for flights like that. I can see that my party hasn't been a success. Do take another of those horrid little cakes. They're really very good, you know."

But I should rather present to you the characters you don't yet know, the one above all who plays the most important part and brings about the climax, Albertine. You will see her when she is just "a young girl in bloom," in whose shadow I spend such happy hours at Balbec. Then when I become suspicious of her over nothing at all and then, for no good reason, either, I trust her again, "for it is the property of love to make us at once more distrustful and more credulous."

I should have stopped there. "The wiser course would have been to consider with curiosity, to possess with delight that little parcel of happiness, failing which I should have died without ever suspecting what it could mean to hearts less difficult to please or more highly favored. I ought to have gone away, to have shut myself up in solitude, to have remained so in harmony with the voice that I had contrived to render amorous for an instant, to render loving, and of which I should have asked nothing more than that it might never again address another word to me, for fear that an additional word, which now could only be different, might shatter with a discord the sensitive silence in which, as though by the pressure of a pedal, there might long have survived in me the ebbing chord of happiness." Then, little by little, I tire of her, the project of marrying her no longer pleases me: when, one night, after one of those dinners at "the Verdurin's in the country," where you will finally discover the real nature of M. de Charlus, she tells me, while saying goodnight, that the childhood friend of whom she had often spoken to me and with whom she still maintains such affectionate relations, is Mlle Vinteuil. You will see the dreadful night I then spend, at the end of which I come weeping to my mother to ask permission to be engaged to Albertine. Then you will see our life together during this long engagement, the slavery to which my jealousy reduced her, and which, succeeding in calming my jealousy, dissipates my desire to marry her, or, at least, so I think. But one day when it is so lovely that my imagination is filled with delight by every passing woman, by thoughts of all the possible journeys I could make, I decide to ask Albertine to leave us. Françoise comes into my room and hands me a letter from my fiancée who has decided to break with me and has been gone since morning. It was what I thought I had wanted. Yet I suffered so much that I was obliged to promise myself that some means of making her return would be found before evening. "Just a little while ago I had believed that this was what I wanted. In seeing how I had deceived myself, I understood how much more deeply suffering delves into psychology than does the best psychologist, and that the knowledge of the component elements of our soul is given us not through the most subtle perceptions of our intelligence, but—hard, brilliant, strange, like salt suddenly crystallized—by the abrupt reaction of pain." The next few days I can barely even take a few steps around my room. "I tried not to brush by the chairs, not to see the piano or any of the other objects she had used and which, in the special language that made them my souvenirs, seemed to wish to impress her departure on me all over again. I sank into a chair, I couldn't stay there, the last time I had sat in it she was still there; and so, at every instant, one or another of the innumerable and humble selves that compose our entity must be informed of her departure, be forced to listen to the words, as yet unknown to that particular self:

'Albertine has gone.' And so with every trifling act that had formerly been suffused with the atmosphere of her presence I was obliged to begin again with renewed effort and the same sorrow the apprenticeship of separation. Then the struggle for other patterns of life. . . . As soon as I became aware of them, I was panic-stricken. This calm, which I had just savored, was the first harbinger of that great intermittent strength, which would struggle against pain, against love, and which would end by mastering them."

This part deals with forgetting, but the page is already half filled and I shall have to skip all that if I am to tell you the end. Albertine does not come back. I arrive at a point of wishing for her death so that she shan't belong to others. "How could Swann formerly have believed that if Odette were killed in an accident he would have regained, if not happiness, at least the peace which comes from the suppression of suffering? The suppression of suffering? Could I really have believed it, believed that death blots out only what exists!" I learn of Albertine's death. "—For the death of Albertine to be able to suppress my suffering, the shock of her fall would have had to kill her not only outside of me, as it did, but inside myself. There, never had she been more alive. In order to enter into us, another person must first have assumed the form, have entered into the surroundings of the moment; appearing to us only in a succession of momentary flashes, he has never been able to furnish us with more than one aspect of himself at a time, to present us with more than a single photograph of himself. A great weakness, no doubt, for a person to consist merely in a collection of moments; a great strength, also; for it is dependent upon memory, and our memory of a particular moment is not informed of everything that has happened since; this moment which it has registered endures still, lives still, and with it the person whose form is outlined in it. Disintegration, moreover, not only makes the dead person live but multiplies him." Each time that I had reached a point where I could bear the sorrow of having lost one of these Albertines, the whole process had to be gone through all over again with another Albertine, with a hundred others. So that what up to then had composed the sweetness of my life, the perpetual rebirth of bygone moments, became its torment (changing hours, seasons). I wait for summer to end, then autumn. But the first frosts recall to my mind other such cruel memories that "like a consumptive who chooses the best place from the physical point of view for his lungs, his cough (but in my case making a moral choice), I then realized that what I had most to dread for my grief, for my heart, was the return of winter. Bound up with each of the seasons in order for me to discard the memory of Albertine, I should have had first to forget them all, prepared to learn them again, as a man who has had a stroke again learns to read. Only an actual extinction of myself would have consoled me for hers. But one's own death is not such an extraordinary thing, it is effected in spite of ourselves every day. —Since, merely by thinking of her, I brought her back to life, her infidelities could never be those of a dead woman; the moments at which she had been guilty of them became the present moment, not only for her but for that one of my various selves who was thinking of her. So that no anachronism could ever separate the indissoluble couple in which to each fresh culprit was immediately meted a jealous lover, always contemporaneous." After all, it is no more absurd to regret that a dead person doesn't know that she has not succeeded in betraying you, than to wish that in two hundred years your own name shall be known. What we think exists only for us, we project into the past, into the future, without permitting ourselves to be impeded by the supposed barriers of death. And when my deepest recollections of her no longer recall her, little insignificant things will have this power. "For the memories of love are no exception to the general laws of Memory itself, ruled by habit, which weakens everything. And so what most recalls a person is precisely the thing we have forgotten, because it was without importance." I start to experience, little by little, the strength of forgetting, this mighty instrument of adaptation to reality, destroying in us that surviving past that is its constant denial. "Not that I no longer loved Albertine. But already I no longer loved her as I had in the final phase, but as in the earliest times of our love. Before forgetting entirely, before reaching the initial stage of indifference, I should have, like a traveler who returns by the same route to his starting point, have to traverse in the return direction, all the sentiments through which I had passed. But the way stations do not seem immobile. While our train is halting at one of them, we feel the illusion that the train is setting out again, but in the direction of the place from which we have come, as on the former journey. Such is the cruelty of memory." There was nothing Albertine could have reproached me for. One can only be faithful to what one remembers, one can only remember what one has known. My new self, although it grew up in the shadow of the old one who died, had often heard that other self talk about Albertine. Through the accounts of the dying self it believed that it knew her, loved her. But this was only a secondhand affection. "As there are strokes of good fortune, so there are misfortunes that happen to us too late, when they can no longer assume all the importance that they would have had in our lives a little earlier." By the time I had realized that, I was already consoled. And there was no reason to be surprised about it. "Regret is really a physical ailment, but among physical maladies it is possible to distinguish those which act upon the body only through the channel of memory. In the first instance, the prognosis is generally favorable. At the end of a given period a man who has been attacked by cancer will be dead. It is very seldom that in the same length of time the grief of an inconsolable widower is not healed."—Alas, Madame, I have no more paper now just when this wasn't going too badly!

Your

Marcel Proust

170: TO JACQUES-EMILE BLANCHE

102, BOULEVARD HAUSSMANN
WEDNESDAY [JUNE OR EARLY JULY, 1915]

Cher ami,

. . . .

I know the novels we like best, published in the last fifty years, have accustomed us to the idea that it was not irrelevant to mention along with a special state of mind or an important truth, some little event, neither special nor important, which drifted into our train of thought at that moment. But this is what has made the "aesthetic" novel so easy to do and has deprived it of all logical value. Your excellent habit, since it is personal and characteristic, of continually writing sentences without verbs (which grammatically I would not advise anyone to imitate, but which I like in you) leads you more than anything into this temptation of observation for observation's sake. It is just about the only grammatical form naturally suited to pure observation (and with good reason, since anyone satisfied with mere recording has no use for verbs). But chiefly this results in such condensation that an insignificant detail (forgive me for talking this way, I mean insignificant in relation to the rest, speaking absolutely; nothing that springs from a mind like yours is insignificant), which you would perhaps hesitate to bring into a more deliberately constructed sentence, seems to you acceptable in this rapid style, like those almost unnecessary objects that we hesitate to put in our trunk, but end by taking along because they don't occupy much space. Underneath all this there is doubtless a drama or at least a painful episode, but since *it is not indicated at all*, one cannot tie it up with what it undoubtedly controls. When you can, please send me back the proof sheets and I can perhaps show you better (although I think I have done it) what (without having great faith in my own judgment) seemed to me useless. As for my memory, I am sure that you intend neither irony nor cruelty when you speak of it to an unfortunate man whose illness (increased by the autointoxication) is just manifesting itself in a very *painful* amnesia. But I am afraid that my criticisms are not accurate. You were at one time, in your criticisms, and the parallel is exact, the Sainte-Beuve of painting (I say parallel simply for your writings, the parallel ceases since you are foremost a painter, and Sainte-Beuve was only accessorily a poet); you showed us the unexpected human truth in Manet, in Fantin, as Sainte-Beuve did for Chateaubriand, for Vigny; you gave us the joy of delightful discoveries and the chance of being mistaken, which we always run when we talk about art or history, when we deal with the man himself, and within the man, not exactly with the essential part he expresses in his work. (Possible mistake against which your marvelous knowledge of the works insures you; we hold you firmly by the hand while you allow us to lean, as over a precipice, over such and such a year, such and such a "*vernissage*," where we see the "ambitions" of Manet and the "shyness" of Fantin.) Now the war (I don't understand how, but the fact that I cannot understand is an additional reason for my mistrusting my own judgment) has wrought in us a crisis of the soul. Perhaps it will need to be more *defined*. I know very well that that is easy to say and that it is often characteristic of spiritual crises not to permit of definition. From the time a "piece," portrait, or landscape appears, we rediscover the delightful colors, the traits of an inimitable character, of the beloved writer. Elsewhere we are on "*terra incognita*" where we readily lose our way, perhaps because you give us too little guidance, leaving us without any knowledge of the characters and the events. . . .

Your admirer,
Marcel Proust

171: TO LUCIEN DAUDET

Mon cher petit,

. . . . I have thought over our conversation of the other evening. Yes, I am sure that for the aesthetic discovery of realities we must place ourselves outside them and know, for example, how not to be a Parisian when we speak of Paris, the way your father so delightfully and terribly knew how not to be of the South when he talked about the South. If you will allow me for a moment to compare an earthworm to the Himalayas, I have always been careful in speaking of the Guermantes not to regard them as would a man of the world or at least a man who is or was in society, but from the point of view of whatever *there may be of poetry* in snobbery. I have not spoken of them in the glib style of a man of the world, but in the dazzled tones of someone for whom it is all very remote, otherwise one would write like —— and not even as well. One must temporarily belong to Nîmes (as your father did) to know how to talk about the charm of the Parisienne, and so it is right to come from Nîmes to prove that the charm of the Parisienne exists.

Forgive this "teacher's" tone.

Mille tendresses,

Marcel

172: TO LUCIEN DAUDET

[1916]

Mon cher petit,

I don't believe in letters that don't arrive, and at the same time I can see that that was the fate of mine, the only one that mattered to me, because I wrote if after having seen your unhappiness, which, although it caused me profound suffering, left me speechless in your presence for reasons which I haven't room to explain here. Since you were going to come back forty minutes later, I thought I should talk to you about them then, but I listened to every sound like Musset in "La Nuit d'Octobre"; *Il me semblait, dans l'ombre, entendre un faible bruit.* You didn't come back. So I wrote you. And obviously Céleste couldn't easily give a clue. There are several messengers, and even she herself can't always remember who has taken which letter, for she pretends not to look at the addresses. But your letter reminding me of a departure for Florence (which, however, didn't take place) disheartened me. All the more because this "detachment" of which you speak (sincerely, I suppose), I found in you. And, besides, even "objectively" and from the point of view merely of your journey, it was I who was right, because during the time I have been rooted here in my eternally sedentary state, I have seen you skate off to slide around the world in 48 hours, successively to "do" Holland, to go to England, to Nice, return to England, all in the time it would take me to decide to change my room.

. . . .

Mon cher petit, don't go away thinking that there are recriminations and reproaches on my part, for you have always overwhelmed me with kindness. But then I believed in friendship; today you will see what I say about it in *Swann*, and that it no longer exists for me, and I am not saying that it is anyone's fault: it would take too long to explain.

Just as it would be too complicated to explain the physical reasons (like a woman who can't declare her passion on a certain day because the skirt she is wearing is too long) that keep me from expressing what I feel when you tell me things that fill me with emotion, like the first day I saw you again, or when you talked to me about my book, or like the other evening. Moreover, it would be too stupid of me to play the savant and the teacher with you. But I know so well that your unhappiness is the result of a wrong mental attitude. Your sublime father who, in the midst of the greatest creative work (when one went into his study to ask if you were coming back from Julian's), seemed no more disturbed than if he had been in the process of sharpening a pencil, had wonderful intuitions about each of our destinies. With prophetic wisdom he said to me: "Your stumbling block, my little one, will be your health." The things he said to Reynaldo were equally apt, and your style and your painting he predicted in advance. Alas, unlike him I cannot look straight into your soul, but such meager little prescriptions as I cannot use myself I should love to give you. . . .

Marcel

173: TO RENÉ BLUM

102, BOULEVARD HAUSSMANN
MAY 31, 1916

Cher ami,

You very kindly offered the other day to break off the ties with Grasset (which I was, nevertheless, very grateful to you for having arranged at a time when I had no publisher). I replied that ethically I could not break with him. And then it happened (I don't like to act like the man who is sought after, but actually in this instance it is true, more so even than I am saying) that the kind solicitations of the *Nouvelle revue française* started again. And in examining my conscience, and remembering the money I enabled Grasset to make by accepting a much smaller amount than he offered for the translations, and thinking of lots of other things, I find that I am in no way behaving badly by asking you to arrange a divorce. You can give Grasset a reason that he will know perfectly well was not invented after the fact. Indeed, I remember very well (and he certainly remembers) that some time after having refused, at his request, the offers of the N.R.F. and having decided to stay with him, I said to him one day in the postscript to a letter, rather in fun (although it was true and embarrassing), that I had just been ruined. The same day (and very nicely I must say) Grasset made a point of telephoning me. I couldn't at all understand his compassionate tone, his circumlocutions, and fearing that he had had some trouble, I ended by asking him what was wrong. He replied, still on the telephone (and I do find that charming and retain a feeling of sympathy for him, although he imagines, I think, that I am "prejudiced" against him), "There is—there is what you wrote me about." I no longer remembered what I had written him. Finally, after forcing him to be specific, I understood that his condolence had to do with my financial losses; I thanked him effusively for being interested in them, begged him not to be any more alarmed by them than I was; I hardly dared add that he should not aggravate them by failing to keep a careful enough eye on the sales. —But, in any case, we can use this story as a pretext. Without bringing it up, it will be convincing enough so that he will believe you when you say to him, "Marcel Proust has lost a large part of what he had. He can no longer be as indifferent as he was to earning a little money. Your firm is closed, the N.R.F. isn't and can publish right away. He is asking you, because of the war, to release him from his promise to publish his other volumes with you and consequently also to take back the first without your being angry or hurt; this is legitimate because I paid for the publication and reserved the rights. I can't remember whether since then I made a new contract with Grasset just before the war, but I don't think so. I think we merely exchanged some words and some letters, in which I expressed my desire to emigrate to the N.R.F. and he, with skillful delicacy, leaving me free while telling me the pain I would cause him, and my being conquered by this procedure and remaining in the fold and rejecting the offers of the N.R.F. I will add (for your benefit) that the reason I am giving you is not true, because even if the N.R.F. had offered to publish me at once, I said that I preferred not to appear until after the peace. However, they were already doing a lot of work on the proofs (there are four volumes!), since I was to have them all appear simultaneously. I will add again that I will not accept terms from the N.R.F. one cent better than Grasset's (which, however, *after* the first volume had become good). They were, besides, prepared for the necessity of giving Grasset an indemnity. But is that really necessary with a book the very expensive printing of which I paid for and on the sale of which Grasset, in spite of all that, made some very good royalties. It is true that the proof of the second volume (several pages) was started several days ago, but so badly done, with such bad mistakes that Brun, Grasset's associate, told me he was going to have the whole thing started over without even discussing it with Grasset. At which point war broke out. It has changed and broken up so many things that it seems to me Grasset cannot be hurt (a thing which would distress me very much) if it makes me change publishers and for purely literary reasons. For Fasquelle had more or less asked me through Maurice Rostand to publish the succeeding volumes, and I didn't even consider it. But my book was for Gide, for poor Rivière, who has it in his prison in Germany, for Copeau, etc., a friend who would be well treated by them. Don't insist too much on the matter of appearing right away, because all he will have to say is that he will give orders to his press. *Cher ami*, if you can bring about this divorce without hurting Grasset, it would give me great satisfaction. I have taken the liberty of telling Gallimard that I was going to ask you to try to arrange this with Grasset. I hope I was not indiscreet in mentioning you; it was to explain why I didn't write myself. I hope that you are still looking well and not getting too tired. I no longer know whether we have talked about poor Bertrand [de Fénelon], because my medication has made me lose my memory to such an extent. The uncertainty, today almost a certainty, about his fate has been for me the same sorrow that I think it has been for you—I mean an inconsolable one. What has made it bearable is that I hadn't seen Bertrand for two years, that memory nourishes the heart, and grief abates. In the same way, a little before the war, I lost the person I loved best. In spite of that, since what happened to Bertrand is not known, it is impossible for me to stay in bed without quantities of veronal, so cruel is my anguish (not only the uncertainty, but the memory confronted with the contradictory reality). I never expected to see him again, and I would even rather not have (that is why I never saw him when he went through Paris), for I prefer to keep the memory of a life when we saw each other all day long and every evening, and that could no longer be. But if I was resigned to his absence, my joy lay in thinking that he was happy, that all his ambitions were gradually being realized. But the idea that he may be—alas, almost certainly is—cut off from the happiness of living, that for him, who had such varied capacities for being happy, for "success," none of the sweetness of thinking or feeling any longer exists—that is a thought I can't bear and for that very reason, just as one moves in the one way that causes one pain, I constantly return to it. *Cher ami*, I never speak of him. But I know with what affection he loved you, loved us, if one really must use the past tense, and it is a great sorrow but a great compensation to talk to you about him.

Always yours,
Marcel Proust

Paul Souday (1869–1929) was a journalist, who, after having served many years as political editor of *Le Temps,* became its chief literary critic in 1912. Noted for his prejudices, his hot temper, and his vanity, an assiduous devotee of the salons of Mme de Noailles, Mme de Caillavet, the Princesse Bibesco, and others, his qualities as a literary critic are here perhaps most relevantly illustrated by his own remarks written in his copy of the first edition of *Swann's Way.* "Idiotic!" was Souday's comment, penciled on the margin of the page (Part I, p. 160) where the narrator describes his Aunt Eulalie, showing how by her "whole-hearted obedience to her own irresistible eccentricities, and to a spirit of mischief engendered by the utter idleness of her existence [she] could see, without ever having given a thought to Louis XIV . . . something of the interest that was to be found in what Saint-Simon used to call the 'mechanics' of life at Versailles. . . ."

Of the highly satirical passage (*ibid.,* p. 178) where Legrandin describes Balbec in grandiose language of his own, which he attributes to Anatole France, Souday wrote, "Obviously not accurately quoted. *Alors?* Why so many insignificant details under the pretext of the exact truth?"

Although the far from laudatory review by Souday of *Swann's Way* in *Le Temps*, December 10, 1913, was instigated by the editor-in-chief, Adrien Hébrard, a friend of Mme Scheikévitch, Souday later claimed to have been the first critic to "discover" Proust.

174: TO PAUL SOUDAY

[1917]

Monsieur,

Quite often I fail to relish your criticism in *Le Temps*. Some of my reasons for this are personal (but by no means egotistical), others are not. So I find all the more satisfaction in telling you how much I appreciate the truth, the spirit, the courage of your articles in which you, practically alone, of all the press, I think, have known how to say and dared to say what we must think, what many people do think of Wagner and of Saint-Saëns, of M. R. Strauss and of M. Zamacoïs, and above all in a paper which really does rather abuse "*Kultur*," "scrap of paper," "aggressor nation," and "*kolossal*." Certainly in comparison to the hardships endured by those who are fighting and even those who are not fighting, the irritation of reading such untruths every day is a matter of small importance. And the gratitude due Boileau, avenger of good sense (a very "advanced" kind of good sense) would be less if we didn't consider the spiritual impoverishment of our young men or our descendants that would result from a system to which certain "doctors" mean to subject and restrict us. Contemporary German literature is so worthless that this system aims practically only at music. (If Russia had been against us in this war, what much more convenient subjects Tolstoy and Dostoevsky would have offered some preachers of journalism, certain philosophers of the serial novel!) But you have talked about music as it should be done. If M. Saint-Saëns feels such an antipathy to Strauss, it would nevertheless seem that he comes close to him in terms of a certain incapacity or laxity in controlling the sources of melodic inspiration (and in that alone). M. Strauss should have denied himself certain memories of *La Dame blanche* in *Salomé*; of *Le Petit Duc* in *La Légende de Joseph*. But can this objection be brought by the excellent musical author who has based his most majestic symphony on an air from *La Mascotte*? However, I don't wish to broach these subjects in a mere letter (which I need hardly tell you is not written for publication). I only wanted to congratulate you, to thank you. I envy you, too: it is unusual to be the unique voice, however little one may want to be, of what I cannot call the *élite*, since I have already ranged myself with them. Taste, artistic truth, which will be no less useful after the war than it was before, will emerge from this eclipse. I have no hard feelings in regard to M. Zamacoïs, whom I have not the honor of knowing, but a victory, the sole result of which would be to substitute for Wagner's aesthetic that of M. Zamacoïs would not be fruitful. In the meantime, your articles will have served to bring you the honor of being a link in the chain and of countering the dictates.

Please accept, Monsieur, my most distinguished respects,

Marcel Proust

175: TO MADAME SCHEIKÉVITCH

AUGUST 5, 1917

Madame,

The very excess of what I shall have to reply to you imprisons me in silence. I hope that you have worked or are going to work, since you are voluntarily depriving yourself of your son. The sacrifice will be less cruel if you work. Montesquiou's bad temper was not aimed at you but against a woman whom it grieves me to see upset (this doesn't mean that I shouldn't have been grieved if it had been you). In fact, I received a letter or rather a whole memorandum of explanation from him. Unfortunately, he is unyielding in his pretensions and is perhaps the only person towards whom my will to peace fails. It can be made to reign on earth among men of good will. But his is not altogether good. I also had some letters from X—, and he came here but I was unable to receive him. His letters were very nice, but they amazed me. He told me particularly that this reading was something sacred. I can't vouch for the sentence, but the adjective was there. Well, if I had X—'s talent, which I should very much like to have, it seems to me I should attach no importance whatsoever to my work and even less to its being read or the rites pertaining thereto. And I imagine that the first time Virgil read the *Aeneid* aloud, if Maecenas had arrived nearly at the end with some friends, the author would have celebrated their arrival and have offered them wine. Please keep to yourself my conclusions about all this, as well as the adjective "sacred," for each of us understands art in his own fashion. I admire and like X—; I should be most unhappy to pain him, and even reproach myself for having left his letters unanswered. I received Mr. W. Berry's lecture, which literally dazzled me by the discovery of the unsuspected race of men creating like Michelangelos fifty thousand years before Christ. (It's overpowering that an American jurist writes so admirably in French. Who wouldn't be proud to have written that?)

I come back from the H—'s exhausted and leave you, respectfully kissing your hands.

Marcel Proust

176: TO MADAME SCHEIKÉVITCH

AUGUST 28, 1917

Madame,

. . . . I am shattered by Emmanuel Bibesco's death. It didn't surprise me. I had guessed and predicted it all long ago; Céleste and perhaps Morand know this. I was astonished, not a week ago, at the optimism of de Brancovan and de Beaumont. I wanted to believe it. But, whether or not it is foreseen, such a misfortune is no less shattering to me, who should have been stricken sooner than Emmanuel. My shrunken life could end without causing regret to anyone; his was full of promise. I am not like Mme Verdurin to whom music gave neuralgia, sorrow does not bring on my attacks of asthma. Nevertheless, until there is a slight abatement in my condition, I am too shocked to attempt this drive, which for me, because of the time of day, is a journey. A journey which I postpone from year to year and which I should take even if you were not at Versailles, where I long to return. All the more so now that you are there. Please believe, Madame, in my tender affection and share my regards with Mme Bordeau, whom I knew in the past at her mother's and at Mme Lemaire's.

Marcel Proust

177: TO MADAME STRAUS

OCTOBER 11, 1917

Madame,

X— must sometime have quoted (what has he not?) this saying of Mme de Sévigné: "How charming a thing is a leaf that sings." I myself should say, "How charming a thing is a leaf of paper that sings." And there is, in fact, nothing as charming as a letter from you. (Please don't think when you see the word I have crossed out here that I was going to say as X— would have said, "from Geneviève Straus." I repeated the word "paper" by mistake.) I am less a scholar than X——, but less ill mannered, too. I must confess he appears to try to be. . . . He quotes some verses of Mme de Noailles in one of his articles and says, "These verses of Anna de Noailles." I don't think this would have occurred to anyone else since she has never signed a single verse "Anna de Noailles." I have known her since she was a young girl, and it has never occurred to me to speak of her except as Mme de Noailles. Since I told you the last time I saw you that I was again going out a little, you will not be surprised to hear that on one occasion I met X——. But what is surprising is that I met him at the only unfashionable dinner I attended. In evening dress he always has a little the air of "Consul," that monkey who could smoke, pay the check, and who dined out. Even in poor X—— with his whitening hair, the majesty of age seems to have caught up with this inferior brother, and from time to time an almost human glimmer crosses his face; it seemed to me that he was leaving the zoo for the Institute (which he must prefer). If he is, at the moment, your "guest," this letter will doubtless serve to put me in his good graces; and yet I shall need them because I still haven't the information about Napoleon and General Negrier for my book. He seemed to me to have assumed such authority and to have said so often, "I am the state," that he ended by convincing people of it, that is to say, by making it come true. Such as he is I might even like him if I had seen him again, but he left after dinner and we didn't speak. Besides, it was particularly regrettable that he left, because an astonishing hypnotic séance followed. At the end of the party there was an air raid warning. I shan't tell you whether the planes flew to the right or left of Cassiopeia, I only know that I caught cold because I went out on the balcony and stayed there over an hour to see this wonderful Apocalypse with the soaring and descending aeroplanes seeming to complement or eclipse the constellations. Even if we had only had a view of the sky there would have been more than enough beauty, it was so marvelous. But the fantastic thing was that like the Greco painting in which there is the celestial scene above and the terrestrial below, we were watching this sublime "Plein Ciel" from the balcony high up; underneath, the Ritz Hotel (where all this happened) appeared to have become a sort of "Liberty Hall." Ladies in nightgowns or even in bathrobes roamed the "vaulted" hall, as they clutched their pearl necklaces to their bosoms. As for the hypnotic séance, it was even funnier because it was conducted by an "amateur," a M. Delagarde, who—picture this—when Princesse Murat (X— would say "Violette") came out of the trance of her own accord, he, the hypnotist, to prove that he was waking her up, rushed to perform the proper awakening gestures to try and get there ahead of her. What's more, this lady who (like everyone else) had so much to ask and such an absolute faith in hypnotism, found nothing more to ask finally (through lack of imagination, no doubt) than that she might stop grinding her teeth. It seemed to me a modest request. But the degree of mediocrity produced by contact with mystery is incredible. Beaumont, who, when awake, has plenty of wit and color, asleep spoke hardly as well as Chabert would have. True, he didn't feel it when the pins were stuck into him, but this privilege would have been valuable only if one had been obliged to stick the pins into him anywhere or everywhere. Besides, the hypnotist, who was ignorant of anatomy, had a casual way of saying, to those who were doing the pin-pricking, in the jolly tone that Thiron or Guy might have used: "Try not to prick him in an artery." It made one shudder. . . .

Please share (unequally) with M. Straus my affectionate respects.

Marcel Proust

P.S. *Chère Mme Straus*. After due reflection, I am sending you this letter, which I have kept over a week, because I found the expressions I used in relation to X. went beyond my thought, which was not malicious, but I have not the strength to begin over. I trust you to *burn it as soon as you've read it*.

Attached to this letter is *Sesame*, with its preface ("Sur la lecture").

178: TO MADAME SCHEIKÉVITCH

OCTOBER 28, 1917

Madame,

I had been hoping to see you one of these days, but my health is wretched. I have been out twice since I saw you and then only at eleven o'clock in the evening. Besides (if even earlier there hadn't been the word of M. Carolus Duran), before that I might not even have telephoned you, for I was a little irritated about something. I feel just as you do about sentimentality. If I dare quote myself, you, having read *Swann*, will know (and will find again in succeeding volumes) a certain Bloch, as disagreeably provided with "*empfindelei*" as he is destitute of "*empfindung*" (I don't know the spelling of these *Boche* words very well. I read them, I believe, in the correspondence of Mendelssohn, who, alas, lacked the second more than he realized). I should like to know how your novel is going, whether you have contrived a way (which you didn't much want to do) of saving your hero. In the meantime, M. de N— is dead. H— in an incredible Dostoevskian scene, wanted me to write to the lady, an even more grotesque idea because I barely know her. I fell back on generalizations about sorrow (refraining from remembering that I had seen them together in your car in front of my door), which are sincerely enough felt, for I am sorry about her grief. I know it is cruel. I imagine it will be short. Also I was afraid that it would not be very kind to write to the lady. It was like saying to her: "I don't at all value your favor because I know very well that as soon as you are consoled, you will not forgive my letter, and therefore, if I write you, it means I don't care whether or not you soon regard me as an enemy." But now she is not thinking of that. And it is helpful, if one has the courage, to give people who are suffering the kind of understanding that, by the time they have changed, will appear to have been criticism. . . .

Your respectful admirer,
Marcel Proust

179: TO CLÉMENT DE MAUGNY

1918

Mon cher Clément,

I am very much touched by your kind letter and abashed that mine should have come to you at this moment of which I wasn't even aware. I hope, with all my heart, that the robust oak of Savoy, which is the Comte de Maugny, will resist this blow, rendered all the more terrible by the time when it is happening. Long ago I compared the war to those organic conditions like diabetes and albuminuria, which aggravate everything else. It is a comfort to me to think that during these painful days your incomparable wife is close to you. Just as your letter came, a young man, a nephew of your cousin Ludre, was paying me a visit. He is charming, extremely intelligent and with a courage equal to his intelligence, which, alas, makes me tremble for him. It was the first time I had seen him. I need hardly tell you that he has no connection whatsoever with the boy of whom I was telling you, who is splendid but wholly of the people. He was recommended to me, but is a little rough-and-ready, so it would be helpful if you could say a good word for him to his colonel or to someone in his regiment (164th Infantry). —He is, as I say, entirely of the people but none the less interesting for that reason, in fact, in my opinion all the more so. He is one of a number of soldiers to whom I send tobacco, cakes, and chocolate every week. I should like to have it made possible for him to go, from time to time, to see his sick parents in the suburbs of Paris—a word of encouragement would cheer him up greatly. He can't spell, but has a very beautiful handwriting. I assume—I fear—that this will be of no use to him, for doubtless there are regulations that would prevent his doing anything but drill.

He hopes not to stay at Laval, and since he had a brother who was killed, he thinks it might be possible to go to Angers in the colonial artillery, where he has another brother.

Thank you again, my dear Clément, for your kindness, which has moved me deeply. I shall send you the exact address of the soldier.

Believe me always,

Ton

Marcel

I have a godson at Dreux. Do you know anyone there? My long letter will have the advantage of sparing you the trouble of coming to see me.

Walter Berry (1859–1927), after having been a lawyer in Washington and, from 1908 to 1911, Judge of the International Tribunal in Egypt, returned to Paris, his birthplace, and became president of the American Chamber of Commerce, an office he held from 1916 to 1923. A friend of Henry Adams, Henry James, and many other writers, an intimate of Edith Wharton's, he met Proust through Mme Scheikévitch, who, after discovering in his library a book binding stamped with the Guermantes arms, arranged a meeting between the two men. Mr. Berry presented Proust with the book and was subsequently most helpful to him in certain financial matters. In 1919 Proust dedicated *Pastiches et Mélanges* to Mr. Berry.

180: TO WALTER BERRY

[1918]

Cher monsieur et ami,

Your letter is the expression of a marvelous poet. Hugo said to Saint-Victor: "One would compose a whole volume to make you write a page." I dare not assume the glorious and tiring role of Hugo. For to write a book is really a bore. But I shall say more modestly that in order to make you write a few lines, I should send you many a box of cigars. Yes, you are a poet. Before I had seen any of Chardin's works, I had never realized what was beautiful in my parents' house about the table after dinner, with one corner of the cloth tucked back and a knife lying against an empty oyster-shell. Before your letter I had read in innumerable stories: "My friend said to me, flicking the ash of his cigar." I had seen *Carmen* and Mme de Salverte, who is black and rolled like a royal cigar. Yet never had I believed that there was beauty in cigars. Since you have described them to me "aligned like the verses of a sublime poem," I dream of looking at, if not of smoking, cigars. I had sent you, as an ironic reminder of the smoke clouds you couldn't blow up to the firmament of the Beaumont ceiling, a few cigars. But you, by your beautiful letter, have given me all the cigars in the world, just as Chardin enabled me to enjoy all the still lives in actual life. But you did even more by sending me a copy of your lecture. Ali Baba's Cave contains no treasure comparable to the one into which you led me. I never for a moment suspected the existence of those prehistoric Giottos. I hope to see a reproduction of the bison at your house. It all makes me dream in the most extraordinary way, for it raises so many problems. But you yourself said that monarchy is the diplodocus, and if that creature even then was a Picasso, it is no more impossible that it too will return. . . .I can't even dream of telling you all that your lecture inspires in me, this marvelous and precise machine for exploring time. Are you really the President of a Chamber of Commerce or are you some homonym, *homo triplex*? This Walter is worthy of him who was called Pater, or Scott, or even just Walter, he who, although a *Boche*, flung on Nuremberg, more real than the bombs in 1914, a certain *Preislied*, which wasn't at all bad. And in that connection I see that you are a thousand times worse than Capus, who suppresses Strauss, Wagner, Hegel, Fichte, but who, by admitting Goethe and Beethoven, cancels in the long run only one century. You declare that the Germans were infected with an irreducible militarism even as far back as 50,000 years before Christ, and someday you will retrace the offensive they hurled against those peaceful illuminators of caves whom I dream about. Nevertheless, your Mediterranean does not seem so peaceful to me. The way in which she swallows up the blasphemer is rather like a certain speech of Theramenes on the death of Theseus. I think she is just as ferocious, but less constant; four years ago she swallowed up my dear secretary, who fell from an aeroplane; he was Italian and was typing the manuscript of *Swann*. Neither he nor his employer had a drop of German blood in their veins, no matter how many generations back their descent is traced. Why, in speaking of those sublime prehistoric artists who painted animals without models, didn't you evoke the artists you saw working in the Hindu temple you plundered?

Please accept, *cher* Monsieur, my admiring, grateful and devoted respects.

Marcel Proust

181: TO WALTER BERRY

JANUARY [1918]

Cher Monsieur et ami,

I am very behindhand in thanking you for your charming little note. My head has been in a whirl these days because of the bad state of health of someone I love very much. Because of this, too, the year has, as you say, gotten off to a murky start. If it weren't for that, I should have asked you to come and dine at the Ritz. But I have barely enough courage to do anything more than walk a few steps in the snow in front of my house. However, things are going well now. May that other murkiness, the one to which you refer, the War, go well, too! If it can (in the sense that a war can "go well," with the dead piling up and the living left ruined; but, after all, people would die just as much if we were beaten, and it would be a thousand times worse), our debt is to the Americans set in motion by Walter Berry. I don't know whether you read in *Les Débats* a week ago an article of Daniel Halévy's on the Americans. . . . In it we see how the women of the North are moved by the thought that they (the Americans) have come "from so far away." The article is short, however, and, all in all, unimportant. But the tone is good, sober, and deeply felt. . . . This must be the twentieth time the war has changed its aspect even in the eyes of those who conduct it. Lloyd George says: "Victory is now a question of tonnage." That is a specialty of yours (among so many others). Nevertheless, I find each of these successive formulas too exclusive. Styles change in strategy as in medicine, even while a war is being fought. I don't care for medical theories that have faith exclusively in serums, etc. . . . Our wish is the same, however; for a successful termination of the war. . . .

Please accept, *cher* Monsieur, my affectionate and devoted respects.

Marcel Proust

P.S. Night before last, while walking in the snow and slipping on the icy pavement, I was approached by two American soldiers who asked me where the Hotel Bedford was. I didn't know it was in the rue de l'Arcade, just a few steps from my house. They spoke little French, I speak no English, so it was silently that I went in search of the Hotel Bedford, which we soon found. And like the women of the North, I, too, was moved by the thought: "They come from so far away."

182: TO MADAME STRAUS

MONDAY [JANUARY 14, 1918]

Madame,

. . . . I very much hope that you will see me again before seeing *Swann*. Nevertheless, I am anxious to have it reappear before it is entirely forgotten, but I have had so many worries that I haven't had the courage to revise the proofs of this second part. When I am not too sad to listen, music is my consolation. I have bought a pianola to add to my *théâtrophone*. Unfortunately they don't have the pieces I should like to play. The sublime Fourteenth Quartet of Beethoven doesn't exist in their rolls. They replied to my order that "never in ten years had a single one of their fifteen thousand subscribers asked for that quartet." I wasn't able to tell whether they were drawing an invidious conclusion in regard to their fifteen thousand subcribers or to the Fourteenth Quartet. But I am afraid that I bore you by telling you my little stories like Mme Sichel's, and that you are no longer listening to me except as you do to her, with that "cruel pity" which is the subject of Gluck's *Divinités du Styx. Adieu,* Madame, I admire and love no one more than you.

Your respectful
Marcel Proust

183: TO MADAME STRAUS

[1st or 2nd of February, 1918]

Chère Madame Straus,

. . . .

I shall, as you suggest, try to come to see you some evening when there are no Gothas, although I never seem to find myself outdoors except on evenings when there are Zeppelins, storms, etc. The night of the Gothas I had gone to hear Borodin's Second Quartet at the Gabriel de la Rochefoucaulds'. Since I was leaving just as the siren started, I could have gone back at once and have avoided (it would have been the first time) being in the street at that moment. But the old chauffeur I had taken couldn't get started for half an hour in the avenue de Messina, so that, standing beside the car—since I didn't have the patience to wait inside it—I heard everything perfectly. But the old chauffeur must have been deaf because after we reached my house when I told him that if he was afraid to go back I could arrange to have him sleep in my little salon, he answered: "Oh, no, I am leaving for Grenelle. It was only a false alarm and nothing at all came over Paris." While he was saying this a bomb exploded in the rue d'Athènes, just five minutes away. *Adieu*, Madame, above all don't answer this.

Your respectful and grateful,
Marcel Proust

184: TO PRINCESSE MARTHE BIBESCO

[AFTER APRIL 4, 1918]

Princesse,

The feeling that I have for you resembles, at least in this, the one of which Musset spoke when he said: "When by so many other ties you are to sorrow bound." The sorrow that Antoine's letter causes me cannot, naturally, be double like that which (uncured, incurable, I hope) I felt at Emmanuel's death. For I suffered then not only at the thought of Antoine's unhappiness, but at having to accept the idea of never again seeing one of my dearest companions on this earth. That half of my experience I cannot go through again, or at least only vaguely, since I didn't know Mademoiselle Lahovary. But this, perhaps, renders my other grief even more cruel, the part that relates to you. For I know very well that my not having known her whom you have just lost alienates me from you, who must, as one always does at such a time, feel far closer to an old servant who knew her, to a gardener who talked to her, to a dressmaker who made her a dress than you do to me. From now on, the people or the things in which you do not find a little of her will seem irrelevant to you. Perhaps, however, I am not entirely so because my restless and implacable thought is so given over to conjuring up the memory of her whom you will never see again. One very recent mutual sorrow has so united us, if I may say so, in the memory of Emmanuel that you will lead me, without realizing it, to her whom I so wanted to know. Even though she remains beyond my perception, I shall always think of her. This misfortune hits me in so much the same way as Emmanuel's did such a short time ago that at times I believe it hasn't happened and that I am suffering double, as one sees double, so that, in the medium of time, the same sorrow seems split in two. But, Princesse, what can my thought mean to you? I am neither the gardener nor the old servant; and even the reassurances that I could bring you through my own personal experience, that you will be not cured, but that one day—an idea which will horrify you now—this intolerable misfortune will become a blessed memory of a being who will never again leave you. But you are in a stage of unhappiness where it is impossible for you to have faith in these reassurances. I can only be disconsolate at your suffering and lay at your feet my grief and my respect.

Marcel Proust

185: TO MADAME STRAUS

MAY 31, 1918

Chére Madame Straus,

. . . .

I shan't talk to you about current events. Never before had I been conscious of the extent to which I love France. You, who love the roads near Trouville, will understand what the countryside of Amiens, of Rheims, of Laon where I went so often, mean to me. Laon was with Emmanuel Bibesco. He is dead now. And we must love men more than things, and I admire and weep more for the soldiers than for the churches which were only the recording of an heroic gesture which today is reenacted at every moment. . . .

I gave the *History of the Dreyfus Affair* to one of my friends who was leaving for Madrid as secretary of the Embassy there. He writes to me from time to time, "the task you imposed on me for the holidays interests me deeply. I spend nights reading Reinach." But because he is very young and because he made Polybe's [Reinach's] acquaintance at the houses of various duchesses, he is very much surprised to find the names of the same ladies at the foot of the list of subscriptions for the Widow Henry where they ask to have Reinach "gutted." Since my friend wants to like *Swann*, he sees in the change of the attitude of these ladies in regard to Polybe a significant form of the elapsing of time. As for me, I preferred the Reinach they wanted to eviscerate. But I must add that I am happier that he dines comfortably at the Lévys. I am speaking of the Mirepoix. Polybe must have forgotten that they are not the only ones whose name is Lévy.

Adieu, Madame, forgive my gossip. I hope that Jacques at least is well, and I send you, in deep communion with all the emotions of these days when we are living through the laceration of the land that is so dear to us, my most respectful and grateful regards.

Marcel Proust

186: TO LUCIEN DAUDET

[CIRCA END OF SEPTEMBER, 1918]

Mon cher petit,

. . . .

The story of the last act of *L'Arlésienne* should be called to the attention of all authors so that they may know the futility of writing. I know of nothing so discouraging. And the example strikes me even more forcibly in relation to *L'Arlésienne*, a work in which I have never found solace. The mortal sorrow it engenders is the cause of practically all the follies I have committed in life and of those which are still left for me to commit. Instead of my little boy in my book having been deluded by the example of Swann, *L'Arlésienne* is what I should have said. *L'Arlésienne* and *Sapho*, do you know any other works that cause such incurable wounds? . . .

Tendrement à toi,
Marcel

187: TO MADAME STRAUS

OCTOBER 9, 1918

Chère Madame Straus,

Ever since your letter came I have not stopped thinking about you with such tenderness and sorrow that this evening—I don't know why—I am reduced to tears, tears which I can't hold back and which almost prevent my writing the words of this letter. I hope that they will be more legible because I have been wanting to write you the last few days about a matter which is in no way part of the infinite melancholy I feel today, but to which a reply is rather pressing. I have done, still on the Affaire Lemoine, a *pastiche*, this time of Saint-Simon, and I have put in it, unless you object, a passage about you. As a rule I don't believe in putting into a seventeenth-century *pastiche* names that evoke as powerfully as yours does the graces of the twentieth century. It makes for dissonance, which is inconsistent in a *pastiche*. But in another way my heart and my mind triumph over this technical reason. Now, I need only know that it does not offend you to figure in this *pastiche*. That alone would stop me, but it seems to me that, considering the infinite pleasure it gives me to talk about you, you should experience at least a little in what I say. If I didn't write you on the very day I wanted to about this *pastiche*, it is because just as I was going to do it (write you), I learned of my brother's being in a terrible motor accident. The poor boy, who for four years has always been in the most dangerous places without being wounded, was in a collision of two automobiles near the front (I mean the military front). These two cars ran into each other and the crash was so dreadful that my brother's head, projecting against the framework of his car, broke it. I naturally prefer this to having had the framework break his head. But, in the end, he did have a deep wound and he lost such enormous quantities of blood that if there hadn't fortunately been a château two kilometers away to which he could be carried on a stretcher and taken care of, he would have bled to death like Calmette. He is doing well now and will soon be taken to Paris, but this two-kilometer journey was very painful. The anxiety that this caused me for several days prevented my writing to ask your permission for the *pastiche*. But it isn't urgent; if during the next two weeks you could write me your assent, that would be time enough. . . .

Marcel Proust

188: TO MADAME STRAUS

[NOVEMBER 13, 1918]

Chère Madame,

What a beautiful letter! . . . Your evocation of Shakespeare in relation to the present tragedy is so profound and is so imbued with a great literary tradition that it immediately brings to mind Sainte-Beuve's calling your father the greatest scholar of his time and this scholar's having been permanent secretary of the Institute. Only in plays of Shakespeare does one see all the events culminating in a single scene: Wilhelm II: "I abdicate." The King of Bavaria: "I am the heir of the most ancient race in the world, I abdicate." The Crown Prince cries out, signs his abdication, his soldiers assassinate him. One must not recriminate against Destiny, particularly when the delayed action of clockwork, which had seemed motionless for four years, gives us this final shower of triumphs. Still I, who am so much the friend of peace because I experience man's suffering too deeply, I believe, just the same, that since we wanted a total victory and a hard peace, it would have been better had it been a little harder.

I prefer, among all the different kinds of peace, those which leave no bitterness in anyone's heart. But since we are not dealing with that kind of peace, since it will perpetuate the desire for revenge, it might then have been wise to make it impossible. Perhaps it is being done. However, I find President Wilson pretty gentle, and since there is no question of a conciliatory peace, and never could have been, through Germany's own fault, I should have liked more rigorous terms; I am a little afraid of German Austria's coming to fill out Germany as a compensation for the possible loss of Alsace-Lorraine. But these are only suppositions and perhaps I am mistaken, and we already have a lot to be thankful for as things stand. General Galliffet said of General Roget: "He talks well, but he talks too much." President Wilson doesn't talk very well, but he talks a great deal too much; there are times in the lives of nations, as in the lives of men (I have, alas, had occasion to apply this to myself), when the right motto is de Vigny's verse: "Only silence is great, all else is weakness." You know that is in "The Death of the Wolf," and you remember all those bloody and stoical verses. But I myself have right now been too long unfaithful to the law of silence, which must also be your doctor's prescription, and I must have tired you. So I bid you *adieu*, begging you to accept and to share with M. Straus my expressions of respectful, grateful, and ardent devotion.

Marcel Proust

PART FOUR

Fame and Death, 1918–1922

At the end of the war in 1918, only four years of life remained to Proust, insufficient time for a final revision of the last two volumes of his novel, *The Sweet Cheat Gone* and *The Past Recaptured*.

The Goncourt Prize, which was awarded him in 1919 for *Within a Budding Grove,* was only one manifestation of the recognition that he at last received, a recognition as warm, if not warmer, abroad than in France. But his health had deteriorated; his dependence upon alternate sedatives and stimulants had increased. He would see no doctor, not even his brother. In rare moments of intense gaiety, he would, perhaps, spend five thousand francs, the entire Goncourt Prize award, in one night of celebration at the Ritz. But practically all of his time he devoted to the concentrated and feverish effort to complete his work before his death, aware always of its imminence.

189: TO MADAME STRAUS

[NOVEMBER 20 ? 1918]

Chère Madame Straus,

. . . .

I haven't the proofs yet of the *pastiches* in which you figure and which I could only lend you for a day, anyway. Besides I hardly mention you (relatively speaking, that is, for I think the part about you amounts to about a page), but in the right tone, it seems to me, the one I frequently use in society when I speak of you. Less disillusioned about the vanities of this world when they concern you than you yourself are, I rather enjoy dazzling such members of the Harcourt, Boisgelin, young Arenberg, etc. circles, whom you have had no reason to see, by showing them the kings and queens besieging your door, which you keep shut in order to try to sleep. And I have tried to indicate this in the *pastiche* of Saint-Simon by saying that princesses of the blood go to your house without your putting yourself out to return their visits and that (as well as I can remember these lines written quite a long time ago and of which I have no copy) under the pretext of illness, turned into a special privilege, you do not escort the Dauphine (the Duchesse of Burgundy) out when she comes to see you. None of this is naturally expanded; you can imagine how little space there is in a *pastiche*, all the more so because too many artistic reasons oblige one to give most of it to seventeenth-century names. Otherwise it is no longer a *pastiche* of Saint-Simon. But since I intend writing some long things about you (and those are to be based on the essence of your personality), it has amused me no less, in the meantime, to allow a side of you to be glimpsed in this Louis-fourteenth crowd.

. . . Please accept, Madame, and ask M. Straus to accept my respectful compliments.

Marcel Proust

Dr. Abel Desjardins, born in 1870, well known as a surgeon and lover of the arts, was influential in the Cubist movement around 1910 and was also an amateur musician.

190: TO DR. ABEL DESJARDINS

1919

While I was still little more than a child there was one joyful experience that brightened those sad years; it was the gift from Abel Desjardins of a photograph on the back of which he inscribed these words: "To my best friend." Unfortunately this joy was marred during two years because after the words, "To my best friend," there was this reservation, "except (I no longer remember the Christian name) X." This X, whom I had never even seen, seemed to me the most enviable man in the world. But, at last, without my ever having known wherein lay the infinite grace of X in comparison with whom I lost favor with Abel, one day Abel asked for the photograph back, then returned it to me with the words, "except X," crossed out. And in my benedictions I made no distinction between Abel for having been so kind and X for having had defects.

Since that time the mementos have seemed so dead to me that latterly, forced to leave the boulevard Haussmann, I burned precious autographs, manuscripts, no copies of which exist—even photographs which have become rare. But all of a sudden I stopped in front of a little boy with a thin nose, a bantering look, and a three-cornered hat, and I exclaimed to the person who was burning up all the things I was taking out of big valises: "No! not that!" It was the photograph in which I was Abel's best friend except for X—then just best friend, nothing more. And that I couldn't have burned, for it was still living.

Marcel Proust

Violet Schiff, a woman of extraordinary charm, cultivation and graciousness, is the widow of Sydney Schiff (1871–1946), who, under the pseudonym Stephen Hudson, translated the English edition of *Le Temps retrouvé.* He was the editor of the review *Arts and Letters,* and the author of a series of novels, *Richard Kurt*, *Elinor Colhouse*, *Prince Hempseed*, and *Tony.*

191: TO MRS. SYDNEY SCHIFF

[JULY, 1919]

8 BIS, RUE LAURENT-PICHAT

(But 37, rue Madame, Please Forward, would be safer because I am not sure that I shall stay here. If you forget 37, rue Madame, you could, if necessary write me at the Ritz Hotel, where they would undoubtedly forward my mail.)

Madame,

I am in complete despair over your having ordered *A l'ombre des jeunes filles en fleurs* and *Pastiches*. Even if I could have answered your enchanting letter a month ago, I should, in any case, have sent you my books. But having been unable to write you for reasons which I shall now explain, I was doubly anxious that my first copy of each of these books should go to you. First, however, let me tell you what kept me from writing. I think I told M. Schiff—with that propensity to uninteresting confidences we indulge towards those who show us sympathy—that since the place where I lived had to be rebuilt (changed into a bank), I was going to be obliged to move out. I didn't try to do anything about it until the day before I had to leave, and then I realized with horror that I had enough belongings to furnish several houses. To this first problem which the movers simplified by stealing part and breaking the rest, I was forced to add another. There was not a single empty house in Paris. It was by a real miracle that Mme Réjane, hearing of my desperation (I could see the time when I should go to live at the Ritz and people would invite me to lunch in the corridors), offered to rent me a floor of her house. And I rushed into it. Only the moving out having already three-quarters killed me, Mme Réjane's house consumed the last quarter. It is next to the Bois, which has given me hay fever, and the partitions are so thin that one can hear everything the neighbors say and feel all the drafts; the Gothas, which never once during the war drove me down cellar, made much less noise even when they fell on the neighboring house than does one blow of a hammer on the floor above here. So that I have not as yet slept a single minute, and I am in such a weakened condition that tonight I have taken all the caffeine possible to be able to write you this letter. I send with it *A l'ombre des jeunes filles en fleurs* and *Pastiches et mélanges*. The worst of it is that you will have too many copies but I can't bear not to send them to you. The *Nouvelle revue française* sent me only second and third editions! Such an effort to get even one first!

I want to ask your advice, which could be infinitely valuable to me, about my book. Since neither I nor anyone else can have a single deluxe copy because all of them were subscribed for in advance by a hateful society of bibliophiles, the *Nouvelle revue française* intends to publish another deluxe edition. But one of much greater luxe. In each copy will be inserted several pages of my manuscript (not facsimiles, the actual original manuscript) and also a heliogravure to be reproduced from my portrait by Jacques Blanche. Only this will be excessively expensive (perhaps 500 francs a copy) because everything has to be reset and the format enlarged so as not to destroy the manuscript, which, in spite of my hideous handwriting (Montesquiou used to say: "There are some people who have ugly but legible handwriting; others, writing that is illegible but attractive; Marcel's succeeds in being at the same time illegible and hideous"), is charming and has the look of a palimpsest, because of the infinite taste of the person who mounted it. The *Nouvelle revue française* naturally hesitates to go to this expense before making sure that it will be covered, all the more because I rather regret not selling the complete manuscript of *the episode* to a collector instead of cutting it up like this. Since you have told me that you are surrounded by friends who like *Swann* so much, perhaps you could advise me and tell me whether you think I could find subscribers and whether the edition would be worth the trouble of producing it (the manuscript is part of *A l'ombre des jeunes filles en fleurs*, perhaps of the whole book, I am not sure because it isn't here). I am sure that you will know admirably how to "sound out" the members of your circle who like what I write and to inform me fairly accurately of what I might expect, what I should advise the *Nouvelle revue française* to do. I can feel that my caffeine is no longer strong enough to help me write you. But before saying *adieu*, I should like to reply to an objection of yours which moved me very much: "I feel that I shall have many sorrows." I think perhaps by that you mean, since you so graciously regard Swann as a living person, that you were disappointed to see him become less sympathetic and even ridiculous. I can assure you that it has caused me great pain thus to transform him.

But I am not free to go against the truth and to modify the laws that control the characters. "*Amicus Swann, sed magis amica Veritas.*" The nicest people sometimes go through nasty phases. I promise you that in the following volume when he becomes a Dreyfusard, Swann once more starts being sympathetic. Unhappily, and this causes me much sorrow, he dies in the fourth volume. And he is not the principal character in the book. I should have liked him to be. But art is the perpetual sacrificing of inclination to truth.

Marcel Proust

192: TO MRS. SYDNEY SCHIFF

[CIRCA AUGUST, 1919]

8 BIS, RUE LAURENT-PICHAT (VERY TEMPORARILY)

Madame,

. . . . A thousand thanks (brief ones because of the dreadful state of my health) for permitting me to make Swann submit to the cruel laws of psychology rather than to my own desire, which would be never to see him ridiculous and, above all, never to let him die. In order not to tire myself too much, I shall not speak to you again about the deluxe edition. You didn't understand me; I never thought such a limited edition could spread the work abroad, but, in spite of that, I thought a fairly large number of people might like it. But there is no assurance at all that there would be enough of them. Jacques Blanche claims this is so. For England I shall consult L. A. Nicholson. . . . Mr. Schiff is as indulgent as you and gives me his permission to make Swann as ridiculous as it is consistent with his character to be. Even marvelously well versed in French letters as you are, I do not know whether my *Pastiches* would amuse you. The one on Saint-Simon would, I think, in any case. Please accept, Madame, my most respectful compliments and all the gratitude of Swann for having endowed him with possibilities of moral stature that are not realized in him in any constant way, but which could have been; for the world of the possible is more extended than the real world, said Leibnitz. Forgive me for quoting a German philosopher in spite of the war, but I do not in the least think that it has removed the meaning from the *Monadology*, the *Tetralogy*, and even from many other things which are no longer fashionable.

Please remember me to M. Schiff.
Your respectful
Marcel Proust

193: TO PAUL SOUDAY

NOVEMBER 10, 1919

Cher Monsieur,

I was very much touched by the friendly way you discussed my opinion of Saint-Beuve, and I should have thanked you immediately if a prolonged attack of asthma had not rendered me incapable of making the slightest move these last few days. I was all the more touched by your kindness because since the misfortune which has struck you [Souday's wife had died recently], since I have heard of your moving sorrow which is so like the ones I have known, you are now as close to my heart, if I may say so, as in the past you were to my mind. I do not believe that it is a strain on you for me to speak of your bereavement again, for there is no more ridiculous custom than the one that makes you express sympathy once and for all on a given day to a person whose sorrow will endure as long as his life. Such grief, felt in such a way is always "present," it is never too late to talk about it, never repetitious to mention it again.

To come back to Sainte-Beuve (and you will find, in addition, in my *Pastiches* another expression of what I think of him; not more analytical, it is true, but more exact, I think). I do not say that every one of his *Lundis* taken separately is absolutely false. I don't doubt but what the Comte de Molé or Chancellor Pasquier were men of parts. I think they do less honor to French literature than Flaubert and Baudelaire, about whom Sainte-Beuve spoke in a way that implied that personal friendship, respect for their characters, dictated at least in part the slight praise he granted them. I don't think that to make a mistake about the value of a work of art is always very serious. Flaubert despised Stendhal, who himself found certain cities in the South disfigured by their sublime Romanesque churches. But Saint-Beuve was a critic, and, moreover, proclaimed at every turn that criticism manifests itself in the exact appreciation of contemporary works.

It is easy enough, he says, not to be mistaken about Virgil or about Racine, but about the book which has just been published, etc.

One can therefore apply to him the same judgment he brought to bear on the critics who praised only the past! Also I was distressed when I saw my friend Daniel Halévy extol Sainte-Beuve as the most trustworthy of guides. If I had not overwhelmed him with letters of reproach for having signed the stupid manifesto of the party of the intelligentsia, I should have replied to him in a newspaper. But, in any case, I was too sick to take up my pen and do it.

Thank you for announcing that you will discuss *A l'ombre des jeunes filles en fleurs*. I shall naturally be very happy to have an article by you, if it doesn't tire you too much. To live with your sorrow, to permit your cruel suffering to metamorphose into luminous and sad meditation, that is the most important thing for you at this time. If writing such a long article, full of such sad passages, would tire you, thereby postponing for even an hour the blessed miracle by which the memory that causes so much pain is transformed into your gentle companion for all time, I should prefer not to have you write this article. Besides, I am afraid that the architecture of *A la recherche du temps perdu* will be no more perceptible than in *Swann*. I can picture readers thinking that I am writing the history of my life, relying on an arbitrary and fortuitous association of ideas.

My structure is concealed and all the less immediately perceptible because it is developed on a large scale (forgive this style. I have not had the strength for a long time even to sign an inscription. This first interminable letter shows my fatigue); but in order to see how rigorous this structure is, I need only recall a criticism of yours, ill-founded in my opinion, in which you disapproved of certain morbid and useless scenes in *Swann*. If it was a question in your mind of a scene between two young girls (M. Francis Jammes begged me passionately to leave it out of my book), it was, in fact, "useless" in the first volume. But the remembrance of it is the mainstay of volumes IV and V (through the jealousy it inspires, etc.). By suppressing it I should not have changed much in the first volume; I should, on the other hand, because of the solidarity of each part, have dropped on the reader's head two whole volumes of which that scene is the keystone.

I am growing tired, *cher* Monsieur, and I am afraid I have tired you. But above all don't take the trouble to answer this letter, and accept my admiring and grateful respects.

Marcel Proust

194: TO LAURE HAYMAN

44, RUE HAMELIN
[OCTOBER OR NOVEMBER 1919]

Chère amie, you who are one of the most precious parts of my past, please believe that if I had had the strength to write you a letter I should not have delayed answering yours for a moment. But I am a poor, sick man who, since he has been wandering from one furnished apartment to another, is not clear-headed two hours a week, even when he stays in bed. I know that for more than twenty-five years, one misunderstanding after another has come between us, as though a wicked sorcerer had sworn to make us dislike each other. As far as I am concerned he has never succeeded. I know that in the opinions of me that you expressed to my dear father, which may have disillusioned him about me and rather cast a shadow over our family life, there was no tinge of ill will. On the other hand, I know how many of the tokens of your consideration were spontaneous and genuine, and I remember them most tenderly. Would you be kind enough not to give out my address, because I must not receive visitors; but if some evening when I am not too ill you would be willing to receive me very late, you would find that your caller was not a ghost but a man who has never ceased thinking of you constantly with equal affection and respect.

Your old admirer,
Marcel Proust

195: TO GASTON GALLIMARD

[PROBABLY DECEMBER, 1919]

. . . . Dear friend and publisher, you seem to reproach me for my system of revisions. I know that it complicates everything (but not in the matter of the *Revue* at least!). But when you asked me to leave Grasset to come to you, you knew about it because you came with Copeau, who, in face of the revised proofs from Grasset, exclaimed, "But this is a new book!" I apologize to you in two ways; the first is to say that the function of all intellectual excellence is diversity of material. Since you have had the kindness to find a certain richness in my books which pleases you, be assured that it is due precisely to this additional nourishment with which I reinfuse them, to my own experience, which literally translates itself into these additions. Be assured, too, that if you gave me great proof of friendship in asking me for my books, it is also out of friendship that I gave them to you. When I sent you the manuscript of *Swann* and you refused it, there could have been self-interest on my part in thinking what the renown of your house might have done in honoring my book a little. After Grasset published it, it made—I don't know how—so many friends that Grasset could have published the rest with no fear of their going unnoticed. In withdrawing them, I followed an impulse of friendship, as you did. Alas, you went away. I continued to receive the books of other writers (for there are publishers who have printers, witness the pile of works received and uncut in my room), but no proof sheets. I think they will come. I am no longer as strong as I was and now perhaps I, in my turn, will be a little slow. Provided everything appears while I am alive, it will be all right; and if it should happen otherwise, I have numbered all my notebooks, which you will take, and which I count on your then publishing in full. I have not yet come to the other points in your letter. But I am too tired to go on so I leave you with an affectionate handshake.

Marcel Proust

196: TO GASTON GALLIMARD

DECEMBER 2, 1919

Cher ami,

Forgive me, one should never reproach a person without explaining oneself immediately. I was so sick this time that really to write a line, to autograph a book was more than my hateful misery could stand. Today I can write a little, for I seem to be having a brief lull. Nevertheless, how difficult to go into the matter of reproaches! I have tried always to preserve our friendship, the potentiality of our friendship, since, alas, you have never yet had the leisure, nor I the health, to fulfill its possibilities. It has survived so many little things—which in the long run become large ones (you yourself have, moreover, preserved it by so much kindness)—I hesitate to put between us any hot-headed crystallization of long-suspended grievances. Permit me to adjourn this discussion, perhaps *sine die*. But I must hold to two points, one of which affects my interests directly, the other, presented to me by M. Boylesve, which affects me in no way and does, perhaps, affect your own interests. Here is the first, which affects me directly! Don't you think (you don't think so, else you would have corrected it, so let us rather say, aren't you mistaken in not thinking) that you are misled by your subordinates, printers, I don't know who, about the editions of the book? (When I say *you*, I mean Gallimard and Tronche, for I believe that Rivière is entirely taken up with the *Revue* and Copeau with the theatre). This is why. I didn't think that *A l'ombre des jeunes filles en fleurs* would be successful. If you remember, I told you that I was a little ashamed of having this languid interlude appear by itself. But by an extraordinary accident, this book has had a hundred times as much success as *Swann*. I was very much moved by the valuable sympathies that *Swann* brought me, but they were isolated. I learned of them indirectly. *Jeunes filles en fleurs* is an entirely different matter. I should seem to be copying my own Goncourt parody if I told you that the book is on all the tables in China and Japan. Nevertheless, it is partly true. In France and the neighboring countries it is not just partly true, it is entirely so. I don't know a single banker who hasn't found it on his cashier's table, nor have I any traveling friends who haven't seen it in their friends' houses in the Pyrenees or in the North, in Normandy or in Auvergne. I have a direct daily contact with the reader, which I never had with *Swann*; there is also a daily demand for articles in the papers. I derive no self-satisfaction from this, knowing that the worst books are often the most popular, but I had hoped to derive some money. But here is where I fear Tronche and you have been misled by subordinates. The number of editions is not the only sign of popularity, but it is one, just as market-prices are indications of the condition of the stock exchange, or the degree of temperature of the condition of a sick man. Very well then, the more *Jeunes filles* sells, the smaller the number of new editions. As early as the first week (in June or July, I can no longer remember, July, I think), even if one couldn't find a single first edition, the sixth, on the other hand, had already come along. We are approaching December and they are selling chiefly the third! I admit that they are also selling the fifth and sixth as in July. But that shows that nothing has been done during these five months, for it is only since the sixth edition that all the articles have appeared in the English (*The Times*, although, according to you, very warm, was the coldest), Italian, Spanish, and Belgian reviews. All this, and four articles by Hermant and everything else wouldn't explain one edition in five months when there had been six in eight days! I admit that from the beginning, books were put on sale before the earlier ones had been sold out. Nevertheless, *everyone* at the present time is reading the book, even those who have not read it have bought it because it's a fashionable book. *All this should translate itself into editions.* Where are they?

At the same time, tell me whether you have chosen a translator for England. It is very important. If you haven't dealt with the lady whose letter I gave you, I shall be able on the 7th to tell you the name of the translator of *Jean-Christophe*, who might be good. They like my books better in England than in France; a translation would be very successful there.

I believe I have not told you of Régnier's charming behavior towards me, but, *cher ami*, I am too exhausted to go on. I am still very ill and, in a hurry, because my strength is waning. I must close in assuring you only of tender and faithful friendship.

Marcel Proust

If you have received the proof sheets of *Le côté de Guermantes* or the typescript of *Sodome et Gomorrhe*, you would help me by sending them without delay to make up for lost time.

197: TO PAUL SOUDAY

DECEMBER 18, 1919

Cher Monsieur,

It was too good of you to write me about the Goncourt Prize, which to you must seem so trivial! For me, who do not command your mediums for spreading ideas and who have only been able to follow the advice given in the first hemistich of Hugo's line, *Ami, cache ta vie et répands ton esprit*, the prize would have been very precious if, just at that moment, the edition of my book had not been exhausted. They are reprinting it so rapidly that this evening, I hope, at the time when your article about which you were kind enough to tell me, appears, there will be new editions on sale. I don't know whether you are the P.S. who signed a witty and profound article on the questionnaire of the review, *Littérature*. What you say about the reason one writes is admirable, as is the interpretation of M. Mille's reply. But secondarily, one hopes to become a member of the Société des Esprits and, therefore, to be read. That is why I did not take the advice of the journalists who found it unworthy of me at my age and with my "literary position (?)." Let a prize lower my position, if it causes me to be read; that I prefer immediately to all the honors. The truth is, as P.S. guesses, I had not thought of the prize. But when I found out that Léon Daudet, M. Rosny the elder, etc., would vote for me in any case, I hastened to send my book to the other members of the Academy [Goncourt]. It was, as M. de Goncourt used to say, "*au petit bonheur*." I didn't know when it was to be awarded. And I was really astonished when they came to wake me up and tell me that I was the incumbent. Since my state of health did not permit of my receiving the journalists, the ones who came to "offer me the front page of their papers" filled them with a sudden reversal to disagreeable articles. I really believe that I was the first Dreyfusard, since it was I who went to ask

Anatole France for his signature; but I was awarded the Goncourt Prize and they say it can only have been as reward for former services as a reactionary and a clerical! Like a character in a fairy tale (or that one of Boileau's, a greybeard to the last) I have seen my age increase hour by hour. On the eve of the awarding of the prize, there was little chance of my getting it because I was forty-seven. The day after, I didn't deserve it because I was fifty-six. . . . Nevertheless, now when I am too tired to write any more, I should like to assure you that it is not necessary for me to die, as one critic would have it, to stop writing *A la recherche du temps perdu*. This work (the badly chosen title of which is rather deceptive) is so meticulously "composed" (I could give you numerous proofs of this), that the last chapter of the last volume was written immediately after the first chapter of the first volume. All the "in-between" part was written subsequently, but a long time ago. The war prevented my getting proofs; illness now prevents my correcting them. Otherwise, the time would be past when critics need any longer trouble themselves about me. . . .

Marcel Proust

Louis Martin-Chauffier, today Foreign News editor of the *Parisien Libéré,* between 1921 and 1940 contributed many critical essays to the *Nouvelle revue française.* Author of a life of Chateaubriand, recipient in 1947 of the *Grand Prix de la Société des Gens de Lettres,* his latest work, *L'Homme et la bête,* is an account of the year he spent in the Belsen Concentration Camp.

198: TO LOUIS MARTIN-CHAUFFIER

44, RUE HAMELIN
(CONFIDENTIAL ADDRESS)
[CIRCA END DECEMBER, 1919]

Monsieur,

I am extremely ill, I am eight hundred letters behind. If I make an exception for you and answer immediately, you will draw the conclusion implicit in this act. It is this: your letter enchanted me. Your *pastiche* completed the enchantment. That is no slight compliment. I am very severe about *pastiches*. Particularly the ones I have read that pretend to imitate me seem to me extremely feeble. Yours is a rare and delightful exception. I find the general spirit wrong (I am really too sick to explain to you what I mean. Perhaps if you say to yourself: not that he looks through a microscope but through a telescope, you will fathom my thought) and this first error makes the *pastiche* a little flat now and then. But what astonishing discoveries! You have discriminated with such precision, parodied with such infinite comic sense certain peculiarities of syntax which I think are known only to us two. You make delightful fun of my comparisons. The gentleman decorated by a minister friend, the resemblance between fathers and sons, a woman's various veils, the positive and the negative, it is all enough to make one die laughing.

Monsieur, I shall perhaps in the course of time have some advice to ask you about etymologies. I asked it of M. Dimier (whom I don't know, however), who answered me kindly and offered to bring me into communication with M. Longnon. And there is no dearth of people who can inform me about all the etymologies. But it would be more amusing to have it be you, now that your letter and your *pastiche* have given me a glimpse into your mind. In any case, I shan't need it until later. I am too ill to remember the proper names that I mentioned to M. Dimier. On the other hand, there is some historical information that would be very useful to me at the present time (I am in a furnished apartment without any books). True, it is long after the Carolingians. This is it. I remember having read some time ago in *Les Débats* (was it an article by André Hallays, I no longer know anything about it) that a Montmorency or, rather, I think, the widow of a Montmorency, ended her days as an abbess. Wasn't she born a Condé? What was the name of the abbey? I think this happened at the time of Richelieu. If you know about it, it would be kind of you to write me. If you don't know, don't take the trouble to answer. In any case, I beseech you not to think that I wrote you just for this. A letter at this time causes me frightful fatigue. There are essential ones which will never be written. If it had only been a matter of Mme Montmorency or Condé, I should not have troubled. One of my friends would have looked up the information. But your letter was so attractive, your modesty so exaggerated that I have set myself the task of thanking you for the one and curing you of the other.

Good luck with your Carolingians. Is it they or others who are destined to monopolize your literary gift? I am not familiar with it, but it is definite and charming.

Your devoted
Marcel Proust

Naturally it makes no difference to me which article in *Les Débats* it was. What I wanted to know was whether a Montmorency, etc. . . . The main thing is that if you knew of an abbess of any period at all, in a chapter as strict as Remiremont, who wasn't related to the d'Haussonvilles, it would do me as well as the Montmorency. It is to give Mme de Villeparisis (I started to say "de la Villetournois") the opportunity to show a portrait of the Abbess and to shock her visitors a little.

Your devoted
Marcel Proust

Marcel Boulenger, a critic and historian, was the brother of Jacques Boulenger (see p. 429).

199: TO MARCEL BOULENGER

[CIRCA JANUARY, 1920]

Cher ami,

I have been gasping for breath so continuously (incessant attacks of asthma for several days) that it is not very easy for me to write. I do, however, want to find sufficient strength to tell you that I received a "clipping" forwarded from the boulevard Haussmann and held over from rue Laurent-Pichat: it is an article signed "M. Boulenger," and it is so nice of you to have wanted to speak of me and to say such pleasant things about me that I wanted to thank you with all my heart. But when we see each other, I shall explain to you why this article, so poetically and wittily written, seems to me, insofar as it applies to my work, wholly and completely untrue. The only excuse, in my opinion, that you could offer (you understand, of course, that I am using the word "excuse" in its intellectual and logical sense) is that you know only, assuming that you have read them, the first two volumes of *Temps perdu*. And since I don't remember very well (veronal, etc.) these two volumes written six years ago, which I have not tried to reread (too small print, bad glasses, etc. again), I am perhaps mistaken in placing in these volumes sentences, scenes, characters that occur only in volumes yet to appear. And you are not the Pythoness of Thebes. But it seems to me very unlikely that in the first two volumes the tone of the rest is not already apparent. So, in spite of my desire to be extremely fair and impersonal, it happens, things being what they are, that in *Temps perdu* the class that is slandered, that is always wrong, talks only nonsense, the vulgar and hateful class, is *le "monde."* I think that for this impression to become incontrovertible, one must wait for *Côté de Guermantes*, but it seems to me that even in *Jeunes filles en fleurs*, Mme Cambremer is vulgarity personified; Saint-Loup, "intellectual," but rather silly; the guests at the Sainte-Euverte *soirée*, mediocre; the Marquis de Norpois, ridiculous; Mme de Villeparisis, literary, but judging everything by false standards and much less *gentille* than my grandmother with her humble origin. And M. de Forcheville (this I am sure has been published; it's at a Verdurin dinner in *Swann*), grotesque. The Duc de Guermantes equally grotesque in the N.R.F. for 1914 (extracts to be published in book form). There remains only Charlus. But he is, from the outset, a person apart who exists in every *milieu. . . . Cher ami,* I am too tired to go on. I must leave you. I thank you. . . .

Marcel Proust

200: TO GASTON GALLIMARD

[EARLY 1920]

Cher ami,

I shall try to answer your questions. Forgive my dictating this letter. Since I am very tired, I am afraid my writing would be illegible.

As for the translations. I have no preference at all for the lady, so choose whoever seems to you best. But above all, don't delay too much, for the edge wears off a certain kind of curiosity. . . .

From the literary point of view, the translator of *Jean-Christophe* has been recommended to me; but the literary point of view is not the only one; you are a publisher and have to concern yourself with the translator's publishers. Nevertheless, I hold at your disposal the address of the translator of *Jean-Christophe*.

. . . .

Your affectionate and devoted friend,

Marcel Proust

201: TO LOUIS MARTIN-CHAUFFIER

44, RUE HAMELIN
[EARLY 1920]

Cher Monsieur et ami,

I must appear ungrateful when really I am not at all. I am merely very ill, and up until now have been in no state to thank you for your amusing Mme de Bassompierre. You won't be annoyed with me for not making use of her and for standing by my Montmorency who, because I have no detailed information about her, I have left rather in a vacuum. Above all one must subordinate, and not let oneself be carried away by the amusement value of an anecdote, nor give to any detail a single line more than it needs to insure the balance of the whole. If I hadn't, alas, stopped seeing M. France so many years ago, he is the person rather than myself who should have profited by your Bassompierre. He loves these decamerons, which I myself hold in no low esteem, but if you do me the honor of reading *Côté de Guermantes*, you will see for yourself that this parasite story would—like vegetation run amuck—have hidden entirely the architectural line which is in itself already sufficiently complex. . . .

Please believe me your sincere friend,
Marcel Proust

202: TO JEAN-LOUIS VAUDOYER

44, RUE HAMELIN
[EARLY FEBRUARY, 1920]

Cher ami,

. . . . I have recently received your questionnaire about the Louvre. . . . Here is the problem: I should like very much to reply, but I haven't been at the Louvre in over fifteen years. I shall go soon, as soon as I can get up during the day, but I understand that you can't wait until then. So, may I answer that, without judging any galleries that I haven't seen (I shan't say it is because of my health, it would interest no one), I am not, in principle, a partisan of art's moving in the direction of the art-lovers' convenience rather than requiring him to come to art. (Naturally, this is not arbitrary: but as one extreme against another, I prefer the inconveniences of *Rheingold*, which one went to hear without taking time for dinner, even with the condescension of the musicians who, themselves, can't bear to listen to the last quartets of Beethoven and who fear that any piece that lasts more than five minutes will tire a listener whose powers, on the contrary, are increased tenfold by the beauty offered him.) While commending the alterations, I advise against the Museum's becoming in any way a Porgès collection. If this kind of reply does not suit your purpose (I can't even find the text of the questionnaire, lost among so many "Inquiries" that I haven't answered and shan't), I could then only limit myself to enumerating eight pictures which I think would be: "Portrait of Chardin" by himself. "Portrait of Mme Chardin" by Chardin. "Still Life" by Chardin. "Spring" by Millet. The "Olympia" by Manet. "The Cliffs of Etretat" by Monet (if it is in the Louvre). A Renoir, or "Dante's Boat," or "The Chartres Cathedral" by Corot. Watteau's "The Indifferent Man" or "The Embarcation." May I say that *if* Austro-German pictures are requested, I should prefer the Dresden and the Vienna (?) Vermeers to additional Watteaus. Under those circumstances, I should ask that Vermeer's "Lacemaker" be hung, not with the painters of his country, but as a separate masterpiece. (None of this means that I prefer Vermeer to Watteau, I shall explain myself) . . .

Yours always,
Marcel Proust

203: TO MADAME STRAUS

44, RUE HAMELIN
[MAY 4–5, 1920]

Chère Madame Straus,

(If you don't find it too familiar of me not to be satisfied with a "Madame" which does not express the feeling in my heart.) . . . How sad to learn—if the information is correct—that Bakst, who did that inspired *Scheherazade* (a great friend of Montesquiou's, too; well worthy of that honor and was appraised and put in his right place by Montesquiou, as no one else would ever know how to), will be put away and for an illness which is bound to last several years (general paralysis). There was not much better news of Nijinsky, who was the bounding creator of those Russian ballets. But that news appears to be less certain. What to believe, anyway, now, when the grand-duchesses declare that the Czar, his wife, and his children are alive, and the son of that unhappy Grand-Duke Paul! The performance at the Opera was dreadful (at least the part I saw; I didn't arrive until 10 o'clock), even *Scheherazade* disfigured which, if the report of Bakst's health is true is, in the face of his powerlessness to defend his work, a terrible sacrilege. The only beautiful thing I caught sight of was in a seat not far from the box (where I sat with one of his nieces) the silhouette and the head of your friend, M. d'Haussonville. I barely caught sight of him (and he didn't see me), but it seemed to me that the years had given his head, without modifying the arch, a majesty which it didn't used to have to such a marked degree. I found him more virile, more the way one pictures the delightful old huntsman his father must have been, as he appeared in the volume of *Souvenirs* I once made you read. . . . Please deign to accept and ask M. Straus to accept my grateful respects.

Marcel Proust

204: TO SYDNEY SCHIFF

44, RUE HAMELIN
[SUMMER, 1920]

Cher Monsieur (do we add "and Friend"? Your letter isn't at hand. But "Friend" would seem to be both pleasant and true). Your letter distresses me because it is wonderful and forces me to answer you this way. It enchants me, shocks me, etc.

First, Enchants me: because of the gallery of portraits you draw, which is splendid, and also for your profound views on humanity, so savory and so sharp. What intensity! You do X— a slight injustice. He has, I think, more nobility of spirit than you say. Unfortunately, since he talks about the stars, he has attached himself not to one of them but to the autos of Mlles X— and Y— (I am too tired, otherwise I should modify slightly even what I am saying). I envy his capacity for nonreaction. I am sick, but I feel myself capable of fighting a duel every day of my life. You don't suspect the extent of my energy (not for work). He reacts to everything as if it were the gentle breath of a rose, and even that seems too much to him. What I reproach him with is being a liar. He made my acquaintance by means of a lie and has never stopped since. But there is no malice in him, only gentleness, understanding, the desire for culture. My indignation (not against him, against you) rises from the way you criticize the selling of deluxe editions. Do you really find it necessary for authors to die of hunger? I am writing my present *Swann* in a hovel, it's true, but because of the housing shortage this hovel costs 2600 francs a month. (And my secretary left me.) The ferocity of readers reminds me of some pages of Ruskin that you may know. And without doubt you also know the anecdote about Whistler's having several of the richest people in England for lunch. Enter bailiffs to attach his property.

There were a great many unsold paintings there, a quarter of which would have sent the bailiff away, but none of the rich art-lovers thought of buying even the smallest grey and silver harmony. Except for that point, I am entirely of your opinion, deluxe editions do not interest me in the least, nor do autographs. But not for the same reason as yours. They seem to you to have something sacred about them (and your idea is very beautifully and very well expressed). But granting that they have for someone who likes the author's books, they don't for the author himself, who doesn't even recognize it (see the will of the Goncourts, asking that the collection they had acquired with such loving care be sold at auction so that instead of decaying in the indifferent atmosphere of a museum each object might be bought by someone who really wished to possess it). Your remarks on people in general, their boredom, make me die laughing. They are so like me! However, I am much more in sympathy with Mme Schiff (I adore the touching tenderness with which you speak of her) when it comes to the selection of these people. I mean to say that I do my intellectual work inside myself, and once I am with my fellow creatures it is more or less a matter of indifference to me whether or not they are intelligent as long as they are kind, sincere, etc.

Were you ever formerly a Dreyfusard? I was—passionately. Nevertheless, since in my book I am absolutely objective it turns out that *Côté de Guermantes* appears anti-Dreyfusard. But *Sodome et Gomorrhe II* will be entirely Dreyfusard and corrective. Certainly I shall send you a copy of *Côté de Guermantes* as soon as it appears. You are too kind to have ordered a copy of the deluxe edition of *Jeunes filles*. I do hope that you can have one. In order to find out, I should have to write to the *Nouvelle revue française*. And it is much more fun writing to you. It would be useless anyway, because you tell me you are writing to them. They will certainly answer. To conclude, for I am overcome with exhaustion, I was appalled that you should attribute my silence to any lack of sympathy. It's like Robert de Montesquiou, who said that I never answered any of his letters because I was *à la mode* (!) and was afraid he would dedicate his next book to me! How could you have thought that I didn't like you right away? There is no one else I should have taken so much trouble to see as I did you during your stay in Paris. . . . Do you know that many English newspapers are very kind to me and allude to the slightest details in a way so familiar as to demonstrate a real understanding? What a misfortune that it isn't translated. Much to tell you about the Asquiths. (Do you know the extraordinary intelligence of the daughter?) But I can go no farther, as this desultory ending shows. Thank you again with all my heart for the deluxe copy.

My respectful compliments to Mme Schiff.

Your friend,

Marcel Proust

205: TO PAUL SOUDAY

SEPTEMBER, 1920

Cher Monsieur et ami,

. . . . I don't know whether I shall be decorated (and I should, indeed, be very happy to be), but I do know what is the greatest pleasure I have already enjoyed; it was your "pneumatic." —I am not very well informed about my decoration since none of my friends who concerned themselves with it have talked to me about it. I know that Léon Blum, whom I used to see sometimes twenty years ago, hoped that I would get this cross [of the Legion of Honor] and took active steps about it. And as I think Léon Daudet, whom I never see, but whom I know better, had the same desire, it cannot be called a political decoration. Barrès, too, must have spoken a word for me, and Régnier. I shall find out about all this to make sure of not being ungrateful to anyone.

Gratitude is a pleasant duty, and I beg of you, *cher monsieur et ami*, to accept my warmest and deepest to you.

Marcel Proust

206: TO PAUL SOUDAY

OCTOBER 8, 1920

Cher Monsieur et ami,

. . . .

It is possible that a book of mine (*Le Côté de Guermantes*), which should have appeared much sooner or much later, will come out very soon. In any case, I shall send it to you at once. This volume will still be "proper." After that the book will be less so without its being my fault. My characters do not turn out well; I am obliged to follow them wherever their flaws or their aggravated vices lead me. . . .

Please accept, *cher monsieur et ami*, my grateful regards.

Marcel Proust

207: MADAME STRAUS TO PROUST

VERSAILLES

OCTOBER 23, 1920

So, mon petit *Marcel* cher, *not only do you not forget me, but you send me a* wonderful rare *copy of your* not *yet published book and write me a delightful letter. In spite of my being in a state of "chronic death," the book gives me* immense pleasure. *I wish I knew how to thank you, but I feel so acutely what I say to you that I can't find the words I want to say. My ideas are badly organized in my poor head. I should like to talk to you about all sorts of contradictory things. First, of my sorrow at knowing that you are ill, and then of my annoyance at being dead, which is quite a handicap in life, and also of the happiness I shall have in rediscovering my friends* chez *Swann. This joy will be as intense as though I were alive, nor is my tender friendship for you that of a dead person. You see how difficult all this is to say and how complicated to write. I feel very "Aunt Léonie." But you can understand me and forgive all the crossed-out words.*

Mon cher petit *Marcel, why do you have 104° temperature when you haven't been "operated on" by a monkey? But you certainly eat less than the Mayor of Cork since the latter takes communion all the time, and the wafer, it would seem, is very nourishing. . . .*

Au revoir, mon cher cher *Marcel, I leave you to read you; I should be acting more wisely by going "Deschanel's way." The grand canal attracts me. . . . However, my melancholy has not yet arrived at the state of delirious notions, only at* sad *ones.*

Thank you again. How I should love to see you! How can I believe that we shall never be well enough to meet again! With all my heart I hope we shall, and I am happy that you have not forgotten your old and faithful friend.

Geneviève H. S.

My husband sends you his best wishes. He has bronchitis and is very unhappy about his daily cuppings. We shall wrangle over the beautiful book which I refuse to lend him. He can only have it when I am resting, and only then because he is sick! I shall lend it to nobody else.

208: TO THE COMTESSE DE MAUGNY

[OCTOBER OR NOVEMBER, 1920]

Madame,

I am disappointed, having received some pages from your soon-to-be-published album, to see that, on the one hand, your caricatures are no longer in color like the ones you sent me two years ago; that on the other hand, several of them are missing, particularly that astonishing, "He isn't handsome, but he is somebody" (Jaurès), a worthy counterpart to, "Much will be forgiven her because she has taken care of many," in which you rival Abel Faivre while both retaining your originality and differing from him greatly.

The omission of the color disappointed me because

it involved the landscapes. You see, long before you knew Clément, he was one of my three best friends. What evenings we spent together in Savoie, watching Mont-Blanc, as the sun set, assume the colors of an illusive Mont-Rose, which the night would engulf. Then we had to get back to Lake Geneva and, before reaching Thonon, we climbed on a sturdy little railroad, not unlike the one I have depicted in one of my not-yet-published books, which you will receive, as they come out, if God grants me life. A nice, patient, good-natured little railroad, which waited for the convenient time, for the laggards and even, once it had started, would stop, when signaled, to pick up the ones who, puffing like the engine itself, would catch up with it at full speed. At full speed, which was where the resemblance ceased, for the train always moved at a prudent pace. At Thonon, long stop, we would shake hands with some person who might have come to the station to see off his guests, with another who wanted to buy newspapers, with many whom I always suspected of having nothing better to do than to greet acquaintances. A form of social life like any other, this stop at the station at Thonon.

But the Château de Maugny, the old home of your husband's ancestors, was way above Thonon but enshrined in the emerald of this wonderful country. That was a long time ago; since then you have been an admirable nurse, and, nevertheless, cheerful in your tireless devotion, you have extracted a very special comic effect from the environment in which you held such an heroic place. A drawing like: "Wake up, my friend, it's time for you to take your sleeping potion," deserves to stay in as much as your repentant fat ladies who illustrate a whole chapter of your *Splendeur et misère* certainly not of courtesans but of some great ladies who become virtuous only late in life.

And the Château de Maugny, you will say, what has happened to it in all this? I have not lost sight of it. Do you remember at the beginning of *Capitaine Fracasse*, the doleful castle where Sigognac lived? Frankly Maugny was admirable, but it was no longer gay. Gautier, who planned on having Sigognac return to the vast castle to finish in gloom a book which he had started in gloom, was a little disconcerted when his publishers demanded a gay, light, triumphant ending. To his daughter above all (Judith Gautier) this seemed less true, less "like real life." He yielded, nevertheless. You have come along since then to prove him right. In marrying Clément you have brought happiness into a sad house; your wit, your shared love have forced the old stones to smile.

All my respects, Madame.
Marcel Proust

209: TO PAUL SOUDAY

6–8 NOVEMBER, 1920

Cher Monsieur,
Let us not mix life (and the feelings of respectful admiration to which it gives birth) with literature. Hence.

1st: Life

Did anyone tell you about two weeks ago that when my pain cleared up for an evening, I sent a taxi to see if you would dine with me that same night at the Ritz, a taxi which, after leaving the rue Guénégaud went to various places in search of congenial friends with whom I hoped to surround you? I shall try again when I can. And couldn't you suggest some "Sesame" for success?

2nd: Literature

Three or four days ago I had what is called a "bad Souday." In the past I should have found it so. But since I have come to know you, since I have shared in your sorrow, since I have felt such sympathy for you, the annoyance of not seeing you is the only thing that counts, and that of a "bad Souday" is trifling. I should wish for fifty worse if only I could dine with you from time to time.

But common sense likes to argue. Therefore, I can't help saying this to you: How, knowing as you probably do, that I have known Guermantes duchesses all my life, have you failed to understand the effort I have had to make to put myself in the place of someone who never knew them, but always hoped to? There, as in the case of dreams, etc., etc., I have tried to see things from the inside, to study the imagination. Snob novelists are those who depict ironically from the outside the snobbishness they practice. Since you are a friend of the Princesse Lucien Murat, she can tell you at how early an age Guermantes of every kind were my familiars. I add that if M. de Guermantes says, "*spirituel*" (but no, that would be too long to write and for you to read). In any case, society people are so stupid that the following occurred to me: irritated at seeing Saint-Simon always talking about the language so peculiar to the Mortemarts, without ever explaining to us wherein the peculiarity consisted, I wanted to go him one better and try to create a "Guermantes wit." However, I could find my model only in a woman not to the manor born, Mme Straus, Bizet's widow. Not only are the words quoted hers (she didn't wish me to use her name in the book), but I have patterned them on her conversation. I shall tell you something even more curious. In *Guermantes II*, which you don't know, my hero receives an invitation from the Princesse de Guermantes (cousin of the Duchesse). This invitation seems to him so elegant that he is afraid a joke is being played on him. But I have not invented this incident. M. d'Haussonville, senior, tells in his memoirs he and his friend, M. d'Aramon, were so eager to be invited to M. Delessert's that when they actually were invited, each, on his own, asked around to find out if it was really true, for they were unable to believe their good fortune. These are perhaps the only two times in my whole work that I have not "invented" out of whole cloth. Finally, if Mme de Guermantes is not gracious to my hero, it is not because he is middle class, but because she feels he is in love with her. In *Guermantes II* (printed but not yet published), as soon as she is no longer loved, she flings herself at her former admirer and continually invites him to dinner.

3rd: Relation between Literary Criticism and Life

One thing hurt me, which you certainly did not say out of malice! At the moment when I am about to publish *Sodome et Gomorrhe*, and when, because I talk about Sodome no one will have the courage to defend me, you (without malice, I am sure) blaze the trail in advance for all the mischief-makers by calling me "feminine." From feminine to effeminate is a mere step. My seconds in duels can tell you whether I behave with the weakness of an effeminate man. Again, I am sure that you said this without malice aforethought.

Please accept, dear sir, with this long letter (entirely confidential and private, naturally, and not at all intended to be quoted), the expression of my very admiring regard and my devoted gratitude. You will have those books in May, but I do hope we shall see each other before then.

Marcel Proust

210: TO PAUL SOUDAY

NOVEMBER 15, 1920

Cher Monsieur et ami,

. . . .

"Feminine," applied to me, has made inroads, as I feared it would; I have learned this from clippings, notably the *Figaro*, and the road to *Sodome* is also becoming a *leitmotiv*. They have not yet withdrawn my cross of the Legion of Honor (but that may come). None of this is a reproach. If you find me feminine, you have every reason to say so. You very kindly place me at the head of a pleiad of talented people, which flatters me very much. . . . I have thought a great deal about that article on *Du côté de Guermantes*; I compared it with the article on *Du côté de chez Swann*, as I remember it. It seems to me possible to extract from them the thing I find reprehensible in your criticism (along with so many things I like to praise there). One might, it seems to me, say that you do not lend yourself to the transfiguration intended by the author, that you place the work of art (and it is all the more bizarre since you have very sound aesthetic preferences) on the same plane as everyday life. . . .

But rather than a boring letter, all this would make good talk!

Your entirely devoted,
Marcel Proust

Jacques Boulenger (1879–1944) was a voluminous critic and journalist. The author of a life of Marceline Desbordes-Valmore, studies of Renan, Rabelais, and social life under Louis Philippe, he was in 1920 editor of *Opinion.* His book reviews were published in book form under the title *Mais l'art est difficile!*

211: TO JACQUES BOULENGER

NOVEMBER, 1920

Cher ami,

. . . .

It is true that because of my own excessive fatigue caused by purely physical details I dispense with inventing any for my hero, and I do take actual characteristics from myself. But would a snob author (and not an analyst of the imagination) say that he wished to meet Mme de Guermantes? He would portray himself favorably, at least as a *Grand Seigneur* or as scornful of society.

In *Guermantes II*, when Mme de Guermantes is no longer loved by my hero (who has also been quite in love with the little bourgeoise, Albertine, whom later on he will love a thousand times more), she sends endless invitations to the said hero, whom she scorned only because she felt that he was in love with her.

I portray so many different things in my work that people really can't think everything in it is myself. Without swooning like the "Dadas" over my pages about deafness (which I find very mediocre in spite of the praise given them), they are nevertheless, true. But I am not at all deaf and only wish that I had as good eyesight as I have hearing. . . .

Yours very affectionately,
Marcel Proust

212: TO LOUIS MARTIN-CHAUFFIER

[EARLY DECEMBER, 1920]

Cher ami,

. . . You were speaking to me about doing an article (presumably for the January 1st number) on *Guermantes*. I wasn't much in favor of it, but didn't wish to influence you in any way. I find your articles remarkable (your Bourget amazing, of the first order), and I think you would make it very clear that *Guermantes* is not a snob book, for when a snob writes a novel he portrays himself as a man of fashion and assumes a derisive air towards fashionable people. The truth is that by a natural logical sequence after having put the poetry of the place-name "Balbec" on a level with the banality of the Balbec countryside, I had to go ahead and do the same thing for the Guermantes family name. And these are books that are said to have very little or no structure. . . . What's more, ever since Hervieu, Hermant, etc., snobbism has been so frequently represented from the outside that I wanted to try to show it inside the person, like a wonderful kind of imagination. Notice (that doesn't mean "notice in your article," because I hope you won't do it) that the only thing I do not say about the character of the narrator is that at the end he is a writer, because the whole book could be called a vocation (?), but this isn't known until the last volume. I am so exhausted I must end this letter, which as it now stands makes no sense at all, but which I am sending anyway, so that you will not think I have forgotten you and will know that I am very fond of you.

Marcel Proust

The following letter was written to the editor of *La Renaissance politique, littéraire, artistique* in answer to a questionnaire on romanticism and classicism, and was published January 8, 1921.

213: [TOWARDS THE END OF 1920]

Monsieur,

I believe that all true art is classic, but the dictates of the mind rarely permit of its being recognized as such when it first appears. From this point of view, art is like life. The language of the unhappy lover, of the political partisan, of sensible parents, seems to those who use it, to be irrefutably self-evident. Yet it does not appear to convince those to whom it appeals; a truth does not force itself from the outside on minds that must first be made akin to the one where the truth originated. In vain Manet insisted that his "Olympia" was classic, saying to those who looked at it, "There is just what you admire in the masters," while the public saw only mockery in the remark. But today, when looking at the "Olympia," one experiences the same kind of pleasure as in looking at the masterpieces among which it is hung; and in reading Baudelaire one feels the same kind of pleasure as in reading Racine. Baudelaire does not know how, or does not wish to finish a work and, also, perhaps, in no one piece of his can one find the accumulated truths which succeed and verge upon one another with such great richness, in Phèdre's single declaration. But the style of the condemned poems, which is exactly that of the tragedies, surpasses them, perhaps, in nobility of feeling. These great innovators are the only real classics and present an almost continuous succession. The imitators of the classics, in their finest moments, provide us only with the pleasures of erudition and of taste which have no great value. That the innovators, worthy of one day becoming classics, submit themselves to a severe inner discipline and are, above all else, builders, cannot be doubted. But just because their architecture is novel, it may remain undetected for a long time. These not-yet-recognized classics and the ancients practiced so much the same art that the former are still those who have done the best criticism of the latter. No doubt this criticism must not be allowed to run counter to the tendencies, to the line of growth of an artist. Nothing is stupider than to say, as did Théophile Gautier, himself a third-rate poet, that Racine's most beautiful line is *La fille de Minos et de Pasiphaé*. But we are permitted to enjoy in Racine's tragedies, in his *Cantiques*, in the letters of Mme de Sévigné, in Boileau, a beauty which is really there and which the 17th century barely perceived.

To sum up, the great artists who were called romantics, realists, decadents, etc., as long as they were not understood, are just the very ones I should call classic, if M. Charles Maurras, in the magnificent studies that he signed with the name Criton, had not warned us of the dangers that lie in thus multiplying more-or-less-arbitrary labels.

Marcel Proust

Jacques de Lacretelle, born in 1888, is a French writer, best known for his novel, *Silbermann.*

214: TO JACQUES DE LACRETELLE

[PROBABLY 1921]

Cher ami,

There are no keys to the characters of this book; or rather there are eight or ten for each one; the same is true of the church of Combray; many churches posed for me in memory. I could no longer tell you which ones. I no longer even remember whether the paving comes from Saint-Pierre-sur-Dives or from Lisieux. Certain windows are certainly those of Evreux, others from the Sainte Chapelle and some from Pont-Audemer. For the sonata my recollections are more exact. To whatever extent I made use of reality—actually, a very slight extent—(starting at the end) at the Sainte-Euverte *soirée*, the little phrase of the sonata is, and I have never told this to anyone, the charming but infinitely mediocre phrase of a sonata for piano and violin by Saint-Saëns, a musician I don't like. (I will show you the exact passage, which recurs several times and which was the triumph of Jacques Thibaud.) At the same *soirée*, a little later on, I shouldn't be surprised if, in speaking of the little phrase, I had thought of the "Good Friday Spell." Again at this same *soirée* (page 241), when the piano and the violin sigh like two birds answering each other's call, I thought of the Franck sonata (particularly as played by Enesco), whose quartet will appear in subsequent volumes. The tremolos that overlay the little phrase at the Verdurins were suggested to me by a prelude to *Lohengrin*, but the prelude itself, at that moment, was suggested by something of Schubert. In that same *soirée* at Verdurin's there is a ravishing piano piece of Fauré.

I can tell you that (at the Sainte-Euverte *soirée*) for M. de Sainte-Candé's monocle I thought of M. de Bethmann's (not the German—though he may perhaps have been originally—but the relative of the Hottinguers); for M. de Forestelle's monocle, I thought of one worn by an officer brother of a musician who was called M. de Tinseau. M. de Palancy's monocle is poor, dear Louis de Turenne's, who never expected the day would come when he would be related to Arthur Meyer, to judge by the way he treated him one day at my house. The same monocle of de Turenne's becomes M. de Bréauté's in *Côté de Guermantes*, I think. Finally, for the friendship with Gilberte in the Champs-Elysees in snowtime, I thought of a person who (unknown to herself) was the great love of my life (or the other great love, for that matter, for there were at least two), Mademoiselle Benardaky, who is now today, Princesse Radziwill (though I haven't seen her for I don't know how many years). But, I need hardly say, the freest passages about Gilberte at the beginning of *A l'ombre des jeunes filles en fleurs* are in no way applicable to this person, for I never had anything but the most respectable relationship with her. For a minute, when Mme Swann walks near the pigeon-shooting gallery, I thought of a wonderfully beautiful cocotte of the period, called Closmenil. I will show you some photographs of her. I repeat, the characters are entirely invented and there is no key, so that no one is less like Madame Verdurin than Madame de B——. Nevertheless, she does laugh the same way. *Cher ami*, I am very ineptly showing my gratitude for the touching pains you have taken to get a copy of this volume by messing it up with these handwritten notes. There is no room for what you asked me to copy, but, if you like, I could put it on some separate pages for you to interpolate. While waiting to hear from you, I send you my friendliest gratitude.

Marcel Proust

Decidedly, reality is reproduced by division, like infusoria, as well as by amalgamation, M. de Bréauté's monocle is also Louis de Turenne's.

215: TO ROBERT DE MONTESQUIOU

[PROBABLY THE END OF APRIL, 1921]

Cher Monsieur,

How kind of you to have written me that magnificent letter! I could have no greater honor. To divert you with trifles, I reply to what you said to me about the false keys in my book. In the whole work (I am not speaking of single volumes, but all the volumes together), there are barely two or three keys, and they figure only for a moment. Thus, there is no key whatsoever for Saint-Loup; but in a passage of the book not yet published, which appeared in *La Revue hebdomadaire*, I called to mind his promenading along the seats of a café, a promenade indulged in by my poor friend Bertrand de Fénelon who was killed in 1914. Otherwise, there are none of his characteristics.

If you remember vaguely *A l'ombre des jeunes filles en fleurs* (forgive me for speaking this way of my forgotten books, but you invited it) at the time when M. de Charlus stares at me steadily and vacantly near the Casino, I thought for a moment of the late Baron D[oasan], an habitué of the Aubernon salon and rather that type. But I dropped it later and constructed a much vaster, entirely invented Charlus. As for Blocqueville, Janzé, etc., I knew them only by name, and Mme de Villeparisis is rather Mme de Beaulaincourt (with a touch of Mme de Chaponay-Courval). I even said she painted flowers so as not to say that she made them, for Mme de Beaulaincourt made artificial ones and it would have been too recognizable. My Charlus does not amount to much in the next volume, but later he takes on a certain fullness (I like to think!).

Many people believe that Saint-Loup is d'Albuféra, but I never thought of him. I suppose he believes it himself; it's the only explanation I can find for his quarrel with me, which makes me very unhappy, all the more so because he had just done me a favor. Curious coincidence. I received your letter just when I had written (I, who never write any more) to the editor of an important review—or, at least an important enough review—and, after having discussed other matters, I said: How unfortunate that an important work of art criticism isn't entrusted to the greatest art critic of our epoch, M. de Montesquiou!

Cher Monsieur, what a strange idea you have of my life! "Huge dividends" made me smile sadly, for I earn nothing from my books. And even if the opposite were true, it would amount to the same thing, for what pleasure can a person have who can no longer even enunciate words clearly! Lately, I ventured into a restaurant, and I had to repeat the word Contrexéville ten times in order to make myself understood. Since I have never had syphilis, this painful disorder is quite unaccountable. This doesn't necessarily prevent our seeing each other because it gives way for a few hours after several days of taking caffeine and adrenalin. My brother says "intoxication." It's a good promissory note to reassure invalids. I can only say to myself, in turning my face to the wall, like Baudelaire: *Dors ton sommeil de brute*.

Cher Monsieur, I offer up prayers for your prompt recovery (you do not tell me what illness you have), and I thank you again respectfully and gratefully for having sent these beautiful flowers of praise to the invalid "who is not embittered."

Marcel Proust

P.S. I can't find the pages I wrote so I am starting over again, this time on large paper. . . . Also, even for inanimate objects (or those considered so) I draw a generalization from a thousand unconscious memories.

I can't tell you how many churches have "posed" for my church at Combray, in *Du côté de chez Swann*. The people are more invented; the monuments come gently, one bringing its spire, another its paving, another its dome. . . .

216: TO JEAN-LOUIS VAUDOYER

44, RUE HAMELIN
[EARLY MAY, 1921]

Cher ami,

I am expressing very badly (but in such a state of health that even one letter, requiring a preliminary *piqûre*, is real martyrdom) what I have wanted to write you for such a long time. It is that I never have seen such a continuous ascent as you achieve from one article to the next. I should have written you after the masterpiece on Watteau if I hadn't been quasi dead (my publishers are obliged to correct the proofs of my books themselves). Everything you said about analogous geniuses touched by death was true! Yesterday I read a Vermeer in which you had, perhaps, less occasion to express yourself fully, but it touched me more than any other. Ever since I saw the "View of Delft" at the Museum of the Hague, I knew I had seen the most beautiful picture in the world. In *Du côté de chez Swann*, I couldn't keep myself from having Swann work on a study of Vermeer. I hardly dared hope that you would render such justice to this wonderful master. For I know your ideas (very sound) on the hierarchy in art, and I was afraid he was a little too Chardin for you. So what a joy for me to read that page. And yet I know hardly anything about Vermeer. I can remember giving a letter to Vuillard about fifteen years ago so that he would go and see a copy of Vermeer I didn't know at Paul Baignères'. I am too exhausted to go on. . . .

Marcel Proust

217: TO JACQUES BOULENGER

MAY 17, 1921

Cher ami,

You are infinitely kind to have quoted that thing of Gide's. But I have so many things to tell you that I shall come back to it later. First, I don't know whether I told you that I made up my mind—on an evening when I was in the worst kind of pain—to dash off an idiotic article on Baudelaire for the N.R.F., which regretted having been the only review not to have spoken of Baudelaire. . . . But, alas, it is not finished because I didn't say anything I wanted to about Baudelaire.

. . . . I didn't understand very clearly from your letter whether you wanted to meet Gide, whether you wanted to have him know it, etc. So I was very much embarrassed because after he had come to see me every day without my having been able to receive him, I finally did receive him the other evening (Saturday, I think) and then and there he spoke of Martin-Chauffier, quoting to me a "remarkable" (?) article of his on Stendhal. But all the time I was saying to myself: "Should I say that Jacques Boulenger (of whom Martin-Chauffier's name made me think) spoke to me about Gide in his letter?" For various reasons, which I shall tell you, I kept still, but it is quite possible that tomorrow, Tuesday, I shall in any case have Gide sent for around half-past ten. If he comes (his arrival is as uncertain as my sending for him), would you like to have me send for you either way at night at rue Oudinot, and you would drink a little champagne at my bedside while he would drink Evian water.

Another thing: the little notice in *Opinion* (which he doesn't at all know that I instigated) seemed to me to have hostile implications (very slightly hostile, however), which took away none of the pleasure the notice gave me. It occurs to me that I had not thought to ask you whether that section of *Opinion* was paying (don't be offended by this, every paper, every review has its commercial side). If it is, I beg of you to tell me how much I owe you. By doing so you would be doubly kind. —You know that I have angered many homosexuals by my last chapter. I feel very sorry about it. But it isn't my fault that M. de Charlus is a *vieux monsieur*. I couldn't suddenly give him the countenance of a Sicilian shepherd like the ones in the Taormina engravings. In any case, you see that even though I think through to the last drop when the defining and reproducing of the Guermantes wit is involved, the other subjects are neither spared nor glossed over. —I am very tired.

Adieu,
Your
Marcel Proust

218: MADAME STRAUS TO PROUST

SATURDAY, MAY 27, 1921

Mon petit cher Marcel,

I may be almost dead *but you don't leave me under a tombstone, which touches me deeply. Your sending me the beautiful copy of your daring and magnificent book* [The Guermantes Way II] *has made me see that I haven't "crumbled into dust" in your heart, and I am very happy about it. It is true that I am not yet in my coffin . . . but only* on my way.

I can't write you all that I should like to say because I am too tired and it would be too long. If only we were two ordinary living people *and* out of bed *at the same time, what fun it would be!*

Reading your beautiful book, I find myself suddenly transported back to the boulevard Haussmann twenty or perhaps twenty-five years ago! And then I shall reread it slowly to make my pleasure last and not to have to part with it. I can never make up my mind to finish a book I like and above all to put it away. *When it is set on the library shelves, I am in despair and it seems lost to me! I seem to need to open it every day! I await the next one impatiently . . . but I should like to buy it and then send it to you to be* inscribed. *These presents you send me are too extravagant! Marcel,* mon cher petit *Marcel, I leave you with such regret! I thank you again with all my heart, and reiterate my tender and true friendship.*

Geneviève H. S.

I am not at all shocked by the subject. *Besides, we have often discussed it when you came to see me in the evening. We should still have many things to say to each other . . . but you will say them in the next volume. My husband asks me to thank you for your affectionate dedication. Won't you be coming to stay in the country (you will find that I talk like Albertine) at Versailles? We are going to move there next week. If only we could see each other again. It is as hard for me to close this letter as to close your book. But I must.*

The following letter is in the form of a dedication written in a copy of *The Guermantes Way II.*

219: TO JEAN-LOUIS VAUDOYER

(CIRCA END OF MAY, 1921)

Cher ami,

I am sending you this and shall look for a first edition. Céleste tells me that you have *Les Plaisirs et les Jours*. In it you will find the only verses on Cuyp which I remembered. They were written before a class at Condorcet, after my coming out of the Louvre where I had just seen the cavaliers with the pink feathers in their hats. I have since been assured that the Duke of Richmond's suit was not pale blue but white. You will see in *Guermantes II* that the Duchesse was no more pleased with her portrait by Elstir than the models of the great painters were with theirs. And in saying this, I couldn't have been copying you, since the book was printed and on sale a month before the incomparable walk through the gallery, for which I remain profoundly and affectionately grateful to you. I regret not having looked more carefully at the view of Rome in which one of the men painted by Ingres stands out conspicuously. Since I don't know Rome I wanted through views of this kind and any amount of Corot, etc., to imagine it. I have talked a great deal with Gide and a little with everyone about your marvelous articles on Vermeer. Who is the imbecile who maligned them in the *Débats*?

Always yours,
Marcel Proust

220: TO PAUL SOUDAY

JUNE 17, 1921

Cher Monsieur et ami,

Your fine article gave me great pleasure, and I am very grateful to you for thus attaching importance to a book of mine, even though you find it "less substantial." Here, again, you crush me, as you did before (as long ago even as *Du côté de chez Swann*), with the sentence about "*chapeau.*" I recognize that what you quoted of mine (in absolute agreement with the text of *Guermantes II*) is absolutely unintelligible. But as my proofs are, to start with, very badly corrected by me, when a book like this one appears, set into print straight from my indecipherable rough draft, my publishers might at least be kind enough to do their best about supervising the printing; it is still terribly incorrect.

I am not trying thus to absolve myself from the very justifiable reproach of frequently making sentences too long, too sinuously bound to the meanderings of my thought. You made me smile with your: "It is limpid." But I have found you too benevolent in pretending that at a third reading it becomes clear; as for me, I understand none of it. You wonder whether I was honored to read my name beside those of Bergson and of Einstein. A thousand other things in this article also touched me. What I object to in your articles is your beginning with criticisms or quotations which discourage the reader in advance from undertaking such a book. But so many profound and more than favorable remarks afterwards move the author so deeply that he no longer thinks of wondering whether it is good, he feels so strongly that it is a beautiful article and one, too, where the kind heart of the critic impels him to give praise which his reason alone might not bestow. As to the end of the book, I was hoping, since you charged my noncommissioned officer, Saint-Loup, with extreme naïveté for having been irritated at being "propositioned," that you would have beaten about the bush less with my Baron de Charlus. But I know that you speak from the heights of a rostrum that addresses itself to all, and that a certain reserve is required, which has nothing to do with timidity. . . . In a literary way, you seem to congratulate Saint-Simon for having remained more "summary." I naturally haven't the mad notion that I am on a par with the man of genius who wrote the *Memoirs*. I know only too well by how many thousand leagues I am removed from his heights. But I do believe another writer performs his duty in trying to probe into the subject matter where Saint-Simon's treatment is summary. I don't know whether or not I have already told you that what impelled me to set down copybook fashion so many of the Duchesse de Guermantes's replies and to make the *Guermantes* wit coherent and always identical, was the sense of being cheated that I felt when Saint-Simon was always talking about the "Mortemart wit," of the "turn of speech so peculiar" to M. de Montespan, to M. de Thianges, to the Abbess of Fontevrault, without finding, in a single word, the slightest hint to enable us to know wherein this singularity of language peculiar to the Mortemart's consisted. Unable to reconstruct "the Mortemart wit" in the past, I gambled on inventing "the Guermantes wit." Alas, I do not have Saint-Simon's genius. But, at least my readers will know what "the Guermantes wit" is, which was a far more difficult thing to do than to say: "Such a very curious wit," without giving the slightest idea of what it was like. So, for M. de Charlus I did the same thing as for the Duchesse de Guermantes: I don't think it necessary to be "summary." But I am beginning to feel tired and, even more, that I am boring you, and I ask only that you accept my affectionately admiring and grateful sentiments.

Marcel Proust

221: TO SYDNEY SCHIFF

[OCTOBER, 1921]

Cher ami,

Your letters are filled with more faces than a museum and more human beings than a city. So I don't understand your not turning to account these astonishing gifts by writing some books. Consider that I live in such a state of pain that I can no longer receive a visitor in spite of the loyalty which friends, whom I have not seen for twenty years, have kept for me; that I never write letters (you are one of the rare exceptions) and, at the risk of seeing today's praise change to tomorrow's "panning," I reply to none of the journalists; that I haven't the strength three quarters of the time to get up to sign a business paper or a check; and then, consider with your magnificent and robust health what I should do if I were as healthy as you. Come now, a little courage, work!

One part of your letter threw me into profound despair. It is the admirable sentence on the friendship that cannot be concretely realized (the sentence which ends with the heartrending words, worthy of the greatest writer: "So as not to have to endure the ending"). You can't imagine the sorrow that sentence caused me. You can understand, however, that not even having seen my family for several years, being unable to read, or write, or eat, or get up, except for an occasional and very rare outing like the one I made one day to see you, the only way I can persevere in such a hideous existence is by cherishing the illusion, shattered each day but renewed on the morrow, that all this will change. I have lived for the last fifteen years on day-to-day hopes. And your letter, confronting me with the reality I am unwilling to face, stunned me for a few minutes with an overwhelming grief. Don't regret it; the truth is always salutary, and anyway I regained my courage quickly and started working so as not to think. I beg of you to keep this confidence to yourself (by "yourself," I mean you and Mme Schiff, whom I do not separate). For I never talk about myself. And when occasionally by chance I see a human being, I say that the only reason I don't see anyone is because of my work. I dislike having anyone think otherwise. . . .

Please lay my respects at the feet of Mme Schiff,

Your friend who admires you,
Marcel Proust

222: TO JACQUES BOULENGER

[END OF JUNE, 1921]

Cher ami,

. . . . You say that my feelings for you have changed; well, that implies two things, one of which I didn't even want to allude to since I could not talk to you about it for a very, very long time and, therefore, found it idiotic not quite simply to keep quiet.

The second thing is nothing, simply what I said to you the night you were here. I hadn't pictured you the way you were when I saw you. Which proves solely that I had thought about you for years and that like all the people, all the cities, all the things one has thought about for a long time—when one sees them, one is surprised to find them different. It was fatal. So then one changes one's course quickly, starting from the real instead of from the imaginary and one restores to the person, the city, etc., all the feelings one had devoted to them, which merely pass over from the dream world to the world of experience. I think though that not my disappointment, but my "change" springs from something nice. And I am sure that if we see each other often, you will sense my friendship for the new Jacques Boulenger (please don't imagine anything of a Charlus nature about this!).

I should like, tired as I am, to ask you a favor, not for myself, I need hardly tell you, but for someone whom I haven't seen for many years (don't tell him that I sometimes see people), someone who is so ill-tempered (not with me, for I am one of the few people with whom he has never had any quarrels) that in no time he may turn my good intentions into a grievance, but in the end, I think, I shall have given him great pleasure and thereby some to myself as well. It is Robert de Montesquiou. A most unjust silence is closing in around his old age (which is stripped of money, too, I believe), for he is an art critic, a marvelous essayist who paints in prose as no one else does the work of a painter or a sculptor he loves. And bear this in mind, too (everything that follows is confidential): at eighteen when I was still a mere youngster under my parents' domination and had written nothing but *Les Plaisirs et les Jours* (much better written, it is true, than *Swann*), I met Robert de Montesquiou, who believed himself on the road to glory and to whom I was so much a child that he has remained for me what to children seems a "grown-up." You can still see this in the fact that (although there is [not] an enormous difference in our ages) I never end a letter to him without the adjective "respectful," which I would not use with anyone of the same difference in age whom I had met later and who didn't come to my parents' home as he did. —So, because I am distressed by the sort of ostracism of which he is the victim, I think each time I am mentioned in a newspaper: "How that must anger him." And I should so much like to have his name reappear. Since he really deserves it, I thought you might perhaps ask him for some essays on artists. Even if this couldn't be carried out for practical reasons, I am sure that just your request would comfort him in his old age, which must be very hard on him. If you don't know him, you could write him: "We were just saying the other evening with Marcel Proust how unfortunate it is that you are so miserly with your essays on art, etc.," but put rather: "We were saying," than, "Marcel Proust said to me," for he would be offended at appearing to have been recommended. And also at having been pitied. So that it would be more tactful to regard his inactivity as voluntary. This is only a small part of what I wanted to say to you on this subject, but I am too tired, and, in any case, it seems to me sufficient if you still have room for him and the desire to ask him. I started writing him again, even more cordial letters, because people have been absurd enough to say that I portrayed him in Charlus, a statement which is even more unforgivable, because, although I have known an enormous number of inverts in society, none of whom anyone suspected, never in the years and years that I have known Montesquiou have I ever seen him either at home or in a crowd give the slightest indication of it. In spite of that, I think (?) that he imagines I wanted to portray him. But since he is infinitely intelligent, rather than to appear to believe it, he was the first to write me the warmest letters about *Guermantes* and *Sodome*. But I believe he thinks so nonetheless. So the kindness of his letters martyrizes me. All the more so since I should be offering him the greatest insult if I even appeared to suspect that this is being said and to beg his pardon for it. He is a wicked man, who through his folly has caused suffering to many of his relations. But his sad old age, divested not only of the glory to which he fancies he had the right, but even of strict justice, cuts me to the quick.

Adieu, Jacques Boulenger,
Marcel Proust

. . . . His address, in any case, is: "*Palais rose*, Le Vésinet, Seine-et-Oise." I have never been at the *Palais rose*, which shows you that it is a long time since we have seen each other. Our last interview dates from a visit he paid me the first year of the war when, having promised to stay only five minutes, he stayed next to my bed for seven hours at the boulevard Haussmann where I was still living. —So don't tell him that it is possible to penetrate into the rue Hamelin, an address which he knows perfectly well, but which he doesn't make use of because I told him I was too ill.

Burn this letter because there are things in it that would enrage to the point of damnation this Count for whom I should so like to do a good turn.

223: TO JACQUES BOULENGER

NOVEMBER 26, 1921

Cher ami,

Before asking Gallimard's "permission," I should like to know whether one of your magazines (*L'Opinion* or the *Revue de la Semaine*) would be disposed to accept an article—very dithyrambic—which I might do on Léon Daudet, not about his politics, naturally, except in as far as there are certain scenes in the manner of Saint-Simon, showing the deputies not knowing whether to rise or sit when they ask for a vote of censure, or whether to put a blue or a white ballot in the box, and then end by abstaining from voting. Admirable articles and irresistibly funny. But mine will have no political complexion, because I am not involved in politics and never have been, unless having signed my name twenty-five years ago to a petition for the revision of the Dreyfus case can be called being involved in politics. If for reasons of principle or other reasons neither *L'Opinion* nor the *Revue de la Semaine* would take the article, it is useless for me to wear myself out writing it, at least for your magazines; useless to ask Gallimard, who is barely convalescent from *Oeuvres libres*, a permission which he might perhaps refuse me, for, even though he expresses it in a charming formula (which doesn't prevent my being very fond of him), the exclusive rights of the N.R.F. are not in our contract but "in the spirit of the contracting party." This use of the singular unquestionably means that it is in his spirit but not in mine. However, if it would distress him, I shan't do it. I have sworn by Christ never again to write for *Oeuvres libres*.

Cher ami, I particularly shouldn't want you to get the idea in your head that I conceived the project of doing this article while dedicating to you as a sort of hazing, my next excerpt, a terribly long one. No, it was because when I received a book of Léon Daudet's which he dedicated to me, and I thought of his persistent propaganda in my behalf, the idea which I formerly had of doing this article came back to me. I know that Léon Daudet is detested and that by praising him I shall put up the backs of the few people who are loyal to me. But admiration and gratitude are both very strong feelings that demand expression. If you like my idea, I shall not speak of his novel, but work hard on his *Souvenirs*. I never do articles; it is like opening a wound from which the rest of my blood will flow. But it so irritates me that he is never mentioned, that people pretend to ignore, or to take for a simple Rochefort, such a remarkable journalist. Of course, his ideas are not mine. But since he never held against me the Dreyfusism with which I formerly pestered him relentlessly, I thought I should emulate his impartiality by being simply a man of letters.

But if this bothers or embarrasses you, say so frankly.

From many points of view it would be a relief not to have this article to do.

Your very devoted friend,
Marcel Proust

Naturally (I know that you don't care but I insist anyway) I should not accept a penny for this article. It is a modest little present. But there are presents that are not welcome. So, I beg of you, do not do this to "give me pleasure." Say no squarely. But remember deep down that when the whole press (except Binet-Valmer) deserted me about *Sodome et Gomorrhe*, Léon Daudet, in *L'Action française*, a ridiculously straightlaced paper, never failed for a single day to support me. So that, since he never reads his own paper, while he was extolling me far above my merits on the front page, on the third page one read: "This book, the title of which we cannot even bring ourselves to pronounce (title taken from Vigny)." Naturally I have never called to Léon Daudet's attention the curious opinion of his collaborator. And he won't know to his dying day that there were "reservations" (in the sense the word is used in the American Senate) made about me in his own paper.

224: TO WALTER BERRY

DECEMBER 9, 1921

Cher Monsieur et ami,

. . . .

You have strange compatriots. An American girl who assures me she is very beautiful, twenty-seven years old (since she lives in Rome, the Villa Wolkonsky, I have forgotten her name, I don't give a hang, anyway) writes me that for three years she has done nothing night and day but read my books. I shouldn't repeat what she said (because I never repeat this sort of thing) except for the conclusion which, if it doesn't belittle her, humiliates me: "And after three years of uninterrupted reading, my conclusion is this: I understand nothing, but absolutely nothing. Dear Marcel Proust, don't be a *poseur*, descend for just once from your empyrean. Tell me in two lines what you wished to say." Since she didn't understand it in two thousand lines, or rather since I didn't know how to express it, I decided it was useless to reply. And she will find me a *poseur*. Do you know who she is (although it is of no importance)? . . .

Your compatriot who asks me to tell her (perhaps to telephone her) in two lines what she didn't understand in two thousand doesn't seem to be very Parisianized. She says to me: "Your great writers, France, Baudelaire, G—, Loti, Renan." G— is a literary man after M. Constant Say's heart. (Do you know whether one should sell Say Refineries? I was no sooner told not to sell Egyptian Refineries than they dropped from 1600 to 500). . . .

I am afraid that our eloquent orator, Briand, hasn't made a very good impression on your compatriots. In spite of which I do not like his being so frequently referred to as a pimp and myself as a genius in the same article. . . .

Marcel Proust

225: TO THE DUCHESSE DE CLERMONT-TONNERRE

44, RUE HAMELIN
(QUASI-CONFIDENTIAL ADDRESS)
[SOON AFTER DECEMBER 21, 1921]

Madame,

I am told that you were almost the only one of his friends who went to poor Montesquiou's funeral. I say poor Montesquiou, although I am quite convinced that he is not dead and that at his funeral at the Charles-Quint, the coffin was happily empty. Which is what makes me wait to write the study I intend consecrating to him. I had not seen him in a long time, but he wrote me the nicest letters, and I had tried to do something to please him, since he had told me that he was ill. It was arranging to have him published in a review, which acceded to my request to take some of his pieces that he rightly deemed unfairly neglected. Unfortunately he was the most difficult man in the world to please. Twenty-four hours later he brusquely changed his mind and wrote a letter, as amusing for me as it was dreadful for the editor of the review on whom I had imposed the most deferential terms in his dealings with Montesquiou. Then he sent me his last book; I was too ill to write him how much I liked it, and if, contrary to all expectations, he is really dead, I shall be inconsolable over not having told him about it in time. But, once again, I have every reason to believe in a final theatrical performance staged in masterly fashion by this marvelous impresario. *Adieu*, Madame, I have too much to tell you and too little strength to go on. Please accept my admiring and respectful greetings.

Marcel Proust

The following letter, published in *Les Annales*, February 26, 1922, was a reply to two questions submitted by the editor.

1. Are there still schools of writing?

2. When a distinction is drawn between the analytical novel and the adventure novel, does it, in your opinion, mean anything, and what?

226: TO THE EDITOR "LES ANNALES"

[LATE 1921 OR EARLY 1922]

Monsieur et cher confrère,

The expression, "analytical novel," is not much to my taste. It has come to mean a study under a microscope, a word which itself has taken on a false significance in ordinary speech, since infinitesimal beings are not—as the science of medicine shows—without significance. As for me, the instrument I prefer is the telescope rather than the microscope. But I was unfortunate enough to start a book with the word, "I," and immediately it was assumed that instead of trying to discover universal laws, I was "analysing myself," in the personal and odious sense of the word. I shall therefore, if you are willing, replace the term "analytical novel" by "introspective novel." As for the "adventure novel," certainly there are in life, in external life, great laws, too, and if the adventure novel can unravel them, it is as good as the introspective novel. Everything that can help discover laws, to throw light on the unknown, to bring about a more profound knowledge of life, is equally valuable. Only, such an adventure novel is, under another name, introspective, too. It is in ourselves that we discover the seemingly external. *Cosa mentale*, applied by Leonardo da Vinci to painting, can be applied to every work of art. One must concede, however, that the adventure novel, even when it does not have these high aims, is easily impregnated with the distinction of the mind that handles it. Stevenson wrote great masterpieces, but he also wrote simple adventure stories, which are delightful and charming. They revolve around Prince Florizel of Bohemia, who, in order to rid his character of the slightest fatuousness that might be attributed to him by snobbishness, is in the end placed by the author in a shop in London where he sells cigarettes.

To say a last word about the so-called analytical novel, it must in my view, never be a novel of pure intellect. It has to do with drawing a reality out of the unconscious in such a way as to make it enter into the realm of the intellect, while trying to preserve its life, not to garble it, to subject it to the least possible shrinkage—a reality which the light of intellect alone would be enough to destroy, so it seems. To succeed in this work of salvage, all the forces of the mind and even of the body, are not superfluous. It is a little like the cautious, docile, intrepid effort necessary to someone who, while still asleep, would like to explore his sleep with his mind without this intervention leading to his awakening. Here precautions must be taken. But although it apparently embodies a contradiction, this form of work is not impossible.

Finally, you ask me about the "schools." They are only a material symbol of the time it takes for a great artist to be understood and placed among his peers, for the repudiated *Olympia* to hang next to Ingres; for Baudelaire, the judgment against him reversed, to fraternize with Racine (whom he, for that matter, resembles, especially in form). Racine is more fertile in psychological discoveries, Baudelaire teaches us more about the laws of memory, which, for that matter, I find set forth in a more living fashion in Chateaubriand or Nerval. With Baudelaire, remembering is static, it already exists when the poem starts (*Quand les deux yeux fermés, etc., O toison moutonnant, etc.*). Final and slight difference: Racine is more immoral.

As soon as the innovator is understood, the school for which there is no longer any need is disbanded. Besides, no matter how long the school lasts, the innovator's taste is always much broader. Hugo vaunted Romanticism as his school, but appreciated perfectly Boileau and Regnard. Wagner never regarded Italian music with the severity of the Wagnerians.

Please accept, etc.

Marcel Proust

227: TO SYDNEY SCHIFF

NIGHT OF FRIDAY OR SATURDAY

[APRIL 28 OR 29, 1922]

Cher ami,

You will now behold all the tragedy, as the German critic, Curtius, would say, of my predicament. Your letter said: "We are here." I understood here to mean, "arrived in Paris." Immediately, in spite of a high temperature, I started my inoculations so as to be able to get up and go to see you at the Ritz where you told me you were going to stop. The thought of dressing annoyed me so I engaged a room where I thought you would come and see me or I you, to be specific No. 12, which is reserved for new arrivals at 7 Saturday morning, but which would leave me all Friday evening to see you and to return to bed at rue Hamelin. I arrive at the Ritz—no Elles, no Olivier, whose day off it was. I go up to No. 12 and ask the bellboy to go find out which apartment is occupied by M. and Mme Sydney Schiff. The boy returns at the end of half an hour, M. Schiff is indeed here but without his wife. I begin to be astonished, I send him back downstairs where a footman was taking the place of the sick porter (the Ritz is actually a desert without oasis, the staff is nonexistent). I was beginning to be consumed by uncertainty and a presentiment. Eventually the boy returns: Yes, M. Schiff is here, M. Mortimer Schiff. Alas, it was not the beloved (forgive me this familiarity) Sydney Schiff. After a little while I left and returned home. Then I took up your letter again and saw that the envelope had the name of the restaurant Foyot. Perhaps even if I had noticed this when I received it, I should have thought (you were so explicit in your: "We shall stop at the Ritz") that you wrote from Foyot but were staying at the Ritz. (All the more because Olivier kept saying that you were "expected.") But there is no point in my wondering whether or not I should have thought that this Foyot address was just a stop on the way to Luxembourg, or a residence, because I didn't look at the envelope. Partly because in the stupor out of which my inoculations pull me for a few hours in the evening, I read my mail, when I read it at all, without even half opening my eyes; partly because, the porter's daughter having measles and whooping cough, I avoid holding the envelopes in my hand. If I had had the luck to find yours, with the name, "Foyot," on it, it was because your envelope happened to be immersed with the rest of my correspondence, which that very day was plunged for two hours into a formaldehyde disinfectant. Alas, is the twice magic name of "Foyot," which evokes memories of excellent lunches down there in my youth, during the days of my general and final examination, a good omen? I hardly think so. First, how soon shall I be able to get up again after this evening's visit to the Ritz? Not for a week at least, even supposing things work out well, and it doesn't look as though they would (Céleste is talking to me, so it is not my thought but my writing that has changed in the last line). And in another week shall I be able to take the inoculations again? Another thing, by the time I can manage to go out, it is very late. (If I see M. Elles and say to him: "How do you happen to be here so late?" he replies, "But it is very early for you.") Besides I am afraid that at Foyot's, a delightful place, a thousand times superior to the Ritz, but "early closing," they wouldn't open up for me late at night. It would be very kind of you to let me know their time schedule. . . . Have you read the fine essay Curtius devoted to me in the Munich *Neue Merkur*? Also Gide copied out for me a letter he had written him about me (the word "tragic," which he applies to my life, is the reason why I said, "tragic," to you in mentioning Curtius at the beginning of this letter). Finally there is still another letter from this same Curtius, bathing in formaldehyde, which I haven't yet read. I still haven't been able to write to Mr. Middleton Murry and, for that matter, can no longer write at all except by dictating to my typist (a niece of Céleste's). But with you I didn't dare. *Cher ami* (who told me that you weren't coming until May, otherwise I should have started my treatments earlier). I still have a thousand things to tell you. But I am too exhausted for more than one. Don't mention my health to Elles, Olivier, etc. . . . I don't like being pitied and you are the only person, or almost the only one, in whom I confide this way. For that matter, I might not do it even with you if I didn't want you to know that if it weren't for my dreadful state of health my affection would often take me to London for twenty-four hours to see you. But in general I don't like to talk about my health.

Prier, pleurer, gémir est également lâche,
Fais énergiquement ta courte et lourde tâche,
Puis après comme moi, souffre et meurs sans parler.

Cher ami, please lay my respects at the feet of Mme Schiff and share with her my grateful admiration.

Your wholehearted friend,
Marcel Proust

Madame Sert was at this time the wife of the Spanish painter José-Maria Sert (1876–1945), from whom she was later divorced.

228: TO MADAME SERT

THURSDAY NIGHT [1921 OR 1922]

Madame,

. . . . Even the sentence "Are you a snob?" which seemed to me very stupid the first time, may now become dear to me because I heard you speak it. In itself, it makes no sense; if among the very few friends who from force of habit continue to come and ask for news of me, an occasional duke or a prince comes and goes, he is amply counterbalanced by other friends, one of whom is a *valet de chambre*, another a chauffeur, and whom I treat with more consideration. Besides one is as good as the other. *Valets de chambre* are better informed than dukes and speak a prettier French, but they are more punctilious about etiquette and less simple, more sensitive. All in all, they are worth it. The chauffeur has more distinction. "Are you a snob?" pleased me as a last year's dress would because I found you pretty when you wore it. But I assure you that the only person's company that could cause me to be labeled a snob is yours. It would not be true. And you would be the only one to believe that I associate with you out of vanity rather than admiration. Don't be so modest.

If you are still on good terms with Sert, tell him I am bursting with fanaticism for him.

Very respectfully yours,
Marcel Proust

229: MADAME STRAUS TO MARCEL PROUST

SATURDAY MAY 13, 1922

Mon petit Marcel si cher,

Laying all weariness aside for at least a few moments, I must explain to you a phenomenon which occurs each time I receive one of your books.

Here's how it happens:

I take the book, I cut the pages and say to myself: I shall read for a quarter of an hour; and then the quarter hour goes by. . . . I read. . . . I continue to read. Dinner is announced I say: "I am coming," . . . and I go on reading. The servant returns timidly and does not leave—so, embarrassed by her pejorative presence, I go downstairs. After dinner we come back up, and very quietly, as though I were doing nothing, I discreetly draw out the precious book . . . and there I am, plunged back into reading, until the impetuous lawyer, whom you know so well, cries out with a vehemence of which you are also not unaware: "But this is abominable, this woman who reads all the time, morning, noon, and night she reads, she reads, she reads, all the time!"

This little picture of my life in the last two days will express more than all the compliments in the world, and will even explain the reason why I haven't thanked you sooner for having sent me these three last rare copies of Sodome et Gomorrhe. *I am taking the time to do it today because I am alone; I have decided not to go, which is reasonable enough since I didn't sleep all night and am in a really very bad state. But that is not the* real reason for my reason. *The real reason is that I want to go back to the end of Volume II and start the third . . . perhaps finish it—with regret. Marcel,* mon petit *Marcel, how I should love to see you! It seemed as though we had so many things to say to each other! But it would be altogether too amusing—and too sad—and I believe it will never happen.* Never! *What a cruel word! I cannot get used to the idea of never seeing you again; the beautiful Céleste has, however, left me a little hope by telling me that perhaps you might come one day before I leave for Versailles (the end of June if the weather is good).*

Au revoir, mon cher petit *Marcel, because I cannot bring myself to bid you* adieu. *It depresses me to know that you are ill all the time. Not that I don't imitate you, but with me it's more natural.*

Thank you again for the tremendous joy I owe you. I love you dearly,

Your old and faithful friend,
Geneviève H. S.

. . . . Thank you for remembering the words of La Juive *so well. I am touched by it.*

So many questions I still want to ask you about your books! —But one must talk *and not* write.

230: TO JACQUES BOULENGER

[CIRCA MAY 15, 1922]

Cher ami,

. . . .

You are too charming! You say that my book "is charming (?)." In any case your moral sense will be satisfied, for you will see that my hero, scorning *Sodome*, is about to be married when the book ends. There will be only my hero's passion for women in the subsequent volumes of *Sodome*, which I also intend giving titles less inspired by Vigny. For the next I thought of *La Prisonnière*, but I don't know that it isn't rather banal. I shall ask your advice before it appears. I am no judge of titles. I should like to have one you would like.

A thousand admiring and affectionate greetings.

Marcel Proust

231: TO SYDNEY SCHIFF

[END OF MAY, 1922]

Cher ami,

. . . . We talk much too much about serious things. Serious conversation is intended for people who have no intellectual life. People like the three of us, on the contrary, who have an intellectual life need frivolity when they escape from themselves and from hard inner labor. We should, as you say, talk about all the little things and leave philosophy to solitude.

On the subject of Mr. Lloyd George, there can be no disagreement between us, and on that point I see you are mistaken. It concerns impressions too trifling to cause either agreement or disagreement. I never saw or heard him, probably if I knew him as I know Asquith's daughter, my impressions would change. . . . I don't mean to say that there is no notable personality on the staff of the *Nouvelle revue française*, but it is neutralized by the rest and makes for a mediocre average, as are all averages, less mediocre than most and fortunately sufficiently elastic. . . .

Marcel Proust

232: TO LAURE HAYMAN

MAY 19, 1922

Chère Madame,

After an accident that happened to me last week (I failed to notice that some medicine had to be diluted, took it neat and as a result had pain enough to make me faint), I had hoped to suffer peacefully without writing a single letter. But since several persons, whose names you have not told me, have been malicious enough to revive this legend, and since you are so devoid of critical judgment as to credit it, which in you flabbergasts me, I am forced to answer you, to protest once more, with no more hope of success, but through a sense of honor. Odette de Crécy not only is not you, but your exact opposite. This seems to me overwhelmingly obvious in every word she speaks. It is even amazing that no detail inspired by you should have been inserted in a portrait which has nothing to do with you. For there is perhaps not a single other of my most invented-out-of-whole-cloth characters to which the memory of some other person, who bears no relation to the rest of the character, has not come to add its little touch of truth and poetry. For example (it is, I think, in *Jeunes filles en fleurs*), I have put in Odette's drawing room the very special flowers which, as you say, a lady "on the Guermantes side" always has in her drawing room. She recognized her flowers, wrote to thank me, never believed for a second that she might, therefore, be Odette. You say, as a case in point, that your "cage" resembles Odette's. I am very much surprised. Your taste is so sure, so daring! If I needed to know the name of a piece of furniture or of material, I would willingly turn to you rather than to any artist; so perhaps with great clumsiness, but at least in the best way I know how, I have, on the contrary, tried to show that Odette had no more taste in furnishing than in anything else; that she was always (except for her clothes) a generation behind the style. I shouldn't know how to describe the apartment in the avenue Trocadéro or the house in rue La Pérouse, but I remember them as the opposite of Odette's house. If there are details common to the two, it no more proves that I was thinking of you in creating Odette than the ten lines resembling M. Doasan, dovetailed into the life and personality of one of my characters to whom several volumes are devoted, signify that I wanted to portray M. Doasan. I pointed out in an article in *Oeuvres libres* the stupidity of people in society who believe that one can introduce a real person into a book in this way. I should add that they generally choose a person who is exactly the opposite of the character. I have long since ceased saying that Mme G. "was not" the Duchesse de Guermantes, was, indeed, her opposite. I cannot persuade a single goose. You compare yourself to that bird: the memory you have left with me is more that of a swallow for lightness (I mean speed), of a bird of paradise for beauty, of a ringdove for faithful friendship, of a gull or an eagle for courage, of a carrier pigeon for soundness of instinct. Alas, did I overrate you? You read me and find yourself resembling Odette! It is enough to make one give up writing books. Mine are not very much in my mind right now. I can tell you, however, that in *Du côté de chez Swann* when Odette drives to *les Acacias* in her carriage, I thought of certain dresses, gestures, etc. of a woman who was called Closmenil and who was very pretty, but there again, in her trailing garments, her slow walk in front of the clay-pigeon gallery, entirely different from your kind of elegance. Moreover, except at that moment (perhaps half a page), I did not think of Closmenil a single time in speaking of Odette. In the next volume, Odette will have married a "nobleman," her daughter becomes a close relative of the Guermantes with a great title. Only unusual women of the world have any idea of what literary creation is. But unusual was just what you were in my memory. Your letter has disillusioned me. I lack the strength to go on, and in saying good-bye to the cruel correspondent who writes only to cause me pain, I place my respects and my tender memory at the feet of her who used to think better of me.

Marcel Proust

233: TO JACQUES BOULENGER

[CIRCA JUNE 15, 1922]

Mon cher Jacques Boulenger,

. . . .

I have wanted to write to your brother, who didn't understand my book and above all seems not to know what my youth was like, but I should have bored him and tired myself. And besides it would have meant my setting myself in the social world in a way that isn't pleasant. I find it more gracious to assume a "barefoot boy" air in my books and to say, "I wasn't sure of being invited." I have never known this kind of insecurity, but I find it more becoming. Stevenson, after describing the Prince of Bohemia, quickly had him end as a tobacconist in London. I was surprised to see how little the Guermantes who read my book realize how shocking it is. The Guermantes women, highly virtuous, cluster about me. Either they don't understand what they read, or perhaps they have looked around them and said to themselves that the proportion of people tainted with "shameful vices" is a tiny bit larger in society than in my books where at least the Cottards, the Elstirs, the Bergottes, the Norpois, etc., etc., maintain the tradition of what was formerly "normal." I must write to M. Thérive. I have been saying that to myself for two years.

Most friendly greetings,
Marcel Proust

234: TO SYDNEY SCHIFF

[JUNE—EARLY JULY, 1922]

Mon cher Sydney,

You have written me a revolting letter, simply for the purpose of revolting me, so that, in my distress, I should write you. That's what I am doing, wondering at the same time whether I'm not wrong to give in to this blackmail. You know perfectly well that I see nobody, that except for going to one *soirée* about which I told you, I have not seen a living human being for months except you and Mme Schiff. You know I can't write (this letter is an exception; and since my letter paper isn't nearby and Céleste is asleep, I am writing you on the little papers I use to light my powders). You know that you yourself, on the contrary, lead just the kind of life I do not lead, but for which you reproach me. If you would read my book, you would discover in it the infatuations and capricious ill temper of the world of society, which I broke away from at the age of twenty, but which did not prevent the *Nouvelle revue française* twenty years later from rejecting *Swann* as the work of a mere man of the world. But you don't read my book because, like all people in society who don't like it, you are too nervous in Paris, too busy in London, and in the country you have too many guests. Nevertheless, it is not my fault, it is the fault of my book; for if it were really a beautiful book, it would immediately bring harmony to disturbed minds and calm to troubled hearts. Meanwhile, since the day it appeared, the real friends of the book have read it in the subway, in cars, in trains, oblivious of their neighbors, forgetting their destination. I ignore your purely mundane statement that you prefer the man to his work. I could refute that sophism in two minutes, but I am too tired. For that matter, I am not even sure that you like the author. I can remember in the past when I asked you to subscribe for a volume of *Jeunes filles en fleurs*, you replied that it irritated you to think that for the same price anyone could buy that edition. Reasoning that way, we would never buy any books and the authors, lacking the wherewithal to buy bread for the body, would die, and one would oneself decay through refusing to buy bread for the spirit. . . .

But I am too tired. I shall rest content in citing you an example of loyalty; for although I see exclusively the Schiffs, I hold for your inspection fifty or more telegrams from Bibesco since he has been here: "Could you dine with us here tonight or wherever you like with whomever you like?" and I haven't gone a single time.

Please lay my respects at the feet of Mme Violet and believe in my profound affection.

Marcel

One thing more revolting to me than the rest. That you should think I claimed to feel better after you had gone. Your departure could only have caused me tears.

Just as absurd to believe that I improved because you were here. The relationship between the mind and the body is not so simple. One day when I am less tired and have less work to do, I shall enlarge upon the subject, for I have a number of very lucid and perhaps even profound ideas on the subject.

235: TO GASTON GALLIMARD

JULY, 1922

Read to the end

Mon cher Gaston,

. . . That writers of Gide's weight and others comparable to him should be paid as much or more than I am seems to me more than natural. But I was very much pained, I confess (with very sharp material repercussions), to learn that a certain author of yours, an intelligent man, competent in questions of craftsmanship, but whom you yourself deem a third-rate writer (an opinion in which I would, on the contrary, defend him against you, who, to my mind, attach too much importance to his French and to his style) was paid much more than I. I laid no stress at all the other day on regular printings. You were certainly right about it. I had understood that my monthly payments were to settle for the past, but that new works would be paid for at the time of printing, according to the agreement (without which we shall never arrive at another understanding!). Certainly, I misunderstood, I am even ashamed to hark back to my mistake. But that others should have precedence over me seems cruel. Dear Gaston, this eternal question of filthy lucre submerges me like mud, which I should like to wash off in a fraternal hand clasp (the humor of such an incoherent metaphor consoles me a little for saying such vulgar things). And I am sure that if you would give me good practical advice you would be doing me a much greater service than in paying me more. One enriches oneself as much in reducing one's expenditures as in increasing one's income. It is not perhaps very business-wise to tell you this, but it is the outpouring of a friend who is very much yours.

You pain me very much by telling me that your life is feckless. It is superb. You have associated your name with the most striking literary movements of our time. Abroad (and I have good reasons—which I am not telling you because it would rekindle certain divergences of opinion between us on another matter—to know it) the N.R.F. is something like Parnassus or Symbolism. I understand that to have one's name attached to a work can cause no pleasure whatsoever when it is dissipated, as it is in my case by constant physical suffering, which prevents my work's yielding me even the slightest satisfaction. Under these circumstances, cut off from happiness by constant discomfort, one can feel nothing. But this is not, thank God, your situation; not only are you in good health but you are a wise man who takes Vittel water. Besides your name is not attached to just one individual work but to a cycle, the N.R.F. Look at life from this angle and you will be proud and happy. Happiness exists on condition that one doesn't regard it as an end in itself but as a great wellspring. I know people who are unhappy because they figure they are a year older or something of that sort. Happiness regarded as an end destroys itself utterly. It is full to overflowing for those who do not look for satisfaction, but who live their lives outside themselves for the sake of an idea. I repeat that my case is not relevant because it is a sheer exception. Anyone who leads a life like mine and who suffers incessantly is almost a monster (I don't mean of wickedness, for I am quite the contrary). But I must draw my arguments from these exceptions, which are fortunately rare. Otherwise absurd examples can be cited to prove anything. Poverty, a moderate income, may further the life of the intellect. That doesn't mean that black misery, days without bread, nights with no roof over one's head are fruitful. Dear Gaston, I am stopping because, in my desire to persuade you that your life is very beautiful (because I am convinced of it), I have tired myself a little too much. . . . Have you Quincy's [sic] *Confessions of an Opium Eater*? Morand, I think, will lend me *The Possessed*. I can't go on.

Yours always,
Marcel Proust

236: TO SYDNEY SCHIFF

[July, 1922]

Mon cher Sydney,

. . . . Your letter is full of inaccuracies (involuntary of course). I am by no means cured.

I did not cite Antoine Bibesco as a man in society, but to prove that you and Mme Violet were the only infringement of my rule. As for Antoine Bibesco, I should like you to know that he and his brother, after reading parts of the manuscript of *Swann* around 1911, were so very enthusiastic (pardon me for speaking about myself like this) that they begged the *Nouvelle revue française*, where they knew Copeau, to publish some excerpts, which they refused to do, and to publish the book, which they also refused. And so with publisher after publisher I failed. . . . All this to tell you that the two Bibescos (one of them, alas, died in the most hideous way) were the first lovers of *Swann*, and it is a complete travesty to label social the ultra-intellectual relation existing between Bibesco and me. For that matter, there is not a day that he doesn't send me clippings out of foreign newspapers from America. He alone keeps me regularly informed about them.

It is absurd to say that when one sees a person it is unnecessary to read his book, like the human voice and a gramophone. Between what a person *says* and what he extracts by meditation from the depths where the bare spirit lies hidden and veiled, there is a world of difference. It is true that there are people superior to their books, but that is because their books aren't *BOOKS*. It seems to me that Ruskin, who from time to time said sensible things, has expressed at least a part of this fairly well. I no longer remember where, but if you wish I shall find it for you.

If it would interest you to read the rather remarkable (but on the whole idiotic) articles that the various newspapers and reviews are doing about me, I will send them to you. But they're not very interesting.

You speak as though I went out in society. In a year I have gone out the one time of which I told you.

I am too tired to continue. I have not yet written to Mr. Eliot, having seen no one on the *Nouvelle revue française*, since they are all on vacation. *Deus nobis haec otia fecit*, they could say about what they learn from my books, and I not as much about them.

I kiss Mme Violet's hands and send you, my dear Sydney, my tender affection.

Marcel Proust

237: TO SYDNEY SCHIFF

[CIRCA END OF JULY, 1922]

Cher Sydney,

. . . .

You are unjust to the public, limited I admit, that loved *Swann* right away. One of the most favorable articles that I ever had was in the *L. Times* of 1913 or the beginning of 1914, when the *Nouvelle revue française* would have none of

Swann. I am in deep despair at not yet having written to Mr. Eliot; the *Nouvelle revue française* must ask him to forgive me. *Unfortunately* I am not at the moment on good terms with them (but not on *bad* ones either). However, Gallimard and Rivière have been on holiday for a month. But they will return, and if the little prose poems (*Le Voleur*, etc.) are ready, they absolutely must publish them. It would be better to start (me or you) with Rivière (that is to say the *Revue*). A book is more difficult to get and it would be easier if the tales had had a success in the *Revue*. I am always afraid of their deplorable taste, which makes them refuse things and then retrieve them three years later when they realize that they have made a mistake. . . . How lucky you are to be able to work! I can't do anything, not even read. I did, however, open the *Figaro* and, as it was incorrectly paginated, I happened on the society news. There I saw that the daughter of a friend of mine, said daughter having married one of the most detestable of the Rumanians (at least I imagine so because I didn't want to go near him), "gave a *tea* in honor of the Shah of Persia and a *goûter* in honor of the Prince of Greece." I wondered in vain about the difference between a *tea* and a *goûter*. Is one supposed to think that there were *petits fours* at the tea (which would not be nice for the Asiatic sovereign), or that tea was not served at the *goûter*? I found no solution, but I am amazed at the strange wordings in the paper and also that people are courageous enough to have published *urbi et orbi* all the dinners, *goûters*, etc. they eat, while in the next column one learns that hundreds of people (perhaps as interesting as the Shah of Persia) were found dead of starvation in Austria and elsewhere.

A thousand admiring greetings to Mme Schiff.

Your

Marcel

Benjamin Crémieux (1888–1944) was a teacher, lecturer and writer, the author of a number of books, among them *XXième siècle, Du côté de Marcel Proust* and *Panorama de la littérature italienne contemporaine.* He died in the concentration camp at Buchenwald.

238: TO BENJAMIN CRÉMIEUX

AUGUST 6, 1922

Cher ami,

You were a monster because, in offering to point out to me what I have refused to let others show me, you have forced me to be impolite to the whole Italian press (which mentions me daily, much to the despair of M. Barrère who believes that I wanted to portray him in M. de Norpois simply because he dined at our house every week when I was a child. But Norpois is representative of an exactly opposite diplomatic type and, as well as being perfectly detestable, too . . .)

I believe that the anachronisms on which you are kind

enough to congratulate me are not in my book. I don't swear to it, and it would bore me too much to open that tiresome work in order to answer you with certainty. But to sum up as well as I can remember, between the Guermantes *soirée* and the second stay at Balbec there is a long interval of time. But for the sake of convenience, if you like, let us Einstein it [*Einsteinisonble*]. Besides, it seems to me it was after 1900. In any case, I think that I speak of the *Ballets russes* only in the future. And, finally, when Swann chats with the Prince de Guermantes, the revision is over. But it does seem that even so there is a little hiatus. But this had already happened in the preceding volumes because of the flattened form my creatures take in their revolution in time. It would be very complicated to explain this in a letter.

As to the Germanophilia of Caillaux, perhaps, actually, it was a little anticipatory. I shall ask Léon Daudet at what period beforehand he denounced him. Nevertheless, I sometimes fancy it was a good thing then. I haven't followed all that and can't, therefore, have an opinion, but it seems to me that the Caillaux of Kiderlen-Waechter was not the same one as during the war. . . .

Please give my respectful compliments to Madame Crémieux and believe me yours always,

Marcel Proust

P.S. I am brokenhearted over not having talked with you about the "little businesses," which you discovered for me near the Passage des Favorites. For I have just finished in *Sodome et Gomorrhe III* a piece on the "cries" of Paris (food-cries above all, of push-carts, etc. . . .). But the originality of the signs of which you tell me is perhaps complemented in the amusing vegetable and fruit calls, etc. . . . and the sounds of various instruments. I have, however, reaped for myself a fairly abundant, at times quite sonorous harvest, one which you would, no doubt, have completed. . . .

Ernst Robert Curtius (1886–),
Professor of Romance Languages at Heidelberg and Bonn Universities, early admirer and perceptive critic of Proust, is the author of numerous critical essays on French writers, of *Der Französischer Geist im Neuen Europa*, *Balzac*, and other volumes.

239: TO ERNST ROBERT CURTIUS

[SEPTEMBER 18, 1922]

Cher Monsieur,

This little note, which accompanies the gift of *Sodome et Gomorrhe II*, is just an apology for the great delay in sending it to you, whom I admire so much, whom I like so much, if I may say so. But much as I detest talking about myself and my ills, I should detest even more your thinking me indifferent. I have been successively deprived of speech, of sight, of motion (lest I fall down every few steps). I prefer not to expatiate on this hell. But I have said enough so that you will forgive me. And since medicine is really an excessively funny science (?), the explanation of all this would be that they have just discovered that my chimney is cracked and that, since I never open my window, I breathe great quantities of carbon dioxide every day—costly inhalation! I do not wish to speak disrespectfully of doctors; my father was professor of the Faculty of Medicine, and my brother, also professor of the Faculty of Medicine, is the most courageous, the most learned, the most intelligent man. But, alas, my father is dead and, as to my brother, I am too ill to receive him. It is true that on certain days I can have myself conveyed out of doors. But it is always around four o'clock in the morning. And I don't want to waken him then because he has to be at his hospital at eight. Really it is hateful to talk inexhaustibly like this about oneself and one's family. But it is just my admiring friendship for you which makes me unbosom myself. I have read a very fine article of yours in which you speak in profound and magnificent terms of what Germany must be since the war. You see that in spite of the infinitely exaggerated but very touching eulogies which Léon Daudet constantly gives me in *L'Action française*, in spite of my brother's affection for General Mangin, affection sealed on the field of battle, I am not at all (nor is my brother) "nationalist." It is rather ill-bred of me to tell you all this, but it was useful to clear the ground. However, there is no need whatsoever of our talking politics. Our concern is literature and it is a very fruitful concern. Renan would say that we suffer *morbo literario*, that is absurd. Bad literature minimizes. But true literature reveals the yet unknown portion of the spirit. It is a little like Pascal's saying, which I am quoting incorrectly because I have no books here: "A little science removes us from God, much science brings us back again." One must never be afraid of going too far, for the truth is beyond. But you know this much better than your affectionate

Marcel Proust

Camille Vettard (1877–1947), a writer and critic, was a high functionary of the Ministry of the Interior from 1904 to 1937.

240: TO CAMILLE VETTARD

[PROBABLY SEPTEMBER OR OCTOBER, 1922]

Mon cher ami,

I should like to answer your questions at length, but I am practically dead, and my reply would be almost the votive offering of a dying man. What I should like people to see in my book is that it sprang wholly from the application of a special sense (at least that is what I believe), which is very difficult to describe (like trying to describe sight to a blind man) to those who have never exercised it. But that is not true of you and you might understand me if I merely give you the (very imperfect) simile (you will certainly find a much better one yourself), which seems to me the best (at least at the present time) to explain what this special sense is. It is perhaps like a telescope, which is pointed at time, because a telescope reveals stars which are invisible to the naked eye, and I have tried (I don't, however, attach any special value to my simile) to reveal to the conscious mind unconscious phenomena which, wholly forgotten, sometimes lie very far back in the past. (It is perhaps, on thinking it over, this special sense which has sometimes made me concur with Bergson—since it has been said that I do—for there has never been, insofar as I am aware, any direct influence.)

As to style, I have endeavored to reject everything dictated by pure intellect, everything that is rhetoric, embellishment, and, more or less, any deliberate or mannered figures of speech (those figures which I denounced in the preface to Morand's book) to express my deep and authentic impressions and to respect the natural progress of my thought. I am saying this all very poorly because I am forced to dictate in terrific pain, which leaves me only strength enough to tell you again of my admiring and grateful affection.

Marcel Proust

Henri Duvernois, pseudonym of Henri Schabacher, French novelist and critic, was at this time editor of *Les Oeuvres libres.* Of this last published letter of Marcel Proust's M. Duvernois wrote in *Le Petit Parisien,* November 28, 1922, "Here on my table is his last letter, written in a trembling, wavering script by a hand already cold in death, a poor letter that I read then with such emotion, that I reread now with tears in my eyes. . . . The date is of a few days ago." Marcel Proust died November 18, 1922.

241: TO HENRI DUVERNOIS

[NOVEMBER, 1922]

Cher ami,

If you knew the state I am in you would be astonished at the miraculous luck that made me open your letter and that even more miraculously gives me the strength to answer it. To sum up, no checks now, please; time enough if I recover from this inopportune attack. As to the "novel," since there is no more of it, have it arranged as you please or throw it in the fire. I am not surprised that nobody understood my senseless proof marks.

In fact, after I thought I had cut everything, they calculated that there were still nine thousand lines too many. So (my attack having begun) I had them remove all the typed manuscript without counting it. So whether they delete a little more or a little less no longer interests me. My only reason for making the effort to write you all this, is so as not to run the risk of the books (Gallimard) appearing too soon afterwards. There is no one I should more have liked to know than your friend. But all visitors are forbidden and impossible. If I survive, we shall see. The title "Precautions inutiles" is idiotic, but it's the only one that doesn't run into complications. If I have another hour with strength enough, I shall write dear Robert de Flers to spare me, "after a long and serious illness valiantly borne," which would be untrue anyway, because this illness has nothing to do with the other. I still think of pulling through, however. But if I should not, it would be preferable to the convalescence I am promised, which makes me shudder. *Cher ami*, don't trouble to reply. Don't send for news of my condition (which no one knows). I was too sick to write you about Rivière (and the Bourget Prize), my affection and admiration for whom you nevertheless know.

And now everything should be finished.

If anything about my dreams or my sleep has stayed in,

it must be removed. If I left it in, I did so out of forgetfulness and it makes for useless repetition.

Now expect nothing more from me but silence, and follow my example.

Yours always,
Marcel Proust

"O, public, too often ungrateful, readers whom a new style drives to the most bitter and often the most unjust criticism, think of those who devote themselves body and soul to that dangerous trade of working for you! Proust for years spent his life bedridden. From time to time he would go out, at night and in a car. The rest of the time he meditated and wrote behind closed blinds and curtains, the lights turned on, a wood fire burning in the hearth winter and summer. No outer noise penetrated to his room. And when someone was astonished that a man could live like that, with artificial light, without fresh air, the noble woman [Céleste Albaret] who took care of Marcel Proust replied, 'It is the atmosphere that suits Monsieur for his work.' Sometimes when he was not feeling too bad, he would invite a friend to dine—not with him, for he ate practically nothing—but beside him. He would order a superb meal with champagne. And he would urge his companion, 'Do eat! You're not eating enough!' And what conversations then! Or rather what a monologue! The guest, dazzled, would listen in enchantment. And that wonderful laugh of Proust's, that laugh which brought back a little of his health long lost. . . . Another gone, killed by the art he served to his last day! That his colleagues should salute that fine, that noble figure of the writer is more than natural. And it is only right that the public, to whom this victim has left the best of himself, should associate itself with this tribute."

Henri Duvernois

Notes

2, p.8 *gentleman in question:* Dauphiné, Oswald Mathieu François (1846–1924). "M. Dauphiné had a rather strange pronunciation; his 'r's' were soft and blurred. He said . . . 'Monsieur Gouegh . . . Monsieur Halévy, *vous passeouez à la pôte.*'" [*Vous passerez à la porte*. Leave the room.] (Fernand Gregh, *L'Age d'or*. Paris, 1947.)

2, p.9 *Gaucher:* Maxime Gaucher (1829–1888) was literary critic of the *Revue bleue* as well as Professor of Rhetoric at the Lycée Condorcet. "We called him 'Père Gaucher' and loved him like a father. . . . Maxime Gaucher, who scorned neither puns nor a play on words, was quick at repartee. The 'poet' Eugène Manuel, who had vainly attempted to become a member of the Academy, was on the staff of the University as Inspector of Secondary Schools. One day when he was visiting a class of Père Gaucher's, he permitted himself some rather astringent remarks on a French composition by one of the young students.

The professor, piqued, replied to the official critic, 'One thing is sure, Monsieur, I do not teach these young people according to manual [Manuel].' The composition attacked bore the signature 'Marcel Proust.'" (Gabriel Astruc, *Les Pavillons des fantômes*. Paris, 1929.)

2, p.9 *Cucheval:* "In October, 1887, Marcel Proust and I both started our courses in Rhetoric. . . . Of our two professors of literature, MM. Cucheval and Gaucher, the former was incapable of understanding him, the latter fathomed him at once. I can remember some of Marcel's dissertations, rich in impressions and figures of speech, already 'Proustian,' with their incident-laden sentences and the parentheses that exasperated M. Cucheval and interested M. Gaucher so much. I can still see and hear Marcel reading aloud his themes while the excellent, the charming M. Gaucher would comment, praise, criticize, and suddenly burst into roars of laughter at the audacity of the style, which really enchanted him. The discovery among his students of a born writer was one of the joys of his last days." (Pierre Lavallée, *Correspondance générale de Marcel Proust* IV. Paris, 1933.)

2, p.11 *D—— H——:* Halévy, Daniel (1873–), son of Ludovic Halévy, author of biographies of Nietzsche, Michelet, and Charles Péguy with whom he was coeditor of *Les Cahiers de la quinzaine*.

2, p.11 *Bizet:* Bizet, Jacques (1873–1922), son of Georges Bizet and Madame Emile Straus.

2, p.12 *Desjardins:* Paul Desjardins (1859–1940) was the teacher and critic who first introduced Proust to the works of Ruskin, George Eliot, Pater, and other English writers in translation. A regular contributor to the *Revue bleue* at this time, his publications there between January and June, 1888, included some rather negligible short stories, a long eulogistic article on Sully Prudhomme, an essay on the posthumous works of Victor Hugo and *Notes and Impressions on the Reception of M. Gérard into the Académie Française*. What he was "trying to accomplish" was summarized in an article by Anatole France. "According to M. Paul Desjardins," France wrote, "style is evil. And yet M. Paul Desjardins has style, which only shows how true it is that the human soul is an abyss of contradictions. In his present state of mind one must not ask him his opinion on such frivolous and profane subjects as literature. He does not criticize. He anathematizes without hatred. Pale and melancholy, he goes his way, sowing tender maledictions."

Legrandin quotes a poem by Paul Desjardins, *Swann's Way* I, pp. 162–3.

4, p.16 *Ohnet:* Ohnet, Georges (1848–1918), author of countless banal novels, far more popular with the public than the works of Zola and Daudet. His work was described by Anatole France as bearing the same relation to literature as the wax dummies used by hairdressers bear to sculpture. His *Le Maître des forges* and *Serge Panine* were favorites of Odette de Crécy. See *Swann's Way* II, p. 55.

5, p.17 *Closmenil:* See Letter 232.

complicated affair: The partner in the alleged affair was a pretty Viennese girl whom Proust had met in a dance hall.

6, p.20 *fencing:* Proust was at this time doing his military service as a volunteer in the 76th Infantry at Orléans.

6, p.21 *Cazalis:* Cazalis, Dr. Henri (1840–1909), a physician at Aix-les-Bains, who, under the pseudonym Jean Lahor, was one of the Parnassian poets. Henry James mentions, as a "small subject" for a story, "the situation of Cazalis and Jean Lahor: the *médecin de ville d'eau* with his great *talent de poète*, changing his name to a 'pen-name'—at his worldly wife's behest, to write poetry . . . and then when the poetry brings him honour, some money, etc., having to change back again . . ." (Henry James, *The Notebooks of Henry James*, ed. F. O. Matthiessen and K. B. Murdock. New York, 1947.)

10, p.26 *Le Banquet:* This little review was conceived in Madame Straus's salon in 1892. Founded by Fernand Gregh, Robert Dreyfus, Jacques Bizet, Daniel Halévy, Henri Rabaud, and Robert de Flers, it ran for eight numbers and contained most of the writings Proust later collected in *Les Plaisirs et les Jours*. It also published some of the earliest works of Henri Barbusse, Gaston de Caillavet, and Léon Blum.

11, p.30 *Saxe:* Mme Hayman collected *Saxe* china figures and nicknamed Proust "*mon petit Saxe psychologique.*"

13, p.32 *Aubert:* Edgar Aubert was a young Swiss friend of M. de Billy's to whom he had introduced Proust the previous year in Paris.

14, p.35 *Cards:* The word *cartes* in French means both maps and cards.

15, p.36 *Madame Henri Baignères:* "Mme Baignères was often 'at home.' In her salon I saw . . . José-Maria Heredia, sonorous and vibrant; . . . the two Ganderax brothers, Louis and Etienne . . . ; Henri de Régnier, gaunt, melancholy, with one eye that of a dreamer and the other, behind its monocle, that of a penetrating psychologist; Jacques Blanche, always unpredictable, often grumbling, sometimes charming, always intelligent. Pierre Louÿs appeared there one season. I saw André Gide there, wearing a beard at that time, and looking like a thundercloud." (Fernand Gregh, *L'Age d'or*. Paris, 1947.)

15, p.37 *Cour des Comptes:* A government accounting agency, similar to a branch of the Treasury.

16, p.38 *collection of little pieces: Les Plaisirs et les Jours* was not published until 1896.

16, p.38 *Madame Madeleine Lemaire:* Madame Lemaire was doubly famous as painter and hostess whose Tuesdays in May were so crowded that latecomers frequently listened to the music or the recitations from the lilac-hedged garden outside. The list of her guests included everyone from the Prince of Wales and the Empress of Germany to the musicians Massenet, Reynaldo Hahn,

Saint-Saëns, and Harold Bauer, who played and sang. Réjane, Coquelin, and Julie Bartet on one occasion acted out an impromptu scene against a background of Mme Lemaire's paintings of roses. Anatole France wrote of Mme Lemaire's "divine hand that sprinkled roses with their own dew." And Dumas, one of her admirers, remarked that she had created more roses than anyone except God. After Mme Lemaire's death, when her daughter was asked which of her mother's friends had also been her lovers, Mlle Suzette replied, "The only one I was sure of was Dumas. . . . She always called him 'Monsieur.'"

See Marcel Proust, *Chroniques*, Paris, 1927. "La Cour aux lilas et l'atelier des roses: Le salon de Mme Madeleine Lemaire," which also appeared in the *Figaro* May 11, 1903.

18, p.43 *Gaulois:* Proust was at this time writing society notes for the newspaper *Le Gaulois*.

18, p.43 *Yturri:* Yturri, Gabriel d', Montesquiou's secretary and majordomo, according to Proust an "Eckermann," according to Léon Daudet "a Tallemant des Réaux with a Spanish accent." Of rather hazy South American origin, he was thought by some to have encountered Montesquiou while a clerk in the Louvre department store, though it was also said that the first meeting occurred at an exhibition of Whistler's paintings.

18, p.44 *Delafosse:* Léon Delafosse was a pianist, who, it has been suggested, served in part as the model for Morel.

18, p.44 *Madame Potocka:* See Marcel Proust, *Chroniques*, Paris,

1927, "Le Salon de la Comtesse Potocka," which also appeared in the *Figaro*, May 13, 1904.

18, p.44 *Mlle Bartet:* Julie Bartet, pseud. of Jeanne Julia Régnault (1854–1941), played chiefly tragic roles at the Comédie Française between 1879 and 1919. "Definition of Bartet's art: an admirable pearl—but imitation." (*Les Nouvelles Littéraires*, July 21, 1928, *Les Carnets intimes de Robert de Montesquiou*.)

20, p.46 *Reveillon:* Mme Lemaire's château near Dieppe.

21, p.47 *Madame Arman:* Madame Arman de Caillavet (1847–1910), usually known as Mme Arman, was the mother of Proust's friend, Gaston de Caillavet, and the Egeria of Anatole France. An intelligent, dominating woman, with a gift for literary criticism, she centered around Anatole France a salon which was one of the first that Proust attended and one of the most influential in Paris.

23, p.49 *Louis Weil:* Louis Weil was the great-uncle at whose house in Auteuil Proust was born and where the Proust family spent many spring and summer holidays. "In his talks with his uncle," M. de Billy writes, "he learned the details of the structure of Jewish society. There he learned of the existence of Charles Haas whom he had in mind when he created the character of Swann."

26, p.52 *my book: Les Plaisirs et les Jours* was published in 1896. This collection of sketches and stories, most of which had been published in *Le Banquet*, appeared in a large deluxe edition with a preface by Anatole France and illustrations and decorations by Madeleine Lemaire. It included facsimiles of Reynaldo Hahn's scores for Proust's portraits in verse of the painters Cuyp, Paul Potter, Van Dyck, and Watteau, and the composers Chopin, Gluck, Schumann, and Mozart. The book went unnoticed in the literary world, and in society it was regarded as the rather amusing work of a dilettante. Proust, in his own preface to the book, described it as "the empty froth of a troubled life which is now growing calm." But immediately after Proust's death, André Gide wrote, "The talent in this exquisite book seems to me so striking that I am astonished we were not dazzled by it at first."

The book which Proust speaks of having "started" at this time was, according to his brother, an early version of *Swann*. The few published fragments from Proust's early notebooks provide evidence of the truth of this statement.

28, p.54 *Jews:* The Dreyfus Affair was, at this time, at its controversial height. Captain Alfred Dreyfus (1859–1935), the only Jew on the general staff of the French army, had, in 1894, on the evidence of forged documents, been convicted of treason and sentenced to life imprisonment on Devil's Island. The untiring efforts of persons believing in his innocence resulted in his retrial at Rennes in 1899.

Among these persons was Marcel Proust who, although prevented by ill-health from official membership on Dreyfusard committees, was nevertheless most active in gathering and reporting information and also in obtaining signatures for a number of petitions in behalf of Dreyfus and Picquart. The only political event in which Proust ever participated, its importance in his life and work has been almost entirely ignored.

The disillusionment he suffered in observing the violent and prejudiced behavior of members of the social world during the Dreyfus Affair served as a turning point in Proust's attitude towards society. He subsequently used the Affair as the motif or touchstone to the social life and philosophy of most of the characters in *Remembrance of Things Past*, where it is mentioned well over a hundred times. Just as the "*madeleine*" dipped in the tea is the motif of unconscious memory, as the "little phrase" in the Vinteuil sonata (and later in the septet) is the love motif and the clue to Marcel's final understanding of the creative process in art, so the Dreyfus Affair is not only a character-motif, but the gauge applied in measuring and analyzing the social changes occasioned by the other great public event of Proust's lifetime, the First World War.

29, p.55 *Labori:* Labori, Fernand Gustave Gaston (1870–1917), Picquart's and later Dreyfus's lawyer. Also the lawyer who defended Emile Zola in the trial that followed the publication of *J'accuse* in January 1898.

29, p.55 *Picquart:* Georges Picquart (1854–1914), Colonel, later General, former chief of the French Army

Intelligence, who after having discovered that false evidence had been used to convict Captain Alfred Dreyfus, was himself demoted and imprisoned in July, 1898.

29, p.55 *Haussonville:* Haussonville, Gabriel Othenin, Comte d' (1843–1924), grandson of Madame de Staël, great-grandson of Necker, member of the Academy, distinguished essayist and historian, a brilliant and handsome ornament of society, described by Proust as the most sincere and courageous liberal among the conservatives.

29, p.55 *Dufeuille:* Eugène Dufeuille (1855–1912) resigned his position as Chief of Cabinet of the Royalist Pretender, the Duc d'Orléans, because of his belief in the innocence of Dreyfus.

29, p.55 *Ganderax:* Ganderax, Louis (1855–193?), lifelong friend and neighbor of Mme Straus, editor of the *Revue de Paris* from 1894 to 1912. See Letter 111.

29, p.55 *Pozzi:* Pozzi, Samuel Jean (1846–1918), distinguished French surgeon and book collector, extremely popular in the world of society.

29, p.56 *Paty de Clam:* Paty de Clam, Armand Auguste Charles Ferdinand Marie Mercier, Marquis du (1853–1916), Lieutenant Colonel in the French army, was a member of the elaborate plot to establish Dreyfus's guilt.

31, p.61 *Constantin:* Prince Constantin Brancovan was the brother of Comtesse Anna de Noailles, later editor of the magazine *Renaissance Latine*. See Letter 83.

31, p.61 *Noailles:* Noailles, Anna, Comtesse de. See Letter 50.

31, p.61 *Polignac:* Polignac, Edmond de, Prince (1822–1901), a man of great charm and intelligence, a talented musician whom Proust greatly admired and some of whose traits he borrowed for the character of Saint-Loup. In 1919 Proust wished to dedicate *Within a Budding Grove* to the memory of the Prince de Polignac in the following words: "To the cherished and venerated memory of Prince Edmond de Polignac. Homage from one to whom he showed so much kindness and who still, in harvesting his memories, admires the singularity of his art and of a delightful spirit."

The widow of the Prince, born Winnaretta Singer of New York, declined the dedication. See Marcel Proust, *Chroniques*. Paris, 1927. "Le Salon de la Princesse Edmond de Polignac. Musique d'aujourd'hui. Echos d'autrefois." Also published in the *Figaro*, Sept. 6, 1903.

31, p.62 *Brancovan:* The Princesse Brancovan was the mother of the Comtesse de Noailles and the Princesse de Caraman-Chimay, and a very talented musician.

31, p.62 *Haussonville:* See Marcel Proust, *Chroniques*. Paris, 1927. "Le Salon de la Comtesse d'Haussonville." Also published in the *Figaro*, Jan. 4, 1904.

31, p.63 *Robert:* Proust, Robert (1873–1935), brother of Marcel, and a distinguished surgeon.

31, p.63 *Millerand:* Etienne Alexandre Millerand (1859–1943) was a member of the Waldeck-Rousseau cabinet at this time and later became Minister of War, 1914–15, and President of the Republic, 1920–1924.

31, p.63 *Jaurès:* Jaurès, Jean, eminent Socialist leader, assassinated by a nationalist fanatic July 31, 1914.

32, p.63 *Roget:* General Gauderique Roget (–1917) was the officer to whom Colonel Henry, guilty of forging some of the documents used to convict Dreyfus, confessed.

32, p.64 *Meyer:* Meyer, Arthur (1844–1924), editor of the newspaper *Le Gaulois,* a snob, social climber, and bibliophile, a Jew converted to Catholicism and a pet aversion of Proust's.

33, p.65 *Barrès:* Auguste Maurice Barrès (1862–1923), a passionate nationalist, author of many novels, Boulangist member of the Chamber of Deputies from 1889–1893, was a fanatical anti-Dreyfusard. He was also for many years the lover of the Comtesse de Noailles.

33, p.65 *Adam:* Adam, Paul (1862–1920), novelist and one of the earliest defenders of Symbolism. In 1895 he published *Le mystère des foules*, a study in Boulangism.

33, p.65 *League of the Rights of Man:* An organization founded in 1898 during the Zola trial to protect the principles of '89 and to serve as a kind of general staff for the Revisionists, the group who were fighting for the retrial of Dreyfus.

33, p.66 *Bertillon:* Bertillon, Alphonse (1853–1914), inventor of criminal anthropometry and graphologist, who insisted that Dreyfus had written the forged letter for which he was falsely convicted.

34, p.67 *Comte d'Eu:* Eu, Louis Philippe Marie Ferdinand Gaston, Prince d'Orléans, Comte d' (1842–1922), son of the Duc de Nemours; he grew up in exile in Brazil, married Isabel, daughter of Emperor Pedro II, became a Marshal in the Brazilian army, and was permitted to return to France in 1889.

34, p.67 *Mercier:* General Auguste Mercier (1833–1921), Minister of War from 1893 to 1895, appeared as witness against Dreyfus in the trial at Rennes.

35, p.68 *Cuvier:* Cuvier, Georges (1769–1832), French naturalist and anatomist.

35, p.68 *Joubert:* Joubert, Joseph (1754–1824), French moralist and writer, author of *Les Pensées*, one of Proust's favorite books.

36, p.70 *Libre Parole:* Nationalist, anti-Semitic, anti-Dreyfusard newspaper, founded and edited by Edouard Drumont, author of the book, *La France Juive*, an attack on the Jews, parts of which appear to have been borrowed by Hitler for *Mein Kampf*.

36, p.70 *Gohier:* Degoulet, Urbain, called Gohier (1862–?), a liberal journalist associated with Clemenceau on *l'Aurore* and *la Raison*.

36, p.70 *Gérault-Richard:* Gérault-Richard, Alfred Léon (1860–1911), Socialist member of the Chamber of Deputies, editor-in-chief of *La Petite République*.

36, p.70 *Reinach:* Reinach, Joseph (1860–1928), journalist and politician, at one time secretary to Gambetta, member of the Chamber of Deputies, one of the earliest and most active Dreyfusards and historian of the Affair.

37, p.71 *Ruskin:* Proust became interested in Ruskin's ideas while a student and, after reading *Ruskin et la religion de la beauté* by Robert de la Sizeranne in 1897, he immersed himself in Ruskin's works. His French versions of *The Bible of Amiens* and *Sesame and Lilies* are less distinguished for their accuracy as translations than for the brilliance of Proust's notes and prefaces. For it is in the preface to *The Bible of Amiens* that Proust's admiration and sympathy for Ruskin are revealed rather than in *Remembrance of Things Past* where the "preestablished harmony" between the two men is hardly indicated in the unacknowledged quotations from *Modern Painters* and *Stones of Venice* cited in *Swann's Way*. Ruskin's name appears once in *Within a Budding Grove* and once in *The Past Recaptured*, both times in invidious contexts.

The work mentioned in this letter is "Pèlerinages Ruskiniens," which appeared in the *Figaro*, Feb. 13, 1900 and was later used in the preface to *La Bible d'Amiens*.

40, p.79 *symphony in yellow:* A poem by Miss Nordlinger which she had sent to Proust.

40, p.80 *Julien Edouard:* Custodian of the cathedral at Rouen who had guided Ruskin.

41, p.82 *Darlu:* Darlu, Marie Julien Alphonse (1849–1921), the professor of philosophy in whose class at Condorcet in 1889 Proust received a prize and of whom he wrote in *Les Plaisirs et Les Jours*, "M. Darlu, the great philosopher whose inspired lectures, more likely to endure than the written word, awakened in me, as in so many others, the process of thinking."

42, p.83 *"This do and thou shalt live, etc.":* See John Ruskin, *The Bible of Amiens*, Chap. IV, ¶s 54, 55–57.

43, p.84 *Humières:* Humières, Robert Marie Aymeric Eugène, Vicomte d' (1868–1915), French poet and translator of the works of Rudyard Kipling and Sir J. M. Barrie. In the foreword to Proust's translation to Ruskin's *The Bible of Amiens* he wrote of M. d'Humières, "When I was held up by a difficult linguistic construction, I used to go to consult the marvelous translator of Kipling and he would immediately resolve the difficulty with his astonishing understanding of English texts, which he grasps with equal intuition and learning. Often, and always effortlessly, he was thus helpful to me."

44, p.84 *Bernard:* Bernard, Paul called Tristan (1866–1947), novelist and writer of farces and comedies, among them *L'Anglais tel qu'on le parle*.

44, p.85 *Albu:* Albuféra, Louis Joseph Suchet, Duc d' (1877–). In his *Chronique*, "Le Salon de la Princesse Edmond de Polignac," first published in the *Figaro*, Sept. 6, 1903, Proust wrote, ". . . the Marquis d'Albuféra, whom one will soon no longer be able to call a dancer, for he is preparing a volume of *Souvenirs* of his voyage to Tunisia, a thrilling *resumé* of the unpublished *Memoirs* of a celebrated Marshal of the first Empire, memoirs which M. Thiers alone knew and which he did not fail to make use of in writing *Le Consulat et l'Empire*."

In 1907, in a letter to Montesquiou, Proust wrote

of the Duc (then Marquis) d'Albuféra, "Living outside of all literary and artistic culture, he is nonetheless a very fruitful barbarian in his fashion, which is not at all common, since he yields a harvest of the pure essence of goodness, very subtle, too, sincere and the elixir of friendly wisdom. But he reads nothing, and I used every pretext in the world for two years to make him read two lines of *The Bible d'Amiens* without any success."

A friend of both Proust's and M. d'Albuféra's remembers the latter's remarking to him, soon after he and Proust became friends, "I understand why I like Marcel, but I can't see why he likes me."

44, p.85 *Guiche:* Gramont, Armand Agénor Auguste Antoine, Duc de, formerly Duc de Guiche, founder and president of *l'Institut d'Optique théorique*, member of the Academy of Sciences, secretary of the Scientific Commission of the Aéro-Club of France, and author of *The Aviator's Elementary Handbook*. Brother of the Duchesse de Clermont-Tonnerre and a longtime friend of Proust's, the Duc was most helpful to him in finding a new apartment in 1919 when, to his great distress, he was forced to leave the boulevard Haussmann. In acknowledgment of his gratitude Proust included the following characterization of the Duc de Guiche in the *pastiche* of Saint-Simon: ". . . the Frenchman who is most knowledgeable in chemistry as in all sciences, so that he has been recognized by the academies and the astronomers, and whose character, birth, and stainless life also guarantee the integrity of his word." (See *Pastiches et Mélanges*, p. 59 ff.)

The Duc de Guiche married Elaine de Greffülhe, daughter of the Comtesse de Greffülhe, cousin and close friend of Montesquiou, November 14, 1904.

44, p.86 *Tombeau:* This word, used to designate the greatest secrecy, was part of the private vocabulary of Proust, Fénelon, and the Bibesco brothers.

45, p.87 *Gallé:* Gallé, Emile (1846–1904), an artist in manufacturing glass and in furniture designing, the Tiffany of France.

46, p.89 *Combes* (in introductory note): Justin Louis Emile Combes (1835–1921) was Premier of France from 1902 to 1905. A provincial doctor who had chosen the profession of medicine after having failed to be ordained for the priesthood, a fanatical anti-Catholic, he used all his power to carry out the anticlerical law which, while giving complete freedom of association, authorized only five religious orders. The passing of the law caused the closing of many schools and some rioting, especially in Brittany.

46, p.90 *Guyot:* Guyot, Yves (1843–1928), an anti-Socialist economist and politician. Author in 1895 of *L'Innocent et le traitre: Dreyfus et Esterhazy*.

46, p.91 *Cochin:* Cochin, Denys (1851–1922), conservative politician and writer, member of the Chamber of Deputies from 1893.

46, p.91 *Illiers:* Illiers, Eure-et-Loir, village near Chartres, birthplace of Dr. Adrien Proust and the Combray of *Remembrance of Things Past*.

46, p. 91 *Ferry laws:* The Ferry laws, sponsored by Jules Ferry, then Minister of Education, were passed in 1881 and 1882. They provided for free, compulsory primary education. All state schools were to be "secular and neutral," and the state was to train all primary school teachers. Normal schools were to be established to train secondary school teachers, and reforms were to be carried out in technical and higher education.

46, p. 91 *church steeple:* See *Swann's Way* I, p. 77 ff.; *The Past Recaptured*, p. 1.

46, p. 91 *Latin:* See *Swann's Way* I, p. 140 ff.

46, p. 91 *old curé:* See *The Captive*, p. 10.

46, p. 92 *church spire:* See *Swann's Way* I, p. 63, p. 82.

46, p. 92 *Humbert:* Humbert, Alphonse Jean Joseph (1844– ?), French politician and journalist, sentenced to hard labor for life and transported to New Caledonia for militant, radical activity during the Commune. Returned to France in 1879. Member of Chamber of Deputies from 1893. Militarist, nationalist, anti-Dreyfusard.

46, p. 92 *Cavaignac:* Cavaignac, Jacques Marie Eugène Godefroy (1853–1905), Minister of War in 1898. "Godefroy Cavaignac was by birth, by education, by career the model Republican. . . . He had been, as a schoolboy under the Empire, a conspicuous Republican; and under the Republic he was a kind of Cato. It was an anti-Dreyfusard interpellation that gave him the opportunity to declare his conviction of the guilt of Dreyfus . . ." (D. W. Brogan. *France under the Republic* [1870–1939]. New York. n.d.)

46, p.93 *Boutroux:* Boutroux, Emile (1845–1921), professor of philosophy at the Sorbonne. Author of *De la contingence des lois de la nature*.

46, p.93 *Lavisse:* Lavisse, Ernest (1842–1922), professor of modern history at the Sorbonne, tutor to the Prince Imperial, and an habitué of the salon of the Princesse Mathilde Bonaparte.

46, p.93 *Stanislas:* Le Lycée Stanislas, the aristocratic, Royalist school at which most of the young noblemen of Proust's acquaintance had been educated.

46, p.94 *Méline:* Méline, Jules (1838–1925), President of the Council and Minister of Agriculture from 1896–1898, a Conservative anti-Dreyfusard. "My father, a friend of M. Méline, was convinced that Dreyfus was guilty. He had flatly refused to listen to some of his colleagues who had asked him to sign a petition demanding a fresh trial. He never spoke to me for a week, after learning that I had chosen to take a different line. His opinions were well known. He came near to being looked upon as a Nationalist." *The Guermantes Way* I, p. 203.

46, p.94 *L'Aurore:* The liberal, Dreyfusard newspaper, edited by Clemenceau, in which Zola's "J'accuse" had been published in January, 1898.

46, p.95 *General André:* André, Louis Joseph Nicolas (1838–1913), Minister of War from 1901 to 1905.

46, p.96 *Aynard:* Aynard, Edouard (1837–1913), politician, businessman, and banker. A reactionary in politics, opposed to lay teaching, an art collector who endowed a museum in Lyons, and a *membre libre* of the Académie des Beaux-Arts.

48, p.99 *Viollet-le-Duc:* Viollet-le-Duc, Eugène Emmanuel (1814–1879), French architect noted for his restorations of the Cathedral of Notre Dame in Paris, of Carcassonne, of Vézelay, and many other monuments.

50, p.103 *Sabine:* The heroine of Mme de Noailles's novel, *La Nouvelle espérance*.

50, p.104 *Vieux papiers, Vieilles maisons, Batz de Lenôtre:* G. Lenôtre, *Paris revolutionnaire—Vieilles maisons, vieux papiers*. Paris, 1900–1930, 6 series.

G. Lenôtre, *Un conspirateur royaliste pendant la Terreur, le Baron de Batz*. Paris, 1896.

51, p.104 *Rouvier:* Pierre Maurice Rouvier (1842–1911) was Premier in 1887 and again in 1905 and 1906. At this time he was Minister of Finance in the Combes cabinet.

51, p.105 *Calmette:* Calmette, Gaston (1852–1914), editor of the *Figaro*, to whom *Swann's Way* was dedicated in 1913 "as a token of profound and affectionate gratitude." He was shot and killed by Mme Caillaux in 1914.

54, p.111 *nonaromatic balsam:* Miss Nordlinger had sent Proust a small packet of balsam seeds.

57, p.113 *hidden flowers:* The compressed Japanese paper flowers that Miss Nordlinger sent Proust reappeared in *Swann's Way* I, p. 62.

58, p.115 *picture of my father:* Miss Nordlinger made the bronze plaque that marks the grave of Dr. Proust in the Père-Lachaise cemetery.

59, p.118 *America:* The art dealer, Bing, had asked Miss Nordlinger to go to the United States to organize an exhibition of Japanese prints.

59, p.118 *Hermant:* Hermant, Abel (1862–), author of many popular social and psychological novels, playwright and journalist. He became Vichy Minister of Education and in 1948 was in prison.

61, p.120 *Une amitié amoureuse* (introductory note): See Louisa de Mornand, "Mon amitié avec Marcel Proust," *Candide*, Nov. 1, 1928.

62, p.123 *Whistlerian magician:* Miss Nordlinger had gone to Detroit to work in the art collection of Charles Freer.

62, p.124 *Daudet:* Daudet, Lucien (1878–1946), younger son of Alphonse Daudet. See letters to him starting in 1913.

62, p.124 *Boldini:* Boldini, Giovanni (1845–1931), Italian-born painter of fashionable portraits who resided in France after 1872.

63, p.125 *Mâle:* Mâle, Emile (1862–), art historian, noted for his works on religious iconography. The book here mentioned was probably *L'Art religieux du XIII siècle en France*.

64, p.129 *Lorrain:* Duval, Paul, pseud. Jean Lorrain (1855–1906), French writer and journalist with whom Proust fought a duel on February 5, 1897. Lorrain, in a malicious review in his column, "Pall-Mall Semaine," in *Le Journal*, February 3, 1897, implied that Anatole France had written the preface to *Les Plaisirs et les Jours* only because of the insistence of his mistress, Mme Arman de Caillavet, thereby reinforcing the current rumor that Mme de Caillavet, and not France, had actually written the preface.

64, p.130 *catoblépas:* "An animal, so completely stupid that he once ate his own paws." Paul Bourget, quoting Flaubert, in Bourget's story, "Gladys Harvey."

65, p.130 *piece of my work:* "Sur la lecture," preface to the translation of *Sesame and Lilies*.

65, p.132 *Mme Desbordes-Valmore:* Desbordes-Valmore, Marceline Felicité Josèphe (1785–1859), an actress who became a poet. Greatly admired by many writers of her day, among them Balzac, Michelet, and Sainte-Beuve, who wrote her biography, she was an idol of Robert de Montesquiou's, who not only arranged for a statue to be erected in her memory at Douai, her birthplace, but who actually owned her ashes.

65, p.132 *Latouche:* Thabaud, Hyacinthe Joseph Alexandre, pseud. Henri Latouche (1785–1851), a writer who was Mme Desbordes-Valmore's first lover and by whom she had a child who died.

66, p.134 *Psst:* A humorous magazine in which Forain published many of his anti-Semitic drawings.

66, p.134 *Forain:* Forain, Jean-Louis (1852–1931), French painter and caricaturist. "Let us admit at once our admiration for the artist so we can add without delay the full horror with which the man inspires us." (*Les Nouvelles littéraires*, July 21, 1928, "Les Carnets intimes de Robert de Montesquiou.") This remark by Maurice Barrès about Forain is quoted in Montesquiou's notebooks.

67, p.137 *muscadin:* A *muscadin* was one of the smart young men about town who, after the fall of Robespierre, beat up Jacobin sympathizers.

68, p.140 *the great writer:* In a letter to M. Léon Bélugon, Proust wrote in 1906, "I was imprudent enough several months ago to say to M. Maurice Duplay . . . , the author of a very talented novel, *Le Tremplin*—apropos of a book on the lower classes of Paris about which he was talking to me—that Stendhal had one day expressed his sympathy for the thousands of poor people who existed (at Civita-Vecchia, I believe); 'It is the only social level in the city that I would willingly frequent,' is more or less what he said, 'and unfortunately the discretion demanded by my diplomatic position prevents it.' And it turns out that this sentence from I don't know where (perhaps from a very bad book of M. Rod's on Stendhal) and which is perhaps a biographer's sentence and not from Stendhal himself, has germinated in M. Duplay's mind. And recently . . . he told me that it has developed into a splendid epigraph for his book, but that he must have the exact text, context, etc. I assured him that I was absolutely ignorant of where it can be found and that I would resort to your infallible knowledge." (*Les Cahiers Marcel Proust* I, Paris, 1927, p. 315.)

68, p.141 *Daudet:* Daudet, Léon (1868–1942), elder son of Alphonse Daudet, writer, journalist, propagandist, and politician, anti-Dreyfusard and anti-Semite, but an admirer and friend of Proust's. With Charles Maurras, he was founder and editor of the Royalist newspaper, *L'Action française*.

69, p.142 *Ruskin's words: Stones of Venice*, Chap. IV, XLIX. "I believe the man who designed and the men who delighted in that archivolt to have been wise, happy, and holy."

69, p.143 *Blanche:* Blanche, Jacques-Emile (1861–1942), French portrait painter, art critic and author of memoirs. The essay on Whistler appeared in the *Renaissance latine* for March, 1905 and was included in *Propos de Peintre, première série: De David à Degas*, Paris, 1919.

69, p.144 *note:* The text of the note reads, "In giving the essential portions, or actually almost the whole first lecture, I wish to thank publicly Mlle Marie Nordlinger, the eminent English sculptor, who more than once forsook a masterpiece she had started . . . and came to see me to clarify some obscure meaning, to establish some doubtful interpretation. Since her modesty has made her refuse the title of collaborator in this translation, the least I can do is to place it under her gracious invocation."

69, p.145 *Besnard:* Besnard, Paul Albert (1849–1934), French painter and member of the Academy.

69, p.145 *Carrière:* Carrière, Eugène (1849–1906), French painter and lithographer.

73, p.150 *Lemaitre's Contes: La Vieillesse d'Hélène* by Jules Lemaitre.

73, p.151 *Bréal:* Bréal, Michel (1832–1915), French philologist, author of numerous works on the psychological aspects of comparative mythology and grammar. The article here mentioned was called "L'Iliade d'Homère: ses origines."

73, p.151 *Courcelles and Alfred de Vigny:* Proust lived at 45, rue de Courcelles at this time and Hahn at 9, rue Alfred de Vigny.

77, p.157 *She died:* Mme Adrien Proust died September 23, 1905.

80, p.161 *Dubois:* Dr. Dubois was a renowned Swiss nerve specialist whose works Proust had been reading at this time. Since it is generally agreed by the medical profession that asthma is a symptom and not a disease, since the present conception of allergy was only defined by von Pirquet in 1906, and since the concept of psychosomatic illness has only been fully developed in recent years, the following footnote from Proust's translation of *Sesame and Lilies*, published in 1906, indicates how much time and thought he was giving to the problem of his illness.

". . . we have contemporary medicine appearing to be on the point of telling us also . . . that we are 'born of the Spirit' and that it continues to control our respiration (see Brugelmann's works on asthma), our digestion (see Dubois of Berne's *The Psychoneuroses* and his other works), the co-ordination of our movements (see *Isolation and Psychotherapy* by Drs. Camus and Pagnies, preface by Professor Déjerine). . . . Doctors said not long ago (and the tardy still repeat it) that a pessimist is a man with a bad stomach. Today

Dr. Dubois says in print unmistakably that a man who has a bad stomach is a pessimist. And it is no longer his stomach that must be cured if his philosophy is to be changed, it is his philosophy that must be changed if his stomach is to be cured . . ." (John Ruskin, *Sésame et les Lys*, tr. by Marcel Proust. Paris, 1906, p. 106.)

A more subjective discussion of the therapy of psychoneurotic illness may be found in the preface to *Sésame et les Lys*, reprinted in *Pastiches et Mélanges*, Paris, 1919, under the title "Journées de Lecture," pp. 250–1.

85, p.168 *Venice:* Proust visited Venice in May, 1900 when he and his mother joined Reynaldo Hahn, his mother, and Marie Nordlinger there.

88, p.173 *Dreyfus:* The verdict of Dreyfus's retrial at Rennes in September, 1899 had again been "guilty," but with extenuating circumstances. The life sentence was reduced to ten years, but Dreyfus was pardoned by President Loubet immediately after. For the next six years efforts were made to secure his reinstatement in the army.

89, p.175 *Beaunier:* Beaunier, André (1869–1925), novelist and critic for the *Revue des deux mondes* and the *Figaro*. In an *Instantané*, or brief pen portrait, of Proust, which appeared in the *Figaro* June 5, 1906, he wrote ". . . Marcel Proust has a liking for perfection; this does not make for a comfortable life."

90, p.175 *Beaunier's article:* This article appeared in the *Figaro*, June 14, 1906. Of Proust's work Beaunier wrote, "It is the model of a well-done translation, a masterpiece of intelligent flexibility, a marvelous success."

91, p.179 *M. de Clermont-Tonnerre:* This episode from Saint-Simon is quoted by Sainte-Beuve in *Causeries de Lundi*, Vol. XI.

93, p.181 *Dreyfus affair:* In an elaborate ceremony on July 13, 1906, Dreyfus was reinstated in the army with the rank of Major and given the cross of the Legion of Honor. Picquart was made a General and shortly afterwards was appointed Minister of War.

The "humorous" remark by Mme Straus was borrowed for the Duchesse de Guermantes in *The Guermantes Way* I, p. 328. "'In any case, if this man Dreyfus is innocent,' the Duchess broke in, 'he hasn't done much to prove it. What idiotic, raving letters he writes from that island. I don't know whether M. Esterhazy is any better, but he does show some skill in his choice of words, a different tone altogether. That can't be very pleasant for the supporters of M. Dreyfus. What a pity for them there's no way of changing innocents.'"

99, p.193 *Vogüé:* Vogüé, Eugène Melchior, Vicomte de (1848–1910), writer and diplomat, on the staff of the *Revue des deux mondes* and the *Journal des débats*.

99, p.194 *Briand's law:* As a result of Pope Pius X's refusal, in 1904, to receive President Loubet, and the subsequent immediate withdrawal of the French ambassador to the Vatican, Aristide Briand, as Minister of Public Worship, was able in 1905 to carry through the Separation Law which removed from all religious bodies any official recognition by the state. Inventories of all church property were to be made, an order which so violated the feelings of devout Catholics that Clemenceau in 1906 countermanded it. But the Pope ordered all Catholics to regard the Separation Law as "null and void," thus obliging many religious orders to leave France, and the Church to forfeit its property.

102, p.199 *article:* "Sentiments filiaux d'un parricide" which appeared on the front page of the *Figaro*, February 1, 1907 and was later included in *Pastiches et Mélanges*. A psychological account and analysis of the murder of his mother and subsequent suicide, by an acquaintance of Proust's, it contains the following lines: "'What have you done to me! What have you done to me!' If we should think about it, there is, perhaps, no truly loving mother who might not, on the last day of her life and often long before, reproach her son in these words. Actually we age and kill all those who love us by the anxiety we cause them, by the quality, in itself disturbing, of the affection we inspire and by the state of alarm into which we are always putting them . . ."

103, p.200 *Fauré:* Fauré, Gabriel (1845–1924), French composer and friend of Proust's. See Letter 214.

103, p.200 *Béraud:* Béraud, Jean (1849?–1935), French painter, one of Proust's seconds in his duel with Jean Lorrain.

103, p.202 *Mme de Chevigné:* Comtesse Adhéaume de Chevigné, to whom Proust had been greatly attracted in his youth and of whom he wrote a sketch in *le Banquet*, portions of which he later used in describing the Duchesse de Guermantes.

104, p.204 *Rochefoucauld:* Rochefoucauld, Gabriel, Comte de La (1875–), writer and journalist, author of several novels, contributor of "Chroniques" to the *Figaro* and the *Gaulois*, and winner of an Academy prize for his studies of his ancestor, the author of the *Maxims*.

108, p.212 *Clermont-Tonnerre:* The Duchesse de Clermont-Tonnerre, under her maiden name, Elizabeth de Gramont, is the author of several volumes of memoirs, of *Robert de Montesquiou et Marcel Proust*, and of biographies of Barbey d'Aurevilly and of Marcel Proust.

109, p.213 *homosexuality trial:* Count von Moltke's libel suit against Maximilian Harden, editor of *Zukunft*, who had accused him, as well as Prince Philip zu Eulenberg, "the Kaiser's friend," of sexual perversion, began on October 23, 1907.

109, p.213 *Paléologue:* Maurice Paléologue (1859–1944), French diplomat and writer, was at this time Minister to Bulgaria.

110, p.214 *D—— 's speech:* In his speech, delivered on his entrance to the Academy on December 19, 1907, Maurice Donnay (1859–1945), the French dramatist, recounting the failure in an examination of his predecessor, the historian Albert Sorel, used the expression, ". . . *il lui poussa une colle*."

110, p.214 *Bourget:* Bourget, Paul (1852–1935), French novelist, dramatist, and essayist of great reputation and prestige at this time.

110, p.214 *Porto-Riche:* Porto-Riche, Georges de (1849–1930), popular French playwright.

111, p.215 *Ganderax:* Ganderax's name was deleted in the French edition of Proust's letters, as were the opening paragraph and the portion of the final paragraph beginning "Yes, this intelligent man . . . " to "Madame, what grim folly. . . ." M. Daniel Halévy, Mme Straus's "nephew," who was consulted about editing the original letter, has supplied the following explanation. "The deletions were made out of a very nice consideration for the memory of Louis Ganderax, then only recently dead. This nice consideration, even at the time, I regarded as misplaced, for the memory of Ganderax, dear to those who knew him, and I was very intimately among that number, was in no way injured by Marcel Proust's reflections. I should even say, on the contrary, that that memory could in no way be better honored than by these words.

"Louis Ganderax, a man of great wit and extreme cultivation, was the embodiment of what in the old days in France was called *l'honnête homme*. This very exacting integrity took the form in him of a scrupulousness, pushed, in his later years, to the limits of neurasthenia. As editor of the *Revue de Paris* he applied his scruples to correcting the proof of every number. These proof-sheets finally became prodigious examples of erudite and grammatical subtlety. He knew it, he apologized for it, and I remember having received from him proofs overloaded with observations, which he himself called his 'professional hyperaesthesia.' Things came to such a pass that in order to rid himself of his scruples he gave up the editorship of the *Revue de Paris*."

113, p.220 *Sem:* Goursat, Georges-Marie, pseud. Sem (1863–1934), French caricaturist, illustrator and writer.

115, p.222 *Maspéro:* Maspéro, Gaston (1846–1916), French Egyptologist, author of *Histoire des peuples de l'Orient*.

116, p.223 *Bergson:* Bergson, Henri (1859–1941), French philosopher, related to Proust by marriage. See Letter 121.

116, p.223 *Croiset:* Croiset, Marie Joseph Alfred (1845–1923), Hellenic scholar and Dean of the Faculty of Letters of the University of Paris.

116, p.224 *Abbé Vignot:* Vignot, Pierre (1858–1921), Professor at the Ecole Fénelon. A highly cultivated and devout man, he exercised great influence on his students. His lectures were published under the title, *La Vie pour les autres, la règle des moeurs*.

116, p.224 *Abbé Huvelin:* Huvelin, Henri (1838–1910), Vicar of the Church of Saint Augustin, church historian.

116, p.224 *Brunschvicg:* Brunschvicg, Léon (1869–1944), French philosopher, schoolmate of Proust's at the Lycée Condorcet.

116, p.224 *Régnier:* Régnier, Henri de (1864–1936), French symbolist poet and novelist.

116, p.224 *Boylesve:* René Boylesve (1867–1926), French psychological novelist who, years later, after having first found Proust's novel unreadable, became one of his great admirers.

116, p.224 *Jammes:* Francis Jammes (1868–1938), French idyllic poet and author of novels and memoirs, was greatly admired by Proust.

116, p.224 *Arenberg:* Arenberg, Auguste Louis Albéric, Prince and Duc d' (1837–1924), native-born French duke and mediatized German prince and duke, a man of great wealth and wide interests. President of Suez Canal Co., officer of The Orléans Railroad Co. and The National Agricultural Society. Deputy for Cher and owner of racing stables.

118, p.228 *Anet:* Schopfer, Jean, pseud. Claude Anet (1868–1931), popular French writer of novels and essays. Best known in 1908 for his *Notes sur l'amour* and *Les Roses d' Ispahan*.

118, p.228 *Marguerittes:* Margueritte, Paul (1860–1918), and Victor (1866–1942), French novelists, who collaborated between 1896 and 1908. Victor was one of the original members of the Goncourt Academy.

118, p.228 *Rosnys:* Boex, Joseph Henri Honoré (1856–1940), and Boex, Séraphin Justin François (1859–1948), pseuds. J. H. Rosny *ainé* and Rosny *le jeune*, Belgian-born French novelists, collaborators until 1909. Original members of the Goncourt Academy.

121, p.237 *La Bible d'Amiens:* On May 28, 1904, at the *Institut de sciences morales et politiques* Bergson read a brief critical estimate of *La Bible d'Amiens*, in which he said among other things that Marcel Proust translated Ruskin in "such lively and original language that a person reading the book has no sense of coping with a translation."

124, p.241 *Helleu:* Helleu, Paul (1859–1929), French painter, friend of Robert de Montesquiou, who published (1913) *Paul Helleu, Peintre et Graveur*, illustrated with reproductions of Helleu's work. According to Jacques-Emile Blanche, the description of the landscapes by Elstir which the narrator looks at before his first dinner at the Guermantes' (*The Guermantes Way* II, p. 152 ff.) were actually based on paintings by Helleu.

127, p.245 *Lister:* Lister, Sir Reginald (1865–1912), Minister Plenipotentiary to Tangier, 1908–1912.

128, p.246 *daughter:* Simone de Caillavet, now Mme André Maurois. Proust had been in love with Mme Gaston de Caillavet (née Jeanne Pouquet) at the time her husband was courting her.

130, p.248 *Monnier:* Monnier, Henri (1805–1877), French writer and caricaturist.

130, p.248 *d'Ache:* Porré, Emmanuel, pseud. Caran d'Ache (1858–1909), French caricaturist. Anti-Dreyfusard, associated with Forain during the Dreyfus Affair.

132, p.252 *article:* "Au seuil du printemps: Epines blanches, Epines roses." *Figaro*, Mar. 21, 1912.

132, p.254 *Les Plaisirs et les Jours:* This statement is a slip of memory. *Les Plaisirs et les Jours* was published four years before Ruskin's death. The essay mentioned here was included in *Pastiches et Mélanges* in 1909.

137, p.265 *Prévost:* Prévost, Marcel (1862–1914), popular French novelist and playwright, author of *Les Demi-Vierges* and *Les Don Juanes*. This confusion in names was not eliminated by Proust's achieving fame. For when the Comtesse de Noailles decided to publish Proust's letters to her she had great difficulty in finding them and finally discovered them filed under the name of Marcel Prévost.

138, p.266 *your red dress:* See *The Guermantes Way* II, p. 394.

139, p.270 *théâtrophone:* A device whereby subscribers could listen to theatrical performances and concerts at home by means of telephonic connection.

143, p.282 *Rostand:* Rostand, Maurice (1891–), son of Edmond Rostand, writer, lecturer and critic. Published laudatory article on Proust in *Comoedia*, December 26, 1912.

144, p.289 *Gautier:* Gautier, Théophile (1811–1872), French writer of novels, poetry, critical works and the travel book *Voyage en Espagne*.

146, p.292 *Valmont:* Dr. Widmer's sanitorium.

150, p.301 *second volume:* See *Within a Budding Grove* I, p. 9.

150, p.303 *François le Champi: François le Champi*, a novel by George Sand, published in 1850.

150, p.303 *article:* See *Figaro*, Nov. 23, 1913. Reprinted in Marcel Proust, *Lettres à Madame C.* Ed. Lucien Daudet. Paris, 1947.

150, p.304 *Hébrard:* Hébrard, François Marie Adrien (1833–1914), editor of the newspaper, *Le Temps*.

150, p.305 *Maurras:* Maurras, Charles (1868–), French poet and journalist, Royalist and founder of the *Action*

Française movement. Sentenced in 1945 to life imprisonment as ideologist of the Vichy government.

150, p.305 *miraculous cure:* Daudet had recently witnessed a miraculous cure at Lourdes.

151, p.305 *flowers:* See *Swann's Way* I, p. 192.

151, p.306 *Cocteau:* Cocteau, Jean (1891–), French novelist, critic, playwright, poet, motion picture writer and producer. Proust, who first met Cocteau in 1911, described him as "a most remarkably intelligent and talented young poet."

154, p.312 *sentence on p. 64:* This sentence Proust apparently cut out of the later edition.

155, p.313 *Copeau:* Copeau, Jacques (1879–), French critic and theatrical producer, founder of the *Théâtre du Vieux-Colombier* in 1913 and, with André Gide, of the *Nouvelle revue française* in 1909.

157, p.316 *Haas:* Haas, Charles (1832–1902), a charming, witty and distinguished Jew, associated with the Rothschilds in business. Inspector of Fine Arts, he was elected to the Jockey Club in 1871 as a result of his gallant conduct during the War of 1870. The only Jew except the Rothschilds to become a member of the Jockey Club, he was converted to Catholicism shortly before his death.

Although Proust, in moments of irritation at the efforts of society people to identify his characters with actual persons, occasionally denied Charles Haas's being the model for Swann, he himself divulged the fact in an apostrophe, which in the French edition of *The Captive* (*La Prisonnière*), p. 273, is addressed to Charles Swann, but in the English translation (*The Captive*, p. 269) to Charles ——. The deliberate identification of the fictional Charles with the real Charles is obvious in the text. For in the novel Proust writes, "If in Tissot's picture representing the balcony of the Rue Royale Club, where you figure with Galliffet, Edmond Polignac, and Saint-Maurice, people are always drawing attention to yourself, it is because they know that there are some traces of you in the character of Swann." The portrait of Haas in that painting is well recognized and has been frequently reproduced.

The snob side of Haas is amusingly revealed in an undated letter of Degas to his friend Bartholomé. "Haas may arrive in 8 or 10 days," he writes, "and the attitude he adopts towards me, whether to see me or cut me . . . will either be an effort for him or none at all. He knows that my sight is bad and that when I do see him, it makes no difference. Will he have a line of action and the courage to follow it? You know how droll ladies' men are with other men."

158, p.317 *Agostinelli:* Agostinelli, Alfred (1888–1914). Proust first knew Agostinelli at Cabourg in the summer of 1907 when he employed him as chauffeur. That same year, in an article in the *Figaro* entitled "En Memoire des églises assassinées," he described how, while on a motor tour, wishing to see the sculpture on the Lisieux Cathedral after dark, ". . . my driver, the ingenious Agostinelli, delivering a salutation to the ancient sculptures from the present time, whose light served only to facilitate a clearer reading of the lessons of the past, focussed the headlights of his automobile successively on all the different parts of the porch."

In 1912 Agostinelli applied to Proust in Paris for the position of chauffeur. But not wishing to dismiss his chauffeur, Odilon Albaret, he hired Agostinelli as secretary to type the manuscript of *Swann's Way*. Soon after the publication of *Swann*, Agostinelli became interested in aviation and decided to obtain a pilot's license. Under the pseudonym Marcel Swann, he enrolled in a flying school at Antibes in April, 1914. On May 30, on his second solo flight, his plane crashed into the Mediterranean and not until June 7 was his body found. See Vigneron, Robert, "La Genèse de Swann," *Revue d'histoire de la philosophie*, Jan. 15, 1937, pp. 67–115.

160, p.322 *Gobineau:* Gobineau, Joseph Arthur, Comte de (1816–1882), French writer and diplomat, author of novels and of *L'Essai sur l'inégalité des races humaines*.

161, p.323 *Masson:* Masson, Frédéric (1847–1923), French historian of Napoleon and the Bonaparte family.

161, p.324 *his articles:* Léon Daudet's articles were published in book form in 1914 under the title *L'Avant-Guerre*. Although primarily anti-German, the point of view was sufficiently anti-Semitic, anti-Dreyfusard, and anti-Republican to make it clear that Proust had indeed not read the articles.

161, p.324 *Péladan:* Péladan, Joséphin (1859–1918), French disciple of Barbey d'Aurevilley, Rosicrucian mystic, author of works on aesthetics in which he held that Wagner alone could claim kinship with the geniuses of the Renaissance.

161, p.324 *General Pau:* Pau, Gérald (1848–1932), French general, commanded an army at the beginning of World War I.

161, p.325 *Célimène and Alceste:* These names were inserted by Daudet.

161, p.325 *Psichari:* Psichari, Ernest (1883–1914), grandson of Renan, French writer and officer. He was converted to Catholicism and admitted to the Third Order of Dominicans in 1912. He was also the author of *L'Appel des armes* (1912), a novel defending the military profession, and of *Le Voyage du Centurion* (1913), an account of an African expedition and his conversion to Catholicism. He died in battle.

161, p.325 *Military Situation:* The author of these articles was Henri Bidou (1875–1943).

163, p.328 *Caillaux affair:* On March 16, 1914, the wife of Joseph Caillaux (1863–1913), then Minister of Finance, shot and killed in his office at the *Figaro*, Gaston Calmette, to whom *Swann's Way* had been dedicated. Calmette had accused Caillaux of irregularities in office and was threatening to publish letters Caillaux had written to his wife before her divorce from her first husband. Robert Dreyfus had been a witness to the shooting, and at the trial Doctor Robert Proust testified as outside medical expert for the defense, an act for which he was criticized. Mme Caillaux was acquitted after a trial, the justice of which was widely questioned. Caillaux advocated making peace with Germany during the war and was arrested in 1918, convicted of correspondence with the enemy, and imprisoned for three years.

164, p.330 *Princesse Mathilde:* Bonaparte, Princesse Mathilde (1820–1904), daughter of Jérôme, younger brother of Napoleon. Her salon, of which Sainte-Beuve, Flaubert, Maupassant, and the Goncourt brothers were habitués, was one of the first Proust attended. See *Within a Budding Grove* I, pp. 162–163.

169, p.338 *Scheikévitch:* This letter was inscribed on the blank pages of Mme Scheikévitch's copy of *Swann's Way*. Many of the quotations are cited from the manuscript of the later volumes of *Remembrance of Things Past*, on which Proust was then working, and the changes between the version given here and the final version are of great interest in revealing Proust's method of composition. See "But another reason for this change . . . an immortal youthfulness." *Within a Budding Grove* I, p. 271.

169, p.339 *"But you're looking* . . . They're really very good, you know." *Within a Budding Grove*, pp. 245 and 252.

169, p.340 *"The wiser course* . . . ebbing chord of happiness." *Cities of the Plain*, I, p. 327.

169, p.341 *"Just a little while* . . . abrupt reaction of pain." *The Sweet Cheat Gone*, p. 2.

169, p.341 *"I tried not to brush* . . . by mastering them." *The Sweet Cheat Gone*, p. 17.

169, p.342 *"How could Swann* . . . only what exists!" *The Sweet Cheat Gone*, p. 81.

169, p.342 *"For the death of Albertine* . . . but multiplies him." *The Sweet Cheat Gone*, pp. 85–6.

169, p.343 *". . . like a consumptive* . . . always contemporaneous." *The Sweet Cheat Gone*, p. 94 and pp. 102–3.

169, p.344 *"For the memories of love* . . . without importance." *Within a Budding Grove* I, p. 308.

169, p.344 *"Not that I no longer* . . . cruelty of memory." *The Sweet Cheat Gone*, pp. 195–6. The word "memory" has been changed to "intelligence" in the published version.

169, p.345 *"As there are strokes* . . . a little earlier." *The Sweet Cheat Gone*, p. 254.

169, p.345 *"Regret is really* . . . not healed." *The Sweet Cheat Gone*, p. 313.

170, p.347 *proof sheets:* J.-E. Blanche, *Propos de peintre: De David à Degas*, 1re serie. Paris, 1919. The preface to this book was written by Proust, to whom it was dedicated.

172, p.349 *Céleste:* Albaret, Mme Céleste (1891–), the wife of Proust's chauffeur, Odilon Albaret, who between 1913 and Proust's death was his indispensable and devoted servant, nurse and friend. See *Cities of the Plain* I, pp. 343–5, Ibid II, p. 376.

172, p.350 *I believed in friendship:* See *Within a Budding Grove* II, pp. 46–7, pp. 267–9, *The Guermantes Way* II, pp. 118–19, *The Past Recaptured*, p. 221.

173, p.354 *Rivière:* Rivière, Jacques (1886–1925), French writer, editor of *La Nouvelle revue française* 1919–1925, author of the novel *Aimée*, dedicated to Proust, and of *L'Allemand*, a psychological study of the Germans.

174, p.357 *Strauss:* Strauss, Richard (1864–), German composer.

174, p.357 *Zamacoïs:* Zamacoïs, Miguel (1886–), prolific French writer and dramatist.

174, p.358 *La Dame blanche:* Opera by François Adrien Boieldieu (1775–1834). Text by Scribe based on Sir Walter Scott's *Guy Mannering* and *The Monastery*.

174, p.358 *Le Petit Duc:* Opera by Alexandre Charles Lecocq (1832–1918). Text by Henri Meilhac and Ludovic Halévy.

174, p.358 *La Mascotte:* Opera by Edmond Audran (1842–1901).

176, p.360 *Morand:* Morand, Paul (1888–), French diplomat and writer, Vichy Minister to Switzerland 1942–1945; he was in exile in Switzerland in 1948. In a letter written to Paul Morand during the war Proust said, "I will not talk to you about the war. I have, alas, assimilated it so completely that I can not keep it separate. . . . For me it is less an object, in the philosophic sense of the word, than a substance interposed between myself and objects. As people used to live in God, I live in the war."

177, p.362 *In evening dress:* The sentence starting with these words through the sentence ending "General Négrier for my book," are here published for the first time.

177, p.363 *air raid warning:* See *The Past Recaptured*, p. 72 ff., pp. 126–8.

180, p.368 *Pastiches et Mélanges:* The dedication read: "To Monsieur Walter Berry, lawyer and scholar, who with incomparable energy and talent, before a still undecided America, pleaded the cause of France, and won it. His friend, Marcel Proust."

180, p.370 *Capus:* Capus, Alfred (1858–1922), popular Parisian writer of comedies.

181, p.371 *article of Daniel Halévy's:* Published in pamphlet form under the title *Avec les boys Américains*, Paris, 1918.

184, p.375 *Mlle Lahovary:* Mlle Marguerite Lahovary, the sister of the Princesse Marthe Bibesco, died April 4, 1918.

185, p.376 *Polybe:* Pseudonym under which Joseph Reinach, author of the six-volume history of the Dreyfus Affair, wrote during the war daily articles for the *Figaro*, which Proust called *Polybsonneries*.

185, p.377 *Widow Henry:* A list of subscriptions "for the widow and orphan of Colonel Henry and against the Jew Reinach" was started in 1898 by Edouard Drumont, the notorious anti-Semite and editor of the anti-Dreyfusard newspaper, *Libre Parole*. Colonel Henry had committed suicide in prison in August, 1898 after confessing the forgery of documents used in evidence against Dreyfus. Among the subscribers to the fund were Maurice Barrès, 50 francs, and Paul Valéry, 3 francs, given "not without due consideration."

186, p.377 *L'Arlésienne:* At the first performance of Alphonse Daudet's play, *L'Arlésienne*, with incidental music by Georges Bizet, practically all of the audience had departed by the time the final curtain fell.

186, p.378 *Sapho: Sapho* (1884), a novel by Alphonse Daudet, later dramatized.

187, p.378 *Affaire Lemoine: L'Affaire Lemoine*, which Proust had used as the theme of all his *pastiches*, concerned a charlatan, Lemoine, who extorted from Sir Jules Wernher, the president of De Beers, over a million francs for a formula he claimed to have discovered for the manufacture of synthetic diamonds. Lemoine's manufactured diamonds turned out to be genuine stones. He was found guilty of fraud and sentenced to six years in prison.

189, p.386 *pastiches:* Marcel Proust, *Pastiches et Mélanges*, Paris, 1919. Besides the previously unpublished *pastiche* of Saint-Simon, this volume contained Proust's parodies of Balzac, E´mile Faguet, Michelet, the Goncourt brothers, Flaubert, Sainte-Beuve, Renan and Henri de Régnier, which had appeared at intervals in the *Figaro* between February, 1908 and March, 1909.

193, p.396 *Molé:* Molé, Louis Mathieu, Comte de (1781–1855), French statesman and writer, Prime Minister 1836–1839.

193, p.396 *Pasquier:* Pasquier, Etienne Denis, Duc de (1767–1862), French statesman, President of the Chamber of Peers under Louis-Philippe, Chancellor in 1837.

193, p.397 *scenes in Swann:* See *Swann's Way* I, p. 218 ff.

195, p.400 *my notebooks:* Proust wrote his novel in longhand in large copy-books.

196, p.401 *Goncourt parody:* See *The Past Recaptured*, p. 14 ff.; *Pastiches et Mélanges*, p. 36 ff.

198, p.406 *Your pastiche:* See L. Martin-Chauffier, *Correspondances Apocryphes*. Paris, 1923. "Marcel Proust au Marquis de Saint-Loup."

198, p.407 *telescope:* See *The Past Recaptured*, pp. 393–4.

198, p.408 *Montmorency:* See *The Guermantes Way* I, pp. 269–70.

199, p.410 *To Marcel Boulenger:* This letter appeared in the *Figaro Littéraire*, May 19, 1928.

200, p.412 *translator of Jean-Christophe:* Cannan, Gilbert (1884–), English novelist, drama critic and dramatist. Translator of *Jean-Christophe* by Romain Rolland.

203, p.415 *Bakst:* Bakst, Léon Nicolaevich (original surname Rosenberg) (1866?–1924), Russian painter and scene designer. Known chiefly as scenic artist for Diaghilev's *Ballets russes*.

203, p.416 *Nijinsky:* Nijinksy, Waslaw (1900–), Russian dancer. Appeared first in Paris in 1909 with Diaghilev's *Ballets russes*. Went insane in 1917 and was confined in an asylum at Davos, Switzerland.

204, p.419 *Asquith's daughter:* Elizabeth Asquith (1897–1945), daughter of Lord Oxford and Asquith, British Prime Minister, 1908–1916, became the wife of Prince Antoine Bibesco in 1919. Proust described her in his *pastiche* of Saint-Simon as "most intelligent, resembling one of those beautiful figures that one sees in Italy, painted in fresco."

207, p.421 *monkey:* King Alexander I of Greece was bitten by a monkey October 9th and died October 25, 1920.

207, p.421 *Mayor of Cork:* MacSwiney, Terence (1879–1920), Irish Nationalist politician, Lord Mayor of Cork, leader in Easter Rebellion. Sentenced to two years' imprisonment for sedition by English Government August 17, 1920. Died October 26, 1920 in Brixton jail, London after a 74-day hunger strike.

207, p.422 *"Deschanel's way"*: Paul Deschanel (1855–1922), French politician, President of the Republic, February 18 to September 22, 1920, had recently gone insane.

208, p.422 *To the Comtesse de Maugny*: A portion of this letter was used as preface to *Au Royaume du Bistouri—30 dessins par R. de M. Preface de Marcel Proust*. Geneva, n.d.

208, p.422 *Faivre*: Abel Faivre (1867–1945), French painter, decorator and until 1920 president of the *Société des Artistes humoristes*, was a friend of Proust's.

208, p.423 *little railroad*: See *Cities of the Plain* II, p. 4.

209, p.426 *d'Haussonville*: Haussonville, Othenin, Comte d' (1809–1884), French politician and historian, father of Comte Gabriel Othenin d'Haussonville.

209, p.426 *Delessert*: Delessert, Benjamin (1773–1847), French philanthropist and founder of the savings bank in France.

209, p.427 *"feminine"*: ". . . M. Marcel Proust is above all a nervous aesthete, a little morbid, almost feminine . . ." Paul Souday in *Le Temps*, November 4, 1920.

215, p.437 *Baron Doasan*: Baron Jacques de Doasan served Proust as partial model for Charlus, for whom he borrowed Doasan's "slightly puffy face, his complexion, blotched under its layers of powder, his white hair and his mustache dyed black, his deceptive air of virility." He and Montesquiou were bitter enemies, for d'Yturri, Montesquiou's favorite, had first been Doasan's friend.

215, p.437 *Aubernon*: Mme d'Aubernon was hostess of a famous salon. She was noted for her way of controlling the conversation at her dinners by ringing a bell when any two of her guests drifted into personal conversation away from the subject set for that meal. Her technique is perhaps best illustrated by the account of Mme Straus's late arrival at one of Mme d'Aubernon's dinners to be greeted by her hostess with, "Oh, you have come just in time, my dear! We were discussing adultery." Whereupon Mme Straus replied, "What a pity! I came prepared for incest!" From Mme d'Aubernon Proust borrowed for Mme de Villeparisis her custom of presenting private theatrical performances at home. A number of her characteristics are also found in Mme Verdurin.

215, p.437 *Mme de Beaulaincourt:* Comtesse Sophie de Beaulaincourt (1818–1904), daughter of the Maréchal de Castellane, was by her first marriage the Marquise de Contades. High-spirited, witty, unconventional, and endowed with extraordinary physical magnetism, her love affair with the Marquis de Coislin, by whom she had a son, repudiated by her husband who had been for a year absent in Turkey, was the cause of considerable scandal. Prosper Merimée had been attached to Mme de Beaulaincourt's mother and in his old age he transferred his affections to the daughter to whom he used, almost daily, to send from the Riviera flowers which she used as models for the artificial ones she was always making and presenting to her friends. Among her friends was Proust, whom she regaled with recollections of the famous men she had known.

215, p.438 *Contrexéville:* Proust is referring here to a mineral water from the springs at Contrexéville.

216, p.440 *Vermeer:* See J. L. Vaudoyer, *Le Mystérieux Ver Meer, l'Opinion*, April 30, May 7 and 14, 1921. This article is the one mentioned in *The Captive*, p. 249, the episode of Bergotte's death, where Proust writes, "But one of the critics having written somewhere that in Vermeer's *Street in Delft* (lent by the Gallery at The Hague for an exhibition of Dutch painting) . . ." Proust in earlier days went a number of times to exhibitions with M. Vaudoyer. Because he was so infrequently able to go out in the daytime, he always regarded these visits to museums as a sort of expedition and he would send ahead his "secretary" with a basket of strawberries or some little pastries to be eaten, mostly by M. Vaudoyer, while Proust sat resting or examining some picture he specially liked. At the exhibition of Dutch painting Proust was stricken ill with a sudden attack of the kind he later described in the above-mentioned passage.

216, p.440 *Vuillard:* Vuillard, Edouard Jean (1868–1940), French painter whom Proust had met some twenty years earlier through Prince Antoine Bibesco. In a letter to the latter written around 1903, Proust said, "I should be very happy if M. Vuillard would consent to sell me the sketch of the dinner at Armenonville last year; a unique case of coincidence between his admirable talent, which is often fruitful to my memory, and one perfect and charming hour of my life."

216, p.440 *Baignères:* Paul Baignères, a minor French painter, was a life-long friend of Proust, of whom he made a very amusing drawing in 1892.

217, p.440 *Baudelaire:* See "A propos de Baudelaire," *Nouvelle revue française*, June, 1921. *Chroniques*, p. 212.

219, p.443 *Guermantes II:* See *The Guermantes Way* II, p. 265.

219, p.444 *Ingres:* The model for the man mentioned in this painting by Ingres was the French painter François Marius Granet (1775–1840).

220, p.444 *Your fine article:* See *Nouvelle revue française*, May 1, 1921.

222, p.448 *the night you were here:* Jacques Boulenger paid Proust a single visit in June, 1921 which was described by Charles du Bos in his *Journal*, August, 1921. "Jacques Boulenger maintains a real openness of mind about everything concerning art proper, but one feels that for what everyone today calls 'general ideas' he would no longer budge. . . . Boulenger told me of the evening he went to see Proust (Gide was there and talked to me about it the next day), the conversation had to do with Sainte-Beuve. Boulenger found Proust in bed, enormous under his mass of covers; he was wearing several sweaters and jerseys and over them all a white barman's [sic] jacket." A few days previous to this visit Gide had written in his *Journal*, ". . . when I read Proust I hate the virtuosity, but always it obtrudes itself on me and I should like, in order really to despise it, first to be capable of it myself; I should like to be sure that I am in no way the fox in the fable . . ."

223, p.452 *Léon Daudet:* Proust had dedicated *The Guermantes Way* I to Léon Daudet in the following words: "To Léon Daudet, to the author of *Le Voyage de Shakespeare*, of *Le Partage de l'enfant*, of *L'Astre noir*, of *Fantômes et vivants*, of *Le Monde des images*, of so many masterpieces. To the incomparable friend, as an expression of gratitude and of admiration."

223, p.454 *Vigny:* The title of *Sodome et Gomorrhe* (*Cities of the Plain*) was taken from the following line of Alfred de Vigny's poem, "Colère de Samson": "*La femme aura Gomorrhe et l'homme aura Sodome.*"

226, p.459 *Nerval:* Gérard Labrunie, pseud. Gérard de Nerval (1808–1855), French writer and translator of Goethe's *Faust*, was the author of *Les Filles de feu*, containing the romance "Sylvie," which Proust greatly admired.

227, p.460 *Elles, Olivier:* Manager and maitre d'hôtel, respectively, at the Hotel Ritz.

232, p.468 *Odette de Crécy:* In a letter to his publisher, Gaston Gallimard, written at about this time, Proust said, "A woman I loved thirty years ago has written me a raging letter to tell me that she is Odette, that I am a monster. Such letters (and the replies) are what kill work, not to mention pleasure; the latter I gave up a long time ago."

In May, 1922 Proust also wrote in a letter to Gabriel de La Rochefoucauld, "Because, when I was provoked at having people say to me, 'Don't defend yourself, the Duchesse de Guermantes is Madame

G—' (when the Duchesse de Guermantes who is everybody and nobody is in any case the exact opposite of Mme G.), I wrote in *Oeuvres libres* that people so little understand artistic creation that they fancy you can put a woman in a book just as she is. I didn't know that a woman (this one not a society woman) who is exactly her opposite would claim to recognize herself in Odette de Crécy. These ridiculous similarities irritate me. What fatally happens is that one's memory suggests for one character some trait from one totally opposite. Thus there is nothing in the Duc de Guermantes of the late Marquis de L., but I was thinking of him when I had the Duc shave in front of his window. Certainly my dear friend Mme S[traus] has nothing of Mme Swann about her, and she is too intelligent to think so. But I put in Mme Swann's drawing-room the beautiful snowballs that Mme S. had put in hers, and she thanked me, without thinking that for that reason I identified her with Odette."

235, p.474 *Read to the end:* The handwriting in this letter, the original of which is at the Sterling Library, Yale University, indicates how very ill and troubled Proust must have been while writing it.

236, p.478 *Eliot:* T. S. Eliot was at this time editor of the magazine, *The Criterion*.

238, p.481 *Barrère:* Camille Barrère (1851–1940) was French Ambassador to Italy from 1897 to 1924.

238, p.482 *Kiderlen-Waechter:* Kiderlen-Waechter, Alfred von

(1852–1912), German statesman and diplomat who negotiated with the French on Moroccan affairs and helped bring about the Agadir incident during the premiership of Caillaux in 1911.

238, p.482 *Passage des Favorites:* The name of the street where M. Crémieux lived.

238, p.483 *Sodome et Gomorrhe III:* See *The Captive*, p. 151 ff., p. 164 ff.

239, p.485 *General Mangin:* Charles Marie Emmanuel Mangin (1866–1925) commanded the defense of Verdun in 1916 and the offensive of Chemin des Dames in 1917. He encouraged the Separatist movement in occupied Germany.

241, p.490 *Precautions inutiles:* This excerpt from *The Sweet Cheat Gone* appeared in *Les Oeuvres libres*, February 1923.

241, p.490 *Robert de Flers:* Robert Pellevé de la Motte-Ango, Marquis de Flers (1872–1927), French dramatist, collaborator with Gaston de Caillavet in writing many comedies, was on the staff of the *Figaro*, was a close friend of Proust's for thirty years and was one of the original contributors to *Le Banquet*.

Index

Page references that follow *n* without parentheses refer to names and subjects mentioned only in the Notes.

Names set in small capitals are from *Remembrance of Things Past.*